BLOOD-RED RIVERS

Jean-Christophe Grangé

BLOOD-RED RIVERS

Translated from the French by
Ian Monk

THE HARVILL PRESS
LONDON

First published with the title *Les Rivières Pourpres* by
Éditions Albin Michel S.A., Paris, 1998

First published in Great Britain in 1999 by
The Harvill Press
2 Aztec Row
Berners Road
London N1 0PW

First published in the United States in 2000 by
The Harvill Press

www.harvill.com

1 3 5 7 9 8 6 4 2

Copyright © Éditions Albin Michel S.A., 1998
English translation copyright © Ian Monk, 1999

Jean-Christophe Grangé asserts the moral right to be identified as the author of this book

This edition has been published with the financial assistance
of the French Ministry of Culture

A CIP catalogue record for this book is available from the British Library

ISBN 1 86046 659 1 (hbk)
ISBN 1 86046 660 5 (pbk)

Designed and typeset in Minion at
Libanus Press, Marlborough, Wiltshire

Printed and bound in Great Britain by Butler & Tanner Ltd
at Selwood Printing, Burgess Hill

For Virginie

I

CHAPTER 1

"Ga-na-mos! Ga-na-mos!"

Pierre Niémans, fingers clenched round his VHF transmitter, stared down at the crowds streaming home across the concrete terraces of Paris's Parc des Princes. Thousands of fiery skulls, white hats, brightly colored scarfs, forming a variegated rippling ribbon. An explosion of confetti. Or a legion of demons seen in a haze of LSD. And those three notes, again and again, slow and ear-splitting: *"Ga-na-mos!"*

Standing on the roof of the nursery school across the road from the Parc des Princes, the officer was controlling the maneuvers of the third and fourth brigades of the CRS riot police. The men in dark blue were running below their black helmets, protected by their polycarbonate shields. Standard procedure. Two hundred men stationed at each set of gates and a "screen" of commandos whose job it was to stop the two teams' supporters from colliding, getting close, or even noticing each other's existence . . .

On that evening, for the Saragossa vs Arsenal clash, the only match all year that saw two non-French teams playing against each other in Paris, more than one thousand four hundred policemen and gendarmes had been mobilised. ID checks, body searches, and herding of the forty thousand supporters that had come from the two countries. Superintendent Niémans, his hair cropped, was one of the officers in charge of these maneuvers. It was not his usual line of business, but he enjoyed this sort of exercise. Pure

1

and total surveillance and confrontation. With neither investigations nor procedures. He relished the absolute lack of accountability. And he loved the military look of this marching army.

The supporters had reached the first floor – they could be made out between the concrete fuselage of the construction, just above gates H and G. Niémans looked at his watch. In four minutes' time, they would be outside, spilling across the road. Then would begin the risks of contact, violence, broken ranks. He filled his lungs in one gasp. That October night was seething with tension.

Two minutes. Niémans instinctively turned round and, far away, could see Place de la Porte-de-Saint-Cloud. Completely deserted. Its three fountains soared up in the night, like worried totem poles. All along the avenue, the CRS vans had lined up. In front of them, the men were rolling their shoulder blades, their helmets clipped onto their belts and truncheons slapping against their thighs. The reserve brigades.

The din mounted. The crowd spread out between the iron gratings stuck with spikes. Niémans could not resist smiling. This was what he had come to see. The crowd surged forward. Trumpets broke through the fracas. A rumbling made every inch of the concrete shake. "*Ga-na-mos! Ga-na-mos!*" Niémans pressed the button on his transmitter and spoke to Joachim, the leader of the East Company. "Niémans here. They're coming out. Push them toward the vans, toward Boulevard Murat, the car parks and the *métro*."

From his vantage point, he weighed up the situation. There was practically no risk on this side. The Spanish supporters had won the match, and so were the less dangerous. The English were coming out from the far side, gates A to K, toward the Boulogne stand, the lair of the wild beasts. Niémans would go and see what was going on there, once operations had got well and truly under way.

Suddenly, in the gleam of the street-lights a beer bottle shot high above the crowd. The officer saw a truncheon crack downwards, the compact ranks withdraw, men falling. He screamed into his transmitter: "Joachim, for fuck's sake, control your men!"

Niémans rushed to the back stairs and ran down all eight flights. When he emerged onto the avenue, two lines of CRS were already pushing forward, set to bring the hooligans under control. Niémans dashed in front of the armed men and waved his arms in long circular motions. The truncheons were just a few feet from his face when Joachim, his head jammed in his helmet, appeared to his right. He raised his visor and glanced furiously at him:

"Jesus Christ, Niémans, are you crazy or what? You're not in uniform, you're going to get yourself . . ."

The officer did not deign to reply.

"What the hell's going on here? Control your men, Joachim! Or in three minutes' time we'll have a riot on our hands."

The chubby red-faced captain panted. His little *fin-de-siècle* moustache twitched in rhythm to his gasping breath. The radio juddered: "Ca . . . Calling all units . . . Calling all units . . . The Boulogne turning . . . Rue du Commandant-Guilbaud . . . I . . . We have a problem!" Niémans stared at Joachim as though he alone were responsible for this chaos. His fingers gripped the transmitter: "Niémans here. We're on our way." Then he calmly gave the captain his orders:

"I'll go. Send as many men there as you can. And sort out the situation here."

Without waiting for a response, the superintendent set off to look for the trainee who was acting as his driver. He crossed the square in long strides and, in the distance, noticed that the barmen of the Brasserie des Princes were lowering their iron shutters. The air was racked with tension. He finally spotted the little dark-haired guy in the leather jacket who was hanging around beside the black saloon car. Niémans thumped his fist down onto the bonnet and yelled:

"The Boulogne turning, quick!"

The two men leapt simultaneously into the car. Its tires smoked as it pulled away. The trainee shot round to the left of the stadium so as to reach Gate K as rapidly as possible along a route specially reserved for the security forces. Niémans had a hunch:

"No," he murmured. "Go round the other way. Then we'll bump straight into the action."

The car spun around one hundred and eighty degrees, skidding on the puddles made by the water cannons already set for the counter-attack. Then it sped away down Avenue du Parc-des-Princes through a narrow corridor formed by the gray vans of the flying squad. The men in helmets heading the same way made room for it without even glancing at it. The trainee swerved left by Lycée Claude-Bernard then took the roundabout so as to coast along the third side of the stadium. They had just passed by the Auteuil stand.

As soon as Niémans saw the first flurries of gas floating in the air, he knew he had been right: the fighting had already reached Place de l'Europe. The car swept through the white fog and had to brake hard to avoid the first victims, who were in full flight. Battle had been joined in front of the Presidential stand. Men in ties and ladies with jewelry were running, stumbling, tears pouring down their faces. Some of them were looking for a way out onto the streets, while others were climbing back up the steps toward the stadium gates.

Niémans leapt out of the car. On the square, a pitched battle was in progress. The bright colors of the English team and the dark forms of the CRS could just be made out. Some of the latter were crawling on the ground – like half-crushed slugs – while others, at a distance, were hesitating about whether or not to use their anti-riot guns for fear of injuring their wounded fellow officers.

The superintendent put away his glasses and tied a scarf round his face. He picked the nearest CRS and snatched away his truncheon, at the same time showing his tricolor card. The man was stunned. His breath misted over the translucent visor of his helmet.

Pierre Niémans ran on toward the confrontation. The Arsenal supporters were attacking with their fists, iron bars and steel toecaps, while the CRS hit back and retreated, trying to defend those already laid out on the ground. Bodies gesticulated, faces creased, jawbones hit the asphalt. Batons went up then rained down, juddering under the force of the blows. The officer pushed his way into the scrum.

He struck with his fist, with his truncheon. He knocked down a big thug, then laid straight into him, hitting his ribs, his belly and face. He was suddenly kicked from the right. Screaming, he got to his feet. His baton wrapped itself round his aggressor's throat. His blood boiled in his head, a metallic taste numbed his mouth. His mind was empty. He felt nothing. He was at war and he knew it.

A strange scene suddenly met his eyes. A hundred yards farther off, an oldish man, who was already in a bad way, was struggling to get out of the clutches of two hooligans. Niémans looked at the supporter's blood-splattered face and the mechanical gestures of the two others, taut with hatred.

One second later and Niémans caught on: under their jackets, the aggressed and the aggressors wore the badges of rival clubs.

A settling of old scores.

By this time, the victim had already got away and had escaped down a side road – Rue Nungesser-et-Coli. The two attackers dived after him. Niémans dropped his truncheon, broke through the scrum and followed them.

The race was on.

Down that silent street, Niémans ran, breathing rhythmically, gaining on the two pursuers who were, in turn, gaining on their prey.

They turned right again and had soon reached the Molitor swimming pool, which was entirely walled off. The pair of bastards finally caught up with their victim. Niémans had got as far as Place de la Porte-Molitor, which overlooks the Paris ring road, and could not believe his eyes. One of the attackers had just produced a machete.

In the dim lights of the highway, Niémans could see the blade relentlessly slicing into the man on his knees, who was twitching under the blows. The attackers lifted up the body and hurled it over the railings.

"No!"

The officer yelled and drew his gun at the same instant. He leant on a car, propped his right fist onto his left palm, aimed and held his breath. First shot. Missed. The killer with the machete turned round amazed. Second shot.

Missed again.

Niémans set off again, his gun flat against his thigh in combat posture. He was furious. Without his glasses, he had missed his target twice. Now he, too, was up on the bridge. The man with the machete had already sprinted away into the undergrowth which bordered the ring road. His accomplice stood there, motionless, pale. The policeman rammed the butt of his gun into the man's throat, then dragged him by the hair as far as a road sign. With one hand, he handcuffed him. Only then did he lean down toward the traffic.

The body had fallen down onto the road and several cars had driven over it before a multiple pile-up had brought everything to a halt. A confused crush of vehicles, shattered bodywork . . . Then the jam broke out into a crazed wailing of horns. In the head-lamps, Niémans could see one of the drivers, who was staggering around near his car, his head in his hands. The superintendent lifted his eyes to stare across the ring road. There was the murderer with his colorful arm band, making his way through the trees. Putting his gun away, Niémans set off again at once.

The killer was now glancing back at him through the branches. The policeman made no attempt to hide. The man must now have realised that he, Superintendent Pierre Niémans, was going to make mincemeat of him. Suddenly, the hooligan leapt over an embankment and vanished. The sound of feet running over gravel gave away the direction of his flight: the Auteuil gardens.

The officer followed, seeing the darkness reflected off the gray rocks of the garden. As he passed by some greenhouses, he spotted a figure climbing a wall. He shot after him and found himself looking down on the tennis courts of Roland-Garros.

The gates were not padlocked. The killer was easily able to move from one court to another. Niémans pulled open a gate, ran across the clay surface and leapt over the net. Fifty yards ahead, the man was already slowing, with obvious signs of fatigue. He managed to get over another net, then clamber up the steps between the stands. Niémans, hardly even tired, smoothly followed him up the stairs. He was just a few feet away from him when, from the top of the stand, a shadow jumped into the void. His prey was now on the roof of a private residence. Then he vanished over the farther side. The superintendent took a run up, then jumped after him. He landed on a platform of gravel. Below were lawns, trees, silence.

Not a trace of the killer.

The officer let himself down and rolled over the damp grass. There were just two possibilities: the house from whose roof he had just leapt down, or a massive wooden structure at the end of the garden. He drew his MR73 and leant his back against the door behind him. It put up no resistance.

The superintendent took a step or two, then stopped in amazement. He was in a hall of marble, overhung by a circular slab of stone engraved with strange letters. A gilded banister rail rose up through the shadows of the upper storeys. In the darkness could be seen imperial red velvet hangings, gleaming hieratic vases . . . Niémans realised that he was inside an Asian embassy.

A sudden noise came from outside. The killer was inside the other building. The policeman crossed the garden and reached the wooden structure. The door was still swinging on its hinges. A shadow among the shadows, he entered. And the magic grew a shade more tense. It was a stable, divided into carved boxes, occupied by little horses with brush-like manes.

The swishing of tails. Straw fluttering. With his gun in his hand, Pierre Niémans walked on. He passed one box, two, three . . . A dull thump to his right. He turned. Nothing but the stamp of a hoof. A snarl to his left. He turned once more. Too late. The blade shot down. Niémans got out of its way at the last moment. The machete slid past his shoulder and embedded itself in the rump of a horse. The kick was terrible. The horseshoe flew up into the killer's face. The officer grabbed his chance, threw himself onto the man, turned round his gun and used it as a hammer.

Again and again he hit him, then suddenly stopped and looked down at the hooligan's bloodied features. His bones were sticking up through the shreds of his skin. An eyeball dangled down on a mess of fibers. Still wearing his Arsenal supporter's hat, the murderer was now motionless. Niémans grabbed back hold of his gun, took its blood-stained grip in both hands and rammed its barrel into the man's split mouth. He took off the catch and closed his eyes. He was about to fire when a shrill noise interrupted him. In his pocket, his cell phone was ringing.

CHAPTER 2

Three hours later, amid the overly new and excessively symmetric streets that surround Nanterre's Prefecture, a lamp was shining in the building that housed the police headquarters of the Ministry of the Interior. A shard of light, at once diffuse and concentrated, gleamed softly across the surface of the desk belonging to Antoine Rheims, who was sitting in the shadows. In front of him, behind the halo, stood the tall figure of Pierre Niémans. He had just given a terse resumé of his report concerning the chase. Rheims asked him, skeptically:

"How's the man?"

"The Englishman? In a coma. Multiple facial fractures. I've just called the hospital. They're going to try to perform a skin graft on his face."

"And the victim?"

"Crushed by the cars, on the ring road, just by Porte-Molitor."

"Jesus Christ. What the fuck was going on?"

"Hooligans settling an old score. There were some Chelsea fans among the Arsenal supporters. When the fighting started, our two hooligans with the machete sliced up their victim."

Rheims nodded incredulously. After a moment's silence, he went on:

"And what about our friend here? Was it really a horse's hoof that put him in a state like that?"

Niémans did not answer, but turned toward the window. In the chalky moonlight, the strange pastel designs which covered the façades of the neighboring apartment blocks could be made out: clouds and rainbows drifting above the dark green hills of Nanterre's park. Rheims's voice rose once more:

"I just don't get it, Pierre. Why do you get yourself into messes like this? You were watching the stadium, that's all, I really . . ."

His voice faded out. Niémans remained silent.

"You're getting on," Rheims went on. "And out of your depth. The agreement we had was perfectly clear: no more action, no more violence . . ."

Niémans turned round and walked over toward his boss.

"Come on, out with it, Antoine. Why did you call me in here, in the middle of the night? You couldn't have known anything about this business when you rang me. So what's up?"

Rheims's shadowy figure did not budge. Broad shoulders, gray curly hair, head like a rock face. The build of a lighthouse keeper. For several years now, the chief superintendent had been running the Central Bureau for the Prevention of Trade in Humans – the CBPTH – a complicated name for what was, in fact, the head office of the vice squad. Niémans had first met him long before he had become installed behind this particular administrative desk, when they were two swift and efficient cops on the beat. The officer with the crew cut leant down and repeated:

"So, what's up?"

Rheims breathed in deeply:

"There's been a murder."

"In Paris?"

"No, in Guernon. A small university town in the Isère *département*, near Grenoble."

Niémans grabbed a chair and sat down opposite the chief superintendent.

"I'm listening."

"The body was discovered early yesterday evening. It had been stuck in between some rocks over a stream which runs along the edge of the campus. Everything points to a psychopath."

"What information do you have about the corpse? Is it a woman?"

"No, a man. A young guy. The university librarian, apparently. The body was naked. It bears marks of having been tortured: gashes, lacerations, burns . . . He seems also to have been strangled."

Niémans placed his elbow down on the desk. He fiddled with the ashtray.

"Why are you telling me all this?"

"Because I'm planning on sending you down there."

"What? Because of a murder? The boys in the local Grenoble brigade will rumble this killer within a week and . . ."

"Don't mess with me, Pierre. You know only too well that things are never as straightforward as they look. I've spoken to the magistrate. And he wants a specialist brought in."

"A specialist in what?"

"In murders. And in vice. He suspects a sexual motive. Or something along those lines."

Niémans stretched his neck toward the lamp and smelt the acrid burning of the halogen.

"You're holding something back, Antoine."

"The magistrate's Bernard Terpentes. An old buddy of mine. We're both from the Pyrenees. And, between you and me, he's in a total panic. Plus, he wants to get to the bottom of this as soon as possible. Stop any rumors, the media, all that bullshit. The new academic year starts in a few weeks and we've got to wind things up before then. Get the picture?"

The superintendent stood up and went back to the window. He stared down at the luminous pinpricks of the street-lights and the dark mounds of the park. The violence of the last few hours was still pounding in his temples: the hacking of the machete, the ring road, the chase across Roland-Garros. For the thousandth time, he thought how Rheims's phone call had certainly stopped him

10

from killing someone. He thought about his uncontrollable fits of violence, which blinded his conscience, ripping apart time and space, causing him to commit outrageous acts.

"Well?" Rheims asked.

Niémans turned back and leant on the window frame.

"I haven't been on a case like this for four years now. Why me?"

"I need someone good. And you know that a central office can pick one of its own men and send him anywhere in France." His huge hands did five-finger exercises in the darkness. "I'm making the most of my little bit of power."

The officer smiled behind his iron-rimmed glasses.

"You're releasing the wolf from its cage?"

"Put it that way, if you want. It'll be a breath of fresh air for you. And I'll be doing an old friend a good turn. And, in the meantime, it'll stop you from beating up on people . . ."

Rheims picked up the gleaming pages of a fax that lay on his desk.

"The gendarmes' first conclusions. So is it yes, or no?"

Niémans went over to the desk and crumpled the roll of paper.

"I'll phone you. To get the news from the hospital."

The superintendent immediately left Rue des Trois-Fontanot and returned home to Rue La-Bruyère in the ninth *arrondissement*. A huge, almost empty flat, with an old lady's immaculate polished floor. He had a shower, dressed his – superficial – wounds and examined himself in the mirror. A bony, wrinkled face. A gleaming gray crew cut. Glasses ringed with metal. Niémans smiled at his appearance. He wouldn't have liked to bump into himself down a dark alley.

He stuffed a few clothes into a sports bag, slid a 12-caliber Remington pump-action shotgun in between his shirts and socks, as well as some boxes of cartridges and speedloaders for his Manhurin. Finally, he grabbed his protective bag and folded two winter suits into it, along with a few brightly patterned ties.

On the way to Porte de la Chapelle, Niémans stopped at the all-night McDonald's on Boulevard de Clichy where he rapidly swallowed two quarter pounders with cheese, without taking his eyes off his car, which was double-parked. Three in the morning. In the ghastly neon light a few familiar ghosts were wandering. Blacks in over-ample clothes. Prostitutes with long dreadlocks. Druggies, bums, drunks. All of them were a part of his previous existence, on the beat. That world which Niémans had had to leave for a well-paid, respectable desk job. For any other cop, a post in a central office was a promotion. For him, it was being put out to grass – plush grass, admittedly, but the move had still mortified him. He took another look at the night hawks that surrounded him. These creatures had been the trees of his personal woodland, where he once roamed, in the skin of a hunter.

Niémans drove without stopping, headlights full on, ignoring speed traps and limits. At eight a.m., he took the Grenoble exit on the autoroute. He crossed Saint-Martin-d'Hères, Saint-Martin-d'Uriage and headed toward Guernon, at the foot of the Grand Pic de Belledonne. All along the winding road forests of conifers alternated with industrial zones. A slightly morbid atmosphere hung in the air, as always in the countryside when the beauty of the scenery is insufficient to hide its profound loneliness.

The superintendent drove past the first road signs indicating the university. In the distance, the mountain peaks rose up in the misty light of a stormy morning. Coming out of a bend, he glimpsed the university at the bottom of the valley: its large modern buildings, its fluted blocks of concrete, all ringed off by long lawns. It made Niémans think of a sanatorium the size of a town hall.

He turned off the main road and drove down into the valley. To the west, he could see vertical streams running into each other, their silvery current beating against the dark sides of the mountains. He slowed down, and shuddered at the sight of that icy water, plummeting down, obscured by clumps of brushwood, then reappearing again, white and dazzling, before vanishing once more . . .

Niémans decided to take a short detour. He forked off, drove under a vaulted ceiling of larches and firs, moist from the morning dew, then came across a long plain bordered by lofty black cliffs.

The officer stopped. He got out of his car and grabbed his

binoculars. He took a long look at the scenery. The river had disappeared. Then he realised that when the torrent reached the bottom of the valley it ran on behind the rock face. Gaps in the rock even gave him occasional glimpses of it.

Suddenly he noticed another detail and focused his binoculars on it. No, his eyes had not deceived him. He went back to his car and shot off toward the ravine. In one of the faults in the rock face he had just spotted a fluorescent yellow cordon, of the type used by the *gendarmerie*:

NO ENTRY

CHAPTER 3

Niémans continued down the fault, which bordered a winding, narrow path. Soon, he had to stop, as it was no longer broad enough for his car. He got out, slipped under the yellow cordon and reached the river.

The flow here came to a halt against a natural dam. The torrent, which Niémans was expecting to see boiling over with foam, had turned into a small, limpid lake. As calm as a face from which every sign of anger had just vanished. Farther on, to his right, it set off once more and presumably flowed through the grayish town which could be seen in the pit of the valley.

But Niémans came to a sudden stop. To his left, a man was already there, crouched over the water. Instinctively, Niémans raised the velcro cover of his holster. This gesture made his handcuffs clink together slightly. The man turned round and his face broke into a smile immediately.

"What do you think you're doing here?" Niémans asked him point-blank.

Without answering, the stranger smiled again, got to his feet and dusted off his hands. He was young, with fragile features and fair, brush-like hair. A suede jacket and pleated trousers. In a clear voice, he riposted:

"And you?"

This insolence astonished Niémans. He gruffly declared:

"Police. Didn't you see the cordon? I hope for your sake you've got a good reason to be here, because . . ."

"Eric Joisneau, from the Grenoble brigade. I'm here as a scout. Three more officers will be arriving later today."

Niémans joined him on the narrow bank.

"Where are the orderlies?" he asked.

"I told them to take a break. For breakfast." He shrugged carelessly. "I had work to do here. And I wanted some peace and quiet . . . Superintendent Niémans."

The gray-haired officer twitched. The young man went on imperviously:

"I recognised you at once. Pierre Niémans. The ex-star of the anti-terrorist squad. The ex-head of the vice squad. The ex-hunter of killers and dealers. The ex of a lot of things, in fact . . ."

"Do inspectors always give so much lip these days?"

Joisneau bowed ironically:

"Sorry, superintendent. I was just trying to take the shine off the star. You know you're an idol, don't you? The 'supercop' all young inspectors dream of becoming. Are you here for the murder?"

"What do you reckon?"

The officer bowed once again.

"It'll be an honor to work with you."

Niémans looked down at the glittering surface of the smooth waters, which shimmered at his feet, as though crystallised in the morning light. A glow of jade seemed to rise up from the depths.

"So, tell me what you know about this business."

Joisneau glanced up toward the rock face.

"The body was wedged up there."

"Up there?" Niémans repeated, staring at the wall of rock, whose sharp contours cast jagged shadows.

14

"Yes, fifty feet up. The killer stuffed the body into one of the crevices in the rock face. Then maneuvered it into a weird position."

"What sort of position?"

Joisneau bent his legs, raised his knees and crossed his arms over his torso.

"The foetal position."

"Original."

"Everything's original about this case."

"I was told there were wounds and burns," Niémans went on.

"I haven't seen the body yet. But I have heard that there are multiple traces of torture."

"Was the victim tortured to death?"

"Nothing is certain for the moment. There are also deep marks on his throat. Signs of strangulation."

Niémans turned back toward the little lake. In it, he clearly saw his own reflection – cropped head and blue coat.

"What about here? Have you found anything?"

"No. I've been hunting for a clue, a detail, for the last hour. Nothing doing. I reckon the victim wasn't killed here. The murderer just stuffed the body up there."

"Have you been up inside the crevice?"

"Yes. Nothing to report. The murderer must have climbed up onto the top of the rock face from the other side, then lowered the body down on a rope. He then went down on another rope and wedged his victim inside. It can't have been easy getting him into that dramatic posture. I can't figure it out."

Niémans looked once more at that ruggedly uneven cliff, stuck with ridges. From where he was standing, it was impossible to gauge the distances, but it looked as if the crevice where the body had been found was halfway up the face, as far from the ground as it was from the top. He spun round.

"Let's go."

"Where?"

"The hospital. I want to see the body."

The naked man, uncovered only down to his shoulders, lay on his side on a gleaming table. He was huddled up, as though frightened of being struck in the face by lightning. Shoulders hunched, head down, the body still had its two fists clenched under its chin, between its bent knees. The skin was white, muscles protruding, the epidermis dug with wounds which gave the corpse an almost unbearable reality. The neck bore long lacerations, as though someone had tried to rip open its throat. Puffed up veins stood out in its temples, like swollen streams.

Niémans glanced up at the other men present in the morgue. Bernard Terpentes, the investigating magistrate, spindly with a pencil moustache; Captain Roger Barnes, a colossus, swaying like a merchant ship, who was in charge of the Guernon gendarmerie; René Vermont, another gendarme captain on special mission, a small balding man with a wine-red complexion and bright beady eyes. Joisneau, who was standing back from the rest, looked every inch the zealous student.

"Do we know his ID?" Niémans asked no one in particular.

Barnes took a soldierly step forward and cleared his throat.

"The victim's name is Rémy Caillois, superintendent. He was twenty-five years of age. He had been chief librarian at the University of Guernon for the last three years. The body was officially identified by his wife, Sophie Caillois, this morning."

"Had she reported him missing?"

"Yes, yesterday at the end of the afternoon. Her husband had set out the day before on a trek in the mountains, in the direction of the Pointe du Muret. Alone, as he did every weekend. He would sometimes sleep out in one of the refuges. That's why she wasn't worried. Until yesterday afternoon . . ."

Barnes fell silent. Niémans had just uncovered the corpse.

There was a sort of unspoken horror, a silent scream that stuck in their throats. The victim's abdomen and thorax were riddled with dark wounds of various shapes and depths. Incisions with violet edges, rainbow-colored burns, black clouds of soot. There were also shallower lesions on the arms and wrists, as though the man had been strapped up with a cable.

"Who found the body?"

"A young woman ..." Barnes peered down at his papers, then proceeded. "Fanny Ferreira. A lecturer at the university."

"In what circumstances did she find it?"

Barnes cleared his throat once more.

"She's a sportswoman who goes white-water rafting. You know, you descend the rapids on a board, wearing a wetsuit and flippers. It's a highly dangerous sport and ..."

"And?"

"She wound up just beyond the natural dam in the river, at the foot of the rock face that borders the campus. When she climbed up onto the parapet, she spotted the body wedged into the cliff."

"And that's what she told you?"

Barnes looked uncertainly around the room.

"Well, yes, I ..."

The superintendent completely uncovered the body. He paced around that livid, hunched-up creature, whose closely cropped scalp stuck out like a stone arrow.

Niémans grabbed the death certificate, which Barnes had handed him. He glanced over the typed text. It had been written by the head of the hospital in person. The doctor made no pronouncement concerning the time of death. He simply described the visible wounds and concluded that death had been caused by strangulation. For further information, it would be necessary to unfold the body and perform an autopsy.

"When will forensics be here?"

"Any minute now."

The superintendent approached the victim. He leant down and examined his facial features. He was young, rather handsome, his eyes closed and, most importantly, there was no sign of any blows to the face.

"Has anyone touched his face?"

"No one, superintendent."

"So his eyes were closed?"

Barnes nodded. With his thumb and index finger, Niémans gently opened one of the victim's eyelids. Then the impossible happened: a gleaming teardrop slowly fell from the right eye. The superintendent started up in disgust. The face was crying.

Niémans scrutinised the others. No one else had noticed this extraordinary detail. He kept his calm and, still out of sight of the others, looked again. What he saw proved that he had not gone mad and that this murder was what every policeman dreads or longs for throughout his career, according to his character. He stood back up and swiftly covered the body once more. Then he whispered to the magistrate:

"Tell us how the investigations are to proceed."

Bernard Terpentes rose to his full height.

"Well, gentlemen, you understand how this business may turn out to be difficult and . . . unusual. Which explains why the public prosecutor and I have decided to call in the local Grenoble brigade and also the *gendarmerie nationale*. I have also called in Superintendent Niémans, here present, from Paris. I am sure his name is not unknown to you. The superintendent is currently part of a high-ranking section of the Paris vice squad. For the moment, we know nothing about the motive for this murder, but it may well be a sexual one. And it is clearly the work of a maniac. Niémans's experience will be of great use to us. Which is why I should like him to lead this investigation . . ."

Barnes agreed with a swift nod of his head, Vermont likewise, but less enthusiastically. As for Joisneau, he answered:

"That's fine as far as I'm concerned. But my fellow officers will soon be here and . . ."

"I'll put them right," Terpentes cut in. He turned toward Niémans.

"Well, superintendent?"

The whole business was starting to get on Niémans's nerves. He longed to be out of there, getting on with the investigation and, above all, alone.

"How many men do you have, Captain Barnes?" he asked.

"Eight. No . . . I mean, nine."

"Are they used to questioning witnesses, collecting evidence, organising road-blocks?"

"Um, well . . . that's not the sort of thing we . . ."

"What about you, Captain Vermont? How many men do you have?"

The gendarme's voice cracked out like a ten-gun salute:

"Twenty. And experienced, all of them. They'll fine-toothcomb the area around where the body was found and . . ."

"Fine. I suggest that they also question everybody who lives near the roads leading to the river, that they call into service stations, railway stations, houses beside bus stops . . . Young Caillois sometimes slept in refuges when out trekking. Find them and search them. Maybe he was kidnapped in one."

Niémans turned toward Barnes.

"Captain, I want you to put out a request for information across the entire region. By noon, I want a complete list of all the area's prowlers, petty crooks, tramps and what have you. I want you to check who's just been released from prison in a two-hundred-mile radius. Thefts of cars and thefts of any kind. I want you to ask questions in hotels and restaurants. Fax them a questionnaire. I want to know the slightest strange occurrence, the slightest suspect arrival, the slightest indication. I also want a list of all the events that have occurred here in Guernon over at least the last twenty years which may or may not have something to do with this business."

Barnes noted each request on his pad. Niémans turned to Joisneau:

"Get hold of the Special Branch. Ask them for a list of the cults, gurus and other similar nut cases in this region."

Joisneau nodded. Terpentes too, in a sign of superior agreement, as though all these ideas were being plucked straight out of his head.

"That should keep you busy till we get the results of the autopsy," Niémans concluded. "I don't need to add that this has got to be kept hush-hush. Not a word to the local press. Not a word to a single soul."

They parted company on the steps of the University Hospital, striding off through the morning mist. In the shadow of that huge edifice, which looked at least two hundred years old, they got into their cars, heads down, shoulders hunched, without a word or a glance.

The hunt was on.

CHAPTER 4

Pierre Niémans and Eric Joisneau went straight to the university, which was on the edge of the town. The superintendent asked the inspector to wait for him in the library, in the main building, while he paid a call on the university vice-chancellor, whose office took up the top floor of the administrative block, a hundred yards away.

The officer entered a vast 1970s construction, which had already been renovated, with a lofty ceiling and walls of different pastel colors. On the top floor, in a sort of antechamber occupied by a secretary and her tiny desk, Niémans gave his name and asked to see Monsieur Vincent Luyse. While waiting, he looked at the photographs on the walls, showing triumphant students brandishing cups and medals, on ski slopes or in raging torrents.

A few minutes later, Pierre Niémans was standing in front of the vice-chancellor. A man with wiry hair, a flat nose, and skin the color of talc. Vincent Luyse's face was a strange mixture of Black African characteristics and anaemic pallor. A few sunbeams shone through the stormy gloom, slicing through the half-light. The vice-chancellor asked the policeman to take a seat, then started nervously massaging his wrists.

"So?" he asked in a dry voice.

"So what?"

"Have you discovered anything?"

Niémans stretched his legs.

"I've just got here, vice-chancellor. I need a little time to settle in.

Meanwhile, just answer my questions."

Luyse stiffened in his chair. His entire office was made of wood, dotted with metallic mobiles reminiscent of flower stalks on a steel planet.

"Have you had any other tricky incidents in your university?" Niémans asked calmly.

"Tricky? No, not at all."

"No drugs? No thefts? No fights?"

"No."

"There aren't any gangs, or cliques? No youngsters giving each other funny ideas?"

"I don't understand what you mean."

"I'm thinking about role-playing. You know, games full of ceremonies and rituals . . ."

"No. We don't have any of that sort of thing. Our students are a clearheaded crowd."

Niémans remained silent. The vice-chancellor sized him up: crew cut, big build, grip of an MR73 sticking out of his coat. Luyse wiped his face, then said, as though trying to convince himself:

"I've been told that you are an excellent policeman."

Niémans responded by staring back at the vice-chancellor. Luyse turned away his eyes and went on:

"Superintendent, all I want is for you to find the murderer in as short a time as possible. The new academic year is about to begin and . . ."

"So there are no students on the campus yet?"

"Only a few boarders. They live on the top floor of the main building over there. Then there are also a few lecturers who are preparing their courses."

"Can I have a list of them?"

"Why . . ." a hesitation, "of course . . ."

"What about Rémy Caillois? What was he like?"

"An extremely discreet librarian. A loner."

"Was he popular with the students?"

"Yes, yes of course he was."

21

"Where did he live? In Guernon?"

"No, here on the campus. With his wife, on the top floor of the main building. Alongside the boarders."

"Rémy Caillois was twenty-five. That's rather young to be married these days, isn't it?"

"Rémy and Sophie Caillois were both students here. Before that, I believe they met while at the campus school, which is reserved for our lecturers' children. They are . . . they were childhood sweethearts."

Niémans got briskly to his feet.

"Most helpful, vice-chancellor. Thank you."

The superintendent headed off at once, fleeing the smell of fear that pervaded the place.

Books.

Everywhere, in the large university library, numerous racks of books were piled up under the neon lights. Metal shelving holding up veritable walls of perfectly arranged paper. Dark spines. Gold or silver chasing. Labels, all of which bore the crest of the University of Guernon. In the middle of the deserted room stood formica-topped tables, divided into small glass carrels. As soon as Niémans had entered the room, he was reminded of a prison visiting-room.

The atmosphere was at once luminous and stuffy, spacious and cramped.

"The best lecturers teach at this university," Eric Joisneau explained. "The cream of the south-east of France. Law, economics, literature, psychology, sociology, physics . . . And especially medicine – all the top medics of Isère teach here and consult at the University Hospital, which is in fact where the old university used to be. The buildings have been entirely renovated. Half the people in the *département* go there when they're ill and all the mountain dwellers were born in its maternity clinic."

Niémans listened to him, arms crossed, leaning back onto one of the reading tables.

"Sounds like you know what you're talking about."

Joisneau picked up a book at random.

"I studied at this university. I started doing law . . . I wanted to be a lawyer."

"And you became a policeman?"

The lieutenant looked at Niémans. In the white neon light, his eyes were gleaming.

"When I took my degree, I was suddenly scared that I was going to get shit bored. So I enrolled in the police academy of Toulouse. I reckoned that the police meant an action-packed career, full of risks. A career that would have surprises in store for me . . ."

"And now you're disappointed?"

The lieutenant put the book back on the shelf. His slight smile faded.

"Not today, I'm not. Definitely not today." He stared at Niémans. "That body . . . How could anybody do that?"

Niémans ducked the question.

"What was the atmosphere like here? Anything special?"

"No. Lots of middle-class kids, full of clichés about life, about politics, about the ideas you were supposed to have . . . And the children of farmers and workers, too. Even more idealistic. And more aggressive. Anyway, we were all heading for Welfare, so . . ."

"There wasn't any funny business? No strange cliques?"

"No. Nothing. Except, that is, there was a sort of university elite. A microcosm made up of the children of the lecturers themselves. Some of them were real high fliers. They won all the prizes every year. Even the sports awards. We were completely left standing."

Niémans recalled the photographs of champions in the antechamber of Luyse's office. He asked:

"Did these students make up a real clan? Could they all be working together on some sick idea?"

Joisneau burst out laughing.

"What do you mean? A kind of . . . conspiracy?"

It was Niémans's turn to get up and wander along the bookshelves.

"A librarian is at the center of a university. An ideal target. Imagine a group of students dabbling in some sort of hocus pocus.

23

A sacrifice, a ritual . . . When choosing their victim, they could quite easily have thought of Caillois."

"Then forget about the whiz kids I just mentioned. They were too busy getting firsts in their exams to worry about anything else."

Niémans walked on between the rows of reddish brown books. Joisneau followed him.

"A librarian," he resumed, "is also the person who lends books . . . Who knows what everybody is reading, what everybody is studying . . . Maybe he knew something he shouldn't have."

"You don't kill someone like that for . . . And what sort of secret reading scheme do you imagine these students had?"

Niémans spun round.

"I don't know. But I mistrust intellectuals."

"Have you already got an idea? A suspicion?"

"None at all. Right now, anything is possible. A fight. Revenge. Intellectual weirdoes. Or homosexual ones. Or quite simply a prowler, a maniac, who stumbled onto Caillois quite by chance in the mountains."

The superintendent fingered the spines of the books.

"You see, I'm not biased. But here is where we're going to start. Dig out all the books that could have some bearing on the murder."

"What sort of bearing?"

Niémans went back down the rows of shelving and emerged into the main reading-room. He headed for the librarian's office, which was situated at the far end, on a raised platform, overlooking the carrels. A computer sat on the desk. Ring-binders lay in the drawers. Niémans patted the dark screen.

"In here there must be a list of all the books that are consulted, or borrowed, every day. I want you to put some of your men on the job. The most bookish ones you can find. Get the boarders to help as well. I want them to pick out all the books that deal with evil, violence, torture and religious sacrifices. Look through the ethnology titles, for example. I also want them to note down the names of all the students who have regularly consulted this sort of book. And dig me out Caillois's thesis."

24

"What about me?"

"You question the boarders. One at a time. They live here night and day, so they must know the university from top to bottom. The habits, the feel of the place, any weird kids . . . I want to know what the others thought of Caillois. I also want you to find out about his walks in the mountains. Find his fellow hikers. Discover who knew the routes he took. Who could have met him up there . . ."

Joisneau glanced skeptically at the superintendent. Niémans walked over to him. He was now speaking in whispers:

"I'll tell you what we have on our hands. We have an incredible murder, a pallid, smooth, hunched-up body bearing the traces of unspeakable suffering. The whole thing stinks of craziness. Right now, it's our little secret. We have a few hours, maybe a little longer, to solve this business. After that, the media will get involved, the pressure will build up, and emotions start to run wild. So concentrate. Dive into the nightmare. Give all you've got. That's how we'll unmask the face of evil."

The lieutenant looked terrified.

"You really think that, in a few hours, we can . . ."

"Do you want to work with me, or not?" Niémans butted in. "Look, this is the way I see things. When a murder has been committed, you have to look at every surrounding detail as though it was a mirror. The body of the victim, the people who knew him, the scene of the crime . . . Everything reflects the truth, some particular aspect of the murder, see what I mean?"

He tapped the computer screen.

"This screen, for instance. When it's been switched on, it will become the mirror of Rémy Caillois's daily existence. The mirror of his working life, of his thoughts. It will contain elements, reflections that may be of use to us. We have to dive in. Get through to the other side."

He stood up and opened his arms.

"We're in a hall of mirrors, Joisneau, a labyrinth of reflected images. So take a good look. At everything. Because, somewhere inside one of those mirrors, in a dead angle, the murderer is hiding."

Joisneau gaped.

"You seem a bit clever for a man of action . . ."

The superintendent slapped his chest with the back of his hand.

"This isn't abstract theory, Joisneau. It's purely practical."

"And what about you? Who . . . who are you going to question?"

"Me? I'm going to question our witness, Fanny Ferreira. And then Sophie Caillois, the victim's wife."

Niémans winked.

"The ladies, Joisneau. That's what I call being purely practical."

CHAPTER 5

Under the dreary sky, the asphalt road snaked across the campus, leading to each of its gray buildings with their blue, rusting windows. Niémans drove slowly – he had obtained a map of the university – on the way to an isolated gymnasium. He reached another block of fluted concrete, which looked more like a bunker than a sports center. He got out of his car and breathed deeply. It was drizzling.

He examined the construction of the campus, situated at a few hundred yards' distance. His parents, too, had been teachers, but in small secondary schools in the suburbs of Lyons. He had practically no memories of them. Family ties had soon seemed to him to be a weakness, a lie. He had rapidly realised that he was going to have to fight alone and, accordingly, the sooner the better. From the age of thirteen, he had asked to be sent to a boarding school. They had not dared refuse this voluntary exile, but he could still remember his mother's sobs from the other side of his bedroom wall: it was a sound in his head and, at the same time, a physical sensation, something damp and warm on his skin. So, he had decamped.

Four years spent boarding. Four years of solitude and physical training, apart from his lessons. All his hopes were then pinned on one target: the army. At seventeen, Pierre Niémans, who had passed his exams with flying colors, went for his three days' induction and asked to join the officers' training school. When the military doctor told him that he had been discharged as unfit and explained the reasons for this decision, Niémans suddenly understood. His anxieties were so manifest that they had betrayed him, despite all his ambition. He realised that his destiny would always be that long, seamless corridor, plastered with blood, where, at the very end, dogs howled in the darkness . . .

Other adolescents would have given up and quietly listened to the psychiatrists' opinions. Not Pierre Niémans. He persisted, and he began training again, with a redoubled rage and determination. If Pierre could not be a soldier, then he would pick another battle-field: the streets, the anonymous struggle against everyday evil. He would devote all of his strength and his soul to a war with no flags and no glorious deaths. Niémans would become a policeman. With this in mind, he spent months practising the answers to psychiatric tests. He then enrolled in Cannes-Ecluse police academy. And the era of violence began: top marks at target practice. Niémans continued to improve, to grow stronger. He became an outstanding policeman. Tenacious, violent, vicious.

He started working in local police stations then became a sharpshooter in what was to become the Rapid Intervention Unit. Special operations began.

He killed his first man. At that instant, he made a pact with himself and, for the last time, contemplated his own fate. No, he would never be a proud warrior, a valiant army officer. But he would be a restless, obstinate street fighter, who would drown his own fears in the violence and the fury of the concrete jungle.

Niémans took a deep breath of mountain air. He thought about his mother, who had been dead for years. He thought about his past, which now seemed like an endless canyon, and his memories, which had splintered, then faded, making a last stand against oblivion.

As though lost in a dream, Niémans suddenly noticed a little dog. The creature was muscular, its short coat glistening in the mist. Its eyes, two drops of opaque lacquer, were staring at the policeman.

Waggling its behind, it was approaching. The officer froze. The dog drew ever nearer, just a few steps away. Its moist nose twitched. Then it abruptly started growling. Its eyes shone. It had smelt fear. The fear oozing out of this man.

Niémans was petrified.

His limbs felt as though they had been gripped by a mysterious force. His blood was being sucked away by an invisible siphon, somewhere in his guts. The dog barked, showing its teeth. Niémans understood the process. Fear produced an odor which the dog smelt and which provoked a reaction of dread and hostility. Fear feeding on fear. The dog barked then rolled its neck, grinding its teeth together. The cop drew his gun.

"Clarisse! Clarisse! Come back, Clarisse!"

Niémans re-emerged from his spell in the cooler. Through a red veil, he saw a gray man in a zip-up cardigan. He was approaching rapidly.

"You got a screw loose, or what?"

Niémans mumbled:

"Police. Get lost. And take your mutt with you."

The man was stunned.

"Jesus Christ, I don't believe this. Come on, Clarisse, come on, little darling . . ."

Master and hound moved off. Niémans tried to gulp back his saliva. His throat felt harsh, dry as an oven. He shook his head, put his gun away and paced round the building. As he turned left, he forced himself to remember: how long was it now since he had seen his shrink?

Around the second corner of the gymnasium, the superintendent came across the woman.

Fanny Ferreira was standing near an open door and sanding down a red-colored foam board. The officer imagined that it must be the raft she used to float downstream.

"Good morning," he said with a bow.

He was back among warmth and assurance.

Fanny raised her eyes. She must have been twenty, at most. Her skin was dark and her hair generously curly, with slight ringlets around her temples and a heavy cascade over her shoulders. Her face was somber and velvety, but her eyes had a penetrating, almost indecent, clarity.

"I'm Superintendent Pierre Niémans. I'm investigating the murder of Rémy Caillois."

"Pierre Niémans?" she repeated in astonishment. "But that's amazing!"

"Sorry?"

She nodded toward a small radio, lying on the ground.

"They were just talking about you on the news. Apparently, you arrested two murderers last night, just near the Parc des Princes. Which is rather good. But they also said that one of them was disfigured. Which is not so good. Are you omnipresent, or what?"

"No, I just drove all night."

"But why are you here? Aren't our own local cops up to it?"

"Let's just say I'm part of the reinforcements."

Fanny went back to work – she damped down the oblong surface of the board, then pressed a folded sheet of sandpaper onto it with both palms. Her body looked stocky and solid. She was dressed casually – neoprene diver's leggings, a sailor's jumper, light-colored leather boots, which were tightly laced. The veiled light cast a soft rainbow over the entire scene.

"You seem to have got over the shock quickly enough," Niémans observed.

"What shock?"

"You remember? You discovered a . . ."

"I'm trying not to think about it."

"So would you mind talking about it again?"

"That's why you're here, isn't it?"

She was not looking at the policeman. Her hands continued to run up and down the length of the board. Her movements were jerky and brutal.

"In what circumstances did you find the body?"

"Every weekend I go down the rapids . . ." She pointed at her upturned raft. . . . "on one of these things. I'd just finished one of

29

my little trips. Near the campus, there's a rock face, a natural dam, which blocks the current and lets you land easily. I was pulling out my raft when I noticed it . . ."

"In the rocks?"

"Yup, in the rocks."

"You're lying. I've been up there. I noticed that there's no room to move back. It's impossible to pick out something in the cliffs, fifty feet up . . ."

Fanny threw her sheet of sandpaper into a plastic cup, wiped her hands and lit a cigarette. These simple gestures provoked a feeling of violent desire in Niémans.

The young woman exhaled a long puff of blue smoke.

"The body was in the rock face. But I didn't see it in the rock face."

"Where, then?"

"I noticed it in the waters of the river. As a reflection. A white blotch on the surface of the lake."

Niémans's features relaxed.

"That's just what I thought."

"Is that really important as regards the investigations?"

"No. But I like everything to be clear."

Niémans paused for a moment, then went on:

"You're a rock climber, aren't you?"

"How did you guess?"

"I don't know . . . because of the region. And you do look extremely . . . sporty."

She turned round and opened her arms toward the mountains, which overlooked the valley. It was the first time she had smiled.

"This is my home turf, superintendent. I know these mountains like the back of my hand, from the Grand Pic de Belledonne to the Grandes Rousses. When I'm not shooting the rapids, I'm climbing the summits."

"In your opinion, could only a climber have positioned the body in the rock face?"

Fanny became serious once more. She observed the glowing tip of her cigarette.

30

"No, not necessarily. The rocks almost form a natural staircase. On the other hand, you'd have to be extremely strong to be able to carry the body without losing your balance."

"One of my inspectors thinks that the killer climbed up from the other side instead, where the slope is less steep, then lowered the body down on a rope."

"That would be one hell of a long way round." She hesitated, then went on. "In fact, there's a third possibility, quite simple, if you know a little about climbing."

"Which is?"

Fanny Ferreira stubbed her cigarette out on her heel and threw it away.

"Come with me," she commanded.

They went inside the gymnasium. In the half-light, Niémans made out a heap of mats, the straight shadows of parallel bars, poles, knotted ropes. As they approached the right-hand wall, Fanny remarked:

"This is my den. No one else comes here during the summer. So I keep my equipment here."

She lit a stormlight, which hung over a sort of workbench. On it were various instruments, metal parts with a variety of points and blades, casting silvery reflections or sharp glints. Fanny lit another cigarette.

Niémans asked her:

"What's all this?"

"Picks, snaphooks, triangles, safety catches. Climbing equipment."

"So?"

Fanny exhaled once more, with a sequence of simulated hiccups.

"And so, superintendent, a murderer in possession of this sort of equipment, and who knew how to use it, could quite easily have raised the body up from the river bank."

Niémans crossed his arms and leant back against the wall. While handling her tools, Fanny kept her cigarette in her mouth. This innocent gesture heightened the policeman's craving. He really did find her extremely attractive.

31

"As I told you," she began, "that part of the rock face has a sort of natural staircase. It would be child's play for someone who knew about climbing, or even trekking for that matter, to climb up first without the body."

"And then?"

Fanny grabbed a fluorescent green pulley, with a constellation of tiny openings.

"And then you stick that in the rock, just above the crevice."

"In the rock! But how? With a hammer? That would take ages, wouldn't it?"

Behind her screen of cigarette smoke, she replied:

"You seem to know practically nothing about rock climbing, superintendent." She seized some threaded pitons from the workbench. "Here are some spits. Now, with a rock drill like this one" – she indicated a sort of black, greasy drill – "you can stick several spits into any sort of rock in a matter of seconds. Then you fix your pulley and all you have to do is haul up the body. It's the technique we use for lifting bags up into difficult or narrow spaces."

Niémans pouted skeptically.

"I haven't been up there, but I reckon the crevice is extremely narrow. I don't see how the murderer could have crouched inside, then been able to pull up the body with just his arms, and with no pull from his legs. Which takes us back to the same portrait of our killer: a colossus."

"Who said anything about pulling it up? To raise his victim, all the climber had to do was lower himself down on the other side of the pulley, as a counterweight. The body would then have gone up all on its own."

The policeman suddenly caught on and smiled at such a simple idea.

"But then the killer would have to be heavier than his victim, wouldn't he?"

"Or the same weight. When you throw yourself down, your weight increases. Once the body had been raised, your murderer could have quickly climbed back up, still using the natural steps, then wedged his victim in that theatrical rock fault."

The superintendent took another look at the spits, screws and rings that were lying on the workbench. It reminded him of a burglar's set of tools, but a particular sort of burglar – someone who breaks through altitudes and gravity.

"How long would all that take?"

"I could do it in less than ten minutes."

Niémans nodded. The killer's profile was becoming clearer. The two of them went back outside. The sun was filtering through the clouds, shimmering on the mountain peaks. The policeman asked:

"Do you teach at the university?"

"Geology."

"More exactly?"

"I teach several subjects: rock taxonomy, tectonic displacements and glaciology, too – the evolution of glaciers."

"You look very young."

"I got my PhD when I was twenty. By then, I was already a junior lecturer. I'm the youngest doctor in France. I'm now twenty-five and a tenured professor."

"A real university whiz kid."

"That's right. A whiz kid. Daughter and granddaughter of emeritus professors, here in Guernon."

"So you're part of the clan?"

"What clan?"

"One of my lieutenants studied at Guernon. He told me how the university has a separate elite, made up of the children of the university lecturers . . ."

Fanny shook her head maliciously.

"I'd prefer to call it a big family. The children you're talking about grow up in the university, amidst learning and culture. They then get excellent results. Nothing very surprising about that, is there?"

"Even in sporting competitions?"

She raised her eyebrows.

"That comes from the mountain air."

Niémans pressed on:

33

"I suppose you knew Rémy Caillois. What was he like?"

Without any hesitation, Fanny replied:

"A loner. Introverted. Sullen, even. But extremely brilliant. Dazzlingly cultivated. There was a rumor going round ... that he had read every book in the library."

"Do you think there was any truth in that?"

"I don't know. But he certainly knew the library well enough. It was his cave, his refuge, his earth."

"He was very young, too, wasn't he?"

"He grew up in the library. His father was head librarian before him."

Niémans casually paced forward.

"I didn't know that. Were the Caillois also part of your 'big family'?"

"Definitely not. Rémy was even hostile to us. Despite all his culture, he never got the results he was hoping for. I think ... or rather, I suppose he was jealous of us."

"What was his subject?"

"Philosophy, I believe. He was trying to finish his thesis."

"What was it about?"

"I've no idea."

The superintendent paused. He looked up at the mountains. Under the increasing glare of the sun, they looked like dazzled giants. Another question:

"Is his father still alive?"

"No. He passed on a few years ago. A climbing accident."

"There was nothing suspicious about it?"

"What are you after? He died in an avalanche. The one on the Grande Lance of Allemond, in '93. You're every inch a cop."

"So we have two rock-climbing librarians. Father and son. Who both died in the mountains. That is a bit of a coincidence, isn't it?"

"Who said that Rémy was killed in the mountains?"

"True. But he set off on a hike on Saturday morning. He must have been attacked by the killer up there. Perhaps the murderer knew the route he was taking and ..."

"Rémy wasn't the sort of person who follows regular routes. Nor one who tells others where he's going. He was very ... secretive."

Niémans nodded his head.

"Thank you, young lady. You know the form – if you think of anything that may be of importance, then phone me on one of these numbers."

Niémans jotted down the numbers of his mobile and of a room which the vice-chancellor had given him at the university – he had preferred to set up base inside the university rather than with the *gendarmerie*. He murmured:

"See you soon."

The young woman did not look up. The policeman was leaving when she said:

"Can I ask you a question?"

She stared at him with her eyes of crystal. Niémans felt decidedly uneasy. Her irises were too light. They were made of glass, white water, as chilling as frost.

"Fire away," he replied.

"On the radio, they said . . . Well, is it true that you were one of the team that killed Jacques Mesrine?"

"I was young then. But it's true. I was there."

"I was wondering . . . What does it feel like afterward?"

"After what?"

"After something like that."

Niémans moved toward the young woman. Instinctively, she flinched. But, with a touch of arrogance, she bravely looked back at him.

"It will always be a pleasure talking to you, Fanny. But you will never get a word out of me about that. Nor about what I lost that day."

The questioner lowered her eyes. Softly, she said:

"I see."

"No, you don't see. Which is just as well for you."

CHAPTER 6

The trickling water dripped onto his back. Niémans had borrowed a pair of hiking boots from the *gendarmerie* and was now ascending the natural staircase in the rock face, which was a reasonably easy climb. When he reached the height of the crevice, he took a careful look at the narrow opening where the body had been discovered. Then he examined the surrounding rock face. With his hands protected by Gore-Tex gloves he felt for possible traces of spits in the wall.

Holes in the stone.

The wind, laden with drops of icy water, beat against his face. It was a sensation Niémans liked. Despite the circumstances, he had experienced a strong feeling of fulfilment on reaching the lake. Maybe the killer had chosen this site for that very reason: it was a place of calm and serenity, pure and uncluttered. A place where jade waters soothed violent souls.

The superintendent found nothing. He continued his search around the niche: no trace of any spits. He knelt on the ledge and ran his hands over the inner walls of the cavity. Suddenly, his fingers came across an evident opening, right in the middle of the ceiling. He thought fleetingly of Fanny Ferreira. She had been right: the killer, equipped with spits and pulleys, must have hauled up the corpse by using his own body weight. He shoved his arms inside and located three notched, grooved cavities, about eight inches deep, and which formed a triangle – the three prints of the spits that had carried the pulleys. The circumstances of the murder were becoming clearer. Rémy Caillois had been set upon while out hiking. The murderer had strapped him up, tortured, mutilated then killed him in those lonely heights, and had then gone back down into the valley with his victim's body. How? Niémans glanced down forty feet below, there where the waters turned into a mirror of lacquer. On the stream. The killer must have descended the river in a canoe or something similar. But why had he gone to such lengths? Why had he not just left the body at the scene of the crime?

The policeman cautiously climbed back down. When on the bank, he removed his gloves, turned his back to the rocks and examined the shadow of the crevice on the perfectly smooth water. The reflection was as steady as a picture. He now felt sure that this place was a sanctuary. Calm and pure. And that was perhaps why the killer had chosen it. In any case, the investigator was now certain about one thing.

His killer was an experienced rock climber.

Niémans's saloon car was equipped with a VHF transmitter, but he never used it. No more than he used his cell phone when it came to confidential calls, it being even less secure. For the last few years, he had used a pager, varying from time to time its brand and model. No one else could intercept this form of communication, which necessitated a password. It was a trick he had learnt from Parisian drug dealers, who had immediately caught on to how discreet pagers were. The superintendent had given his number and password to Joisneau, Barnes and Vermont. As he got into his car he took it out of his pocket and switched it on. No messages.

He started his car and drove back to the university.

It was now eleven in the morning. Occasional figures crossed the green esplanade. A few students were running on the track in the stadium, which stood slightly away from the group of concrete blocks.

The officer turned at the crossroads and headed back toward the main building. This immense bunker was eight storeys high and six hundred yards long. He parked and consulted his map. Apart from the library, the huge construction contained the medicine and physics lecture halls. On the upper floors were the rooms set aside for practical work. And on the top floor there were the boarders' rooms. The campus janitor had marked, with a red felt-tip pen, the room occupied by Rémy Caillois and his young wife.

Pierre Niémans walked past the library doors, which were adjacent to the main entrance, and reached the hall: an open-plan construction lit by large bay windows. The walls were decorated with naïve frescoes, which shone in the morning sunlight, and the end of the hall, several hundred yards away, vanished into a sort of mineral haze. It was a place of Stalinist dimensions, utterly unlike the pale marble and brown wood of Parisian universities. Or, at least, that was what Niémans supposed. He had never before set foot in a university in Paris or anywhere else.

He climbed up a staircase of suspended marble steps, each block bent into a hairpin and separated by vertical strips. Something the architect had dreamt up, in the same overwhelming style as the rest. Every other neon light was broken, so Niémans crossed regions of utter darkness before emerging into zones of excessive brilliance.

He finally reached a narrow corridor, punctuated by small doors. He wandered down this black shaft – here, all the light bulbs had given up the ghost – looking for number 34, the Caillois's flat.

The door was ajar.

With two fingers, the policeman pushed the thin piece of plywood open. Silence and half-light welcomed him. Niémans found himself in a little hall. At the end, a stream of light crossed the narrow corridor. It was enough to enable him to make out the frames that hung on the walls. They contained black-and-white photographs, apparently dating from the 1930s or 1940s. Olympic athletes in full flight spiralled into the sky, or dug their heels into the ground, in postures of religious pride. Their faces, figures and positions gave off a sort of worrying perfection, the inhuman purity of statues. Niémans thought of the university architecture. It all fitted together in a rather uneasy way.

Beneath these images, he noticed a portrait of Rémy Caillois and took it down to get a better look. The victim had been a handsome, smiling youth with short hair and drawn features. His eyes shone with an extremely alert sparkle.

"Who are you?"

Niémans turned his head. A female form, draped in a raincoat, stood at the end of the corridor. Still a kid. She, too, could scarcely be twenty-five. Her shoulder-length fair hair framed a thin ravaged face, whose paleness brought out the dark rings around her eyes. Her features were bony, but delicate. This woman's beauty emerged only in moments of crisis, as though it were the echo of a first feeling of uneasiness.

"I'm Superintendent Pierre Niémans," he announced.

"And you come in like that without knocking?"

"I'm sorry. The door was open. You are Rémy Caillois's wife?"

Her reply was to snatch the portrait out of Niémans's hands and hang it back on the wall. Then, walking back into the room to the left, she took off her raincoat. Niémans had a surreptitious glimpse of a pale emaciated chest in the hanging folds of an ancient pullover. He shuddered.

"Come in," she said despite herself.

Niémans found himself in a cramped living-room, with a neat austere decor. Modern paintings hung on the walls. Symmetrical lines, distressing colors, incomprehensible stuff. The policeman took no notice. But one detail did strike him: there was a strong chemical smell in the room. A smell of paste. The Caillois must have just redecorated their flat. This detail cut him to the quick. For the first time he shivered at the thought of this couple's ruined hopes, the ashes of happiness that must still be glowing beneath that woman's grief. He adopted a serious tone:

"I've come from Paris, Madame. I was called in by the investigating magistrate to help in the enquiries into your husband's sad demise. I . . ."

"Do you have a lead?"

The superintendent stared at her, then suddenly felt like breaking something, a window, anything. This woman was full of grief, but her hatred of the police was even stronger.

"No, we don't. Not for the moment," he admitted. "But I'm optimistic that investigations will soon . . ."

"Ask your questions."

Niémans sat down on the sofa-bed, opposite the woman who had chosen a small chair in order to keep her distance from him. To save face, he seized a cushion and fiddled with it for a few seconds.

"I've read your statement," he began. "And I would just like to

39

get a little additional information. Lots of people go hiking in this region I suppose?"

"What else do you think there is to do in Guernon? Everybody goes walking, or climbing."

"Did other hikers know the routes Rémy took?"

"No. He never talked about that. He used to go off on ways known only to him."

"Did he just go walking, or climbing as well?"

"It depended. On Saturday, Rémy set off on foot, at an altitude of less than six thousand feet. He didn't take any equipment with him."

Niémans paused for a moment before getting to the heart of the matter.

"Did your husband have any enemies?"

"No."

The ambiguous tone of the answer led him to ask another question, which took even him by surprise:

"Did he have any friends?"

"No. Rémy was a loner."

"How did he get on with the students who used the library?"

"The only contact he had with them was to give them library tickets."

"Anything strange happen recently?"

The woman did not answer. Niémans pressed the point:

"Your husband wasn't particularly nervy or tense?"

"No."

"Tell me about his father's death."

Sophie Caillois raised her eyes. Her pupils were dull, but her eyelashes and eyebrows were magnificent. She gave a slight shrug of the shoulders. "He died in an avalanche in 1993. We weren't married at the time. I don't know anything much about all that. What are you trying to get at?"

The police officer remained silent and looked round the little room, with its immaculately arranged furniture. He knew this sort of place off by heart. He realised that he was not alone with Sophie Caillois. Memories of the dead man lingered there, as though his soul were packing its bags somewhere, in the next room. The superintendent pointed at the pictures on the walls.

"Your husband didn't keep any books here?"

"Why would he have done that? He worked all day in the library."

"Is that where he worked on his thesis?"

The woman nodded curtly. Niémans could not take his eyes off that beautiful, hard face. He was surprised at meeting two such attractive women in less than one hour.

"What was his thesis about?"

"The Olympic games."

"Hardly an intellectual subject."

An expression of scorn crossed Sophie Caillois's face.

"His thesis was about the relationship between the sporting event and the sacred. Between the body and the mind. He was studying the myth of the *athlon*; the first man who made the earth fertile by his own strength, by transcending the limits of his own body."

"I'm sorry," Niémans huffed. "I don't know much about philosophy . . . Does that have something to do with the photographs in the corridor?"

"Yes and no. They're stills taken from a film by Leni Riefenstahl about the 1936 Berlin Olympic games."

"They're striking images."

"Rémy said that those Games had revived the profound nature of the Games of Olympus, which were based on the marriage of mind and body, of physical effort and philosophical expression."

"And in this case, of Nazi ideology, isn't that so?"

"The nature of the thought being expressed didn't matter to my husband. All he was interested in was that fusion of an idea and a force, of thought and action."

This sort of clap-trap meant nothing to Niémans. The woman leant forward then suddenly spat out:

"Why did they send you here? Why someone like you?"

He ignored the aggressive tone. When questioning, he always used the same cold, inhuman approach, based on intimidation. It is pointless for a policeman – and particularly for a policeman with his mug – to play at being understanding or at amateur psychology. In a commanding voice, he asked:

"In your opinion, was there any reason for anyone to have it in for your husband?"

"Are you crazy, or what?" she yelled. "Haven't you seen the body? Don't you realise that it was a maniac who killed my husband? That Rémy was picked up by a nut? A headcase who laid into him, beat him, mutilated him, tortured him to death?"

The policeman took a deep breath. He was thinking of that quiet, unworldly librarian, and his aggressive wife. A chilling couple. He asked:

"How was your home life?"

"Mind your own fucking business."

"Answer the question, please."

"Am I a suspect?"

"You know damn well you're not. So just answer my question."

The young woman looked daggers at him.

"You want to know how many times a week we fucked?"

Goose-pimples rose over the nape of Niéman's neck.

"Would you co-operate, Madame? I'm only doing my job."

"Get lost, you fucking pig."

Her teeth were far from white, but the contours of her lips were ravishingly moving. Niémans stared at that mouth, her pointed cheek bones, her eyebrows, which shed rays across the pallor of her face. What did the tint of her skin, of her eyes matter? All those illusive plays of light and tone? Beauty lay in the lines. The shape. An incorruptible purity. The policeman stayed put.

"Fuck off!" the woman screamed.

"One last question. Rémy had always lived at the university. When did he do his military service?"

Sophie Caillois froze, taken aback by this unexpected question. She wrapped her arms around her chest, as though suddenly chilled from the inside.

"He didn't."

"He was declared unfit?"

The woman's eyes fixed themselves once more on the superintendent.

"What are you after?"

"For what reasons?"

"Psychiatric, I think."

"He had mental problems?"

"Are you off the last banana boat, or what? Everybody gets dismissed for psychiatric reasons. It doesn't mean a thing. You play up, come out with a load of gibberish, then get dismissed."

Niémans did not utter a word, but his entire bearing must have expressed deep disapproval. The woman suddenly took in his crew cut, his rigid elegance and his lips arching in a grimace of disgust.

"Jesus Christ, just drop it!"

He got up and murmured:

"So, I'll be going then. But I'd just like you to remember one thing."

"What's that?" she spat.

"Whether you like it or not, it's people like me who catch murderers. It's people like me who will avenge your husband."

The woman's features turned to stone for a couple of seconds, then her chin trembled. She collapsed in tears. Niémans turned on his heel.

"I'll get him," he said.

In the doorway, he punched the wall and called back over his shoulder:

"By Christ, I swear it. I'll get the little fucker who killed your husband."

Outside, a silvery flash burst in front of his face. Black spots danced beneath his eyelids. Niémans swayed for a few seconds. Then he forced himself to walk calmly to his car, while the dark halos gradually turned into women's faces. Fanny Ferreira, the brunette. And Sophie Caillois, the blonde. Two strong, intelligent, aggressive women. The sort of women this policeman would probably never hold in his arms.

He aimed a violent kick at an ancient metal bin, riveted to a pylon, then instinctively looked at his pager.

The screen was flashing. The forensic pathologist had just finished the autopsy.

II

CHAPTER 7

At dawn that same day, at a distance of two hundred and thirty miles due west, Police Lieutenant Karim Abdouf had just finished reading a criminology thesis about the use of genetic sampling in cases of rape and murder. The six-hundred-page door-stopper had kept him up practically all night. He now looked at the figures on his quartz alarm clock as it rang: 07.00.

Karim sighed, flung the thesis across the floor, then went into the kitchen to make some black tea. He returned to his living-room – which was also his dining-room and bedroom – and stared out at the shadows through the bay window. Forehead pressed against the pane, he evaluated his chances of being able to conduct a genetic enquiry in the one-horse town to which he had been transferred. They were zero.

The young second-generation Arab looked at the street-lights, which were still nailing down the dark wings of the night. Bitterness knotted his throat. Even when up to his ears in crime, he had always managed to avoid prison. And now, here he was, twenty-nine years old, a cop, and banged up in the lousiest prison of them all: a small provincial town, as boring as shit, in the midst of a rocky plain. A prison with neither walls nor bars. A psychological prison which was gnawing away at his soul.

Karim started daydreaming. He saw himself nicking serial killers, thanks to analyses of DNA and specialised software, just like in American movies. He imagined himself leading a team of scientists who were studying the genetic map of the criminal type. After much research and statistical analysis, the specialists isolated a sort of rupture, a flaw somewhere in the spiral of chromosomes, and identified this split as the key to the criminal mentality. Some time ago, there had already been mention of a double Y chromosome which was supposed to be characteristic of murderers. But this had turned out to be a false lead. Nevertheless, in Karim's daydream, another "spelling mistake" was located in the set of letters which made up the genetic code. And this discovery had been made thanks to Karim and his relentless arrests. A shudder suddenly ran through him. He knew that if such a "flaw" existed, then it was also coursing round his veins.

The word "orphan" had never meant much to Karim. You could miss only what you had experienced and he had never had anything which could even remotely be described as a family. His earliest memories were of a patch of lino and a black-and-white TV in the Rue Maurice-Thorez children's home in Nanterre. Karim had grown up in the midst of a colorless, graceless neighborhood. Detached houses rubbed shoulders with the tower blocks, patches of wasteland gradually turned into housing estates. And he could still remember those games of hide-and-seek with the building sites that were little by little gobbling up the wild nature of his childhood.

Karim was a lost child. Or a foundling. It all depended on which way round you looked at it. Whichever, he had never known his parents and nothing in the education that he subsequently received had served to remind him of his origins. He could not speak Arabic very well and had only the vaguest knowledge of Islam. The adolescent had rapidly rejected his guardians – the carers in the home, whose simplicity and general niceness made him want to puke – and had given himself over to the streets.

He had then discovered Nanterre, a limitless territory crisscrossed by broad avenues, dotted with massive housing estates, factories and local government offices, and populated by a sheepish crowd dressed in rumpled old clothes and who expected no tomorrows. But degradation shocks only the rich. Karim did not even notice the poverty that characterised the town from the tiniest brick to people's deeply wrinkled faces.

His adolescent memories were happy ones. The time of punk rock, of "No Future". Thirteen years old. His first pals. And first dates. Oddly enough, in the loneliness and torments of adolescence, Karim stumbled across a reason to love and to share. After his orphaned childhood, his difficult teenage years gave him a second chance to find himself, open up to others and to the outside world. Even today, Karim could still remember those times with a total clarity. The long hours spent in bars, pushing and shoving over a pinball machine, laughing with his buddies. The endless daydreams, throat in a knot, thinking about a girl he had spotted on the steps at school.

But the suburbs were hiding their true nature. Abdouf had always known that Nanterre was a sad dead-end place. He now discovered that the streets were violent, even lethal.

One Friday evening, a gang burst into the café of the swimming pool, which was open late. Without a word, they kicked the manager's face in, then bottled him. An old story of refused entry, or a beer not paid for, no one knew any more. And no one had lifted a finger. But the stifled cries of the man beneath the counter became resonant echoes in Karim's nerves. That night, things were explained to him. Names, places, rumors. He got a glimpse of another world, the existence of which he had not even suspected. A world peopled by ultra-violent beings, inaccessible estates, blood-stained cellars. On another occasion, just before a concert on Rue de l'Ancienne Mairie, a fight had turned into a slaughter. The tribes were out once again. Karim had seen kids rolling on the asphalt, their faces split open, and girls hiding under cars, their hair sticky with blood.

As he got older, he no longer recognised his town. A tidal wave was swamping it. Everyone spoke in admiration of Victor, a boy from the Cameroons who jacked up on the roofs of the estate. Of Marcel, a nasty piece of work, with a pock-marked face and a blue beauty spot tattooed on his forehead, like an Indian, who had been put away several times for beating up cops. Of Jamel and Saïd who had held up the Caisse d'Epargne. On his way out of school, Karim would sometimes notice these youths. He was struck by their haughty nobility. They were not vulgar, uneducated or coarse. No, they were aristocratic, elegant, with ardent eyes and studied gestures.

He chose his camp. He started out by stealing car radios, then cars and so became truly financially independent. He hung out with the drugged-out Black, his "brothers" the bank robbers, and especially Marcel, a footloose, scary and brutal person, who ran wild from dawn to dusk, but who could also distance himself from the suburbs in a way which fascinated Karim. Marcel, a peroxide skinhead, wore fur-lined jackets and listened to Liszt's *Hungarian Rhapsodies*. He lived in squats and read Blaise Cendrars. He called Nanterre "the octopus" and, as Karim knew, invented for himself a whole set of excuses and explanations for his future, inevitable fall. Strangely enough, this suburban being revealed to Karim the existence of another life, one beyond the suburbs.

The orphan swore that, one day, he would make it his.

While continuing his thieving, he studied hard at school, which surprised everybody. He took Thai boxing lessons – to protect himself from others and from himself, for he was occasionally gripped by uncontrollable fits of violent rage. His destiny had now become a tightrope, along which he walked without losing his balance. Around him, the dark swamps of delinquency and debauchery were swallowing everything up. Karim was seventeen. He was alone again. Silence surrounded him when he walked across the hall of the adolescents' home, or when he had a coffee in the school café, sitting next to the pinball machines. No one dared wind him up. By that stage, he had already been selected for the regional Thai boxing championships. Everyone knew that Karim Abdouf could break your nose with a flick of his foot and with his hands still flat on the zinc counter. Other stories also went round, about hold-ups, drug deals, epic fights . . .

Most of these rumors were unfounded, but they meant that Karim was pretty much left alone. He passed his exams with flying colors. He was even congratulated by the headmaster and suddenly realised that this authoritarian man was also frightened of him. The kid enrolled in Nanterre University to study law. At that time, he was stealing two cars a month. Since he knew several fences, he constantly swapped them around. He was certainly the only second-generation Arab on the estate who had never been arrested, or even bothered by the police. And he still had not used drugs, of any sort.

At twenty-one, Karim passed his law degree. What now? Lawyers would not take on a six-feet-six tall Arab, as slim as a rake, with a goatee, dreadlocks and his ears full of rings, even as a messenger boy. One way or the other, Karim was going to end up on Welfare and find himself right back at square one. Never. So carry on stealing cars? More than anything else, Karim loved those secret hours of the night, the silence of parking lots, the waves of adrenaline that ran through him as he foiled the security systems in BMWs. He realised that he was never going to be able to give up that inscrutable, heightened existence, a tissue of risk and mystery. He also realised that, sooner or later, his luck was going to run out.

It was then that he had a revelation: he would become a cop. He would then live in that same arcane universe, but sheltered from the laws he despised, and hidden from the country he wanted to spit on. One thing he had never forgotten from his childhood was this: he had no origins, no homeland, no family. He was a law unto himself, and his country was limited to his own breathing space.

After national service, he enrolled as a boarder in the Cannes-Ecluse police academy, near Montereau. It was the first time he had left Nanterre, his manor. His grades were excellent from the start. Karim's intellectual capacities were well above average and, above all, he knew more about delinquent behavior, gangland law and the suburban life than anybody else. He also turned into a brilliant marksman and his knowledge of unarmed combat deepened. He became a master of *té* – a quintessential form of close combat, bringing together the most dangerous elements of the various martial arts and sports. The other apprentice cops took an instinctive dislike to him. He was an Arab. He was proud. He knew how to fight, and he spoke better French than most of his classmates, who were generally waifs and strays who had joined the police to stay off Welfare.

One year later, Karim completed his course by holding down a series of posts as a trainee in various Parisian police stations. Still the same no-man's-land, still the same poverty. But this time in Paris. The young trainee moved into a little bed-sitter in the Abbesses quarter. A little perplexed, he realised that he had made it.

But he had not cut all ties with his origins. He regularly went back to Nanterre to hear the news. One disaster after another. Victor had been found on the roof of an eighteen-storey building, as crumpled as a witchdoctor's doll, a syringe sticking into his scrotum. OD. Hassan, a massive blond Berber drummer had blown his brains out with a shotgun. The "brother" bank robbers were doing time in Fleury-Mérogis. And Marcel had become a hopeless junkie.

Karim watched his friends drowning and, with horror, saw the final tidal wave break. AIDS was now hastening the process of destruction. The hospitals, once full of worn-out workmen and bedridden oldsters, were now filling up with dying kids with black gums, mottled skin and withered bodies. He saw most of his friends go that way. He saw the disease gain in power and size, then ally itself with Hepatitis C and mow down the ranks of his generation. Karim retreated, with fear in his guts.

His town was dying.

In June 1992, he got his badge. And was congratulated by the panel – a load of fat bastards with signet rings who filled him full of pity and loathing. But it did call for a celebration. He bought some champagne and headed for Les Fontanelles, Marcel's estate. Still today, he could remember every detail of that late afternoon. He rang the door-bell. Nobody. He asked the kids downstairs, then wandered through the halls of the building, the football fields, the waste tips heaped with old papers . . . Nobody. He kept on looking until evening. In vain. At ten o'clock, Karim went to Nanterre Hospital's AIDS unit – Marcel had been HIV positive for the last two years. He walked through the fumes of ether, past the faces of the sick, and questioned the doctors. He saw death at work. He contemplated the terrible progress of the epidemic.

But he did not find Marcel.

Five days later, he heard that the body of his friend had been found in a cellar, his hands fried, his face sliced into ribbons, his nails bored by an electric drill. Marcel had been tortured almost to death, then finished off with a shotgun blast to his throat. The news did not surprise Karim. His friend had been doing too much and watering down the doses he sold. It had only been a question of time. By coincidence, that very day, he received his bright new tricolor inspector's card. That coincidence was, for him, a sign. He retreated into the shadows, thought of Marcel's killers, and grinned. The little fuckers would never have imagined that one of Marcel's pals was a cop. Nor would they have imagined that this cop would make no bones about killing them, both for old times' sake, and from a personal conviction that life just should not be that fucking awful.

Karim started investigating.

Within a few days, he had got the killers' names. They had been seen with Marcel just before the presumed time of the murder. Thierry Kalder, Eric Masuro and Antonio Donato. He felt disappointed. They were three small-time junkies who probably wanted to get Marcel to reveal where he stashed his gear. Karim collected more detailed information: neither Kalder nor Masuro could have tortured Marcel. Not warped enough. Donato was the guilty party. Extorting money with menaces from little kids. Pimping for under-age girls on building sites. Junked out of his mind.

Karim decided that his death alone would assuage his vengeance.

But he had to work quickly. The Nanterre cops who had given him this information were also after the fuckers. Karim plunged into the streets. He was from Nanterre, he knew the estates, he spoke the kids' language. It took him just one day to find the three junkies. They were holed up in a ruined building, close to one of the autoroute bridges by Nanterre University. A place waiting to be demolished while vibrating from the din of cars shooting past, a few yards from the windows.

He arrived at the wrecked building at noon, ignoring the noise of the traffic and the hot June sun. Children were playing in the dust. They stared at the big guy, with his rasta looks, as he entered the ruins. Karim crossed the hall, full of ripped-open letter boxes, leapt up the stairs four at a time and, through the growling of the cars, distinctly made out the give-away sound of rap. He smilingly recognised *A Tribe Called Quest*, an album he had been listening to for the last few months. He kicked open the door and said simply: "Police." A wave of adrenaline burst into his veins. It was the first time he had played at being the fearless cop.

The three men were frozen with astonishment. The flat was full of rubble, the walls had been torn down, pipes stuck out everywhere, a TV sat on a gutted mattress. A brand-new Sony, obviously stolen the previous night. On the screen, the pale flesh of a porno film. The hi-fi rumbled away in a corner, shaking down dust from the plaster.

Karim felt as if his body had doubled in size and was floating in space. Out of the corner of his eye he saw car radios carelessly heaped up at the far end of the room. He saw torn-open packets of powder on an upturned cardboard box. He saw a pump-action shotgun amid some boxes of cartridges. He immediately picked out Donato, thanks to the photofit portrait he had in his pocket. A pale face with light-blue eyes, protruding bones and scars. Then the other two, hunched up in their efforts to extract themselves from their chemical dreams. Karim still had not drawn his gun.

"Kalder, Masuro, scram!"

The two of them jumped at hearing their names. They dithered, glanced at each other with dilated pupils, then headed for the door. Which left Donato, who was shaking like an insect's wing. He made a rush for the gun. Just as he was about to grab it, Karim crushed his hand and kicked him in the face – he was wearing steel-tipped shoes – without taking his other foot off the trapped hand. The joints in the arm cracked. Donato screamed hoarsely. The cop seized the man and dragged him over to the ancient mattress. The heavy rhythm of *A Tribe Called Quest* pounded on.

Karim took out his automatic, which he wore in a velcro holster on his left side, and wrapped up his carrying hand in a transparent plastic bag – made of a special uninflammable polymer – which he had brought with him. He tightened his hold on the diamond-patterned grip. The man looked up at him.

"What . . . what the fucking hell are you doing?"

Karim loaded a bullet into the cylinder and smiled.

"Cartridge cases, buddy. Ain't you ever seen that on the TV? Never leave cartridge cases lying round . . ."

"What you after? You a cop? You sure you're a cop?"

Karim nodded to each question, then said:

"I'm here for Marcel."

"Who?"

The cop saw the incomprehension in the man's eyes. And he realised that this wop couldn't even remember the person he had tortured to death. He realised that, in this junkie's memory, Marcel did not exist, had never existed.

"Tell him you're sorry."

"Wh . . . What?"

The sunlight spilled in over Donato's gleaming face. Karim lifted his gun in its plastic envelope.

"Ask Marcel to forgive you!" he panted.

The man understood that he was going to die and roared:

"Sorry! Sorry, Marcel! Fucking Jesus! I'm really really sorry, Marcel! I . . ."

Karim shot him twice in the face.

He got the bullets back out of the burnt fibers of the mattress, stuffed the burning-hot cases into his pocket then left without looking back. He figured that the other two would soon be back with reinforcements. In the entrance hall, he waited for a few minutes then saw Kalder and Masuro sprinting his way, accompanied by three other zombies. They rushed into the building through the wobbling doors. Before they had had time to react, Karim was in front of them and flattening Kalder against the letter boxes.

He brandished his gun and yelled:

"One word and you're dead. Come looking for me, and you're dead. Top me, you go down for life. I'm a fucking cop, you dickheads. A cop, get it?"

He threw the man down onto the ground and went out into the sunlight, crushing shards of glass under his feet.

So did Karim bid farewell to Nanterre, the town that had taught him everything.

A few weeks later, he phoned the police station on Place de la Boule to ask about their enquiries. He was told what he already knew. Donato had been killed, apparently by two 9mm caliber bullets from an automatic, but they had found neither the bullets nor their cases. As for his two accomplices, they had vanished. As far as the cops were concerned, the case was closed. As far as Karim was concerned, too.

The Arab asked to join the BRI, Quai des Orfèvres, a unit specialising in tailing, on-the-spot arrests and "jumping" known criminals. But his results played against him. They suggested the Sixth Division – the anti-terrorist brigade – so that he could infiltrate the Islamic fundamentalists in suburban hot spots. Immigrant cops were too rare a commodity to miss out on this chance. He refused. No way was he going to act as a grass, even if it did come to fanatical assassins. Karim wanted to roam through the kingdom of the night, go after killers and face them on their own turf, wander off into that parallel world which was also his own. His refusal was not well received. A few months later, Karim Abdouf, top of his class in the Cannes-Ecluse police academy, and unsuspected killer of a psychopathic junkie, was transferred to Sarzac, in the *département* of the Lot.

The Lot. A region where the trains did not stop any more. A region where ghost villages sprang up around roads, like stone flowers. A land of caves, where even tourism attracted only troglodytes: gorges, pits, cave paintings ... This region was an insult to Karim's personality. He was a second-generation Arab, off the streets, nothing could be stranger to him than this two-bit provincial town.

A dreary daily routine began. Karim had to go through days of tedium, punctuated by menial tasks: writing reports of car accidents, arresting an illicit vendor in a shopping center, nicking gatecrashers in tourist venues ...

So the young Arab started living in his daydreams. He got hold of biographies of great policemen. Whenever he could, he went to the libraries at Figeac or Cahors to pick out newspaper articles dealing with police enquiries, crimes and misdemeanors, anything and everything which reminded him of his true vocation. He also bought old bestsellers, the memoirs of gangsters . . . He subscribed to the police force's professional press, to magazines specialising in guns, ballistics, new technologies. A sea of paper, into which Karim was slowly sinking.

He lived alone, slept alone, worked alone. At the police station, which must have been one of the smallest in France, he was simultaneously feared and hated. His fellow cops called him "Cleopatra" because of his locks. Since he did not drink, they thought he was a fundamentalist. And, because he always declined the obligatory stopover chez Sylvie during their nightly rounds, they imagined he was gay.

Immured in his solitude, Karim ticked off the days, the hours, the seconds. He sometimes spent an entire weekend without saying a word.

That Monday morning, he re-emerged from one of his spates of silence, spent almost entirely in his bed-sitter, apart from a training session in the forest, where he relentlessly practised the murderous gestures of *té*, before emptying a few magazines into some century-old trees.

His door-bell rang. Instinctively, Karim looked at his watch. 07.45. He opened the latch.

It was Sélier, one of the late-duty officers. He looked wretched. A mixture of worry and fatigue. Karim did not offer him any tea. Nor even a seat. He just said:

"Well?"

The man opened his mouth, but nothing came out. Under his cap, his hair was gluey with greasy sweat. At last, he stammered:

"It's . . . it's the school. The primary school."

"What is?"

"Jean-Jaurès School. It was broken into . . . during the night."

Karim smiled. The week was getting off to a fine flying start. Some loafers from a nearby estate must have decided to smash up a school, just for the fun of it.

"Much damage?" Karim asked, while getting dressed.

The uniformed officer grimaced as he saw the clothes Karim was putting on. A sweatshirt, jeans, hooded tracksuit top, then a light-brown leather jacket – a garbage collector's model from the 1950s. He stammered:

"No. That's just it. It was a professional job . . ."

Karim was doing up his boots.

"A professional job? What's that supposed to mean?"

"It wasn't kids mucking about . . . They got into the place with skeleton keys. Took loads of precautions. It was just the head-mistress who noticed something weird. Otherwise . . ."

The Arab got to his feet.

"What did they steal?"

Sélier panted and slipped his index finger under his collar.

"That's what's even weirder. They didn't steal anything."

"Really?"

"Really. They just got into a room, then . . . pfft! . . . Seem to have left just like that."

Karim took a brief look at his reflection in the window panes. His locks tumbled down obliquely on either side of his temples, his narrow face was sharpened by his goatee. He adjusted his woolly hat of Jamaican colors and smiled at his image. A devil. A devil sprung out of the Caribbean. He turned toward Sélier:

"So why did you come running after me?"

"Crozier isn't back from his weekend yet. So Dussard and me . . . We reckoned that you . . . That you ought to come and see . . . Karim, I . . ."

"All right, all right. Let's go."

CHAPTER 8

The sun was rising over Sarzac. An October sun, lukewarm and pallid, like a bad convalescence. In his old five-door Peugeot, Karim followed the police van. They crossed the dead town which, at that hour, still had a ghostly gleam about it, like will-o'-the-wisps.

Sarzac was neither an ancient village nor a modern town. It was spread out over a long plain, with its middle-aged houses and blocks of flats lacking any distinguishing signs. Only the town center had a slight difference: a little tramline ran from one end to the other, alongside the streets of cobblestones. Each time he went by, Karim thought of Switzerland or of Italy, without knowing why. He had not been to either of these countries.

Jean-Jaurès School lay due east, in the poor part of town, near the industrial area. Karim reached a set of incredibly ugly blue and brown buildings, which reminded him of the estates of his childhood. The school stood at the end of a concrete ramp, above a cracked asphalt road.

A woman, wrapped up in a cardigan, was waiting for them on the steps. The headmistress. Karim greeted her and introduced himself. She welcomed him with a frank smile, which took him aback. Generally speaking, he provoked a wave of mistrust. Karim mentally thanked this woman for her spontaneousness and observed her for a few seconds. Her face was as flat as a lake, with big green eyes set in it, like a pair of waterlilies.

Without another word, the headmistress asked him to follow her. The pseudo-modern building looked as if it had never been finished. Or else, as if it was constantly being revamped. The corridors and the extremely low ceiling were made of polystyrene tiles, many of which were out of place. Most of them were covered with children's drawings, pinned there, or else painted directly onto the walls. Little coat pegs were ranged at kids' height. Everything was off kilter. Karim felt as though he was walking in a shoebox that had been crushed under someone's feet.

The headmistress stopped in front of a half-open door. She whispered, in a voice full of mystery:

"This is the only room they visited."

Gingerly, she pushed open the door. They entered an office which had the feel of a waiting-room. Glass-panelled shelving contained numerous registers and school books. A coffee-maker stood on a small fridge. A desk of imitation oak was swamped with green plants standing in saucers full of water. The whole room smelt of moist earth.

"You see," the woman said, pointing at one of the glass panels. "They opened this cupboard. It contains our archives. But it doesn't look as if they stole anything. Or even touched anything."

Karim knelt down and examined the lock on the panel. Ten years of break-ins and car thefts had given him a solid education in burglary. No doubt about it, the intruder who had dealt with this lock knew a trick or two. Karim was astonished: why should a cracksman bother to burgle a primary school in Sarzac? He picked out one of the registers and flicked through it. Lists of names, teachers' comments, administrative notes ... One volume for each year. The lieutenant stood up again.

"And nobody heard anything?"

The woman answered:

"You know, the school isn't heavily guarded. There is a caretaker, but ..."

Karim stared hard at that glass-panelled cupboard, which had been ever so gently forced open.

"Do you think the break-in occurred on the night of Saturday, or of Sunday?"

"Either. Or even during the day. As I just said, during the weekend our little school is hardly Fort Knox. There's nothing worth stealing."

"OK," he concluded. "You'll now have to go down to the police station and make a statement."

"You're undercover, aren't you?"

"Sorry?"

The headmistress was eyeing up Karim attentively. She had another go:

"I mean, the way you're dressed, your appearance. You infiltrate gangs on the estate, and . . ."

Karim burst out laughing.

"We don't have much in the way of gangs round here."

The headmistress ignored this remark and proceeded, in a knowing voice:

"I know all about it. I saw a documentary on TV. Characters like you wear double-sided jackets marked with police badges and . . ."

"Really, Madame," Karim butted in. "You're overestimating your little town."

He turned on his heels and headed off toward the door.

"You're not going to look for clues? Take fingerprints?"

Karim replied:

"Given the seriousness of the crime, I think we'll just make do with your statement and ask one or two questions round the neighborhood."

The woman looked disappointed. She stared attentively at Karim once again:

"You're not from these parts, are you?"

"No."

"So why did they send you here?"

"It's a long story. One of these days, I might drop by and tell you it."

Outside, Karim rejoined the uniformed officers, who were smoking, holding their cigarettes in their closed fists and wearing the hunted expressions of schoolboys. Sélier leapt out of the van.

"Lieutenant, Jesus! There's more!"

"What?"

"Another break-in. I've never seen anything like it . . ."

"Where?"

Sélier hesitated, looking at his colleagues. He was panting under his moustache.

"In . . . In the cemetery. They broke into a tomb."

*

58

The tombs and crosses lay on a slight slope, a mixture of grays and greens, like engraved lichen glistening in the sunlight. Behind the gate, the young Arab breathed in a scent of dew and withered flowers.

"Wait for me here," he mumbled to the others.

While slipping on his latex gloves, Karim said to himself that Sarzac would long remember a Monday such as this one.

This time, he had dropped back into his bed-sitter to pick up his "scientific" equipment: a kit containing powdered aluminum and granite, adhesives and nynhidrine for revealing hidden fingerprints, as well as elastomers to make moulds of possible footprints ... He had decided to collect the slightest possible clue.

He followed the gravel footpaths leading to the desecrated tomb, the position of which had been indicated to him. His first fear was that there had been a genuine profanation. Of the sort that seemed to have become a macabre fashion in France over the last few years. Skulls and mutilated corpses. Not this time. Everything was apparently in perfect order. The desecrators had obviously not touched anything, except for the vault. Karim reached the foot of the granite block: a monument shaped like a chapel.

The door was slightly ajar. He knelt down and examined the lock. As at the primary school, the burglars had been extremely careful about opening the vault. The lieutenant stroked the edge of the wall and observed to himself that this had, once again, been done by professionals. The same ones?

He opened the door a little wider and tried to imagine the scene. Why had the intruders taken such pains to open a tomb and then left without closing up the wall again? The lieutenant pushed in the stone block several times, then understood: some scraps of gravel had slipped under the edge and warped the jamb. It was now impossible to lock the vault. These little chips of stone had given the desecrators away.

The cop now examined the stone aspergillums which made up the lock. A strange structure, presumably typical of this sort of construction, and which only a specialist would know. A specialist? The policeman held back a shiver. Once more, he wondered if this had really been done by the same team that had broken into the primary school. What could be the connection between the two crimes?

The inscription provided him with part of the answer. It read: "Jude Ithero. 23 May 1972 – 14 August 1982". Karim thought it over. Perhaps this little boy had gone to Jean-Jaurès School. He looked at the plaque again: no epitaph, no prayer. Just a small oval frame, made of old silver, had been nailed onto the marble. But there was no picture inside.

"That's a girl's name, isn't it?"

Karim turned around. Sélier was standing there with his beetle-crushers and panic-struck eyes.

"No, a boy's name."

"But it's English, no?"

"No, Jewish."

Sélier wiped his forehead.

"Jesus Christ, is this a desecration like the one at Carpentras? Some extreme right-wing nutters?"

Karim stood up and wiped his gloved hands together.

"No, I don't think so. Do me a favor and go and wait for me at the gate with the rest."

Grumbling, Sélier went off with his cap pointing skywards. Karim watched him as he walked away, then looked back at the slightly opened door.

He decided to do a little caving. He went in, crouching under the roof, and lit his torch. Down the steps he crept, the gravel creaking under his boots. He felt as though he was breaking an ancestral taboo. He reflected on how he had no religious beliefs and, just then, congratulated himself on that fact. The beam of light was already piercing the gloom. Karim went on, then stopped in his tracks. The little wooden coffin, positioned on two trestles, stood out clearly in the beam from his torch.

His throat like sandpaper, Karim went over and examined the coffin. It measured about six feet. Its corners were topped with mouldings and silver arabesques. Despite possible leakages, the whole thing looked in good condition. He felt its joints and said to himself that, without his gloves, he would never have dared touch that coffin. This sensation of fear irritated him. At first sight, the lid had apparently not been taken off.

He gripped his torch between his teeth and set about a close examination of the screws. But a voice boomed out above him:

"Whatcha think you're doing here?"

Karim jumped. He opened his mouth, the torch fell out and rolled onto the coffin lid. As he turned round, the shadows fluttered over him. A man – with low shoulders and a woolly hat – was leaning down through the entrance. The Arab felt for his torch on the ground. He panted:

"Police. I'm a police lieutenant."

The man said nothing, then growled:

"You've no right to be here."

The policeman found his torch and made his way back to the staircase. He stared up at this big sullen character, standing in a frame of light. He must be the cemetery keeper. Karim knew that he was trespassing. Even in such a context, he still needed a written authorisation, signed by the family, or else a special search warrant for tombs. He climbed the steps and said:

"Watch out. I'm coming back up."

The man stood to one side. Karim drank in the sunlight as though it were nectar. He presented his tricolor card and announced:

"Karim Abdouf. From the Sarzac station. Was it you who discovered the profanation?"

The man remained silent. With his colorless eyes, like bubbles in gray water, he observed the Arab.

"You've no right to be here."

Karim nodded absent-mindedly. The morning air was sweeping away his fears.

"All right, old pal. Don't make a scene. Policemen are always right."

The old man licked his lips, which were surrounded by stubble. He stank of booze and damp mud. Karim tried again:

"OK, tell me everything you know. What time did you make your discovery?"

The old man sighed:

"I came here at six this morning. There's to be a burial."

"When was the last time you were here?"

"Friday."

"So the vault could have been opened any time during the weekend?"

"Yup. 'Cept, I reckon it was last night."

"Why?"

"'Cos it rained Sunday afternoon and there's no trace of dampness inside the vault. So the door must still have been closed."

Karim asked:

"Do you live near here?"

"Nobody lives near here."

The Arab glanced round the little cemetery, a paradise of peace and quiet.

"Do you ever get kids hanging out round here?" he pressed on.

"No."

"Never any suspicious visitors? Vandalism? Occult ceremonies?"

"No."

"Tell me about this grave."

The keeper spat on the gravel.

"There's nothing to tell."

"It's a bit odd having a vault just for one child, isn't it?"

"Yup, pretty odd."

"Do you know the parents?"

"No. Never seen them."

"You weren't here in 1982?"

"No. And the guy before me's dead." He sniggered. "Even we have to go sooner or later."

"The vault looks well looked after."

"I didn't say no one ever came here. I said I hadn't seen them. I'm experienced. I know how fast stones get worn away. I know how long flowers survive, even plastic ones. I know how the weeds and brambles and all that mess starts growing. So I can tell you that this vault is looked after regularly. Only I've never seen a soul."

Karim had another think. He knelt down and looked at the little frame, shaped like a cameo. Without lifting his eyes, he said to the keeper:

"I've got the impression that the grave robbers stole the photo of the kid."

"Eh? Yeah, maybe they did."

"Do you remember what the kid looked like?"

"No."

Karim stood up, took his gloves off and concluded:

"A team of specialists will be along later today to take finger-prints, and pick up any clues. So, cancel this morning's funeral. Tell them there's work going on, flooding, whatever you like. I don't want anybody in here today, got it? And definitely no journalists."

The old man nodded his head, but Karim was already on his way to the gate. In the distance, a piercing bell was chiming nine o'clock.

CHAPTER 9

Before going back to the station and writing up his report, Karim decided to drop back in at the school. The sun was now dousing the crests of the houses with its yellow rays. Once again, he said to himself that it looked as if it was going to be a lovely day, and the banality of the thought made him retch.

Upon reaching the school, he asked the headmistress:

"Did a little boy called Jude Ithero come to school here during the 1980s?"

Playing with the ample sleeves of her cardigan, the woman simpered:

"Do you already have a lead, inspector?"

"Just answer my question, please."

"Well . . . We'll have to go and look through the archives."

"Come on then, let's go."

The headmistress led Karim once again to the little office full of plants.

"During the 1980s, you say?" she asked, while running her index finger along the line of registers behind the glass doors.

"1982, 1981, and so on," Karim replied.

He suddenly noticed that she was hesitating.

"What's wrong?"

"How odd. I didn't notice that this morning . . ."

"What?"

"The registers . . . The ones for 1981 and 1982 . . . They're missing."

Karim pushed her aside and examined the spines of the brown volumes, piled up vertically. Each one bore a date. 1979, 1980 . . . the next two were indeed missing.

"What do these books contain exactly?" Karim asked, while flicking through the pages of one of them.

"The pupils in each class. Teachers' comments. They're the school's logbooks . . ."

"If a child was eight in 1980, what class would he have been in?"

"*Cours élémentaire 2*. Or even *Moyen 1*."

Karim read through the corresponding lists. No Jude Ithero. He asked:

"Does the school keep any other documents concerning the years 1981 and 1982?"

The headmistress thought for a second.

"Well . . . We'd have to look upstairs . . . The school canteen records, for example. Or the medical reports. They're all kept up in the attic. Follow me. Nobody ever goes up there."

They leapt up the linoleum-covered steps four at a time. The woman seemed highly excited by all this business. They went down a narrow corridor and reached an iron door. The headmistress stopped in front of it in amazement.

"I . . . I just don't believe it," she said. "This door's been forced open, too . . ."

Karim examined the lock. Broken, but with the same extreme caution. The policeman went inside. It was a large gabled room without any windows, except for a barred-off skylight. Bundles of documents and files were stacked up on metal cases. Karim was struck by the smell of dry, dusty paper.

"Where are the files for 1981 and 1982?" he asked.

Without a word, the headmistress strode off toward some shelving and started rummaging through the heavy bundles and bulging files. Her search took only a few minutes, but her conclusion was categorical:

"They're missing, too."

Karim's skin tingled. The school. The cemetery. The years 1981 and 1982. The name of a little boy: Jude Ithero. All parts of the same puzzle. He asked:

"Were you already here in 1981?"

She giggled flirtatiously:

"Well really, inspector. I was still a student then . . ."

"Did anything strange happen in the school at that time? Anything serious you might have heard about?"

"No. What sort of thing do you mean?"

"The death of a pupil."

"No. I've never heard of anything like that. But I could find out."

"Where?"

"From the local education authority. I'll . . ."

"Could you find out if a little boy called Jude Ithero was at this school during those particular two years?"

The headmistress was now breathing heavily.

"Yes . . . No problem, inspector. I'll . . ."

"And quick about it. I'll be back later."

Karim ran down the stairs, then stopped halfway and turned round:

"Just one other thing, for your information. Nowadays, in France, you don't say 'inspector' any more, you say 'lieutenant'. Just like in America."

The headmistress gaped after the rapidly receding figure.

Of all the cops in the station, Police Chief Crozier was the one Karim detested the least. Not because he was his boss, but because he had plenty of genuine experience and often showed signs of having a true cop's flair.

Henri Crozier came from the Lot, was an ex-soldier and had been on the force for the last twenty-odd years. With his potato nose and his greased-down hair, looking as if it had been combed with a rake, he oozed rigor and severity, but in the right mood he could also be disconcertingly jovial. Crozier was a lone wolf. He had neither a wife, nor any children, and imagining him at the center of a cosy family life was like picturing a slice of the craziest science fiction. This solitude attracted Karim, but it was their only point in common. Apart from that, the Chief was every inch a narrow-minded, chauvinistic policeman. The sort of bloodhound who would like to be reincarnated as a pit-bull.

Karim knocked and entered his office. An iron filing cabinet. The smell of scented tobacco. Posters to the glory of the French police force containing stiff, badly photographed figures. The Arab felt vaguely sick once more.

"What the hell's going on then?" Crozier asked from behind his desk.

"A break-in and a profanation. Two professional, discreet and very strange crimes."

Crozier grimaced.

"What was stolen?"

"From the school, a few files from the archives. From the cemetery, I don't know. We'll have to conduct a detailed search of the vault where . . ."

"You reckon that the two crimes are connected?"

"It's an obvious conclusion. Two break-ins, the same weekend, in Sarzac. We're going to end up in the record books."

"But have you discovered what the connection is?"

Crozier cleaned out the tip of his blackened pipe. Karim grinned to himself: a caricature of the police commissioner in 1950s cop shows.

"I might have a connection, yes," he mumbled. "The link's tenuous, but . . ."

"I'm listening."

"The vault that was desecrated contains a little kid with a weird name: Jude Ithero. He died when he was ten, in 1982. Perhaps you remember something about that?"

"No. Go on."

"Well, the records the burglars lifted were for the years 1981 and 1982. So, I couldn't help wondering if young Jude didn't go to this particular school during those very years and . . ."

"Do you have any supporting evidence for this supposition?"

"No."

"Have you checked the other schools?"

"Not yet."

Crozier blew into his pipe, like Popeye. Karim went over to him and adopted his sweetest tone:

"Let me lead this investigation, superintendent. I just know there's something strange about all this. A link between the various elements. It sounds incredible, but I'm sure that this was a professional job. They were looking for something. Let's start by finding the kid's parents, then I'll give the vault a thorough search. I . . . you agree?"

The superintendent kept his eyes down and set about filling the dark bowl of his pipe. He murmured:

"It was a gang of skins."

"What?"

Crozier looked up at Karim.

"I said, the cemetery job was done by a gang of skinheads."

"What skinheads?"

The superintendent burst out laughing and crossed his arms.

"See? You still have plenty to learn about our little region. There are a good thirty of them. They live in a disused warehouse near Caylus. An old mineral water depot. About twelve miles from here."

As he stared at Crozier, Abdouf thought it over. The sun was shining on the superintendent's oily hair.

"I think you're wrong about that."

"Sélier told me it was a Jewish grave."

"No, it wasn't! I just told him that Jude was originally a Jewish name. That doesn't mean a thing. The vault has no Judaic symbols on it, and Jews prefer to be buried alongside the rest of their family. Superintendent, this child died at the age of ten. In cases like that, Jewish graves always have a design, or pattern, to illustrate this broken destiny. Such as an unfinished pillar, or a felled tree. This tomb is a Christian one."

"Quite a specialist. How come you know all that?"

"I read about it."

But Crozier simply repeated:

"It was a gang of skins."

"But that's ridiculous. This wasn't an act of racism. It wasn't even a piece of vandalism. The grave robbers were looking for something . . ."

"Karim," Crozier cut him off, in a friendly but slightly tense tone of voice. "I always appreciate your judgment and advice. But I'm still the boss here. Trust an old timer. The skins are the ones to question. I reckon if you paid them a little call, then we might learn a thing or two."

Karim stood up and swallowed hard.

"Alone?"

"You're not telling me you're scared of a few kids with short hair, are you?"

Karim did not reply. Crozier liked this sort of test. To his way of thinking, it was playing the bastard, but also a sign of respect. The lieutenant grabbed the edges of the desk. If Crozier wanted to play, then he was willing to play along.

"Let's make a deal, superintendent."

"What kind of deal?"

"I'll grill the skinheads, all on my own. Shake them up a bit and give you a written report by one p.m. In return, you'll get me a warrant to search that vault. All above-board. I also want to question the kid's parents. Today."

"And what if it was the skins?"

68

"It wasn't the skins."

Crozier lit up. His tobacco crackled like straw.

"It's a deal," Crozier wheezed.

"After checking Caylus, I lead the investigation?"

"Only if I have your report by one o'clock. In any case, we'll soon have the regional crime squad on our backs."

The young cop strode over to the door. His fingers were on the handle, when the superintendent called to him:

"You'll see. I'm just sure that your looks are going to go down a storm with the skins."

Karim slammed the door on the old veteran's guffaws.

CHAPTER 10

A good cop needs to know his enemy thoroughly. Inside and out. And Karim was a world expert on the subject of skinheads. During his years in Nanterre he had fought several bloody battles with them. Then he had written a report about them while at the police academy. As he drove at high speed toward Caylus, the Arab ran through what he knew. It was a way to work out what his chances were against those bastards.

The first thing that crossed his mind was the uniforms worn by the two main branches. All skinheads were not extreme right-wingers. There were also the Red Skins, on the extreme left. Multi-racial, highly trained and following a code of honor, they were as dangerous as the neo-Nazis, if not more so. The Fascists wore their pilot's jackets the right way round, green side uppermost. The Reds, on the other hand, wore theirs inside out, fluorescent orange side uppermost. The Nazis tied their Docs with red or white laces. The Lefties with yellow ones.

At about eleven o'clock, Karim came to a halt in front of the disused warehouse, "The Waters of the Valley". With its high walls made of corrugated plastic, the depot faded away into the clear blue sky. A black DS was parked in front of the gate. After a moment's preparation, Karim leapt out. The skins were presumably inside, sleeping off their beer. As he walked over to the warehouse, he forced himself to breathe calmly while reciting the words which would determine his immediate destiny: green jackets and white or red laces meant the Nazis; orange jackets and yellow laces, the Reds.

Only then would he have a chance to get out of there without a fight. He took a deep breath and slid the door along its rail. He did not need to look at their laces to know where he had ended up. The walls were tagged with red swastikas. Nazi symbols were daubed alongside pictures of concentration camps and blow-ups of tortured Algerian POWS. Beneath them, a gang of cropped-hair kids in green jackets was observing him. Their steel-capped Docs gleamed in the darkness. Extreme right-wing, militant tendency. Karim knew that all these characters had the word "SKIN" tattooed on the inside of their lower lips.

Karim concentrated on his own movements and looked round for their weapons. He knew what sort of arsenal these crazies usually had: American knuckledusters, baseball bats and pocket revolvers with a double magazine of buckshot. The bastards probably also had some pump-action shotguns stashed away somewhere, loaded with rubber bullets.

What he then saw looked even worse.

Girls. Female Skins, with shaved heads, except for tufts sticking up over their foreheads and locks dangling down over their cheeks. Fattened up bitches, dowsed in booze and probably even more violent than their men. Karim swallowed hard. He now realised that what he was up against was no group of bored street kids, but a genuine gang which was presumably hiding out there while waiting for some new contract to go and beat someone up. He reckoned his chances of getting out in one piece were diminishing rapidly. One of the girls had a swig from her beer, then opened her mouth to burp. For Karim's benefit. The others burst out laughing. They were all as big as the cop.

The Arab forced himself to speak loudly and clearly:

"All right you lot, I'm a cop. I'm just here to ask you a few questions."

They came over toward him. Cop or not, Karim was first and foremost an Arab. And an Arab's hide was not worth shit in a warehouse full of these bastards. Nor even, perhaps, as far as Crozier and the rest of his fellow officers were concerned. The young lieutenant trembled. For a split second, the earth seemed to fall away from under his feet. It felt as if he was up against an entire town, a country, even the world.

Karim took out his automatic and pointed it toward the ceiling. This gesture stopped his attackers in their tracks.

"I repeat: I'm a cop and I want to play this fair and square with you."

He slowly placed his gun down on a rusty barrel. The skins watched him.

"I'll leave my piece here. And no one'll touch it while we all have a nice little chat."

Karim's automatic was a Glock 21 – one of the newest ultra-light models, made of 70% polymer. It had fifteen rounds in its magazine, plus one in the barrel, and a phosphorescent sight. He was sure that they'd never seen one before. He had got them.

"Who's the boss round here?"

Silence for an answer. Karim took a few steps forward and repeated:

"Who's the frigging boss? We're wasting time here."

The biggest one came forward, his entire body pent up ready to launch into the attack. He spoke in the rocky regional accent.

"What does this little runt want with us, then?"

"I'll forget you said that. Now, let's talk."

Nodding, the skin walked over to him. He was taller and broader than Karim.

The Arab thought of his dreadlocks and what a handicap they were. In a fight, they made for a perfect handhold. The skin kept coming, his hands open, like metallic wrenches. Karim did not budge an inch. A glance to his right: the others were approaching his gun.

"So what does our little A-rab want . . ."

The head-butt shot out like a missile. The skin's nose was flattened into his face. As he doubled up, Karim span round and kicked him in the throat. The hooligan took off and landed again six feet away, rolling in agony. One of the skins grabbed the gun and pressed the trigger. Nothing. Just a click. He tried to load the breech, but the charger was empty. Karim took out a second automatic, a Beretta, from a holster behind his back. With one foot on his victim, he aimed his gun at the gang and yelled:

"Did you really think I was going to leave a loaded gun lying around with little fuckers like you?"

The skins were petrified. The man on the ground gave a strangled groan:

"Fair and square, eh? You cunt."

Karim kicked him in the groin. He screamed. The cop knelt down and twisted his ear. The cartilage cracked between his fingers.

"Fair and square? With shitheads like you?" Karim laughed nervously. "You gotta be joking . . . Now, you bunch of cunts, turn round! Hands against the wall! The bitches too!"

He shot out the neon lights. They went up in a blue flash, the metal casing ricocheted against the ceiling before crashing down onto the ground in an explosion of firecrackers. The hoodlums were now running round left, right and center. Pathetic. Karim yelled fit to bust a gut:

"Empty your pockets! One move, and I'll knee-cap you!"

The room was now a vibrant darkness. Karim stuck his gun into the leader's ribs and quietly asked him:

"What are you lot on?"

The man was spitting blood.

"Wh . . . what?"

Karim dug deeper with his gun.

"What junk are you getting off on?"

"Speed . . . glue . . ."

"What sort of glue?"

"Di . . . Dissoplastine."

"What? For bicycle punctures?"

The skin nodded dumbly.

"Where is it?" Karim went on.

The hooligan rolled his bloodshot eyes.

"In the trash bag . . . over there by the fridge . . ."

"One move, and I'll kill you."

Karim backed off, staring round the room as he went, pointing his gun at the wounded skin, then at the motionless figures facing the wall. With his left hand, he tipped over the bag: thousands of tablets spilled out, as well as some tubes of glue. He picked up the tubes, opened them and walked across the room. He squeezed out gluey snail trails onto the floor, just behind the cornered skins. As he went, he kicked them in the legs and the kidneys while pushing away their knives and other implements to a safe distance.

"Turn round."

Their Docs shuffled uneasily.

"Now, you're all going to show me how many press-ups you can do. The bitches as well. Right on the glue."

Their hands squelched down into the Dissoplastine, which oozed up between their clenched fingers. After three pushes, their palms were stuck firmly. The skins slumped down, chests on the floor, twisting their wrists as they hit the concrete.

Karim went back to his initial attacker. He sat down, cross-legged in the lotus position and breathed deeply to get his calm back. His voice became more relaxed:

"Where were you last night?"

"It . . . it wasn't us."

Karim's ears pricked up. He had humiliated these skins as a challenge and was now asking them questions as a matter of form. He was sure that these shitheads had had nothing to do with desecrating the cemetery. But now this skin seemed to know what he was after. The Arab bent down.

"What are you talking about?"

The leader leant on his elbow.

"The cemetery . . . it wasn't us."

73

"How do you know about it then?"

"We . . . we were over that way . . ."

Karim suddenly caught on. Crozier had a witness. That morning, somebody had tipped him off that the skinheads had been seen round the cemetery the previous night. The superintendent had then packed him off without saying a word. Karim would settle that score later.

"Go on."

"We was hanging round there . . ."

"What time?"

"I dunno . . . about two o'clock, maybe . . ."

"Why?"

"I dunno . . . for a bit of fun . . . we was looking for building site caravans . . . to beat up a few blacks . . ."

Karim shuddered.

"And then?"

"We went by the cemetery . . . and the fucking gate was open . . . we saw these shadows . . . some guys was coming out of one of the graves . . ."

"How many?"

"T . . . two, I reckon."

"Can you describe them?"

The skin sneered.

"We was out of it, man."

Karim gave him a clip round his shattered ear. He stifled a cry, which came out like the hissing of a snake.

"What did they look like?"

"I dunno . . . it was pitch dark!"

Karim thought it over. If there was one thing he was sure of, then it was that this had been a professional job.

"And then?"

"It fucking freaked us out . . . so we beat it . . . I just knew they'd fucking pin this one on us . . . 'Cos of what happened in Carpentras . . ."

"Is that all? You didn't notice anything else? Any other details?"

"No . . . nothing . . . at two in the morning, that dump's totally fucking dead."

Karim imagined the loneliness on that little road, with its solitary streetlamp, a white gash in the night drawing moths. And the gang of skinheads, jostling along, glued out of their minds, singing Nazi songs. He repeated:

"Think again."

"It was . . . a bit later . . . I think we saw one of them East European motors, a Lada, or something like that, it was speeding down the road . . . from the cemetery . . . on the D143 . . ."

"What color was it?"

"Wh . . . white."

"Nothing else?"

"It . . . it was covered in mud."

"Did you get the registration number?"

"What do you think we are? Fucking pigs, or something?"

Karim's heel shot into his guts. The man writhed, blood gurgling from his mouth. The lieutenant got to his feet and dusted off his jeans. There was nothing more to be learnt there. He heard the others groaning behind him. By then, they must have had third or fourth degree burns on their hands. Karim concluded:

"Do me a favor and go along to Sarzac police station later today and make a statement. Tell them I sent you and they'll roll out the red carpet for you."

The skin's panting head nodded; he had the eyes of a cowed animal.

"Why . . . why you doing this, man?"

"So as you'll remember. A cop is always a headache. And an Arab cop is a fucking migraine. Go out beating up on niggers again and your head will be splitting . . . " Karim gave him a last kick " . . . fit to bust."

The Arab backed off, picking up his Glock 21 as he went.

Karim drove off rapidly and then stopped in a small wood a few miles away to let the calm flow back into his veins and think things through. So, the profanation had happened before two o'clock. There were two graverobbers and they were driving – probably – an Eastern European car. He looked at his watch. There was just enough time to get all that down in writing. Enquiries could now get seriously under way. They would have to send out an APB, trace the car, talk to people who lived on the D143 . . .

But his mind was already elsewhere. He had carried out his mission. And Crozier was going to have to give him a free hand. The enquiry could now be run his way. And the first step would be to find out what had happened to a little boy who had died in 1982.

III

CHAPTER 11

"An examination of the anterior facet of the thorax revealed large longitudinal incisions, doubtlessly caused by a sharp instrument. Other lacerations made by the same instrument were also found on the shoulders, arms . . ."

The forensic pathologist was wearing a rumpled calico coat and small glasses. His name was Marc Costes. He was young, with sharp features and vague eyes. Niémans had taken a liking to him at first sight, for he immediately saw that he was a dedicated investigator, lacking in experience perhaps, but certainly not in enthusiasm. He was reading out his report in a slow, methodical voice:

". . . multiple burns: on the torso, shoulders, sides and arms. Approximately twenty-five such marks were located, many of which run into the incisions previously described . . ."

Niémans butted in:

"Which means?"

The doctor looked up timidly over his spectacles.

"I think the murderer cauterised the wounds with a flame. He seems to have sprinkled small amounts of gasoline over the incisions before setting fire to them. I would say that he must have adapted some sort of aerosol to do the job, perhaps a steam cleaner."

Once more, Niémans started pacing up and down the practical studies room, where he had set up his headquarters, on the first floor of the psychology/sociology building. He had decided to hear out the forensic pathologist in this his sanctuary. Captain Barnes and Lieutenant Joisneau were also present, sitting quietly on their school benches.

"Go on," he ordered.

"Numerous swellings, bruises and fractures were also detected. As many as eighteen bruises can be counted on the torso alone. There are four broken ribs. Both clavicles have been reduced to splinters. Three of the fingers on the left hand, and two on the right hand, have been crushed. The genitalia are blue subsequent to beating.

"The weapon used was undoubtedly an iron or lead bar, approximately three inches thick. It is, of course, vital to distinguish these wounds from those which were caused during the transportation of the body and its being 'wedged' into the rock, but such post mortem bruising does not behave in the same way . . ."

Niémans glanced round at the others: eyes staring, foreheads glowing.

" . . . To move on to the upper part of the body. The face is intact. No visible signs of bruising on the nape . . ."

The policeman asked:

"No trace of blows to the face?"

"None. It would even seem as though the killer had avoided touching it."

Costes looked down at his report and started reading again, but Niémans cut in:

"One moment. I suppose there's plenty more still to come."

Fiddling with his report, the doctor blinked nervously.

"Several pages . . ."

"Right. We can all go through it later on our own. Just tell us the cause of death. Did the wounds you mentioned kill him?"

"No. He was strangled to death. There can be no doubt about that. With a metal wire, of a diameter of about a tenth of an inch. A bicycle brake cable I would say, or a piano wire, a cord of that sort. The cable cut into the flesh over a length of six inches, crushed the glottis, sliced through the muscles of the larynx and cut open the carotid causing a haemorrhage."

"And the time of death?"

"Hard to say. Because of the crouched position of the victim. This piece of gymnastics upset the natural process of rigor mortis and ..."

"Just give me an approximate time."

"I would say ... after dusk on Saturday evening, between eight o'clock and midnight."

"So Caillois was jumped on the way home from his expedition?"

"Not necessarily. In my opinion, he was tortured for quite some time. I reckon that it is more likely that Caillois was captured during the morning. And that the torture session lasted all day."

"In your opinion, did the victim try to defend himself?"

"Impossible to say, because of the large number of wounds. But one thing is certain, he was not knocked out. He was tied up and conscious during the entire proceedings. There are clear marks of straps on his arms and wrists. What is more, given that there is no sign of the victim's being gagged, we can suppose that the torturer was sure that no one would hear what was going on."

Niémans sat down on a window sill.

"About the tortures, were they professional?"

"Professional?"

"Are they methods used in the army? Anything known?"

"I am no specialist, but I would say probably not. They look more to me like the actions of a ... a madman. A lunatic who wanted the correct answers to his questions."

"Why do you say that?"

"The killer was trying to make Caillois talk. And Caillois did so."

"How do you know that?"

Costes modestly bowed his head. Despite the temperature in the room, he still had not taken off his parka.

"If the killer had been torturing Rémy Caillois just for sadistic pleasure, then he would have tortured him to death. But, as I have told you, he finished him off in a different way, with a metal wire."

"Any trace of sexual violence?"

"No. Nothing at all of that sort. It is clearly not his department."

Niémans paced along beside the workbench. He was trying to imagine the monster capable of inflicting such torments. He visualised the scene from the outside. He saw nothing. No face, no figure. He then thought of what the tortured man would have seen, when in the throes of suffering and death. He saw savage movements, brown, ochre and red tints. An unbearable storm of blows, fire and blood. What could Caillois's last thoughts have been? He said aloud:

"Tell us about his eyes."

"His eyes?"

The question came from Barnes. His voice had shot up a tone in astonishment. Niémans was good enough to reply:

"Yes, his eyes. Earlier, in the hospital, I noticed that the killer had stolen his victim's eyes. The sockets even seemed to be full of water . . ."

"Precisely," Costes intervened.

"Tell us everything from the beginning," Niémans ordered.

"The killer operated beneath the eyelids. He slipped a cutting instrument under them, severed the oculomotor muscles and the optical nerve. He then extracted the eyes. After that, he then carefully scratched clean the interior of the two sockets."

"Was the victim dead by then?"

"Impossible to say. But I did notice evidence of haemorrhaging in that region, which could indicate that Caillois was still very much alive."

Silence closed over his words. Barnes was ghostly white; Joisneau as though crystallised by terror.

"And then?" Niémans asked to break that feeling of panic, which was rising ever higher.

"Later, when the victim was dead, the killer filled up the sockets with water. From the river, I suppose. Then he carefully closed the eyelids again. Which explains why the eyes were shut and protruding, as though they had not been mutilated in any way."

"Let's get back to the excision. In your opinion, does the killer know about surgery?"

"No. Or, at best, only vaguely. I would say that, as for the torturing, he knows how to apply himself."

"What instruments did he use? The same as for the lacerations?"

"The same sort, in any case."

"What sort?"

"Industrial tools. Carpet cutters."

Niémans stood in front of the doctor.

"Is that all you can tell us? No clues? No obvious lead that arises from your report?"

"No, unfortunately not. The body was thoroughly washed before being wedged into the cliff. It can tell us nothing about the scene of the crime. And even less about the identity of the killer. All we can suppose is that he is strong and dexterous. That is all."

"Which isn't much," Niémans grumbled.

Costes paused for a moment, then went back to his report.

"There is just a further detail which hasn't been discussed yet . . . A detail which has no direct bearing on the crime itself."

The superintendent's ears pricked up.

"Which is?"

"Rémy Caillois had no fingerprints."

"Meaning?"

"That his hands were corroded, worn away to such a point that not a trace of a print was left on his fingertips. Maybe he was burnt in an accident. But the accident must have occurred a long time ago."

Niémans looked questioningly at Barnes, who raised his eyebrows in ignorance.

"We'll check that out," the superintendent said gruffly.

Then he went over to the doctor, so close to him that he brushed against his parka.

"And what is your personal opinion about this murder? What's your feeling? What's your intuition as a medic as regards the torture?"

Costes took off his glasses and rubbed his eyelids. When he put his spectacles back on, his gaze seemed clearer, as though polished bright.

"The murderer carried out some obscure ritual. A ritual which had to finish up with this foetal position in a hollow in a rock. The whole thing seems to have been well worked out, perfectly planned. And so the mutilation of the eyes must be an integral part of it. Then there is the water. The water replacing the eyes under the lids. As though the killer wanted to cleanse and purify the sockets. I am having tests made on that water. Who knows? They might provide us with a clue . . . some chemical lead."

Niémans brushed these words away with a vague gesture. Costes had spoken of a rite of purification. Since visiting that little lake, the superintendent, too, had had an act of catharsis in mind. They were both thinking along the same lines. Above that lake, the killer had tried to purify that defilement – or perhaps wash away his crime?

Several minutes ticked by. Nobody dared to move. In the end, Niémans opened the door of the room and murmured:

"Back to work. We don't have much time. I don't know what Rémy Caillois was forced to admit. I only hope that it won't lead to any more murders."

CHAPTER 12

Niémans and Joisneau went back to the library. Before going in, the superintendent glanced at the lieutenant. His face was haggard. So, blowing out like an athlete, he slapped him on the back. Young Eric replied with an unconvincing smile.

The two of them entered the main room. An unexpected sight was in store for them. Two regional crime squad officers, as well as a horde of uniformed men in shirt sleeves, had invaded the library and were giving it a thorough search. Hundreds of books were piled up in front of them in columns. Joisneau asked, in astonishment:

"What the hell's going on here?"

One of the officers replied:

"We're only following orders . . . We're looking out all the books about evil and religious rituals and . . ."

Joisneau looked across at Niémans. He seemed horrified by this disorderly operation. He yelled at the crime squad:

"But I told you to go through the computer! Not get all the books down from the shelves!"

"We did a computer search, according to title and subject matter. And now we're going through the books looking for clues, or points of similarity with the murder . . ."

Niémans butted in:

"Did you ask the boarders for advice?"

The officer pulled a face.

"They're all philosophers. They just started bullshitting. The first one told us that the notion of evil was a bourgeois concept, and that we'd have to adopt a more social, or even Marxist approach. So we dropped him. The second one went on about frontiers and transgression. But according to him, the frontier was inside us . . . our consciences were in constant negotiation with a higher censor and . . . Well, anyway, it didn't mean much to me. The third one got us going with the Absolute and the quest for the impossible . . . He told us about mystical experiences, which could take place with either good or evil as the goal. So . . . I . . . Well, in fact, we're a bit up to our ears in it, lieutenant."

Niémans burst out laughing.

"Told you so," he whispered to Joisneau. "Never trust an intellectual."

He turned to the confused cop:

"Keep looking. To the key words 'evil', 'violence', 'torture' and 'ritual' you can now add 'water', 'eyes' and 'purity'. Go through the computer. Above all, dig out the names of the students who consulted this sort of book, or who were working on this sort of subject matter, for their PhDs for example. Who's working on the main computer?"

A broad-backed young man, who was shifting his shoulders about inside his jacket replied:

"I am, superintendent."

"What have you found in Caillois's files?"

"There are lists of damaged books, books to be ordered etc. Then lists of students who use the library and the places where they sit."

"Where they sit?"

"Yup. Caillois's job was to place them all . . ." He nodded toward the glass carrels. ". . . in those little boxes over there. He put each seat into his computer's memory."

"You haven't found the thesis he was working on?"

"Yes, I have. A thousand pages about the ancient world and . . ." He looked at a sheet of paper he had scribbled on. ". . . Olympia. It's about the first Olympic games and the religious ceremonies that went on around them . . . Pretty heavy going, I can tell you."

"Print it out and read it."

"Eh?"

Niémans added, ironically:

"Speed-read it, I mean."

The man looked crestfallen. The superintendent immediately went on:

"Nothing else in his machine? No video games? No e-mail?"

The officer shook his head. This came as no surprise to Niémans. He had guessed that Caillois's entire life had been in books. A strict librarian, who allowed just one thing to impinge on his professional responsibilities: the writing of his thesis. What could have been tortured out of such a hermit?

Pierre Niémans turned round to Joisneau:

"Come with me. I want to know where your investigations stand."

They took shelter between two rows of shelving. At the end of the alleyway, an officer in a cap was grappling with a book. Faced with such a sight, the superintendent found it difficult to remain serious. The lieutenant opened his notebook.

"I've questioned several of the boarders and Caillois's two colleagues in the library. Rémy was not very well liked. But he was respected."

"Why was he unpopular?"

"No particular reason. I get the impression that he made people feel uneasy. He was a close, secretive type. He made no effort to communicate with others. And, in a way, it went with the job." Joisneau stared around, almost in fear. "Just imagine it ... Spending all day in this library, staying quiet."

"Did anyone mention his father?"

"You know that he was the previous librarian? Yeah, some mention was made of him. Same sort of guy. Silent, impenetrable. It's like a confessional in here, I suppose it must get to you in the end."

Niémans leant back against the books.

"Did anyone say that he died in the mountains?"

"Of course. But there's nothing suspicious about that. The poor guy was swept away by an avalanche and ..."

"I know. Do you think anybody could have had it in for the Caillois family, father and son?"

"Superintendent, the victim fetched books from the reserve, filled out slips and gave the students the numbers of their reading desks. Who would want to avenge that? A student who hadn't been given the right edition?"

"OK. What about his climbing?"

Joisneau flicked back through his notebook.

"Caillois was both an excellent climber and a highly experienced hiker. Last Saturday, according to the witnesses who saw him leave, he probably set out for a hike, at about six thousand feet, without any equipment."

"Any hiking friends?"

"None. Even his wife never went with him. Caillois was a loner. Practically autistic."

Niémans then relayed what he had learnt:

"I've been back to the river. And I discovered traces of spits in the rock. I think the killer used a climbing technique to winch up the body."

Joisneau's face went tense.

"Shit, I went up there, too, and I didn't . . ."

"The holes are inside the cavity. The killer fixed pulleys into the niche, then lowered himself down to act as a counterweight for the body."

"Shit."

On his face was a mixture of bitterness and admiration. Niémans smiled.

"I don't deserve any praise for that. I was helped by a witness. Fanny Ferreira. She's a real pro." He winked. "And a hot number. I want you to investigate further in that direction. Get a complete list of all the experienced climbers and everyone who has access to that sort of equipment."

"We're talking about thousands of people!"

"Get your team mates to help. Ask Barnes. Who knows? Something might turn up. I also want you to deal with the eyes."

"The eyes?"

"You heard forensics, didn't you? The killer made off with his eyes, and was extremely careful about it. I have no idea why he did that. Fetishism, maybe. Or a particular form of purification. Maybe those eyes reminded the killer of something the victim witnessed. Or the weight of a stare which the murderer had become obsessed with. I don't know. It's all a bit vague and I don't like this sort of psychological bullshit. But I want you to shake up the town and pick up anything that may have something to do with those eyes."

"For instance?"

"For instance, find out if, in the town or university, there have been any accidents involving that part of the anatomy. Go through the statements taken by the local brigade over the last few years, and news stories in the local press. Any fights where someone might have got injured. Or else, animals being mutilated. I don't know, just look. And find out if there are any big eye problems, or cases of blindness in this region."

"You really think I'll be able to . . ."

"I don't think anything," Niémans sighed. "Just do it."

At the end of the row, the uniformed officer was still staring sideways. At last, he dropped his books and made off. Niémans went on in a whisper:

"I also want all of Caillois's comings and goings over the last few weeks. I want to know who he saw, and who he spoke to. I want a list of the phone calls he made, both at home and at work. I want a list of the letters he received. Maybe Caillois knew his murderer. Maybe they even arranged to meet up there."

"What about his wife? Anything interesting?"

Niémans did not answer. Joisneau added:

"I've heard she's a bit of a handful."

Joisneau put his notebook away. His face had gone back to its usual color.

"I don't know if I should tell you this . . . what with that mutilated body . . . and that crazy killer on the loose . . ."

"But?"

"But, I really feel like I'm learning things working with you."

Niémans was flicking through a book: *The Topography and Reliefs of the Isère*. He chucked the volume to the lieutenant and concluded:

"Then just pray we learn as much about the killer."

CHAPTER 13

The curled-up profile of the victim. Muscles as tense as ropes under the skin. Blue and black wounds intermittently slicing into the pallid skin.

Back in his office, Niémans was examining the Polaroid photographs of Rémy Caillois.

The face front on. Eyelids open on the black holes of the sockets.

Still in his coat, he thought of what that man had suffered. Of the violent panic that had suddenly arisen in that innocent region. Without even admitting it to himself, the policeman now feared the worst. Another murder, perhaps. Or, rather, an unpunished crime, swept aside by time and fear, which would help everyone to forget. Rather than to remember.

The victim's hands. Photographed from above, then from below. Beautiful delicate hands, opening out onto their anonymous tips. Not the slightest fingerprint. Traces of cuts into the wrists. Granular. Dark. Stony.

Niémans tipped back his chair and leant against the wall. He folded his hands behind his neck and thought over his own words: "Each element in an investigation is a mirror. And the killer is hiding in one of the dead angles." There was one idea that he could not get out of his mind: Caillois had not been chosen by chance. His death was connected to his past. To someone he had once known. To something he had once done. Or to some secret he had learnt.

What?

Since his childhood, Caillois had spent his life in the university library. Then, every weekend, he used to disappear into the airy heights which overlooked the valley. What could he have done or found out to deserve such punishment?

Niémans decided to make a rapid investigation of the victim's past. Instinctively, or by personal predilection, he chose to begin with a detail which had struck him during his questioning of Sophie Caillois.

After a few phone calls, he managed to get through to the 14th Infantry Regiment, which was stationed near Lyons and which was the place where all the young men from that region went for their three days' national service induction. When he had given his name and explained the reason for his call, he was transferred to archives and got them to dig out the file of Rémy Caillois, who had been declared unfit for service during the 1990s. Niémans could make out the furtive tapping of the keyboard, the distant footfalls in the room, then the shuffling of pieces of paper. He asked the clerk:

"Read me the conclusions in his file."

"I don't know if I can . . . What proof is there that you're really a superintendent?"

Niémans sighed.

"Call the *gendarmerie* in Guernon. Ask for Captain Barnes and . . ."

"OK, OK. Here we go, then." He flicked through the pages. "I won't go into any details, the answers to the tests, and all that. The conclusion is that your man was declared unfit, due to 'schizophrenia'. The psychiatrist added a handwritten note in the margin. It says: 'Therapy requested', which is underlined. Then, after that: 'Contact the Guernon University Hospital'. If you want my opinion, he must really have had a screw loose, because in general we just . . ."

"Do you have the doctor's name?"

"Of course, it's Dr Yvens."

"Does he still work in your unit?"

"Yes. He's upstairs."

"Put me through to him."

"I . . . OK. Hang on."

A synthetic fanfare burst from the receiver, then a basso profondo voice boomed out. Niémans introduced himself and explained what he wanted. Doctor Yvens sounded skeptical. He finally asked:

"What was the recruit's name?"

"Caillois, Rémy. You discharged him five years ago. Acute schizophrenia. You wouldn't remember him by any chance? If you do, what I'd like to know is whether you think he was acting mad or not."

The voice objected:

"This information is strictly confidential."

"We've just found his body wedged into a rock face. Throat slit. Eyes ripped out. Multiple tortures. Bernard Terpentes, the investigating magistrate, has called me in from Paris to lead the enquiries. He could contact you himself, but I'd rather we didn't waste time. Do you remember . . . ?"

"Yes, I remember," Yvens cut in. "He was sick. Crazy. No doubt about it."

This was, in fact, what Niémans had been expecting, but he was still taken aback by the reply. He repeated:

"So he wasn't putting it on?"

"No. I see play-actors all year. Healthy minds are far more imagi-native than sick ones. They come up with the most incredible ideas. The truly sick are easy to spot. They are locked into their madness. Obsessed, consumed by it. Even insanity has its own . . . logic. Rémy Caillois was sick. A textbook case."

"What form did his madness take?"

"Ambivalent thought processes. Loss of contact with the outside world. Surly silences. The classic symptoms of schizophrenia."

"Doctor, that man was librarian at the University of Guernon. Every day, he was in contact with hundreds of students and . . ."

The doctor laughed sardonically.

"Madness is a cunning beast, superintendent. It can hide itself from others, slip away under a harmless-looking exterior. You should know that even better than I do."

"But you've just told me that you found him evidently insane?"

"I'm experienced. And, since then, Caillois perhaps learnt to control himself."

"Why did you note: 'Therapy requested'?"

"I advised him to go and get help. That's all."

"And did you contact Guernon Hospital yourself?"

"To be honest, I can't remember. His case was an interesting one, but I don't think I told the hospital about him. You know, if the sufferer doesn't . . ."

"You said 'interesting'?"

The doctor breathed deeply.

"He was living in an enclosed world of extreme strictness, in which his personality multiplied. Other people probably thought he was fairly laid back, but he was absolutely obsessed by order and precision. Each of his feelings crystallised into a concrete form, a separate personality. He was a one-man army. A fascinating case."

"Was he dangerous?"

"Definitely."

"And you just let him go."

There was a pause, then:

"Oh, you know, the number of madmen on the loose . . ."

"Doctor," Niémans went on in a hushed tone. "The man was married."

"Really? Then I pity his wife."

The policeman hung up. These revelations had opened new horizons. And deepened his anxiety.

Niémans decided to pay another little call.

"You lied to me!"

Sophie Caillois tried to push the door shut, but the superintendent's elbow was wedged in the jamb.

"Why didn't you tell me that your husband was sick?"

"Sick?"

"Schizophrenic. According to the specialists, he needed locking up."

"You bastard."

Her lips tight, the young woman tried once more to close the door, but Niémans had no difficulty staying where he was. Despite her lank hair, despite her unravelled pullover, he found that woman more beautiful than ever.

"Don't you understand?" he yelled. "We're looking for a killer. We're looking for a motive. Maybe Rémy Caillois did something or other which might explain his horrible death. Something he might not even have been able to remember. Please . . . you're the only one who can help me!"

Sophie Caillois opened her eyes wide. All the beauty of her face formed itself into subtle networks of lines and twitched nervously. Particularly her perfectly drawn eyebrows, which had frozen into a splendid, tragic expression.

"You're crazy."

"I have to know about his past . . ."

"You're crazy."

The woman was trembling. Niémans lowered his eyes despite himself. He took in the shape of her shoulder blades, rising up under the wool of the pullover. Through it, he could make out a twisted, almost shrivelled, bra strap. Suddenly, an impulse led him to grab her wrist and pull up her sleeve. Blue marks covered her forearm. Niémans cried:

"He beat you!"

The superintendent looked away from the dark traces and stared into Sophie Caillois's eyes.

"He beat you! Your husband was sick. He liked hurting people. I'm sure of that. He'd done something wrong. I'm sure you have your suspicions. You haven't told me a tenth of what you know!"

The woman spat in his face. Staggering, Niémans pulled back.

She seized her chance and slammed the door. When Niémans's shoulder charged it once more, a sequence of bolts was clicking shut on the other side. In the corridor, the boarders were staring worriedly at him from their doors.

The policeman kicked the jamb.

"I'll be back!" he yelled.

Silence had descended.

Niémans punched the wood one last time, which gave off a hollow echo, then remained motionless for a few seconds.

The woman's voice, quivering with sobs, came from the other side of the door, as though from a deep pit.

"You're crazy."

CHAPTER 14

"I want a plain-clothes cop on her tail. Call the Grenoble crime squad."

"Sophie Caillois? Why?"

Niémans looked at Barnes. They were both in the main hall of the Guernon *gendarmerie*. The captain was wearing the standard royal blue sweater with its white lateral stripe. He looked like a sailor.

"That woman's hiding something," Niémans explained.

"But you surely don't think that it was her who . . ."

"No, I don't. But she isn't telling us everything she knows."

Unconvinced, Barnes nodded, then he handed the superintendent a large cardboard box crammed with faxes, documents and rustling carbon paper.

"The first results of our general investigation," he declared. "For the moment, there's not much to write home about."

Oblivious to the surrounding din of bustling gendarmes, Niémans glanced through the files as he strolled back to his office. He inspected the thick wads of carbon copies summing up Barnes's and Vermont's enquiries. Despite the large number of reports and statements, not a single piece of solid evidence had emerged. The procedures, interrogations, searches, fieldwork . . . had produced nothing. As he entered his glass-walled office, Niémans grumbled to himself. Such a spectacular crime, in such a small town. The superintendent just could not believe that they still had not come up with a serious lead.

He grabbed a chair from behind his metal desk and started reading through it all thoroughly.

The idea of a prowler had led to nothing. The enquiries in prisons, police stations and law courts had all been inconclusive. As for thefts of cars during the previous forty-eight hours, not a single one could be directly associated with the killing. The hunt for murders and other crimes that had occurred during the last twenty years had also drawn a blank. Nobody could remember any other killing which had been so atrocious and so strange, or any other act similar to it. In the town itself, police records contained only a few mountain rescues, petty thefts, accidents, fires etc.

Niémans flicked through the next folder. The systematic questioning of all the hoteliers, via fax, had proved fruitless.

He went on to Vermont's contribution. His men were continuing their search along the banks of the river. For the moment, they had visited only five refuges and there were seventeen of them, according to the map, some of which were perched up on the mountain at an altitude of over nine thousand feet. Did it make any sense to kill someone at such a height? His men had also questioned the nearby country folk. Some of these interviews had already been typed up in the familiar jargon of the *gendarmerie*. Niémans glanced through them and smiled: if the spelling mistakes and turns of phrase were similar to those of policemen, other expressions were redolent of the army. The men had asked questions in service stations, railway stations and at bus stops. Nothing doing. But rumors were now starting to run rife in the streets and chalets. Why all these questions? Why all these gendarmes?

Niémans laid the file down on his desk. Through the window he saw a patrol that had just returned, their cheeks pink and their eyes glassy from the cold. He made a questioning gesture at Captain Vermont, who answered with a clear shake of his head. Nothing.

For a few seconds, the superintendent watched the uniforms as they went past, but his thoughts were already elsewhere. He was thinking about the two women. One of them was as tough as tree-bark. Her muscles must be full, her skin dark and velvety. A taste of resin and rubbed herbs. The other was frail and bitter. She oozed uneasiness, an aggressiveness mixed with fear, which Niémans found equally fascinating. What was the strange beauty of that bony face hiding? Had Rémy Caillois really beaten her? And how much grief did she really feel at the sight of her mutilated husband, whose body had such suffering written all over it?

Niémans got up and looked through one of the windows. Behind the clouds, above the mountains, the sun was shedding yellow beams, which resembled clear gashes dug out in the dark, swollen flesh of the storm. Below, the superintendent gazed at Guernon's identical gray houses. The polygonal roofs to prevent the snow from piling up. The dark windows, small and square like paintings drowned in shadows. The river which crossed the town and ran alongside the detachment of gendarmes.

The image of the two women filled his mind once again. In each enquiry, the same sensation gripped him. The investigations heightened his senses, giving him a feeling of a thrilling, vibrant courtship. He fell in love only when pursuing criminals: with witnesses, suspects, whores, barmaids . . .

The brunette or the blonde?

His cell phone rang. It was Antoine Rheims.

"I've just come back from Hôtel-Dieu Hospital."

Niémans had let the morning pass by without even calling Paris. That business at the Parc des Princes was now going to shoot back toward him like an explosive boomerang. The Chief continued:

"The medics are attempting a fifth skin graft to save his face. Because of this, he now has practically no flesh left on his thighs. But that's not all. Three skull fractures. The loss of one eye. And seven facial fractures. Seven, Niémans. His lower jaw has been pushed back into his larynx. Shards of bone have severed his vocal cords. He's in a coma but, come what may, he'll never talk again. The medics say that even a car accident could not have caused so much damage. So what am I supposed to tell them now? And what about the British Embassy? And the media? The two of us have known each other for a long time. And I think we're friends. But I also think that you're a violent maniac."

Niémans's hands started to tremble.

"That hooligan was a murderer," he replied.

"And what does that make you then?"

The cop did not answer. He passed the phone, which was gleaming with sweat, into his left hand. Rheims went on:

"How are your enquiries progressing?"

"Slowly. No leads. No witnesses. It's going to be much harder than we first thought."

"I told you so! When the press catches on that you're in Guernon, they're going to start buzzing about you like flies round shit. Why the hell did I send you there?"

Rheims slammed the phone down. Niémans sat there for a few minutes, his eyes staring into nothingness, his mouth dry. In blinding flashes, his mind played back the violence of the previous night.

His nerves had cracked. He had beaten that murderer in a fit of rage, which had drowned him, had totally wiped out any other idea than the desire to crush, there and then, what he was holding in his hands.

Pierre Niémans had always lived in a world of violence, a universe of depravity, with cruel and savage borders, and he did not fear to walk where danger lurked. On the contrary, he had always sought it out, flattering it, the better to affront and control it. But he was no longer capable of keeping that control. That violence had now invaded him, had entered his very marrow. He was now weak and under its command. And he had not even managed to master his own fears. In some corner of his head, dogs were still howling.

He suddenly jumped. His mobile was ringing again. It was Marc Costes, the forensic pathologist, his voice triumphant:

"Some good news, superintendent. We have a solid piece of evidence. It's about the water we found under the eyelids. I've just received the laboratory report."

"And?"

"And it doesn't come from the river. Incredible, isn't it? I'm working on the problem with Patrick Astier, a chemist from the specialist branch in Grenoble. He's a real whiz. According to him, the traces of pollution in the water found in the eye-sockets are not at all the same as those found in the river."

"Can you be more precise?"

"The liquid under the eyelids contains H_2SO_4 and HNO_3, that is to say, sulphuric acid and nitric acid. It has a pH of 3. In other words, it's highly acidic. Almost like vinegar. Such a figure is a precious piece of information."

"I don't understand. What do you mean?"

"I don't want to get technical with you, but sulphuric acid and nitric acid are derivatives of SO_2, sulphur dioxide, and NO_2, nitrogen dioxide. According to Astier, only one sort of industry produces such a mixture of dioxides: power stations which burn lignite. That is to say, an extremely old form of power station. Astier's conclusion is that the victim was killed or transported near just such a place. Find a lignite burner in the region, and you'll have located the scene of the crime."

Niémans stared up at the sky. Its dark scales were glittering in the persistent sunlight, like an immense silvery salmon. Maybe he was at last onto something. He ordered:

"Fax me the composition of that water on Barnes's number."

The superintendent was opening his office door when Eric Joisneau appeared.

"I've been looking for you everywhere. I think I've got some vital information."

Was the investigation at last beginning to take off? The two officers retreated into the room and Niémans closed the door. Joisneau was feverishly grasping his notebook.

"I've discovered that there's a home for young blind kids near Les Sept-Laux. A lot of them apparently come from Guernon. They suffer from a variety of complaints. Cataracts, pigmentary retinitis, color blindness. The number of cases in Guernon is way over the national average."

"Go on. What's the reason for that?"

Joisneau cupped his hands together.

"The valley. The isolation. A medic explained that they are genetic problems. Handed down from one generation to the next, because of a certain amount of inbreeding. It's apparently quite common in isolated areas. A sort of genetic contamination."

The lieutenant tore a page off his pad.

"Look, here's the address of the home. The director, Doctor Champelaz, has made an in-depth study of the phenomenon. I thought that you'd . . ."

Niémans pointed a finger at Joisneau.

"You go."

The young officer's face brightened.

"You trust me?"

"Yes, I trust you. Now, split."

Joisneau spun round, then, knitting his brows, changed his mind.

"Superintendent, I . . . Sorry, but why don't you want to question the director yourself? It could be an important lead. Are you onto something better? Or do you think I'll ask more pertinent questions because I'm a local boy? I don't get it."

Niémans leant on the door jamb.

"You're right. I am onto something. But I'll give you a little extra lesson, Joisneau. In an enquiry, external motivations also have a part to play."

"What sort of motivations?"

"Personal ones. I'm not going to that home, because I suffer from a phobia."

"What? Of blind people?"

"No. Of dogs."

The lieutenant looked astonished.

"I don't get it."

"Think about it. Where there are blind folk, there are dogs." Niémans mimed the hunched figure of a blind man being led by an imaginary pooch. "Guide dogs for the blind, follow me? So there's no way I'm setting foot in that place."

With those words, the superintendent left his startled lieutenant.

He knocked on Captain Barnes's office door and opened it at once. The colossus was making separate piles of faxes: answers from hotels, restaurants and garages which were still flooding in. He looked like a grocer going through his stocks.

"Superintendent?" Barnes raised an eyebrow. "Here, I've just received . . ."

"I know."

Niémans grabbed Costes's fax and glanced through it. It was a list of figures and long words, the chemical composition of the water from the eye-sockets.

"Captain," the officer asked him, "Are there any power stations in the area? One that burns lignite?"

Barnes looked skeptical.

"None that I know of. Maybe to the west . . . There are several industrial areas in the direction of Grenoble."

"Where could I find out?"

"There is the Isère Industrial Board," Barnes answered. "But, hang on a second, I've got a better idea. This power station must cause a hell of a lot of pollution, I suppose?"

Niémans grinned and showed him the fax covered with figures. "An acid bath."

Barnes was jotting something down.

"Go and see this guy. Alain Derteaux. He's a gardener who owns the tropical greenhouses on the way out of Guernon. He's our pollution expert. A militant ecologist. He knows the origin, the composition and the environmental consequences of the slightest whiff of gas or smoke in the entire region."

Niémans was on his way out when the gendarme called him back. He was holding up his hands, palms turned toward the superintendent. Two massive mitts.

"I was forgetting . . . I found out about the fingerprint problem. You know, Caillois's hands. He had an accident when he was a kid. He was helping his father repair their little yacht on Lake Annecy and he burnt his hands with some highly corrosive detergent. I contacted the lake authority and they remember all about the accident. Ambulance, hospital, the whole works . . . We could check it out, but in my opinion we'd be wasting our time."

Niémans turned and grabbed the door handle.

"Thanks, captain." He pointed at the faxes. "Keep up the good work."

"You too," Barnes replied. "And good luck. That ecologist is a real pain in the ass."

CHAPTER 15

" . . . the entirety of our region has been poisoned and is now dying! Industrial zones have sprung up across the valleys, on the sides of the mountains, in the forests, contaminating the water table, infecting the soil, infiltrating the very air that we breathe . . .

That's the Isère: gases and poisons at every altitude!"

Alain Derteaux was a wizened man, with a narrow, wizened face. His beard and metallic glasses made him look like an escaped Mormon. Lurking in one of his greenhouses, he was fiddling with some jars which contained cotton wool and loose earth. Niémans butted into the speech, which had got under way as soon as he had introduced himself.

"I'm sorry, but I am in desperate need of some information."

"What? Oh yes, of course . . ." He looked condescending. "After all, you are a police officer . . ."

"Do you know of a power station in the area which burns lignite?"

"Lignite? Brown coal? . . . It's pure poison . . ."

"Do you know of a place like that?"

While planting some minuscule branches in one of his jars, Derteaux shook his head.

"No. There's no lignite in this region, thank heavens. That industry has been declining rapidly both in France and in our neighboring countries since the 1970s. It causes far too much pollution. Acidic fumes which go straight up into the atmosphere and turn every cloud into a chemical bomb . . ."

Niémans searched through his pocket, then handed him Marc Costes's fax.

"Would you mind taking a look at these chemical components? It's the analysis of some water found near here."

While Derteaux was carefully reading it through, the policeman gazed round the vast greenhouse; its panes of glass were misty, cracked, stained with long black streams. Leaves as big as the windows, tentative shoots, as tiny as rebuses, languid creepers, gnarled and interlaced. They seemed to be struggling to acquire the slightest patch of ground. Derteaux lifted his head and looked puzzled.

"You say that this sample comes from this region?"

"Exactly."

Derteaux readjusted his glasses.

"May I ask where? I mean, precisely where?"

"It was found on a corpse. A murdered man."

"Oh, of course . . . How silly of me . . . You are a policeman." He thought it over, looking increasingly skeptical. "A corpse, here, in Guernon?"

The superintendent ignored the question.

"Can you confirm that the composition comes from pollution caused by the burning of lignite?"

"It is certainly a highly acidic form of pollution, in any case. I've attended some seminars on the subject." He read the report once more. "The levels of H_2SO_4 and HNO_3 are . . . exceptional. But, I'll say it again, there are no more power stations of that sort in the region. Not here, nor in France, nor even in Western Europe."

"Could this contamination come from another sort of industry?"

"No, I don't think so."

"Then where could we find an industrial activity that does cause this sort of pollution?"

"More than five hundred miles away. In Eastern Europe."

Niémans clenched his teeth. His first lead was surely not going to come to nothing like this.

"There could be another explanation," Derteaux mumbled.

"Which is?"

"Perhaps this water does come from somewhere else. It might have traveled here from the Czech Republic, or Slovakia, Rumania, Bulgaria . . ." He whispered in a confidential tone. "They're a bunch of barbarians when it comes to the environment."

"You mean in a container? A lorry passing this way, and . . ."

Derteaux burst out laughing, but without the slightest hint of joviality.

"I was thinking of a simpler form of transport. This water could have come our way in a cloud."

"Can you explain yourself?" Niémans asked.

Alain Derteaux opened his arms and raised them toward the ceiling.

"Imagine a power station somewhere in Eastern Europe. Imagine its huge chimneys spouting sulphur dioxide and nitrogen dioxide day in, day out ... These chimneys are sometimes over three hundred feet tall. The thick masses of smoke go up, up, then mix with the clouds ... If there is no wind, then the poison stays where it is. But when the wind rises, to the west for example, then the dioxides travel in the clouds which burst on our mountains and empty themselves. It's what is known as acid rain. It's destroying our forests. As though we weren't producing enough poison ourselves, our trees are being killed off by other people's poison! But, I assure you, we put plenty of toxic substances in our own clouds, too ..."

A clear simple picture engraved itself in Niémans's mind. The killer was sacrificing his victim in the open air, somewhere on the mountains. He was torturing, mutilating, murdering him while a shower of rain fell down on the carnage. The empty eye-sockets, turned up toward the sky, filled with water. With poisonous rain. The killer closed up the eyelids, sealing his macabre operation on those tiny reservoirs of acidic water. It was the only explanation.

It had rained while the monster was carrying out his murder.

"What was the weather like on Saturday?" Niémans asked abruptly.

"I beg your pardon?"

"Do you remember if it rained here on Saturday, toward dusk, or during the night?"

"No, I don't think so. It was a beautiful day. Perfect summer sunshine and ..."

A one-in-a-thousand chance. If the weather had been dry when the murder was probably being committed, then Niémans might be able to locate one single area where there had been a down-pour. A shower of acid rain which would point precisely to the scene of the crime, as clearly as a chalk circle. The officer suddenly realised that to find where the murder had taken place, then he would have to follow the clouds.

"Where is the nearest meteorological station?" he asked hastily.

Derteaux thought for a second.

"Twenty miles from here, near the Mine-de-Fer. You want to

check if it rained? The idea is an interesting one. I'd like to know myself if those barbarians are still sending us toxic bombs. This is out-and-out chemical warfare, superintendent, and nobody cares!"

Derteaux stopped. Niémans was handing him a piece of paper.

"The number of my mobile. If you have any other ideas on the subject, then call me."

Niémans spun round and crossed the greenhouse, the leaves of the ebony trees scratching at his face.

CHAPTER 16

The superintendent drove with his foot down. Despite the menacing sky, the day seemed set to turn fair. A quicksilver light constantly flittered around the clouds. The branches of the fir trees, between black and green, were tipped with wild glimmers, shaken by the relentless wind. As he drove round the bends, Niémans enjoyed the deep, secret vibrancy of the forest, as though it were driven on, lifted up, illumined by that sunny wind.

The superintendent thought of the clouds carrying a poison which was later to be found in a pair of empty eye-sockets. When he left Paris the previous night, he had not imagined being involved in such an investigation.

Forty minutes later, the policeman arrived at Mine-de-Fer. He had no difficulty in locating the meteorological station, a dome jutting out from the side of the mountain. Niémans took the track which led to the scientific center, discovering a surprising sight as he went. About a hundred yards away from the laboratory, some men were struggling to inflate a massive balloon made of transparent plastic. He parked his car and clambered up the slope. Going over to the parka-clad men, with their reddened eyes, he presented his official police card. The meteorologists looked at him dumbly. The long crumpled sections of the balloon looked like streams of silver. Beneath them, a bluish flame was slowly inflating the fabric. The entire scene seemed enchanted, spell-like.

"Superintendent Niémans," the officer bawled over the din from the burner. He pointed at the concrete dome. "I need one of you to come up to the laboratory with me."

One man, obviously the boss, stepped forward.

"What?"

"I want to know if it rained last Saturday. It's part of a criminal investigation."

The meteorologist just stood there, an irritated expression on his face. His hood was slapping against his cheeks. He pointed up at the huge form, which was gradually expanding. Niémans bowed slightly, making an apologetic gesture.

"The balloon can wait."

The scientist headed up toward the laboratory murmuring:

"It didn't rain last Saturday."

"We'll see about that."

The man was right. Once inside, they consulted the central meteorological office, and could not find the slightest trace of turbulence, of precipitation or of a storm over Guernon during those hours in October. The satellite photographs which flickered across the screen were categorical: not a single drop of rain had fallen on the region during that day or during the night of Saturday to Sunday. Other data appeared in a corner of the screen: the level of humidity in the air, the atmospheric pressure, the temperature ... The scientist grudgingly came up with a few explanations. An anti-cyclone had brought about a certain stability in the sky for a period of about forty-eight hours.

So Niémans asked the engineer to extend his search to Sunday morning, then to Sunday afternoon. No storms, no showers. He widened the investigation to a radius of sixty miles. Nothing. Then one hundred. Still nothing. The superintendent banged his fist down on the desk.

"This just isn't possible," he groaned. "It rained somewhere. I have proof of that. In a valley. Or on the top of a hill. Somewhere around here there was a storm."

The meteorologist shrugged and continued clicking his mouse, while shadowy gleams, wavy lines and slight spirals went on crossing the screen, above a map of the mountains, retracing the beginnings of a fine cloudless day in the heart of Isère.

"There must be another explanation," Niémans murmured. "Jesus Christ, I . . ."

His mobile phone started ringing.

"Superintendent? Alain Derteaux speaking. I've been thinking over your lignite business and looking into it myself. I'm sorry, but I was mistaken."

"Mistaken?"

"Yes. Such highly acidic rain cannot possibly have fallen last weekend. Nor indeed at any other moment."

"Why not?"

"I've obtained some information concerning the lignite industry. Even in Eastern Europe, the chimneys where such fuel is burnt now have special filters. Or else the sulphur is extracted from the minerals. In other words, this form of pollution has dropped considerably since the 1960s. Such heavily polluted rain has not fallen anywhere for about thirty-five years. And a good job too! So, I'm sorry. I misled you."

Niémans remained silent. The ecologist went on, in an incredulous tone of voice:

"You are sure that this water was found on a corpse?"

"Certain," Niémans replied.

"Then it sounds incredible, but your corpse comes from the past. It picked up some rainwater which fell over thirty years ago and . . ."

The policeman muttered a vague "good-bye" and hung up.

With slouching shoulders, he went back to his car. For a fleeting moment, he had thought that he had a lead. But it had dissolved away, like that acid-saturated water which had led to an utter absurdity.

Niémans looked up once more at the heavens.

The sun was now darting out transversal beams, making the cotton wool arabesques of the clouds turn golden. The brilliant light ricocheted off the Grand Pic de Belledonne, refracted on the eternal snows. How could he, a professional cop, a rational being, have thought for one moment that a few clouds were going to reveal the scene of the crime?

How could he have imagined that?

Suddenly, he opened his arms toward the gleaming landscape, just like Fanny Ferreira, the young climber. He had just understood where Rémy Caillois had been killed. He had just realised where thirty-five-year-old rainwater could be found.

Not on the earth.

Nor in the sky.

In the ice.

Rémy Caillois had been killed at an altitude of over six thousand feet. He had been executed in the glaciers, at a height of nine thousand feet. In a place where each year's rain is crystallised and remains in the eternal glassiness of the ice.

That was the scene of the crime. And this was a solid lead.

IV

CHAPTER 17

At one o'clock in the afternoon, Karim Abdouf entered Henri Crozier's office and placed his report in front of him. The Chief, who was concentrating on a letter he was writing, did not even glance at the papers and just asked:

"Well?"

"The skins didn't do it. But they saw two figures coming out of the vault. That very night."

"Could they describe them?"

"No. It was too dark."

Crozier deigned to raise his eyes.

"Maybe they're lying."

"Oh no they're not. They did not desecrate that tomb."

Karim paused. The silence between the two men lengthened. Then he went on:

"You had a witness, superintendent." He aimed his index finger at the seated figure. "You had a witness and you didn't tell me. Somebody told you that the skinheads had been seen hanging round the cemetery that night, and you concluded that they had done it. But the truth of the matter is more complex. And if you'd let me question your witness, then I . . ."

Crozier slowly lifted his hand in a sign of peace.

"Calm down, kid. People round here talk to the old brigade. To locals like them. You wouldn't have got a tenth of what I was told without even having to ask. Is that all you learnt from the shaven heads?"

Karim examined the posters to the glory of the "guardians of the peace." On one of the metal cabinets shone the cups which Crozier had won in various shooting competitions. He announced:

"The skins also saw a white car drive off from the area at about two o'clock in the morning. It took the D143."

"What sort of car?"

"A Lada. Or some other East European make. We'll have to put somebody onto that. There can't be that many motors of that sort round here and . . ."

"Why not you?"

"You know what I want, superintendent. I questioned the skins. Now I want to make a thorough search of the vault."

"The cemetery keeper told me that you'd already been inside."

Karim let the remark pass.

"How are investigations in the cemetery going?"

"Zero. No fingerprints. Not the slightest piece of evidence. We're going to continue searching in a larger radius. If it was vandals, then they were extremely cautious ones."

"They weren't vandals. They were professionals. Or, in any case, people who knew what they were looking for. That vault conceals a secret which they wanted to unravel. Have you told the family? What did the parents say? Do they agree to us . . ."

Karim came to a halt. Crozier was looking decidedly uneasy. The lieutenant leant both of his hands on the desk and waited for the superintendent's answers. The man mumbled:

"We haven't found the family. There's nobody by that name in the town. Nor in the rest of the *département*."

"The funeral was in 1982, there must be some record of it somewhere."

"So far, we've drawn a blank."

"What about the death certificate?"

"There's no death certificate. Not in Sarzac."

Karim's face brightened up. He stood up and paced round the room.

"There's something wrong about that grave and about that kid.

I'm sure of it. And this something is linked to the burglary at the primary school."

"You're letting your imagination run away with you, Karim. There are umpteen possible explanations for this mystery. Perhaps little Jude died in a car accident. Maybe he was hospitalised in a nearby town, then buried here, because that was the simplest solution. Perhaps his mother still lives here, but has a different surname. Maybe ..."

"I spoke to the cemetery keeper. The vault has been well looked after, but he's never seen anybody visit it."

Crozier did not respond. He opened a metal drawer and pulled out a bottle of bronze-colored spirits. He rapidly poured himself a shot.

"If we can't find the family," Karim went on, "Then maybe we can get permission to enter the vault?"

"No."

"So let me look for his parents."

"What about the white car? And the search for clues around the cemetery?"

"Reinforcements are on their way. The regional boys can take care of that. Give me a few hours, superintendent. To manage this part of the investigation. On my own."

Crozier raised his glass in front of Karim.

"You don't fancy a drop, I suppose?"

Karim shook his head. Crozier downed his glass in one and clicked his tongue.

"You've got until six this evening. Written report included."

The Arab was gone with a rustling of leather.

CHAPTER 18

Karim phoned back the headmistress of Jean-Jaurès School to see if she had obtained any information about Jude Ithero from the education board. She had made a request, but received nothing.

Not a single file. Not a single mention. Not a trace in any of the area's archives.

"Perhaps you're barking up the wrong tree," she volunteered. "The child you're looking for maybe didn't live in this region."

Karim hung up and looked at his watch. Half past one. He allotted himself two hours to check the archives of the other schools and look through the composition of the classes which matched the boy's age.

In less than an hour, he had completed his tour of the local educational establishments and had found no trace of Jude Ithero. He went back once more to Jean-Jaurès. An idea had occurred to him while rummaging through the other archives. The saucereyed woman welcomed him eagerly.

"I've done some more work for you, lieutenant."

"Oh yes?"

"I looked out the names and addresses of the teachers who were working here at that time."

"And?"

"And bad luck. The previous headmistress is now retired."

"Jude was nine in 1981 and ten in 1982. Could we find who his teachers were?"

The woman looked through her notes.

"Indeed. In fact chance would have it that the 1981 CM1 and the 1982 CM2 classes both had the same teacher. It is quite common for a teacher to 'jump' up a class, from one year to the next . . ."

"Where is she now?"

"I don't know. She left this school at the end of the 1981–1982 academic year."

Karim groaned. The headmistress pulled a serious face.

"I've been thinking about that, too. There is one thing we haven't looked at yet."

"What's that?"

"The school photographs. We keep one copy of each class portrait, you know."

The lieutenant bit his lip. Why had he not thought of that?

The headmistress went on:

"I went through our photographic records. And the portraits of CM1 and CM2 that interest us have also vanished. It's quite incredible."

This revelation filtered slowly into the policeman's mind, like a ray of light. He thought of the oval frame, stuck up on the plaque of the vault. He realised that someone had "obliterated" the little boy, taking away his name, his face. The woman interrupted his train of thought:

"Why are you smiling?"

Karim answered:

"I'm sorry. But I've been waiting for this moment for a long time. I'm onto something big, do you see that?" The lieutenant paused for a moment to get his concentration back. "I've had an idea, too. Do you keep the old class books?"

"The class books?"

"In my day, each class had a sort of daily register, where they noted down who was absent, and the homework to be done for the next day."

"That's what we do here, too."

"So, do you keep them?"

"Yes. But they don't contain a list of the pupils."

"I know, only the ones who were absent."

The woman's face lit up. Her eyes shone like mirrors.

"You're hoping that young Jude was absent one day?"

"What I'm hoping most of all is that our burglars didn't think of that, too."

Once more, the headmistress opened the glass case which contained the archives. Karim ran his finger along the dark green spines and pulled out the class books corresponding to those two years. Another disappointment: not once did they mention the name of Jude Ithero.

Maybe he really was barking up the wrong tree. Despite his firm conviction, nothing proved that the boy had been to school there. Still he flicked backward and forward through the pages, looking for a detail that would confirm that he was on the right track.

It suddenly leapt out in front of him, from the pages of the book which had been numbered in a round, childish hand: some of them were missing. The cop opened wide the book and discovered large scraps of paper sticking up from the binding. The class book of CM2 had had the pages covering the period 8–15 June, 1982 ripped out. These dates seemed like hooks, fishing out a chunk of oblivion. Karim could almost see the child's name, written in that same round hand, on the missing pages . . .

The lieutenant mumbled:

"Get me the phone book."

A few minutes later, Karim was calling round all the doctors in Sarzac, with this certainty written in his blood: if Jude Ithero had been absent from the 8th to the 15th of June 1982, then he must have been ill. He questioned all of them, asking them to look through their records, spelling out, each time, the child's name. None of them remembered the surname. The cop swore. He tried the neighboring towns: Cailhac, Thiermons, Valuc. It was from Cambuse, a town situated at eighteen miles' distance, that a medic finally replied in a flat voice:

"Jude Ithero. Yes, of course. I remember him perfectly."

Karim could not believe his ears.

"Fourteen years later? And you remember him that well?"

"Come to my surgery and I'll explain."

CHAPTER 19

Dr Stéphane Macé was an updated and elegant version of the country physician. Distinguished features, long pale hands, a pricy suit; and a perfect specimen of the alert, understanding, refined bourgeois doctor. From the start, Karim detested this cocksure medic. He sometimes frightened himself with his outbursts of fury, which split away from him as though they were icebergs in his own personal Bering Sea.

Without taking off his leather jacket, he perched on the corner of the chair. A desk of polished wood lay between them. A few vaguely affected knick-knacks, a computer, a dictionary of drugs . . . The surgery was sober, strict and upmarket.

"Go on, doctor," Karim demanded point-blank.

"Perhaps you could tell me what line of investigations you are . . ."

"No." Karim softened his brutality with a smile. "Sorry. I can't."

The doctor tapped his fingers on the edge of his desk, then got to his feet. The sight of this Arab in a woolly hat had obviously taken him aback.

"It was in June 1982. A call just like any other. For a little boy, who was running a temperature. It was my first tour of duty. I was twenty-eight years old."

"Is that why you remember the visit so well?"

The doctor smiled. A grin as wide as a hammock, which exasperated Karim even more.

"No. You'll see why . . . I received the call via a central switchboard and noted down the address without knowing where I was going. In fact, it was to a little house, lost in the middle of a rugged plain, about nine miles from here . . . I still have the address . . . I'll give it to you."

The lieutenant quietly nodded.

"Anyway," the doctor went on, "I came across a completely isolated stone building. The heat was terrible, insects were buzzing in the dried-out shrubbery . . . When the woman opened the door, I immediately had a strange impression, as though she were out of her place in this rustic decor . . ."

"Why?"

"I don't know. There was a gleaming, polished piano in the main room and . . ."

"Aren't yokels allowed to like music?"

"That's not what I meant . . ."

The doctor stopped.

"You apparently do not find me to your taste."

Karim looked up.

"What does that matter?"

The doctor nodded in agreement, still with an affable air. His smile never left his lips, but there was now fear in his eyes. He had just noticed the grip of the Glock 21, snug in its velcro holster. And perhaps the dried blood-stains on the sleeve of Karim's leather jacket. Increasingly uneasy, he started pacing up and down again.

"I went into the child's bedroom and that is when things became decidedly odd."

"Why?"

The doctor shrugged.

"The room was empty. No toys. No pictures. Nothing."

"What did the boy look like?"

"I don't know."

"You don't know?"

"No. That was the oddest part of it. The woman let me into a dark house. All the shutters were down. Not a single light was on. When I went in, my first thought was that she was simply trying to make the place as cool as possible. But there were also sheets over the furniture. It was all . . . very mysterious."

"What did she tell you?"

"That her child was ill. And that the light hurt his eyes."

"Were you able to examine him . . . normally?"

"Yes. In the shadows."

"What was wrong with him?"

"A simple throat infection. In fact, I can remember that . . ."

The doctor bent over and put his fingers to his lips – a dry, scholarly gesture, no doubt designed to impress his clientele. But it left Karim cold.

"It was at that moment that I understood . . . When I got out my pencil light to examine the boy's throat, the woman grabbed my wrist . . . Extremely violently . . . She did not want me to see her child's face."

Karim thought it over. One of his legs was twitching. He was thinking about the empty oval frame, pinned up over the tomb. And the theft of the photos.

"When you said she was violent, what did you mean?"

"I should really have said that she was strong. Abnormally strong. I must add that she was at least six feet tall. A real colossus."

"And did you see her face?"

"No. As I told you, this all happened in semi-darkness."

"And then?"

"I wrote out the prescription and left."

"How did she behave? Toward her son, I mean?"

"She seemed to be both very attentive and distant at the same time . . . The more I think about it . . . the stranger that visit seems."

"And you've never been back to see them?"

The doctor was still pacing round the room. He glanced blackly at Karim. Every trace of joviality had vanished from his face. The policeman then realised why he remembered that visit so clearly. Two months later, little Jude was dead. And the doctor must know that.

"There were the holidays," he went on. "And . . . then I finally returned to the house at the beginning of September. But it was empty. From a distant neighbor I learnt that they had gone."

"Gone? Didn't anybody tell you that the boy had died?"

The doctor shook his head.

"No. The neighbors knew nothing about that. I only found out later, quite by chance."

"How?"

"In Sarzac cemetery, when attending a funeral."

"Another one of your patients?"

"You are starting to become unpleasant, inspector, I . . ."

Karim stood up. The doctor backed off.

"Ever since then," the cop said, "you've been wondering if you didn't miss the symptoms of a more serious disease that day. Ever since, you've been living with that vague remorse. I suppose you must have looked into the matter yourself. Do you know what the kid died of?"

The doctor slid his index finger inside his collar and opened a button. His forehead was running with sweat.

"No, I don't. But you're right . . . I did try to find out for myself, but I found nothing. I contacted my colleagues, the hospitals . . . Nothing. I became obsessed by this story, can you understand that?"

Karim turned on his heel.

"Then you're still in for a few surprises."

"What?"

The doctor was as white as lint.

"You'll find out soon enough," Karim retorted.

"For heaven's sake, what have I ever done to you?"

"Nothing. It's just that I spent my youth stealing cars belonging to guys like you . . ."

"Who are you? What's going on? You . . . You haven't even shown me any official identification, I . . ."

Karim grinned.

"Don't panic. I was only joking."

He slipped out into the corridor. The waiting-room was crammed with people. The doctor caught up with him.

"Wait," he panted. "Is there something you know which I do not? I mean . . . about the cause of death."

"Sorry, no."

The cop turned the handle. The doctor shoved his hand against the door. His suit was trembling like a set of sails.

"What's going on? Why this investigation so long after the event?"

"Someone broke into the kid's tomb last night. And burgled his school."

"Who . . . who do you think did it?"

The lieutenant declared:

"I don't know. But one thing's certain. When it comes to yesterday's crimes, we can't see the wood for the trees yet."

CHAPTER 20

He drove for a long time, along the deserted roads. In that region, A-roads are like B-roads and B-roads like farm lanes. Under the smooth blue sky, the fields stretched away without crops or livestock. Occasional rocky crags poked up across the landscape, revealing silvery hollows, as welcoming as a mantrap. Crossing this land meant going back through time, to a period when agriculture had not yet been invented.

Karim had started out with the idea of visiting Jude's family's house, the address of which Macé had given him. It no longer existed. A heap of ruins and stones, scarcely higher than the bed of grayish grasses, lay there where it had stood. He could then have gone to the land register and found the name of its owner, but he decided to press on to Cahors in order to question Jean-Pierre Cau, Jean-Jaurès School's official photographer, who had taken the missing photos.

He hoped to be able to examine the negatives of the classes that interested him. The boy must be there, among those anonymous faces, and Karim now felt an overwhelming desire to see that face, even if there was no way he would recognise it. He had a secret hope that he would capture something, some obscure hint, a sign, while examining those negatives.

At about four o'clock in the afternoon, he parked his car by the pedestrian precinct in Cahors. Stone porches, cast-iron balconies and gargoyles. All the aristocratic beauty of an historical town center, enough to make Karim, the suburban kid, want to puke.

He wandered through the streets and at last found the shop sign of Jean-Pierre Cau, specialist in "weddings and baptisms".

The photographer was upstairs, in his studio.

Karim leapt up the staircase. The room was in semi-darkness. All he could make out were large frames hanging on the walls, containing smiling couples in their Sunday best. Standardised happiness on glossy paper.

Karim immediately felt bad about the wave of scorn that had passed through him. Was he there to judge people? What did he, the exiled cop, have to offer instead? He had never been able to stare back into a young girl's eyes and now all the love he possessed had turned into a fossilised kernel, isolated from the looks and the warmth of others. For him, sentiment meant the humility and vulnerability he had always rejected, like a proud bird of prey. But, in this domain, pride was a mortal sin. Now, in his lonely shell, he was rapidly drying up.

"Are you getting married?"

Karim turned round toward the voice.

Jean-Pierre was as gray and pock-marked as a pumice stone. He had large curly whiskers, which seemed to be quivering with impatience, in contrast with his tired, baggy eyes. He turned on the light.

"No," he added, sizing up Karim. "You're not getting married."

His voice was gravelly, like that of an old smoker. Cau approached him. Behind his glasses, under his withered eyelids, his gaze wandered between world-weariness and distrust. Karim smiled. He had no warrant, nor any authority in this town. He was going to have to play things smoothly.

"My name's Karim Abdouf," he began. "I'm a police lieutenant. I need some information connected with an investigation . . ."

"Are you from Cahors?" the photographer asked, more intrigued than worried.

"From Sarzac."

"Do you have a card, or anything?"

Karim dived into his pocket and handed him his official papers. The photographer examined them for a few seconds. The Arab sighed. He was sure that the man had never seen a police card close up before, but still that did not stop him from acting the wise guy. Cau gave it back with a forced smile. Wrinkles furrowed his forehead.

"How can I help you?"

"I'm looking for some class photographs."

"Which school?"

"Jean-Jaurès, in Sarzac. I need the class portraits of CM1 in 1981 and of CM2 in 1982, as well as a list of the pupils' names if, by any chance, you have them with the photos. Do you keep that sort of thing?"

The man smiled again.

"I keep everything."

"Could we take a look?" the policeman asked, in the sweetest voice he could drag up from his throat.

Cau pointed at the adjoining room. A ray of light cut into the shadows.

"No problem. Step this way."

The second room was even larger than the studio. A complicated black machine, containing a mess of optical glasses and adjustable instruments, was fixed above a long counter. On the walls were pinned large pictures of baptisms. White, everywhere. Smiles. New-born babies.

Karim followed him as far as his metallic filing cabinets. The man bent down, reading the labels on the drawers, then pulled one open. He removed a wad of thick brown paper envelopes.

"Here we are, Jean-Jaurès."

Cau extricated one envelope, which contained several folders of translucent paper. He looked through them. Then looked again. The wrinkles on his brow multiplied.

"You did say CM1 in '81 and CM2 in '82?"

"That's right."

His weary eyelids widened.

"How odd. I can't . . . They're not here."

Karim shivered. Could the robbers have had the same idea as him? He asked:

"Did you notice anything particular when you opened this morning?"

"What do you mean?"

"Anything like a burglary?"

Cau burst out laughing and pointed at the infra-red detectors at each of the four corners of the studio.

"If anyone tried to break in here, they wouldn't have had an easy time of it, believe you me. I've spent a bit on security . . ."

Karim smiled fleetingly, then declared:

"Check, all the same. I know plenty of guys who would have no more difficulty with your system than with a doormat. You do keep your negatives, don't you?"

Cau's expression changed.

"My negatives? Why?"

"Maybe you still have the ones I'm interested in."

"Sorry, but that's strictly confidential."

The cop noticed a vein twitching in the photographer's neck. It was time to up the tone a bit.

"Your negatives, grandpa. Or I'll get touchy."

The man stared back at Karim, hesitated, then backed away and nodded. They went over to another metal cabinet, this time sealed with a padlock. Cau undid it and opened one of the drawers. His hands were shaking. The lieutenant leant on his elbow and faced him. As the minutes ticked by, he could feel an inexplicable fear and anxiety rising in the man. As though Cau, as he searched, had remembered something which was now bugging him horribly.

The photographer dived once more into his envelopes. Seconds went by. He finally raised his eyes. His face was a contortion of tics.

"I . . . uh, no. I don't seem to have them any more either."

Karim pushed the drawer violently shut. With his hands caught in the metallic trap, the photographer screamed. Never mind about playing things smoothly. Karim squeezed the man by his throat and lifted him off the floor. His voice was still calm:

"Be reasonable, now, Cau. Were you burgled, yes or no?"

"N . . . no. Honestly."

"So what have you done with the fucking pictures?"

Cau stammered:

"I . . . I . . . I sold them."

In his amazement, Karim let him drop. The man groaned and massaged his fists. The cop murmured softly:

"Sold them? But . . . when?"

The man replied:

"Good God . . . All that's ancient history . . . And I can do whatever I like with my . . ."

"When did you sell them?"

"I don't know . . . maybe fifteen years ago . . ."

Karim was reeling from one surprise to another. He pushed the photographer back against the cabinet. Transparent paper folders fluttered around them.

"Tell it from the beginning, grandpa. Because none of this is very clear."

Cau grimaced:

"It was one evening, during summer . . . A woman came here . . . She wanted the photographs . . . The same ones as you . . . It's just come back to me . . ."

This new information completely threw Karim. So, as early as 1982, "they" had been looking for photos of little Jude.

"Did she mention Jude? Jude Ithero? Did she give you his name?"

"No. She just took the photos and the negatives."

"Did she give you any money?"

The man nodded.

"How much?"

"Twenty thousand francs . . . A fortune back then . . . For a few snapshots of kiddies . . ."

"Why did she want the photos?"

"I don't know. We didn't discuss that."

"You must have looked at those photos . . . Was there a kid with some special distinguishing feature? Something she wanted to hide?"

"No. I didn't notice anything . . . I don't know . . . I just don't know . . ."

"What about the woman? What was she like? Was she big and strong? Was she his mother?"

The old man suddenly froze, then burst out laughing. A long deep laugh, from the pit of his stomach. He smirked:

"No chance of that."

Karim grabbed the man with both hands, shoving him back against the filing cabinet.

"WHY NOT?"

Cau's eyes rolled beneath their withered lids.

"She was a nun. A goddam Catholic nun!"

CHAPTER 21

Sarzac had three churches. One was being renovated, the second was run by an old priest with one foot in the grave, while the third had a young minister, about whom the strangest rumors were circulating. People said that he drank in secret with his mother in the presbytery.

The lieutenant, who had a general dislike for the entire population of Sarzac, and in particular for their taste for gossip, did have to admit that this time they were right. He himself had been called in once to separate the mother and the son, who were in the throes of an incredibly violent drunken brawl.

But it was this priest that Karim chose to question.

He braked in front of the presbytery. A charmless bungalow made of cement, abutting a modern church with asymmetric stained-glass windows. The small sign on the door said: "My Parish". Brambles and nettles sprawled over the steps. He rang the doorbell. Several minutes went by. Karim heard muffled cries. He swore to himself. This was all he needed.

Finally, the door opened.

Karim felt as though he was contemplating a shipwreck. It was mid-afternoon, but the priest already stank of booze. His thin features were covered by a shaggy beard and wiry hair, as though sprinkled with ashes. His eyes were nicotine colored. His jacket collar was threadbare, his shirt front gleaming with assorted stains. As a priest, he was finished, used up, burnt out. His religious destiny had lasted no longer than a leaf of smouldering incense, with its stubborn heady odor.

"What can I do for you, my son?"

His voice was cracked, but steady.

"Police Lieutenant Karim Abdouf. We've met before."

The man readjusted his gray collar.

"Ah yes, I seem to . . ." He glanced round with a hunted expression. "Was it the neighbors who called you out?"

Karim smiled.

"No. I need your help. For a police investigation."

"Oh. Really? Then, come on in."

The policeman entered the house. His soles stuck to the floor as he went. He looked down and saw that the linoleum was marked with long, shining traces.

"It's my mother," the priest whispered. "She doesn't do anything any more, except mess the place up with her jam." He scratched his uncombed hair. "It's strange, but it's all she will eat."

The decor was chaotic. Scraps of plastic, stuck up anyhow, imitated wood, ceramics and cloth. Through a half-open door, the policeman noticed rectangles of yellow polystyrene, sliced up with a carpet cutter, and ill-matching cushions, which gave an idea of the character of the living-room. A heap of gardening tools lay on the floor. In front of him, another room contained a formica table, covered with dirty plates, and an unmade bed.

The priest staggered toward the living-room. He tripped, then steadied himself. Karim said:

"Why don't you have a drink? We'll save time that way."

The man turned round, with a hostile stare.

"Look who's talking, my son. You're shaking from your head to your toes."

Karim gulped. He was still in a state of shock. He had not stopped to think, or collect his wits, since slapping the photographer around a bit. All he could hear was a buzzing in his head, and he felt a hammering in his chest. Absent-mindedly, he wiped his face with his sleeve, like a snotty kid.

The priest poured out a glass of spirits.

"Care for a drop?" he asked, with an unpleasant grin.

"Never touch the stuff."

The man in black downed his shot. Blood surged across his haggard face. His fevered eyes shone like sulphur. He sniggered:

"Islam, is it?"

"No. I like to keep my wits about me for my job. That's all."

The priest raised his glass.

"Here's to your job, then."

Karim then spotted the mother, who was coming and going in the corridor. She was hunched over, almost doubled up, and carrying a pot of jam. He thought of the open vault, the skinheads, the nun who had bought the school photographs, and now these two ghouls from a ghost-train. He had opened a Pandora's box, which seemed to be producing an endless stream of nightmares.

The priest intercepted his gaze.

"Leave her, my son. She's all right." He sat down on one of the foam mattresses. "Now, what can I do for you?"

Karim slowly raised a hand.

"Just one thing first. Please, stop calling me 'my son'."

"Sorry," the man answered with a smirk. "It's force of habit."

With an ironic gesture, the priest took another sip. He had recovered his world-weary expression.

"What sort of investigation are you working on?"

Karim was pleased. The priest obviously had not yet heard about the profanation of the cemetery. So Crozier had managed to hush the whole thing up.

"I'm sorry, but it's highly confidential. All I can tell you is that I'm looking for a convent. Near Sarzac, or Cahors. Or even elsewhere in the region. I'm hoping you will help me find it."

"Which order would that be?"

"I don't know."

The man poured himself another shot. His little glass glinted merrily.

"There are several of them around here." He smirked again.

"This region must lend itself to seclusion . . ."

"How many?"

"At least ten, just in this *département*."

Karim made a rapid mental calculation. Going round all these convents, which were no doubt scattered across the region, would take at least an entire day. But it was now already gone four o'clock. He had only two hours left. He was stuck.

The priest stood up and started rummaging through a cupboard.

"Ah, here it is."

He flicked over the pages of a sort of directory, printed on Bible paper. The mother walked into the room and tiptoed over to the bottle. Without looking at Karim, she poured herself a glass. She had eyes only for her son. Eagle-eyes, like triggers, brimming with hatred. As he read through the directory, the priest barked:

"Leave us, mother."

The woman did not respond. She clutched her glass in both hands. Her bony fingers jutted out. Suddenly she noticed Karim. Her dry, bitter voice piped up:

"Who are you?"

"Leave us." The priest turned toward Karim. "I've marked the pages with the ten convents in question, if you'd like to jot them down . . . But they're quite a long way away from one other."

Karim had a look. He vaguely recognised the names of the villages. He got out his notebook and wrote them down.

"Who are you?" the mother repeated.

"Go back to your bedroom, mother!" the priest shouted.

He went over to Karim.

"What are you looking for exactly? I might be able to help you . . ."

Karim raised his pen and stared at this man of the cloth.

"I'm looking for a nun. A nun who's interested in photos."

"What sort of photos?"

Karim noticed a gleam fleetingly light up the priest's eyes.

"Have you ever heard of anything along those lines?"

The man scratched his head.

"Um . . . no."

Karim asked:

"How old are you?"

"Me? I'm . . . I'm twenty-five."

The mother poured herself another drink. She was listening intently. Karim went on:

"Were you born in Sarzac?"

"Yes, I was."

"And did you go to school here?"

The priest shrugged.

"Yes, until secondary school. I then went to . . ."

"Which school? Jean-Jaurès?"

"Yes, but . . ."

He suddenly saw the link.

"She's been here."

"What?"

"The nun. The nun I'm looking for . . . She came here and bought your class photographs. That's it! She's been round all the houses, collecting as many school photos as she could find. Were you in the same class as Jude Ithero? Does that name mean anything to you?"

The priest had gone white.

"I . . . I've no idea what you're talking about."

The mother's voice broke in:

"What is all this?"

Karim wiped his face with his hands, as though he were turning over a fresh page in his features.

"I'll start again. If you had a normal education, then you were in CM2 in 1982, weren't you?"

"But that's almost fifteen years ago!"

"And in CM1 in 1981."

Shoulders bent, the priest stiffened. His fingers grasped the back of a chair. Despite his age, his hands now looked like those of his mother. Old and knotted with blue veins.

"Yes . . . that must be about right . . ."

"So, you were in the same class as a little boy called Ithero. Jude

Ithero. An unusual name. Think it over. This is extremely important."

"No, really, I don't think . . ."

Karim took a step forward.

"But you can remember a nun who was looking for school
photographs, can't you?"

"I . . ."

The mother was lapping it all up.

"Is this Arab telling the truth, you little shit?" she asked.

Then she swung round and hopped off toward the door. Karim
grabbed the chance. He seized the priest by his shoulders and
whispered into his ear:

"Out with it, for Christ's sake!"

The priest slumped down onto a corner of the foam mattress.

"That evening still remains a mystery to me . . ."

Karim knelt down. The priest was articulating slowly:

"She came here . . . one summer evening."

"In July 1982?"

He nodded.

"She knocked at the door . . . It was so hot . . . stifling . . . As if
the last hours of daylight were baking the stones . . . I don't know
why, but I was on my own . . . I opened the door . . . Heaven help
me . . . Just imagine it! I was about ten years old, and that nun
appeared in the half-light, in her black-and-white veil . . ."

"What did she say?"

"She began by speaking about school, the marks I had got, my
favorite subjects. She had an extremely soothing voice . . . Then
she asked to see my school friends . . ." The priest wiped his face,
which was dripping with sweat. "I . . . I went and fetched my school
photograph . . . The one with all of us on it . . . I felt very proud
about showing her my pals, you see? And that's when I realised
that she was after something. She took a long look at the picture,
then asked me if she could keep it . . . As a souvenir, she said . . ."

"Did she ask you for any other photos?"

The priest nodded. His voice thickened.

"She also wanted the portrait of CM1, of the previous year."

Karim was now certain that, if he asked round the parents of the children in those classes, not a single one would still be in possession of those group photographs. But why had that nun made off with all these photos? Karim felt as though a stone jungle was closing around him, cutting off the view.

The mother reappeared in the doorway. She was clutching a shoebox against her chest.

"You little shit. You gave our photographs away. Your school portraits. And you used to be such a good little kid . . ."

"Shut up, mother!" The priest fixed his eyes on Karim's. "I'd already had the call, you see? That huge woman practically hypnotised me . . ."

"Huge? She was big, was she?"

"No . . . Oh, I don't know . . . I was ten . . . But I can still see her, with her black hood. She had such a sweet voice . . . She wanted the photos, and I gave them to her, without a moment's hesitation. She blessed me, then disappeared. It felt like a sign, a . . ."

"You shit!"

Karim glanced round at the mother. She was furious. He looked back at the priest and realised that he was now locked away in his memories. He adopted his sweetest tone:

"Did she tell you why she wanted those pictures?"

"No."

"Did she mention Jude?"

"No."

"Did she give you any money?"

The priest grimaced.

"No, of course not! She asked me for the photos, and I gave them to her, that's all! Good Lord! I . . . I thought that visit was a sign, you follow me? Of divine recognition!"

He was sobbing.

"I didn't yet know that I was a failure. A useless alcoholic. A pickled idiot. The son of this . . . How can one give what one hasn't got?" Clutching onto Karim's leather jacket, he was now imploring him. "How can one shed light, when one is drowning in darkness? How? How?"

The mother dropped the box. Photos spilled across the floor. She threw herself at him violently, raining blows on his back and shoulders.

Terrified, Karim retreated. The entire room was shaking. He realised that he would have to leave. Or else go crazy himself. But he did not have all the answers he needed. He pushed the woman away and leant back over the priest.

"In two seconds, I'll be out of here. And it'll all be over. You've seen that nun since, haven't you?"

Racked with sobs, he nodded.

"What's her name?"

The priest sniffed. The mother was pacing up and down, muttering incomprehensible curses.

"What's her name?"

"Sister Andrée."

"Her convent?"

"Saint-Jean-de-la-Croix. They're Carmelites."

"Where is it?"

The man held his head in his hands. Karim pulled him up by his shoulder.

"Where is it?"

"Between ... between Sète and Cap d'Agde, just by the sea. I go and see her sometimes, when I doubt my faith. She's my succour, you see that? A help ... I ..."

The door was already flapping in the wind. The cop was running toward his car.

V

CHAPTER 22

The sky had darkened once more. Beneath the clouds, the Grand Pic de Belledonne rose up in a huge black wave, its rocky sides frozen rigid. Its slopes, dotted with minuscule trees, seemed to fade away as they ascended into a hazy white mist. The lines of the cable cars stretched downwards, like tiny wires across the snow.

"I reckon that the killer went up there with Rémy Caillois, while his victim was still alive." Niémans smiled. "I think they took a cable car. An experienced climber could easily switch the system on, at any time of the day or night."

"Why are you so sure that they went up there?"

Fanny Ferreira, the young geology lecturer, was looking splendid. Beneath her hood, her face was vibrantly fresh and youthful. Her hair fluttered round her temples and her eyes shone out from the darkness of her skin. Niémans felt a terrible urge to bite into that pure living flesh. He answered:

"We have proof that the body passed through a glacier in one of the mountains. My instinct tells me that the mountain in question was the Grand Pic, and the glacier the amphitheater of Vallernes. Because this is the peak which overlooks the university and the town. And that is the glacier which turns into the river which runs down to the campus. I think that the killer then descended into the valley on the stream, in a dinghy or something of that sort, with his victim on board. He then wedged him in the rocks, so that his reflection appeared in the river . . ."

Fanny looked uneasily around. Gendarmes were bustling about

the cable cars. There were weapons, uniforms, tension. She declared, obtusely:

"All of which still doesn't explain what the hell I'm doing here."

The superintendent grinned. The clouds were drifting across the sky, like a funeral procession on its way to bury the sun. He, too, was wearing a Gore-Tex jacket and waterproof kevlar-tec leggings, which were strapped up round his ankles, above his climbing boots.

"That's simple. I want to go up there, to look for evidence. And I need a guide."

"What?"

"I'm going to explore the amphitheater of Vallernes, until I find something. So I need an experienced guide, and so I quite naturally thought of you." Niémans grinned again. "Didn't you tell me that you knew this mountain like the back of your hand?"

"No way."

"Come on, now. I could demand your presence as a material witness. Or I could quite simply requisition you as a guide. I've heard that you have got your official climbing certificate. So, no arguing. We're just going to fly over the summit and the amphitheatre in a helicopter. It will only take a couple of hours."

Niémans gestured over to the gendarmes who were waiting beside a van. Alongside it, they were laying out large waterproof canvas bags on the slope.

"I've had some equipment brought up. For our expedition. If you'd just like to check . . ."

"Why me?" she persisted, as stubborn as a mule. "One of these gendarmes could easily do it . . ." She pointed at the men who were busying themselves behind her. "They're the mountain rescue guys, aren't they?"

The policeman leant toward her.

"Put it this way, I'm trying to pick you up."

Fanny glared at him.

"Superintendent, less than twenty-four hours ago, I discovered a corpse wedged into a cliff. I've undergone repeated questioning and spent ages in the police station. If I were you, I'd keep the macho chat-up lines to yourself!"

Niémans looked at her. Despite the murder, despite this gloomy atmosphere, he was totally under the charm of this wild, muscular woman. Crossing her arms, Fanny repeated:

"So, I'll ask you again: why me?"

The officer picked up a dead branch, which was lined with lichen, and bent it to and fro nervously.

"Because you're a geologist."

Fanny frowned. Her expression had changed. Niémans explained:

"Analysis has shown that the traces of water we found on the victim's body date back to a period before the 1960s. They contain residues of a form of pollution that no longer exists. Rain that fell in this region over thirty-five years ago. You realise what that means, don't you?"

The young woman looked intrigued, but said nothing. Niémans knelt down and, with his stick, drew some parallel lines on the ground.

"I've done a bit of finding out. Each year's rainfall becomes compressed into an eight inch thick stratum on the ice-caps of the highest glaciers, those which never thaw." He pointed at the various layers in his drawing. "These strata are preserved up there eternally, like a crystal archive. Therefore, the body spent some time in one of these glaciers, where it picked up this water from the past."

He looked at Fanny.

"I want to dive into the ice, Fanny. I want to go down into those ancient waters. Because the killer murdered his victim there. Or else transported him there. I don't know. And I need a scientist capable of finding the crevasses which lead to this buried ice."

One knee on the ground, Fanny was now staring at the drawing in the grass. The light was gray, stony, riddled with reflections. The young woman's eyes were sparkling like snowdrops. It was impossible to read her thoughts. She murmured:

"What if it's a trap? What if the killer only picked up those crystals in order to attract you onto the summit? The strata you're talking about are at an altitude of over ten thousand feet. This is going to be no picnic. Up there, you'll be vulnerable and ..."

"That did occur to me," Niémans admitted. "Which would mean that this is a message. That the murderer wants us to go up there. And go up there we will. Do you know of any crevasses in the amphitheater of Vallernes through which we could reach the older ice?"

Fanny nodded curtly.

"How many of them are there?" Niémans asked.

"On this glacier, I'm thinking of one extremely deep crevasse in particular."

"Perfect. What are our chances of being able to go down inside it?"

The whirring of a helicopter suddenly filled the sky. As its blades approached, the grass turned into billowing waves and, a few yards from them, the surface of the stream rippled.

"Do we have a chance, Fanny?"

She glanced across at the deafening machine and ran a hand through her curls. As she bent down, her profile sent shivers through Niémans's spine.

She smiled:

"You'll have to hang on tight, officer."

CHAPTER 23

Seen from above, the earth, rocks and trees shared out the territory in a succession of peaks and depressions, of light and shade. As the helicopter flew over this landscape, a marvelling Niémans observed these changes for the first time. He admired the lakes of dark conifers, the shipwrecked moraines, the stony heights. Crossing these lonely horizons, he felt as if he had grasped a hidden truth about our planet. A violent, incorruptible truth that had abruptly been exposed, which would always resist the will of mankind.

The helicopter made its precise way through the labyrinth of reliefs, following the course of the river, as all of its effluents now converged into one single sparkling flow. Beside the pilot, Fanny stared down at these waters, which, now and then, sent back fleeting glints. She was the person who was now in charge.

The green of the forests fell away. The trees retreated, fading into their own shadows, as though abandoning the chase. Then came the black earth – a sterile surface, which must have been frozen for much of the year. Dark mosses, gloomy lichens, stagnant marshes, which gave off an intense feeling of desolation. Soon, large gray ridges appeared. Rocky crests which had surged up as though propelled by the earth's sighing. Then more shadowlands, like the black moat of some forbidden fortress. The mountain was there. It extended, stretched and exposed its abyssal spurs.

Finally, their eyes were dazzled. Immaculate whiteness. Snow-covered domes. Icy fissures, the lips of which had begun to close up with early fall. Niémans saw streams which became petrified as they flowed. Despite the grayness of the sky, the surface of this snake of light was brilliant, as though white-hot. He pulled down his polycarbonate goggles, buttoned down their protective shells and looked at the scarred river. On its immaculate bed could be seen flashes of blue, like imprisoned memories of the sky. The din of the blades was now being swallowed up by the snow.

In front, Fanny did not take her eyes off her GPS, a receptor with a quartz dial, which allowed her to position herself in relation to a satellite's signals. She grabbed the microphone that was connected to her helmet and spoke to the pilot:

"Over there, to the north-east. That's the amphitheater."

The pilot nodded and the chopper swerved off, with all the lightness of a toy, toward a large nine-hundred-feet-long crater, shaped like a boomerang, which seemed to be wallowing on the top slope of the peak. Inside this basin lay a massive tongue of ice, casting brilliant reflections into the heights and darker glimmers down the slopes, where the ice was building up, becoming compressed before splintering into frozen shards. Fanny shouted at the pilot:

"Here. Just down there. The big crevasse."

The helicopter flew toward the confines of the glacier, where the translucent ledges piled up into a staircase, before opening out into a long fault – a monster from hell whose snowy face seemed to be grinning. The chopper touched down in a whirlwind of powdery flakes, its blades plowing out large furrows in the drifts.

"Two hours!" the pilot bellowed. "I'll be back in two hours. Just before nightfall."

Adjusting her GPS, Fanny handed it to the man and indicated the point where she wanted him to pick them up. The man nodded. Niémans and Fanny leapt down onto the ground, each holding a large waterproof bag.

The helicopter took off again at once, as though drawn up by the heavens, leaving those two figures alone amid the eternal snows.

They took stock for a moment. Niémans raised his eyes and examined the precipice of ice just by where they were standing, like two human particles in a white desert. The policeman was dazzled, his every sense alert. In contrast with the hugeness of the landscape, he seemed to be able to hear the slightest murmuring of the snow as its flakes crunched together into snugly hidden crystals.

He glanced at the young woman. Her body tense, shoulders stretched, she was breathing in deeply, as though gorging herself on that cold purity. The mountain seemed to have put her back into a good mood. He supposed that she was happy only among those glinting reflections, that headier atmosphere. She made him think of an oread. A creature of the mountains. He pointed at the crevasse and asked:

"Why this one, rather than another?"

"Because it's the only one deep enough to reach the strata that you're interested in. It goes down to a depth of three hundred feet."

Niémans went over to her.

"Three hundred feet? But we only have to descend a few feet to reach the layers dating to the 1960s. According to my calculations, at an average of eight inches per year, we . . ."

Fanny smiled.

"That's fine in theory. But this glacier doesn't obey the averages. The ice in its basin becomes crushed and oblique. In other words, it widens out and lengthens. In fact, one year in this gulf produces a layer of about three feet. So count again, officer. To go back thirty-five years, we're going to have to descend . . ."

" . . . at least a hundred feet."

The young woman nodded. Somewhere, in a blue-tinted niche, a stream could be heard flowing. The slight laughter of trickling water. Fanny pointed at the gulf behind them.

"There's also another reason why I chose this fault. The last stop of the cable car is just eight hundred yards away. If you're right, and the killer really did lure his victim up to a crevasse, then the chances are it was to this one. It's the easiest one to get to on foot."

Fanny bent down and opened her bag. She produced two pairs of laminated steel crampons and tossed one to Niémans.

"Fix these on your boots."

Niémans did so. He covered both soles with the metallic points, adjusting them to meet the edges of his boots. He then buckled up the neoprene straps as though they were spurs. It reminded him of putting on roller-skates when he was a kid.

Fanny had already removed from her bag some hollow threaded rods, which ended in oblong loops.

"Ice spits," she commented laconically.

Her breath froze into a shining mist. She then took out a piton hammer with a broad handle, its nickel-plated parts apparently removable, then she handed a helmet to Niémans, who was look-ing at all these objects with mounting curiosity. These tools looked highly sophisticated and, at the same time, perfectly simple. They seemed to be made of unknown, revolutionary materials, and were as brightly colored as sugar drops.

"Come here."

Fanny put a cushioned harness around his waist and thighs, which looked like a maze of straps and buckles. But she had it done up in a matter of seconds. She stood back, as though she were a dress designer sizing up a model.

"You'll do," she smiled.

Next, she picked up a strange lamp, with thin metal strips, an electronic system plus a stubby wick in front of a reflector. Niémans caught a glance of himself in this mirror: in a balaclava, helmet, harness and steel points, he looked like a futuristic Yeti. Fanny screwed the lamp into his helmet, then dangled a pipe behind his shoulder. She tied the reservoir at its end onto Niémans's belt and murmured:

"It's an acetylene lamp, fueled by vapor. I'll show you how it works, when the moment comes."

Then she lifted her eyes and addressed Niémans in a serious tone of voice:

"Ice is a world apart, superintendent," she began. "Forget your reflexes, your habits, and ways of thinking. Trust nothing: not its reflections, not its hardness, nor the appearance of its walls." She pointed to the gulf while doing up her own harness. "Down there, in that gulch, everything will become extraordinary, stupefying. But there are traps everywhere. You've never encountered ice like this before. It's ultra-compressed, harder than concrete, but half an inch of it can also conceal a pit. You will have to follow my instructions to the letter."

Fanny stopped, allowing her words to sink in. The condensation formed a magical halo around her face. She pulled her hair back into a bun and put on her balaclava.

"We're going to enter the pothole this way," she went on. "The level drops here, so it will be easier. I'll go in first and position the spits. The imprisoned gases which I shall release when breaking into the ice will form a huge crack covering several yards. This fault could run vertically, or horizontally. So you must stand away from the wall. It'll make one hell of a din, which is nothing in itself, but it could loosen some blocks of ice or stalactites. Keep your eyes peeled, superintendent. Stay constantly on your guard and don't touch anything."

Niémans drank in the young woman's instructions. It was certainly the first time that he had ever been under the orders of a curly-haired girl. Fanny seemed to notice this quiver of pride. She continued in a tone of voice that mixed amusement and authority:

"We're going to lose all notion of time and space. Our only point of reference is the rope. I have several bags each containing one hundred yards of rope, and I alone will be able to measure the distance we've covered. You will follow in my steps and obey my orders. No personal initiative. No spontaneous actions. Clear?"

"OK," Niémans sighed. "Is that all?"

"No."

Fanny examined the cloud-laden sky.

"I only agreed to this expedition because of the storm. If the sun comes out again, then we'll have to come back up at once."

"Why?"

"Because the ice will melt. The streams will reawaken and pour down on top of us, along the walls. The temperature of the water will be less than two degrees. Now, the physical effort will have made our bodies baking hot. That will be the first shock, which may well give us both heart attacks. If we survive that, then our limbs will start to go limp, we'll slow down and gradually lose consciousness . . . Get the picture? Within a few minutes, we'll be frozen solid, like statues, on the end of our rope. So, whatever happens, and whatever we discover, at the first sign of sunshine, we come back up."

Niémans thought this new phenomenon over.

"Doesn't that mean that the killer also needed a storm to be able to go down inside the fault?"

"A storm. Or nightfall."

The superintendent remembered that, when he had been following the cloud hypothesis, he had found out that the sun had shone all Saturday in that area. If the killer had really gone down into the ice with his victim, then he must have waited for it to be night. Why had he made things so difficult for himself? And why then bring the corpse back down into the valley?

Unused to the crampons, Niémans staggered clumsily over to the edge of the fault. He risked a glance down. The canyon did not seem vertiginous. After fifteen feet, the walls swelled out until they were almost touching each other. The gulf was then but a narrow slit, like the opening of an infinitely deep shell.

Fanny joined him and, while attaching a large number of snap-hooks and spits onto her belt, observed:

"The stream slides into the crevasse then widens a few feet lower down. Which explains why the gulf is far wider after this initial fault. Beneath it, the water splashes against the walls and erodes them. We'll have to slip between its jaws to get inside."

Niémans looked at the two icy edges, which seemed to open up reluctantly over the pit.

"If we went down even deeper into the glacier, would we find water from past centuries?"

"Absolutely. In the Arctic, it's possible to descend as far as extremely distant eras. At a depth of over ten thousand feet lie, still intact, the rainwaters which pushed Noah into constructing his Ark. And the air he breathed, too."

"The air?"

"Bubbles of oxygen, imprisoned in the ice."

Niémans was astonished. Fanny put on her rucksack and knelt down by the edge of the crevasse. She screwed in her first spit, attached a snaphook, then played the rope through it. She looked up at the storm clouds, then playfully declared:

"Welcome to the time machine, superintendent."

CHAPTER 24

They roped down.

The policeman was suspended on the rope, which slid through a self-locking grip. To go down, all he had to do was press the handle, which then slowly played it out. As soon as he released the pressure, it became blocked. Sitting in his harness, he was now dangling in the void.

Keeping his mind on this simple gesture, Niémans listened to Fanny's instructions. Several feet beneath him, she told him when to lower himself down. When he reached the next spit, the policeman changed ropes, taking care to attach himself first by the short cord tied to his harness. With all these straps, Niémans looked like an octopus decked with sparkling Christmas decorations.

As the descent continued, the superintendent remained above the young woman and, although he could not see her, instinctively trusted himself to her experience. As he progressed along the wall, he heard her working a few feet below him. His mind emptied. Outside his own concentration, all he felt was a mixture of strange vivid sensations. The chill breath of the wall. The support of his harness as his body hung in the air. The beauty of the ice, with its dark blue sheen, like a lump of night torn from the heavens.

Soon, the daylight faded. They passed between the swollen edges of the fault and into the very heart of the gulf. Niémans felt as though he were diving into the crystallised belly of a huge animal. Under that bell-jar of ice, made up of one hundred per cent water, his sensations became even sharper and more intense. He quietly admired the dark, translucent walls which cast off jagged glints of light, like echoes of the day. In the darkness, each of their movements resonated deeply in the vault.

Finally, Fanny touched down on a sort of almost horizontal gallery, which ran along the wall. Niémans followed her onto that natural landing. The two sides of the crevasse had narrowed again until they were just a few yards apart.

"Come here," she ordered.

He did so. Fanny pressed a button on the top of his helmet – just as if she had flicked on a lighter – a sudden bright ray gleamed out. The policeman caught another glimpse of himself in the reflector on the young woman's helmet. What he saw most clearly was the acetylene flame, a sort of inverted cone, which was shedding this strong light by refraction. Fanny cautiously turned on her lamp, too, then said:

"If your killer came into this gulf, then this is the route he took."

Baffled, Niémans stared at her. The yellowy gleam of her lamp shone down on her face, deforming it into a pattern of disturbing, brutal shadows.

"We've reached the right depth," she continued, indicating the smooth surface of the wall. "Ninety feet below the dome. The crystallised snow from the 1960s. And then, below it . . ."

Fanny opened another bag of rope then fixed a spit into the wall. After having hammered it home, she screwed it into place by sliding a snaphook into its end, and twisting its threaded point. Just as she would have done with a corkscrew. Niémans was astonished by her strength. He looked at the displaced ice, which emerged from the spit through a side opening, and thought how few men he knew would be capable of such a feat.

They roped off again, but this time horizontally, along that glittering tunnel. Tied one to the other, they were walking above the precipice. Their reflections mingled in the wall opposite them. Every twenty yards, Fanny fractioned off the rope, digging another spit into the wall and separating off the next section. She repeated this action several times, and they progressed a hundred yards.

"Shall we go on?" she asked.

The policeman looked at her. Her face, hardened by the brutal light from the lamp, now seemed distinctly sinister. He nodded, pointing at the corridor of ice which led away into an infinite succession of reflections. She opened another bag and carried out her maneuver once more. Spit, rope, twenty yards, then spit, rope, twenty yards . . .

They thus covered four hundred yards. Not a sign, not a trace of the killer having gone that way before them. Soon, the walls seemed to be wandering in front of Niémans's eyes. Slight clicking noises and distant sardonic laughter came to his ears. The world had become luminous, resonant, shaky. Did ice vertigo exist? He peered at Fanny, who was opening a fresh bag of rope. She did not seem to have noticed anything.

A vague panic gripped him. Perhaps he was starting to lose his wits. His body, his brain, were perhaps so tired that they were showing signs of cracking up. Niémans began to tremble. The cold bit into his bones in waves. His hands seized the next spit. His feet shuffled on clumsily. With tears in his eyes, he tried to catch up with Fanny. He suddenly felt that he was about to fall, that his legs could no longer support him. His wits wandered even further. The bluish walls seemed to be undulating rapidly in the light of his lamp, and the distant laughter to echo around him. He was going to fall. Into the pit. Into his own madness. He managed to give a suffocated shout:

"Fanny!"

She turned round and Niémans realised that he was not going crazy. Her face was no longer disfigured by the shadows from the lamp. A brilliant light, so intense that its source was unfathomable, was raining down on her features. Fanny's beaming, majestic beauty had returned. Niémans peered around. The wall was now afire with light. And a torrent was pouring down the walls, in a ghostly flood.

No, he was not going crazy. On the contrary, he had noticed something which Fanny had been too busy with her ropes to see. The sun. Up on the surface, the storm clouds must have scattered and the sun had come out. Hence the diffuse light which had crept in through the cracks in the glacier. Hence the gleams and the laughter from the niches. The temperature was rising. The glacier was beginning to melt.

"Shit," muttered Fanny, who had just caught on.

She immediately examined the nearest spit. The thread of the screw was standing out from the wall, which was disappearing in long drips. The two of them were going to become unhooked. Fall straight down into the bottom of the pit. Fanny barked:

"Step back!"

Niémans tried to move backward, then to his left. His foot slipped, he stood upright, his back over the void and pulled violently on the rope to recover his balance. He heard it all at the same instant: the sound of the spit coming out, his crampons scratching along the wall, the shock of Fanny's hand grabbing him by the nape of the neck at the last moment. She pinned him against the wall.

Icy water gnawed into his face. Fanny whispered into his ear: "Don't move."

Hunched up, panting, Niémans froze. Fanny straddled him. He felt her breath, the softness of her curls, smelt her sweat. She roped him up again and stuck two more spits into the wall at lightning speed. By the time she had done so, the whispering from the gulf had turned into groans, the rivulets a waterfall. All around them, the flow beat thunderously against the walls. Entire sections of the ice fell away, breaking into pieces on the gallery. Niémans closed his eyes. He felt himself drift away, slip, faint into that hall of mirrors in which angles, distance and perspective had vanished.

It was Fanny's scream which brought him back to reality.

He turned his head and saw her bent on the rope, trying to distance herself from the wall. Niémans made a superhuman effort, got to his feet and, through the sheets of water which were pouring down with the force of a cataract, approached her. His fingers clasped round the rope, he let himself swing out like a hanged man and passed through the vertical stream. Why was she trying to get away from the wall, even when the crevasse was swallowing them up? Fanny pointed at the wall of ice.

"There," she panted. "It's there."

Niémans maneuvered himself into the young climber's line of vision.

Then he drank in the impossible.

In the transparent wall, a veritable mirror of white water, the shape of a body imprisoned in the ice suddenly surged out. In the foetal position. Its mouth was voicing a silent scream. The incessant shallow torrent that passed over the image distorted that vision of a bruised and battered corpse.

Despite his astonishment, despite the cold that was freezing them both to the bone, the superintendent immediately grasped that what they were looking at was a mere mirror image of reality. He checked his balance on the gallery, then swung round, describing a perfect arc to get a look at the other ice face, just opposite.

"No," he murmured. "There."

He could now no longer take his eyes off the real body, stuck in the facing wall of ice, its bloody contours mingling with its own reflection.

CHAPTER 25

Niémans put the file back down on the desk and asked Captain Barnes:

"Why are you so sure that this man's our new victim?"

The gendarme shrugged and opened his arms.

"His mother's just been in to see us. She says that he disappeared last night . . ."

The superintendent was once again in a *gendarmerie* office, on the first floor. Dressed in a tight woolen pullover, with a roll-neck collar, he was only just starting to warm up. One hour before, Fanny had managed to get the two of them out of that gulf, just about in one piece. Luck had been on their side: the helicopter had reappeared above their position at that very instant.

Since then, mountain rescue teams had been working on extracting the body from its icy mausoleum, while the superintendent and Fanny Ferreira had returned to the town and undergone a routine medical check-up.

Barnes had then immediately mentioned another missing person, whose identity could well match that of the body they had discovered: Philippe Sertys, aged twenty-six, single, a nursing auxiliary at Guernon Hospital. While sipping at his scalding coffee, Niémans repeated his question:

"How can you be so certain that this is our man, before we've even established the victim's identity?"

Barnes fumbled through his papers, then stammered:

"It's . . . it's because of the resemblance."

"What resemblance?"

The captain handed Niémans a photograph of a young man, with narrow features and a crew cut. He was smiling keenly, the darkness of his eyes was tainted with gentleness. His face made him look youthful, almost boyish, but also tense. The superintendent saw where Barnes was coming from: he looked just like Rémy Caillois, the first victim. Same age. Same pointed features. Same hair cut. Two slim, handsome young men whose expressions seemed to conceal some hidden anxieties.

"This is a series, superintendent."

Niémans drank some coffee. It felt as if his still-frozen throat was going to crack from the contact of such violent heat. He raised his eyes.

"Sorry?"

Barnes was swaying from one foot to the other. His shoes could be heard creaking, like the bridge of a ship.

"I lack your experience, of course, but . . . Look, if the second victim does turn out to be Philippe Sertys, then this is obviously a series. The work of a serial killer, I mean. Who chooses his victims according to their appearance. This sort of face must remind him of some traumatic experience, or . . ."

The captain stopped dead under Niémans's furious stare. The superintendent smiled broadly in an attempt to wipe out his irritation.

"Captain, we are not going to turn this resemblance into some big theory. Least of all when we have not yet identified the second victim."

"I . . . You're right, superintendent."

The gendarme fidgeted nervously with his file, which seemed to contain the existence of the entire town. He looked embarrassed and, at the same time, jumpy. Niémans could read his mind. In it, "Serial Killer in Guernon" was written up in flashing letters. This gendarme was going to remain traumatised until his retirement, and even beyond it. The policeman asked:

"How are the rescue teams doing?"

"They're on the point of bringing the victim to the surface. The . . . the ice had frozen over the body. My colleagues think that the man was placed up there last night. The temperature must have been very low for the ice to harden so much."

"When are we likely to be able to see it?"

"We'll have to wait about another hour, superintendent. Sorry."

Niémans got up and opened the window. Cold air billowed into the room. Six o'clock.

Night was already falling over the town. Thick darkness that was slowly absorbing the slate roofs and the wooden façades. The river slid between the shadows, like a snake between two rocks.

The superintendent shivered in his sweater. Provincial life was definitely not for him. And particularly not this variety: stuck at the foot of the mountains, beaten by the cold and the storms, divided between the black sludge of the snow and the incessant dripping of stalactites. A secret, hostile, sullen world, locked up in its silence like the kernel of an iced fruit.

Turning toward Barnes, he asked:

"Where do we stand now, twelve hours into our enquiries?"

"Nowhere. All our checking has produced nothing. No prowlers. No recently released prisoners whose profile might match that of the killer. Nothing from the hotels, bus or railway stations. And our road-blocks have also failed to produce."

"What about the library?"

"The library?"

Now that there was a second corpse, the book angle was starting to look secondary. But Niémans wanted to see each part of the investigation through to its conclusion. He explained:

"The regional boys are checking through the books consulted by the students."

The captain shrugged.

"Oh, that . . . That's not our business. You'll have to ask Joisneau . . ."

"Where is he?"

"I've no idea."

Niémans then tried to call the young lieutenant on his cell phone. No answer. Switched off. Annoyed, he asked again:

"And Vermont?"

"Still up on the heights with his brigade. They're searching the refuges and the sides of the mountain. Now even more so . . ."

Niémans sighed.

"Ask Grenoble for some more men. I want another fifty. At least. I want the search to be concentrated around the amphitheater of Vallernes and the cable car that runs up there. I want the entire mountain to be fine-toothcombed up to its tip."

"I'll get onto it."

"How many road-blocks are there?"

"Eight. The toll booth on the autoroute. Two on the A-roads and five on the B-roads. Guernon is under close watch. But, as I just told you, it . . ."

The policeman stared straight into Barnes's eyes.

"Captain, we are sure of only one thing: the killer is an experienced mountain climber. Question everybody in Guernon, and in the environs, who's capable of crossing a glacier."

"There'll be quite a crowd. Climbing is the local sport and . . ."

"I'm talking about an expert, Barnes. A man who is able to descend a hundred feet under the ice and transport a dead body there. I've already asked Joisneau to check that out. Find him and ask him what he's found."

Barnes nodded.

"Very well. But I must repeat that we are mountain folk. You'll find experienced climbers in every village, inside every house, on the sides of every summit. It's a tradition with us. Some of our locals are still crystal makers, or shepherds . . . But all of us still have a passion for the heights. It's only really in Guernon, in the university town, that these traditions are dying out."

"What are you getting at?"

"All I mean is that we'll have to extend the radius of our search. To the upper villages. And that it will take us days."

"Ask for extra reinforcements. Set up a post in each hamlet. Check people's movements, their equipment, their expeditions. And, for Christ's sake, find me some suspects."

The superintendent opened the door and concluded:

"Get the mother in for me."

"The mother?"

"Philippe Sertys's mother. I want to speak to her."

CHAPTER 26

Niémans went down to the ground floor. The *gendarmerie* offices looked like any other police station in France or, probably, in the world. Through the windows in the partitions, Niémans could see metal filing cabinets, an assortment of formica-topped desks, and filthy lino stained with cigarette burns. He liked such monochrome, neon-filled places. Because they were a reminder of the police's real vocation – the streets, the outside world. These grim buildings were merely the antechamber of the policeman's life, his dark warren, from which he emerged, sirens blaring.

That was when he noticed her, sitting in the corridor, wrapped up in a heavy blanket and dressed in a gendarme's royal blue sweater. He shivered and found himself back under the ice, beside her, and he felt her warm breath against the nape of his neck. Half anxious, half flirtatiously, he readjusted his glasses.

"Haven't you gone home yet?"

Fanny Ferreira's clear eyes looked up at him.

"I have to sign my statement. I'm getting used to it now. But don't count on me to discover the third one."

"The third one?"

"The third corpse."

"So you think there will be more murders?"

"Don't you?"

The young woman must have noticed a pained expression flicker across Niémans's face. She murmured:

"Sorry. I was being sarcastic. It helps me to handle the situation."

As she spoke, she patted the place next to her on the bench, as though inviting a child to sit with her. Niémans did so. His head down, hands together, feet twitching slightly.

"I didn't thank you," he mumbled between his teeth. "If it hadn't been for you, in the ice . . ."

"I just did my job as a guide."

"True. Not only did you save my life, but you also took me exactly where I wanted to go."

Fanny's expression became serious. Gendarmes marched up and down the corridor. Boots thumping and oil-skins creaking. She asked:

"Where are you? I mean, in your investigations? Why this terrible violence? Why such . . . weird killings?"

Niémans tried to smile, but failed.

"We're getting nowhere. All I know is what my nose tells me."

"Meaning?"

"My nose tells me that this is a series. But not in the usual sense of the term. This isn't a killer who strikes at the whim of his obsessions. This series has a motive. A precise, established, rational motive."

"What sort of motive?"

The policeman gazed at Fanny. The shadows of the passing guards flickered across her face, like the wings of a bird.

"I don't know. Yet."

Silence descended. Fanny lit a cigarette, then abruptly asked:

"How long have you been in the force?"

"About twenty years."

"What made you join? The idea of putting the bad guys in prison?"

Niémans smiled, spontaneously this time. From the corner of his eye, he saw another squad arriving, with rain pearling from their capes. A glance at them was enough to tell him that they had found nothing. He looked back toward Fanny, who was inhaling a long drag.

"That sort of idea gets quickly lost along the way, you know. Anyway, justice and all that bullshit never interested me very much."

"So why? Power? Job security?"

Niémans was astonished.

"You really do have funny ideas. No, I think I joined for the sensations."

"Sensations? Like the one we've just had?"

"For example."

"I see," she nodded ironically, exhaling the pale smoke. "Action Man. Who only feels alive when he risks his life every day . . ."

"And what's wrong with that?"

Fanny aped Niémans's posture – shoulders hunched and hands linked, as though in prayer. She had stopped laughing. She seemed to guess that Niémans, behind these generalisations, was revealing a part of himself. Cigarette in her mouth, she murmured:

"Nothing. Nothing whatsoever . . ."

The policeman lowered his eyes and, through the curved lenses of his glasses, observed the young woman's hands. No ring. Only dressings, marks and cracked skin. As though she was married to the mountain, the elements, violent emotions.

"Nobody understands cops," he went on, gloomily. "And so nobody can judge them. Our world is closed, brutal, incoherent. A dangerous universe with well-established frontiers. If you are on the outside, you are incapable of understanding. And on the inside, you lose your objectivity. That's the life of a cop. A sealed existence. A crater of barbed wire. Incomprehensible. It's the very nature of the thing. But one point at least is clear: we have nothing to learn from a load of bureaucrats who wouldn't even risk getting their fingers caught in their car doors."

Fanny stretched, ran her hands through her curls and pushed them back. The gesture made Niémans think of roots, mixed with the earth. Roots of a heady sensual nature. The policeman trembled. Icy pinpricks were battling against the warmth of his blood.

The young woman quietly asked:

"What are you going to do? What's your next step?"

"Keep looking. And waiting."

"For what?" she picked him up aggressively. "Another victim?"

Ignoring this provocation, Niémans got to his feet.

"I'm waiting for the body to be brought down from the mountain. The killer made an appointment with us up there. He placed a pointer in the first corpse which led me to that glacier. I think he will have put a fresh clue in the second body, which will lead us to the third . . . and so on. It's a sort of game, which we are supposed to lose."

Fanny stood up as well and grabbed her parka, which was drying on the end of the bench.

"You must agree to give me an interview."

"What are you talking about?"

"I'm the chief editor of *Tempo*, the university magazine."

Niémans felt his nerves tightening under his skin.

"Don't tell me that you . . ."

"Don't panic. I couldn't care less about the magazine. Anyway, like it or not, at the rate your investigations are going, the whole of the national press is going to be here soon. You'll then have a load of journalists on your trail who are far more tenacious than I am."

The superintendent waved away this possibility.

"Where do you live?" he suddenly asked.

"At the university."

"Where, exactly?"

"On the top floor of the main building. I have a flat, near the boarders' rooms."

"Where the Caillois live?"

"Precisely."

"What's your opinion of Sophie Caillois?"

Fanny smiled in admiration.

"She's a strange girl. Silent. But extremely pretty. The two of them were as thick as thieves. Almost as if . . . as if they had a secret."

Niémans nodded.

"That's what I think, too. And the motive for the murders perhaps lies in that secret. I'll call round to see you later this evening, if that's all right."

"Are you still trying to pick me up?"

The superintendent grinned.

"More than ever. And I'll give you exclusive rights to everything I know, for your rag."

"I told you. I couldn't care less about that magazine. I'm incorruptible."

"See you this evening," he said over his shoulder, as he turned on his heel.

CHAPTER 27

One hour later, the body of the second victim had still not been extracted from the ice.

Niémans was furious. He had just listened to Philippe Sertys's old mother's laconic testimony, told in a thick local accent. The previous evening, her son had left home as usual at about nine o'clock in his car, a recently purchased second-hand Lada. Philippe worked nights at the Guernon University Hospital, and began his shift at ten o'clock. She had started to become worried only the next morning, when she found his car in the garage, but no Philippe in his bedroom. This meant that he had come home, then gone out again. But another surprise was in store for her. She contacted the hospital and was told that Sertys had taken the night off. So, he had gone somewhere else, had returned home, then left again on foot. What the hell did it all mean? The woman was frantic, and clutched at Niémans's arm. Where was her boy? According to her, this was extremely worrying. Her son did not have a girlfriend, never went out, and slept every day "at home".

The superintendent unenthusiastically made a mental note of this information. All the same, if Sertys did turn out to be the prisoner in the ice, her testimony would help them to fix the possible time of the murder. The killer must have kidnapped the young man in the early hours of the morning, murdered him, probably mutilated him, then transported him to the amphitheater of Vallernes. It was the chill air of dawn that had sealed the ice wall over the victim. But this was all pure speculation.

The superintendent took the old woman to speak to a gendarme, so that he could take down a detailed statement. As for him, he decided to return with his files to his little den in the university.

Once there, he changed back into a suit then, alone in his office, laid out on his desk the various documents he had brought with him. His first step was to conduct a detailed comparative study of Rémy Caillois and Philippe Sertys, in an attempt to establish a link between the first victim and the probable second one.

The two men did not seem to have that much in common. They were both aged about twenty-five. They were both tall, slim, with regular and yet rather tormented features topped off by a crew cut. They had both lost their fathers: Philippe Sertys's had died two years before of liver cancer. But Rémy Caillois had also lost his mother, who had died when he was eight years old. Their final point in common was that they had both followed in their fathers' footsteps – as a librarian for Caillois, and as a nursing auxiliary for Sertys.

Their differences, on the other hand, abounded. Caillois and Sertys had not gone to the same school. They had grown up in different parts of town and did not belong to the same social class. Rémy Caillois was middle-class and had grown up among the intellectuals of the university. Philippe Sertys had been born into the lower classes and had started work at the age of fifteen, in the hospital with his father. He was practically illiterate and still lived in the small family home on the outskirts of Guernon.

Rémy Caillois was a bookworm and Philippe Sertys a night-owl at the hospital. The latter did not seem to have any hobbies, apart from hanging around in the aseptic corridors where he worked, and playing video games at the end of the afternoon in the bar across the road from the hospital. Caillois had been dismissed as unfit from the army. Sertys had served in the infantry. One was married; the other single. One was an enthusiastic mountain walker; the other apparently never went out. One was schizophrenic and undoubtedly violent; the other was, according to everybody, "as gentle as a lamb".

Therefore, the only thing the two of them had in common was their looks. The sharp features they both had, the crew cut, and the slender build. As Barnes had said, the killer must be choosing his prey according to their physical appearance.

The idea of a sex crime crossed Niémans's mind: the killer could be a closet homosexual who was attracted by this sort of young man. But the superintendent remained skeptical, and the forensic pathologist had been categoric: "It is clearly not his department." In the wounds and mutilations of the first victim's body, the doctor had seen a cold cruelty, a dogged application that had nothing to do with a pervert's frenzied desires. What was more, no trace of sexual assault had been found on the corpse.

So, what then?

The killer's madness presumably ran along other lines. In any case, the resemblance between the two presumed victims and the beginnings of a series – two murders in two days – now made it likely that they were the work of a psychopath, in the throes of some demonic obsession, who would kill again. There were other factors to support this hypothesis: the presence of a clue in the first body which had led to the second one, the foetal position, the mutilation of the eyes and the positioning of the bodies in wild, dramatic locations: the cliff overlooking the river, the transparent prison of ice . . .

And yet, Niémans still did not accept this thesis.

In the first place, because of his daily experience as a police officer.

While serial killers had been imported from America and now peopled the world's books and films, that terrible trend had never really taken off in France. During his twenty years of service, Niémans had arrested paedophiles, whose lusts had occasionally driven them to commit murder, rapists who had killed in a frenzy of violence, sadomasochists whose cruel games had gone too far, but never, in the strict sense of the term, a serial killer who had committed a long list of motiveless murders. It was not a French specialty. Whichever way you looked at it, the facts were there: the last French killers who had murdered repeatedly had been lower-middle-class men, like Landru or Dr Petiot, chasing after a small inheritance or stealing from their victims. But nothing in common with that American nightmare, those bloodthirsty monsters who haunted the United States.

The superintendent looked again at the photographs of Philippe Sertys, then those of Rémy Caillois, spread out over the students' work-top. In the cardboard folder, there also lay the images of the first corpse. A red-hot iron burned his conscience: he could not just sit there, doing nothing. At that very moment, while he was examining these Polaroids, a third person might be undergoing unspeakable tortures. His eye-sockets were perhaps being cleaned out with a carpet cutter, his eyeballs torn out by rubber-gloved hands.

It was seven o'clock. Night was falling. Niémans stood up and turned out the neon light. He decided to explore Philippe Sertys's life thoroughly. Perhaps he might find out something. A clue. A sign.

Or, quite simply, another common factor linking the two victims.

CHAPTER 28

Philippe Sertys lived with his mother in a small detached house on the outskirts of town, near a housing estate of shabby buildings, down a deserted street. A brown polygonal roof, a dirty white façade, curtains of yellowed lace, which framed the interior darkness like a smiling set of rotten teeth. Niémans knew that the old woman was still going through her statement at the station and there was no light from inside. But he still rang the bell, as a precaution.

No answer.

Niémans walked around the house. A violent, icy wind was blowing, carrying a first hint of winter. A little garage stood next to it, to the left. He peered inside and found an ancient muddy Lada. He walked on. A few square feet of cropped grass lay behind the dwelling: the garden.

The policeman glanced round again, on the look-out for nosy neighbors. Nobody. He went up the three steps and examined the lock. A standard, downmarket job. The policeman forced it open without any difficulty, wiped his feet on the mat and entered the presumed victim's home.

After the hall, he reached a cramped living-room and switched on his torch. Its white beam revealed a green carpet, covered with small dark rugs, a sofa-bed stuck under some hunter's shotguns on the wall, some ill-assorted furniture and a collection of hideous rustic knick-knacks. It smelt to him of airless comfort, a jealously guarded daily existence.

He put on his latex gloves and went carefully through the drawers. He found nothing of interest. Silver-plated cutlery, embroidered handkerchiefs, personal papers – tax returns, prescriptions . . . He glanced over them, then made a rapid search for further information. Nothing. It was a dull, run-of-the-mill family sitting-room.

Niémans went upstairs.

He easily located Philippe Sertys's bedroom. Animal posters, color magazines heaped up in a chest, TV guides: it all gave off an impression of intellectual poverty which verged on the inane. Niémans searched more thoroughly. He found nothing, apart from a few details which revealed Sertys's totally nocturnal existence. A large collection of lamps, of varying voltages, took up an entire shelf – as though the man wanted to create a different light to go with each season. He also noticed the solid reinforced shutters, as a protection against daylight, or else to conceal his own night-time movements. Then Niémans came across some eye-masks, like those used in aeroplanes, to block out the slightest glimmer of light. Either Sertys found it hard to sleep. Or he had the nature of a vampire.

Niémans turned over the blankets, sheets and mattress. He slid his fingers under the rugs and ran his hands over the wallpaper. He found nothing. And, above all, not the slightest trace of a girlfriend.

The policeman looked hastily round the mother's bedroom. The atmosphere in that house was starting to get to him. He went back downstairs for a quick inspection of the kitchen, bathroom and cellar. Nothing doing.

Outside, the wind was still raging, making the windows rattle slightly.

He turned off his torch and experienced an unexpected agreeable sensation, the feeling of a secret intrusion, a hidden refuge.

Niémans stopped to think. He could not have got it wrong. Not to that point. There had to be some sign lurking there, somewhere. He told himself that he had been mistaken after all, then immediately changed his mind. He had to dig out the truth, find the link between Caillois and Sertys.

Another idea then occurred to him.

The changing-room in the hospital was a vague bluish-gray color. Succeeding ranks of rusty metallic cupboards stood precariously to attention. The place was deserted. Niémans silently walked on. He read the names in the little iron frames until he found Philippe Sertys.

He put his gloves back on and felt the padlock. Memories streamed through his mind: the time of nocturnal missions, dressed in black, with the boys of the Antigang Brigade. He did not feel particularly nostalgic about that period. What Niémans loved more than anything else was penetrating the mood of the night, mastering its vital hours, but only as a real intruder: on his own, in silence, and undercover.

The lock clicked, and the door opened. White coats. Confectionery. Old magazines. And more lamps and eye-masks. Careful not to make the metal clang, Niémans felt round the interior partitions and searched into the corners. Nothing. He checked to see if the cupboard had a false bottom, or top.

Swearing to himself, Niémans knelt down. He was clearly not on the right track. There was nothing to be learnt from this young man's existence. What was more, he did not even know if that deep-frozen body, up in the mountains, was really Philippe Sertys. Perhaps the auxiliary would reappear in a few days' time, coming back home after his first elopement, on the arm of a beautiful nurse.

Niémans could not help smiling at his own stubbornness. He decided to get out of there before anybody noticed him. It was when he was standing up that he noticed a square of linoleum that had moved slightly out of place under the cupboard. He felt the roughness of the concrete below it, then an object. He heard a metallic sound, pushed his fingers further and closed his fist. When he opened it again, his hand was holding a key on a ring, which had been carefully concealed beneath the cabinet.

Along its shaft, Niémans recognised the characteristic indentations for opening a reinforced metal door.

If Sertys had a secret, then this was the key to it.

At the town hall, he just managed to catch the land register clerk, who was about to go home. When he mentioned the name "Sertys", the man did not blink. Word of the murder had obviously not got out yet, nor the presumed identity of the second victim. The town clerk, who already had his coat on, grudgingly looked for the information the policeman required.

While waiting, Niémans ran back over the hypothesis which had led him there, as though this would increase its chances of turning out right. Philippe Sertys had concealed the key to a reinforced lock under his cupboard in the changing-room. Now, the front door of the house had no armor-plating. This key could have been cut for any number of doors, cupboards or stock-rooms, maybe in the hospital. But why hide it? A hunch had led Niémans to pay a call on the land register to see if Philippe Sertys might own another house, a shack, a barn, anything that might have a reinforced door concealing a second existence.

The grumbling clerk placed a battered cardboard box onto the counter. On its top, in a thin brass frame, was a label which read: "Sertys". Holding back his excitement, Niémans opened it and leafed through the official documents, the solicitors' contracts, the title deeds. He read them carefully, looked at the numbers of the plots and located them on a map of the region which was included in the file. He stared at the address again and again.

So, it was as simple as that.

Philippe Sertys and his mother rented the house they lived in, but the young man also owned another property, which he had inherited from his father.

CHAPTER 29

It was not a dwelling, but an isolated warehouse near the foot of the Grand Doménon, encircled by arid conifers. On the walls of the building, pale paint was flaking off, like the scales of an iguana, presumably untouched for an untold number of years.

Niémans approached it cautiously. The windows had metal bars and were blocked by sacks of concrete. There was a cumbersome gate and, to its right, a reinforced door. It was a place to store barrels, metal drums, or sacks of building material. Something to do with industry. But this warehouse belonged to a taciturn auxiliary nurse, who had presumably just been murdered in a high-altitude glacier.

The policeman began by pacing round the building, then he went back to the reinforced door. He slid the key into the lock. He heard the mechanism give a slight click, then the sound of the bolt gliding out of its metal surround.

The door swung open. Before going in, Niémans took a deep breath. Inside, the bluish gleam of the night filtered in softly through the few gaps left between the sacks of concrete stacked up against the metal bars. It was several hundred square yards in area, somber, run-down, lined by transversal shadows cast by the metallic structure of the roof. Tall pillars rose up toward the tip.

Niémans advanced with his torch on. The place was completely empty. Or, rather, had recently been emptied. There were dust marks everywhere, furrows had been dug out in the concrete floor, presumably by some heavy furniture which had been pulled toward the door. It was filled with a strange atmosphere, an echo of panic, of a mad rush.

The superintendent went on, peering, sniffing, feeling. It was, indeed, an industrial site, but it was extraordinarily clean. An antiseptic odor still hung there. But there was also the vague scent of a wild animal.

Niémans continued. He was now walking on white dust, like crushed chalk. He knelt down and found some tiny wire meshes.

Perhaps they came from some fencing, or were bits of an air filter. He slipped some of them into his plastic envelopes, then took samples of the dust and crushed matter, but without being able to identify their neutral dull odor. Yeast. Or plaster. Not drugs, in any case.

His next discovery showed that the place had been well heated for many years. Electric sockets were situated in each corner of the room, undoubtedly used for heaters, the positions of which could still be made out from the black patches they had left on the walls.

Niémans's mind raced with several contradictory hypotheses. The high temperature could mean that animals had been raised there. He also imagined that it could have been used as a laboratory for experiments, in sterile conditions. Hence the strong hospital smell. He did not know why, but the place gave him the creeps. A stronger, more violent fear than that which he had experienced in the glacier.

He was now sure of two things. The first was that shy little Philippe Sertys had used this place for some occult practices. The second was that the young man had been forced to move everything out in a great hurry, just before he had been killed.

The officer stood up and, playing his torch across the walls, examined them closely. There might be a hiding place there, a niche in which Sertys may have left something. He brushed his palms over them, tapped them, listened to their resonance, watched for changes in their make-up. The walls were covered with thick paper, over a layer of compressed glass wool. Insulation, presumably.

Niémans had now covered two entire sides. Then, at a height of nearly six feet, he felt a hollow which was out of line with the rest of that bulging surface. He ran his index finger along the edge of it and noticed that someone had plastered it over. He tore off the wallpaper and discovered some hinges. He squeezed his fingers into the central gap and managed to force this priest hole open. Shelves. Dust. Mould.

The superintendent felt along the planks and, on one of them, encountered something flat, covered with a layer of dust. He grabbed the object. It was a small exercise book with ring-binding.

His flesh blazing, he flicked through it at once. The pages were covered with tiny, incomprehensible figures. But one of them bore a large inscription at the top. The letters looked as though they had been written in blood, and with such violence that the pen had occasionally ripped through the paper. Niémans thought of a frenetic rage, a boiling geyser. As if the author of these scarlet lines had not been able to contain his madness. Niémans read:

WE ARE THE MASTERS, WE ARE THE SLAVES.

WE ARE EVERYWHERE, WE ARE NOWHERE.

WE ARE THE SURVEYORS.

WE CONTROL THE BLOOD-RED RIVERS.

The policeman leant against the wall, on the scraps of brown paper and shreds of glass wool. He turned off his torch, and a flash glowed in his mind. He had not found a link between Rémy Caillois and Philippe Sertys. He had found something better: a shadow, a secret at the heart of that young hospital worker's existence. What did those figures and strange sentences in that exercise book mean? What had Sertys been doing in his mysterious warehouse?

Niémans briefly took stock of his investigations, as though bringing together the first smouldering twigs of a fire in a blizzard. Rémy Caillois was an acute schizophrenic, a violent man who had – perhaps – once committed some terrible crime. As for Philippe Sertys, he had indulged in some sort of undercover activity in this sinister workshop, then tried to remove all trace of it shortly before his death.

The superintendent had no solid proof, no evidence, but it was certain that neither Caillois nor Sertys had been as straightforward as their public lives suggested.

Neither the librarian nor the nursing auxiliary had been an innocent victim.

VI

CHAPTER 30

Karim, his guts in a knot, had now been driving for almost two hours. He was thinking of that face. A child's face. Sometimes he imagined it as being that of a monster. Perfectly smooth, with neither a nose nor cheekbones, pierced by two shiny white eyeballs. Or then again, he pictured it as being that of a perfectly ordinary cute little boy. So ordinary, that it left no mark on people's memories. Or else, Karim saw a set of impossible features. Wavy, unstable, reflecting the face of the person examining them. A sparkling appearance which mirrored other people's looks, revealing the deepest secrets concealed beneath the hypocrisy of their smiles. The cop shivered. He was now sure about one thing: the key to this mystery lay in that face. And nowhere else.

He had taken the autoroute from Agen to Toulouse and had then driven alongside the Canal du Midi, taking him past Carcassonne and Narbonne. His car was a terrible old jalopy. A sort of coughing fit made of cylinders and rattling parts. He could not get it to go over one hundred and thirty kilometers per hour, even with the wind behind him. He could not stop thinking over this enigma. He was now approaching Sète, along the coast road, and nearing the Convent of Saint-Jean-de-la-Croix. The gray, vague landscape by the sea had a calming effect on him. His foot hard down, he was now mulling over the rational information he had gathered.

His visits to the photographer and the priest had cast new light on the case. Karim had suddenly realised that the documents missing from Jean-Jaurès School could well have been stolen long before last night's break-in. On the road, he phoned back the headmistress. When asked "is it possible that those documents have been missing since 1982 and that nobody noticed during all those years?" the headmistress had answered "yes". When asked "is it possible that their disappearance was only noticed today, thanks to the burglary?" she had answered "yes". When asked "have you ever heard of a nun who was trying to get hold of school photos from that period?" she had answered "no".

And yet . . . Before setting out, Karim had conducted a final piece of research in Sarzac. Thanks to papers in the registry office – dates of birth and home addresses – he had contacted several former pupils of those two fateful classes: CM1 and CM2, 1981 and 1982. Not one of them still had his old school photos. In certain cases, a fire had started in the room where the photos were kept. In others, there had been a burglary. The thieves had stolen nothing except for a few photographs. Or, yet again, though this was rare, people remembered a nun, who had called by to look for the pictures. It had been at night, and nobody was able to describe her. All of these events had occurred during the same short period: July 1982. One month before little Jude's death.

At about half past six in the evening, as he was driving past the Bassin de Thau, Karim spotted a phone box and rang up Crozier. He was now outside his jurisdiction. And it was a feeling he liked. He was casting off. The superintendent yelled:

"I hope you're on your way here, Karim. We did say six o'clock."

"I have a lead, superintendent."

"What lead?"

"Let me follow it up. Every step I take confirms what I suspected. Do you have anything new concerning the cemetery?"

"You're playing at being the lone ranger, and now you expect me to . . ."

"Just answer. Have you found the car?"

Crozier sighed.

"We have come up with seven owners of Ladas, two of Trabants and one of a Skoda in the *départements* of the Lot, Lot-et-Garonne,

Dordogne, Aveyron and Vaucluse. And not one of them is our car."

"You've already checked the owners' alibis?"

"No, but we found some scraps from the tires near the cemetery. They're extremely low-grade carbon jobs. The owner of our car still uses the original tires and all the ones we've located run on Michelin or Goodyear. It's the first thing people change on that sort of motor. We're still looking. In other regions."

"Is that all?"

"That's all for now. What about you?"

"I'm advancing backward."

"Backward?"

"The less I find, the more sure I am that I'm on the right track. Last night's break-ins are linked to a much more serious business, superintendent."

"What do you mean?"

"I don't know. Something to do with a boy. With his kidnapping or murder. I don't know. I'll call you back."

Without giving the superintendent time to ask another question, Karim hung up.

On the outskirts of Sète, he drove through a small village by the sea. Here, the waters of the Golfe du Lion mingled with the earth in a huge area of marshland, bordered with reeds. The policeman slowed down as he passed a strange port, apparently without any boats, but with long, dark fishing nets suspended between the houses with their shuttered windows.

Everything was deserted.

A pungent smell filled the atmosphere, not of the sea, but rather of some sort of fertiliser, laden with acid and excrement.

Karim Abdouf was nearing his destination. The direction of the convent was now indicated. The setting sun lit up the sharply glinting saline pools on the surface of the marshes. Eight miles further on, he noticed another road sign, indicating a tarmac lane leading up to the right. He drove on, taking the winding bends which were bordered by a confusion of reeds and furze.

At last, the buildings of the cloister emerged. Karim was astonished.

Between these dark sand dunes and rampant weeds stood two massive churches. One of them had finely sculpted towers topped by fluted domes, like monumental cream-cakes. The other was large and red, made of a multitude of small stones, culminating in a wide tower with a flat roof. Two cathedrals which, in that salty sea air, made him think of pieces of flotsam. The Arab just could not understand what they were doing in such a lonely, desperate place.

As he approached, he saw that a third building stretched out between them. A one-storey construction with a rank of narrow, over-ornate windows. Presumably it was the convent itself, which was seemingly drawing in its bricks so as to avoid any contact with the two churches.

Karim parked. He thought how he had never before been so closely confronted by religion – at least, not so often in such a short period of time. This reminded him of a piece of reasoning he had once heard. At the Cannes-Ecluse police academy, senior officers sometimes came to lecture about their experiences. One of them had made a deep impression on Karim. He was tall, with a crew cut, and small iron-rimmed spectacles. His talk had been fascinating. The officer had explained how a crime is always reflected in the minds of the witnesses or loved ones. That they should be seen as mirrors, with the murderer hiding in one of the dead angles.

The officer had sounded crazy, but the students had all been riveted. He had also spoken about atomic structures. According to him, when even apparently trivial details or elements regularly reappeared during the course of an enquiry, then it was necessary to pay attention to them, for they certainly concealed a deeper meaning. Each crime was an atomic nucleus and the recurrent elements were its electrons, revolving around it and drawing out a subliminal truth. Karim smiled. That cop with metal spectacles had been right. It was a good description of this present investigation. And religion had now become a recurring element. It no doubt contained some part of the truth which he was going to have to dig out.

He walked over to a small stone porch and rang the bell. A few seconds later, a smile appeared in the doorway. It was an ancient smile, framed in black and white. Before Karim even opened his mouth, the nun drew back and said:

"Come in, my son."

The cop found himself in a dark hall. On one of the white walls, a crucifix could be made out, over a somberly glinting painting. To his right, Abdouf could see gray light coming out of a few open doors down a corridor. And, through a nearby opening, he noticed lines of varnished chairs, a floor covered with linoleum – the impeccably harsh appearance of a place of prayer.

"This way," the nun said. "We are having dinner."

"At this time?"

The nun stifled a slight laugh. She seemed as wicked as a little girl.

"You don't know the Carmelites' daily routine? Every day, we go back to prayer at seven o'clock."

Karim followed her. Their shadows flitted across the linoleum, as though over the waters of a lake. They then reached a large room, where about thirty nuns were eating and chatting away in a brutally strong light. Their faces and veils had a slightly cardboard look about them, like communion wafers. Some of them glanced or smiled at the policeman, but none of them interrupted their conversations. Karim made out a number of different languages, French, English and a Slavic tongue too, perhaps Polish. Karim did as he was told and sat down at the end of the table, in front of a bowl full of lumpy yellow soup.

"Eat, my son. A big boy like you needs feeding . . ."

"My son", again . . . But Karim did not have the heart to snap at the nun.

He looked down at his bowl and remembered that he had not eaten since yesterday. He swallowed the soup in no time, then devoured several pieces of bread and cheese. Each part of the meal had that particular taste of homemade food, concocted with whatever was to hand. He poured himself some water, from a stainless steel jug, then looked up. The nun was watching him, and exchanging a few observations with her neighbors. She murmured:

"We were talking about your hair-do . . ."

"And?"

The nun giggled.

"How do you go about making those plaits?"

"They're natural," he replied. "Frizzy hair naturally goes into plaits like this. In Jamaica, they're called dreadlocks. The men never cut their hair and never shave. It's against their religion, just like with rabbis. When the locks are long enough, they fill them up with earth to make them heavier and . . ."

Karim came to a sudden stop. The reason for his visit had just forced itself back into his mind. He opened his mouth to explain what he was investigating, but the nun got in first:

"Why did you come here, my son? And why do you have a gun under your jacket?"

"I'm a police officer. I need to talk to Sister Andrée. Badly."

The nuns went on chatting, but the lieutenant saw that they had heard his request. The woman declared:

"We'll go and call on her." She signalled discreetly to one of her neighbors, then turned back to Karim. "Follow me."

The cop bowed to the table in a sign of farewell and gratitude. A highwayman thanking those who had offered him their hospitality. They went back down the bright corridor. Their footsteps made not a sound. Suddenly, the nun turned to him:

"You have been told, I suppose?"

"About what?"

"You can speak to her, but you cannot see her. You can listen to her, but you cannot go near her."

Karim examined the edges of the veil, arched up like a shadowy vault. It reminded him of a nave, an illuminated azure dome, the churches protruding on the Rome skyline, the sort of clichés which come into your mind when you try to put a face to the God of the Catholics.

"Darkness," she whispered. "Sister Andrée has made a vow of

darkness. We have not seen her now for the last fourteen years. She must be blind by now."

Outside, the last rays of sunlight were disappearing behind the huge edifices. A wave of cold surged over the empty courtyard. They were walking toward the church with high towers. On its right-hand side, there was a small wooden door. The nun searched through the folds of her robe. Karim heard the clinking of keys, scratching against the stone.

Then she left him in front of the half-open door.

The darkness seemed inhabited, peopled by damp smells, fluttering candles, worn stones. Karim took a few steps inside then raised his eyes. He could not make out the top of the vault. The scattered gleams from the stained-glass windows were already being consumed by the dusk, the flames of the candles seemed to be prisoners of the cold, overwhelming immensity of the church.

He walked past a font, shaped like a seashell, then the confessionals and alcoves, which seemed to be hiding secret religious artifacts. He noticed another dark candelabrum, supporting a large quantity of candles burning in pools of wax.

The place reawoke vague memories in him. Despite his origins and the color of his skin, his subconscious was drenched in the Catholic faith. He remembered the chill Wednesdays in the children's home, where the afternoon TV session was always preceded by catechism. The suffering of the Way of the Cross. Christ's goodness. The feeding of the five thousand. All that bullshit . . . Karim felt a wave of nostalgia rise inside him and a strange sensation of tenderness for the staff at the home. He hated himself for such sentiments. The Arab wanted no memories or weaknesses from his past. He was a son of the present. A being of the here and now. Or, that was at least how he liked to imagine himself.

He paced on under the vaults. Behind a wooden trellis, at the back of the alcoves, he could make out some dark rugs, white rubble, pictures woven in gold. A scent of dust enveloped him as he went. Suddenly, a low sound made him spin round. It took him a few seconds to distinguish the shadow from the surrounding darkness – and to release the grip of his Glock, which he had instinctively seized.

In the hollow of an alcove, perfectly motionless, stood Sister Andrée.

CHAPTER 31

She lowered her head, and her veil completely obscured her features. Karim realised that he would never be able to see that face, and he had a flash of inspiration. Perhaps both the nun and the little boy bore a sign, a mark which revealed their kinship. The nun and the little boy were perhaps mother and son. That thought sank like a dagger into his mind, to such a point that he did not hear the woman's opening words:

"What did you say?" he whispered.

"I asked you what you wanted."

Her voice was deep, but pleasant. The horsehair of a bow sweeping across the strings of a violin.

"I am a police officer, sister. I want to talk to you about Jude."

The dark veil did not move.

"Fourteen years ago," Karim went on, "in a small town called Sarzac, you stole or destroyed all of the photographs featuring a little boy called Jude Ithero. In Cahors, you bribed a photographer. You tricked children. You created accidents, committed burglaries. And all with the intention of obliterating a face on a few photos. Why?"

The nun remained motionless. Her veil formed an arc of nothingness.

"I was obeying orders," she finally declared.

"Orders? Who from?"

"From the boy's mother."

Karim felt pinpricks all across his skin. He knew that she was telling the truth. At once, he gave up his sister/mother/son hypothesis.

The nun opened the wooden gate which separated her from Karim. She walked in front of him then strode over toward some cane-bottomed chairs. She knelt beside a column on a prayer-stool, with her head bent down. Karim went along the next row and sat in front of her. A smell of woven straw, of ashes and incense assailed him.

"Go on," he said, while staring at that patch of darkness where her face should have been.

"She came to see me one Sunday evening, in June 1982."

"Did you know her?"

"No. This is the very place where we met. I did not see her face. She did not tell me her name, nor give me any other information. She just told me that she needed me. For a particular task . . . She wanted me to destroy the school photographs of her son. She wanted to wipe out all trace of his face."

"Why did she want to do that?"

"She was mad."

"Come on. You can do better than that."

"She said that her son was being pursued by demons."

"By demons?"

"Those were her very words. She said they were looking for his face . . ."

"She didn't explain it more clearly?"

"No. She said that her son was cursed. That his face was proof, a piece of evidence which reflected the evil of those demons. She also said that she and her son had gained two years' reprieve from the curse, but that the evil had caught up with them and now the demons were on their heels again. It made no sense at all. She was mad. Totally mad."

Karim drank in every word. He did not understand what this business about "proof" meant, but one thing at least was clear: those two years' reprieve had been the ones spent in Sarzac, in the most absolute anonymity. So where had this mother and son come from?

"If little Jude was really being pursued by dangerous people, then why give this secret mission to a nun who everybody would remember?"

The woman did not reply.

"Please, sister," Karim whispered.

"She said that she had tried everything to hide her child, but the demons were far more powerful than she was. She said that the only thing left now was to exorcise his face."

"What?"

"According to her, I had to be the one who obtained the photographs then burnt them. It would be an exorcism. In that way, I would free her son's face."

"This is all totally beyond me, sister."

"I told you. She was mad."

"But why you? For heaven's sake, your convent is over a hundred and twenty-five miles away from Sarzac!"

The nun remained silent, then said:

"She had searched for me. She had chosen me."

"What do you mean?"

"I have not always been a Carmelite. Before receiving the call, I was a mother. I had to abandon my husband and my son. The woman thought that this would make me likely to accept her request. She was right."

Karim stared on into that pit of darkness. He pressed her:

"You're not telling me everything. If you thought she was mad, then why did you do as she asked? Why cover hundreds of miles to get a handful of photos? Why lie, steal, destroy?"

"Because of the child. Despite that woman's madness, despite her wild words, I . . . I sensed that the child was in danger. And that the only way to help him was to carry out his mother's instructions. Even if it just served to calm her down."

Karim swallowed hard. The pinpricks were covering his skin once again. He approached her and adopted his sweetest tone of voice:

"Tell me about the mother. What did she look like?"

"She was very tall, and big. She must have been at least six feet. Her shoulders were broad. I never saw her face, but I remember that she had a gleaming, black, wavy head of hair. She also wore glasses, with thick frames. She was always dressed in black. In pullovers made of cotton, or wool ..."

"What about Jude's father? Did she ever mention him?"

"No, never."

Karim gripped the wood of the prayer-stool and bent further over. Instinctively, the woman pulled back.

"How often did she come here?" he asked.

"Four or five times. Always on a Sunday. In the morning. She gave me a list of names and addresses – the photographer, and families that might possess the photographs. During the week, I set about obtaining the pictures. I went to see the families. I lied. I stole. I bribed the photographer with money she had given me ..."

"Did she then take the photos away?"

"No. I've already told you. She wanted me to burn them ... When she came here, she simply crossed off the names on her list ... When all the names had been gone through, she seemed relieved. Then she completely disappeared. As for me, I took the path of the shadows. I chose darkness, isolation. The only eyes I can bear are God's. Since that time, I have prayed for the little boy every day. I ..."

She broke off, apparently suddenly catching onto something.

"What brought you here? Why all these questions? My God, Jude isn't ..."

Karim stood up. The incense was burning his throat. He suddenly realized that he was panting, with his mouth agape. He swallowed hard, then glanced at Sister Andrée.

"You did what you could," he said blankly. "But it served no purpose. A month later, the kid was dead. I don't know how. I don't know why. But that woman wasn't as mad as you think. And yesterday, in Sarzac, Jude's grave was desecrated. I am now practically certain that the demons she was afraid of were the persons responsible. That woman was living in a nightmare, sister. And that nightmare has just been resurrected."

Head down, the nun groaned. Her veil was a cascade of black-and-white silk.

Karim went on, his voice growing louder and louder. His harsh tones rose up in the church and he no longer knew on whose behalf he was speaking, for her, for himself, or for Jude.

"I'm an inexperienced officer, sister. I'm a thug, and I work as a loner. But, in some respects, that's bad news for last night's bastards." He grabbed the prayer-stool again. "Because I promised that kid something, understand? Because I come from nowhere and nothing, and nobody's going to stop me. This is personal business, now, get it? Personal business!"

The policeman leant down. He felt the wood crack into splinters beneath his fingers.

"It's time for you to get thinking, sister. Come up with something, anything that will put me on the right track. I have to get to Jude's mother."

Still bent over, the nun shook her head.

"I don't know anything."

"Think! Where could I find that woman? Where did she go after Sarzac? And before all that, where had she come from? Give me a detail, a lead, to help me continue my enquiries!"

Sister Andrée was swallowing back her tears.

"I . . . I think she came here with him."

"With him?"

"With the boy."

"Did you see him?"

"No. She left him in town, near the station, in an amusement park. The fairground is still there, but I have never worked up the courage to go and see the stall-keepers. Perhaps . . . Perhaps one of them might remember the boy . . . That's all I know . . ."

"Thank you, sister."

Karim ran off. His steel-capped shoes rang like pieces of flint across the huge courtyard. He stopped in the icy air, as stiff as a rake, and stared up at the sky. In a fleeting moment of panic, his lips mumbled:

"Jesus Christ . . . where am I? . . . Where the fuck am I?"

CHAPTER 32

The amusement park stretched out in the dusk beside a railway line, on the limits of that small, deserted town. The stands spat out their light and music into nothingness. There was not one single idler, not one family that had come out for a stroll there that Monday evening. Far off, the dark sea opened its white jaws in a succession of violent waves.

Karim walked on. A big wheel was slowly rotating. Its spokes were dotted with little fairy lights which were alternating, one lot on, the other lot off, as though in the throes of a series of short circuits. Musical horses cantered riderless around the carousel; identical-looking attractions, covered with tarpaulin, were being whipped by the wind: bran tubs, arcade games, pathetic amusements . . . Abdouf would have been unable to say whether he found the church or this fair the more depressing.

Without hoping for much, he started questioning the stall-keepers. He mentioned a kid called Jude Ithero, then the date: July 1982. Generally, the faces remained as inscrutable as mummies. Sometimes he got a negative grunt. On other occasions, signs of incredulity: "Fourteen years ago! Whatcha expect?" Karim felt increasingly discouraged. Who was likely to remember? How many Sundays had Jude in fact spent there in all? Three? Four? Five?

Telling himself that the kid might well have taken a liking to one attraction in particular, or become friendly with a stall-keeper, he stubbornly asked round the entire park . . .

But he completed his circuit without the slightest success. He stared at the coast. The waves were still spitting out their tongues of foam around the piles under the seafront. It looked like an ocean of tar. He felt as if he had entered a no-man's-land, where nothing whatever was to be learnt. A childhood memory resurfaced in his mind: the magical town in *Pinocchio*, to which all the naughty little boys were drawn by wonderful attractions, before being captured and then turned into donkeys.

What had Jude been turned into?

He was about to go back to his car when, across the wasteland, he spotted a small circus.

He told himself that, in the name of his enquiry, he was going to have to explore every possible avenue. Shoulders slouching, he marched over to the canvas dome. It was not a real circus – more like a shabby tent containing a series of miserable turns. Above the entrance, a plastic banner announced, in twisted lettering: "The Fire-eaters". With two fingers, the cop raised the piece of cloth that served as a door.

He stopped dead before the blinding spectacle inside. Flames. Dull sounds of scraping. The smell of gasoline in the air. The lieutenant had a fleeting image of a souped-up machine, made of muscle and fire, of brands and human torsos. Then he realised that, under the pale stage lights, he was watching a sort of waltz of the fire-eaters. Men with bare chests, gleaming with sweat and gasoline, were exhaling their inflammable breath onto the crackling torches. They then formed themselves into a menacing-looking semi-circle. Another swig of gasoline. More flames. Some of them bent down, while others leapt over their backs, spitting out a further dazzling incantation.

The cop thought of the demons that had been pursuing Jude's mother.

Every element in this long nightmare kept up the same atmospheric pressure, the same disturbing deadliness.

"Each crime is an atomic nucleus," the cop with the crew cut had said.

Karim sat down on one of the wooden benches and contemplated these apprentice dragons for a while. He sensed that he should wait there, then question these men. But why, he had no idea. At last, one of the fire-eaters deigned to notice his presence. He stopped his performance and, holding his blackened torch which was still spitting with fire, walked over to him. He must have been under thirty, but the lines on his face seemed to have been dug out by twice that number of years. Thanks to a spell inside, no doubt. His hair was brown, his skin brown, his eyes brown. And the piercing stare of someone who was always on the look-out for trouble.

"You one of us?" he asked.

"What?"

"A traveler. You looking for work?"

Karim pressed his hands together.

"No, I'm a cop."

"A cop?"

The fire-eater approached and propped one heel on the bench just below Karim.

"Well you sure don't look like one."

The Arab could smell the man's flaming torso.

"What's a cop supposed to look like?"

"What are you after? It can't be illegal immigrants, can it?"

Karim did not reply. He glanced round the patchwork canvas dome, the performers in the ring, then the thought occurred to him that this character must have been about fifteen in 1982. What were the chances of his having run into Jude? Zero. But he just had to ask.

"Were you already here fourteen years back?"

"Yeah, probably. This circus belongs to my folks."

Karim said, in one breath:

"I'm on the trail of a little boy who might have come here round that time. In July 1982, to be precise. On several successive Sundays. I'm looking for someone who might remember him."

The fire-eater searched for the truth in Karim's eyes.

"You're not serious, are you?"

"Don't I look it?"

"What was this kid's name?"

176

"Jude. Jude Ithero."

"And you really expect someone to remember a kid who might have dropped into our circus fourteen years back?"

Karim stood up and strode over the benches.

"Forget it."

The young man suddenly grabbed him by the jacket.

"Jude came here a few times. He used to stay sitting there while we were rehearsing. Like he was hypnotised, or something."

"What?"

The man climbed up a row and stood beside Karim. His breath stank of gasoline. He went on:

"It was one hell of a hot summer, that one. Like you could fry eggs on the sidewalk. Jude turned up here four Sundays in a row. We were about the same age. We played together. I taught him to spit out fire. It was kid's stuff. What's the big deal?"

Karim stared at the young fire-eater.

"And you remember him, just like that, fourteen years later?"

"That's what you were hoping, isn't it?"

The cop raised his voice:

"All I want to know is why you remember."

The man leapt down onto the circle of beaten earth, clicked his heels together and raised his torch to his lips. He sprinkled it with saliva tinged with gasoline. A shower of sparks flew out.

"It's because there was something a bit special about Jude."

Karim trembled.

"Something about his face?"

"No, not his face."

"What then?"

The young man spat out another volley of flames, then cackled:

"Listen, man, Jude was a girl."

CHAPTER 33

Slowly, the truth was taking shape.

According to the fire-eater, the child he had met on four occasions was a young girl, carefully disguised as a boy. Hair clipped short, boyish clothes, boyish manners. The man was categorical:

"She never told me she was a girl . . . It was her secret, see? But I noticed at once that something was odd. First off, she was really beautiful. A stunner, in fact. And then there was her voice. And her shape. She must have been about ten, or twelve. And it was beginning to show. Then there were other things. She had lenses in her eyes that changed their color. They were dark, but as black as ink. Artificial looking. Even though I was a kid, I still spotted that. And she was always complaining that her eyes hurt. They were stinging right into her head, that's what she said . . ."

Karim gathered the evidence. Jude's mother's greatest fear was that the demons were going to destroy her child. Which is presumably why she had left her town and ended up in Sarzac. Once there, she must have adopted a new identity. And Karim should have realised that before. She had changed her child's name, thoroughly altered its appearance, and even its sex. That way, nobody could possibly find her out. But, two years later, the demons had turned up again in her new town, Sarzac. They were still looking for the child and were about to unmask him.

To unmask her.

The mother had panicked. She had destroyed all the documents, all the school registers, all the files that contained her daughter's assumed name. And, in particular, the photographs. Because, if the demons did not know her child's new name, they certainly knew her face. It was, in fact, the face they were looking for. The proof of her identity. That was why they must first have wanted to examine the school photos so as to pick out the features they were after. But where had these pursuing demons come from?

And who were they?

Karim questioned the young fire-eater, who was still brandishing his torch:

"And did this little girl ever say anything about demons?"

"Demons? No, the demons . . ." He pointed at the troop and chuckled. ". . . that was us. And Jude didn't say a lot. I told you, we were kids. I just taught her to spit out fire . . ."

"And that interested her?"

"Not half. She said she wanted to learn . . . so as to protect herself. And protect her mum, too . . . A bit of a funny kid."

"She didn't say anything else about her mother?"

"No . . . And I never saw her either . . . Jude stayed with us for a couple of hours then, all of a sudden, she was gone . . . Like Cinderella. She vanished like that a few times, then never came back."

"Do you remember anything else? A detail I could find useful?"

"No."

"Her name, for instance . . . She never told you her name, her real one, I mean."

"No, but now I stop and think, there was something . . ."

"What?"

"I started by calling her 'Joode', like in the Beatles song. But that wound her up. She insisted on being called 'Ju-de', with a French pronunciation. I can still see her little mouth pouting: 'Ju-de'."

The fire-eater smiled nostalgically, his eyes seemed to mist over. Karim figured that this dragon must have been head-over-heels in love with the girl. The man then asked him a question:

"So what are you investigating? What's up with her? These days, she must be at least . . ."

Karim was no longer listening. He was thinking of little Jude, who had been to school for two years under an assumed name. How had the mother managed to fake her identity papers and enrol her in that school? How had she managed to pass her off as a little boy and so fool everyone, in particular the teacher she saw every day?

He had a sudden idea. He looked up and asked the human torch:

"Is there a phone round here?"

"Course there is. What do you take us for, bums?"

Abdouf followed him as he led the way.

He then found himself in a small shed of painted wood at the end of the ring. There was a telephone on a small shelf. He dialled the number of the headmistress of Jean-Jaurès School. The wind was slapping against the edges of the tent. In the distance, the fire-eaters continued their rehearsal. It rang three times, then a man's voice answered.

"I'd like to speak to the headmistress, please," Karim explained, mastering his excitement.

"Who shall I say is calling?"

"Lieutenant Karim Abdouf."

A few seconds later, the woman's breathless voice panted into the receiver. The policeman asked point-blank:

"Do you remember the teacher you mentioned, who left Sarzac at the end of the 1982 school year?"

"Of course."

"You told me that she'd taken CM1 in 1981, then CM2 in 1982."

"That's correct."

"So, she followed Jude Ithero from one class to the next?"

"Yes. You could put it that way. But, as I told you, it's common practice . . ."

"What was her name?"

"Hang on, I'll look at my notes . . ."

The headmistress rummaged through her papers.

"Fabienne Pascaud."

This name, of course, meant nothing to Karim. What was more, it had nothing in common with the child's assumed name. With each new piece of information, he ran up against a brick wall. He asked:

"Do you have her maiden name?"

"That is her maiden name."

"She wasn't married?"

"She was a widow. Or, according to my files, she was. How odd. She seems to have started to use her old surname again."

"What was her married name?"

"Hang on . . . There it is: Hérault. H.E.R.A.U.L.T."

Another dead end. Karim was barking up the wrong tree again. "OK. Thanks, I'll . . ."

There then came a blinding flash. If he was right, if this woman really was Jude's mother, then the little girl's surname must originally have been Hérault. And her first name . . .

Karim thought again of the fire-eater's remark about the pronunciation of the kid's name. She had been adamant that it should be pronounced in the French way. Why? Because it reminded her of her real name? Her real, girl's name?

Karim panted into the receiver:

"Hang on a second."

He knelt down and, his hand shaking, wrote the two names in the sand, in block capitals, one above the other:

FABIENNE HERAULT

JUDE ITHERO

The last two syllables rhymed. He thought for a moment then, with his hand, wiped out what he had just written in the dust. He started again, this time separating the syllables:

JU DI THE RO

Then:

JUDITH HERAULT

He almost roared in triumph. Jude Ithero's real name was Judith Hérault. The little boy was a little girl. And her mother had definitely been her school teacher. She had readopted her maiden name and masculinised her daughter's first name, so as not to confuse her child or run the risk of her making mistakes in company.

Karim clenched his fists. He was sure that that was how things had been worked out. The woman had been able to change her child's identity at the school, because that was where she taught. This hypothesis explained everything: the ease with which she had fooled everyone in Sarzac, the discreet way in which she had made off with the official documents. His voice trembled, as he asked the headmistress:

"Could you obtain some more information about that teacher, from the education board?"

"This evening?"

"Yes, this evening."

"I . . . Well, I do have friends there. Maybe I can. What do you want to know?"

"I want to know where Fabienne Pascaud/Hérault moved after leaving Sarzac. And I also want to know where she taught before arriving in your town. Dig out some people that knew her. Do you have a cell phone?"

The woman gave him her number. She sounded a little out of her depth. Karim went on:

"How long will it take you to go to the board, and find all that out?"

"A couple of hours."

"Take your cell phone with you. I'll call you back in two hours."

Karim ran out of the hut and waved good-bye to the fire-eaters, who had started up their St Vitus's dance once again.

CHAPTER 34

Two hours to kill.

Karim adjusted his woolly hat and strolled back to his car. The shadows were being swept away by a wind laden with maritime miasma which seemed to freeze the earth and the tarmac. Two hours to kill. He wondered if this region had given up all of its secrets yet.

He tried to imagine Fabienne and Judith Hérault, those two lonely people coming here each Sunday during that summer. He pictured the scene exactly, replaying it from different angles, searching for a clue that might reveal a new lead for him to follow up. He could see the mother and her daughter in the morning light, walking cautiously through a region in which nobody would recognise them. That determined woman, obsessed by her child's face. And the androgynous child itself, locked up in its fear.

Abdouf did not know why, but he imagined that strange couple to be united by their common distress. He saw them hand in hand, walking in silence . . . How did they get here? By train? By road?

The lieutenant decided to pay a visit to all the nearby railway stations, service stations on the autoroutes and *gendarmerie* headquarters, in search of a trace, a police report, a memory . . .

Two hours to kill. There was nothing else he could do.

He drove off under a sky that was reddened by the last fires of the setting sun. The October nights were already beginning to lengthen into a shrivelled darkness.

He found a phone box and called the Rodez police in the hope of finding a car registered under the name Fabienne Pascaud or Hérault in the *département* of the Lot in 1982. In vain. Nobody by that name was on record. He got back into his car and started looking round the local railway stations, while still keeping open the possibility of a privately owned vehicle.

He visited four stations. And drew four total blanks. Abdouf lapped up the miles, in concentric circles, around the convent and the amusement park. All he saw in the beam of his headlamps was the tall, ghostly shapes of trees, rocks, tunnels . . . He felt good. Adrenaline was warming his limbs and the excitement was keeping all of his senses alert. The Arab was back with the sensations he loved, of the night, and of fear. Those sensations he had discovered in the middle of car parks when, hidden behind the pillars, he had filed down his first set of keys. Karim was not afraid of the dark. It was his world, his cloak, his deep waters. It made him feel safe, as tense as a tightrope, as powerful as a predator.

At the fifth station, all the cop found was a freight loading zone, full of ancient wagons and blue turbines. He drove off at once, but then immediately braked. He was on a bridge, above the autoroute, at the Sète (west) exit. He gazed down at the little toll-booth, three hundred yards away. His instinct told him to check it out.

Explore every avenue. Always.

He took the approach road and at once turned right, passing between some privet hedges. Behind them were several prefabricated huts: the offices of the toll company. Not a single light. But, by some nearby sheds, he spotted a man. He braked again, parked his car and marched straight toward the figure, which was busying itself at the back of a tall truck.

The bitter wind doubled in intensity. Everything was dry, dull, dusty, as though enclosed in an envelope of sea air. The cop clambered over the road signs, the buckets, the plastic sheeting. He banged on the side of the lorry – a consignment of salt – producing a loud metallic din.

The man jumped. All that was visible through his balaclava was his eyes. His graying brows frowned.

"What's all this? Who are you?"

"The Devil."

"What?"

Karim smiled and leant against the container.

"Only joking. I'm from the police, grandpa. I need some information."

"Information? There's nobody here till tomorrow, I . . ."

"Autoroute toll-booths are open round the clock."

"The collector's in his booth, and as for me, I work here . . ."

"That's just what I said. Now, the two of us are going into the office. You're then going to get yourself a nice cup of coffee, while I take a look at the computer."

"The computer? . . . What for?"

"I'll explain once we're nice and warm inside."

The offices resembled the rest of the establishment: cramped and makeshift. Thin walls, cardboard doors, formica-topped desks. Everything was switched off. Dead. Apart from the computer which was humming away in the shadows. It contained the central information unit which continued to run, day in day out, relaying everything that needed to be known about the local autoroute network. Every accident, each breakdown, all the toings and froings of the autoroute services were recorded in its memory.

The old man was all for handling the computer himself. He pulled up his balaclava and Karim whispered into his ear:

"July 1982. Dig out the whole lot for me. Accidents, repairs, the number of users, the slightest thing out of the ordinary. The works."

The old man took off his gloves and blew on his fingers to warm them up. He tapped on the keyboard for a few seconds. A list appeared for the month of July, 1982. Figures, data, breakdowns. Nothing of any interest.

"Can you do a name search?" Karim asked, leaning over his shoulder.

"Spell it."

"I've got several: Jude Ithero, Judith Hérault, Fabienne Pascaud, Fabienne Hérault."

"Is that all?" the man grumbled, entering the names into the machine.

But, after a couple of seconds, an answer flashed up. Karim bent nearer.

"What's happening?"

"There's something on record under one of those names, but not in July 1982."

"Keep looking."

The man touched a few more keys. The information arrived in glowing letters on the dark screen. The cop's body stiffened. The date sprang out into his face: 14 August, 1982. The same as the one on Jude's grave. And the name on the file was also the same: Jude Ithero.

"I couldn't remember the name," the old boy panted. "But I do remember the accident. It was awful. Just near Héron-Cendré.

The car skidded. It went straight through the central divide and smashed into the corner of a sound-proofed wall just opposite. We found them, the mother and her son, crushed inside the bodywork. But only the kid didn't make it. He was in the front seat. The mother escaped with a few cuts and bruises. There was a stream of blood across both sides of the road. Two times three lanes, can you imagine it?"

Karim could no longer control his trembling limbs. So this was how Fabienne and Judith Hérault's years on the run had ended. At eighty miles per hour, against a roadside wall. It was that absurd. That simple. He choked down a cry of anger. He just could not believe that the whole adventure, all the precautions that that woman had taken, had been wiped out by a skidding car.

And yet, he had known it right from the start: Judith had died in August 1982, just as her grave indicated. All he was now doing was finding out the exact circumstances of her death. Tears welled up under his eyelids, as though he had just lost someone he loved. Someone he had loved for a mere few hours, but with a raging violence. Beyond words and years. Beyond space and time.

"Go on," he commanded. "Describe the body of the child."

"He ... he was completely crammed inside the wreckage. A mess of flesh and bodywork. Jesus Christ! It took them more than six hours to ... I mean ... I'll never forget it ... His face was ... I mean ... He didn't have a face any more, no head, nothing."

"What about his mother?"

"His mother? I don't even know if it was his mother. Anyway, she didn't have the same name as ..."

"I know. Was she injured?"

"No. Like I said, she got away with just cuts and bruises ... Nothing really. What happened was the car span round, see? It hit the wall bang on the passenger side. Typical on that bend and ..."

"Describe her to me."

"Who?"

"The woman."

"I'm not likely to forget her. She was very tall. With brown hair and a big face. And enormous glasses. All dressed in baggy black clothes. It was really weird. She didn't cry. She seemed very distant. Maybe she was in shock, I dunno . . ."

"What was her face like?"

"Pretty."

"Meaning?"

"With sort of chubby cheeks . . . I dunno . . . And very white skin, almost transparent."

Abdouf changed tack.

"You keep a file on each accident, don't you? A report, with the death certificate and so on?"

The bristly old man looked at Karim. His eyes were sparkling in the darkness.

"What exactly are you after, buddy?"

"Show me the file."

The man wiped his hands on his anorak and opened a filing cabinet with doors like shutters. Karim watched him read his way through the names of the victims, mumbling them out loud.

"Jude Ithero. This is the one. But I'll warn you, it's not a . . ."

Karim seized it and flicked through the pages. Reports from witnesses, certificates, police particulars, insurance claims. The whole scenario. Fabienne Pascaud had been driving a hired car, which she had rented in Sarzac. The home address was the same as the one he had been given by Dr Macé – that lonely ruin in a rocky valley. Nothing new there. But what was surprising was that the mother had declared her child's death under the name of Jude Ithero, sex male.

"I don't get it," the cop said. "So the child was a boy?"

"Um, yeah . . ." The old man was looking at the file over Karim's shoulder. "That's what she said, anyway . . ."

"You don't remember there being any problem about that?"

"Problem? What on earth do you mean?"

The cop struggled to control his voice:

"Look, all I'm asking is: was it possible to determine the sex of the child?"

"Hey, I'm no doctor! But really, I don't reckon it was. The body was in pieces ... A real autoroute smash ..." He wiped his hand over his face. "... Look, bud, I'm not going into details ... Lord knows how many accidents I've seen in the last twenty-five years ... And it's always the same bloody mess." He waved his hands in the air, miming layers of fog. "It's like an underground war, get me? Which breaks out from time to time in horrific violence."

Karim understood that the state of the body had allowed the mother to keep her secret, even to the grave. But what had been the point? Had she still been afraid? Even now her little girl was dead?

The lieutenant grabbed the file once more and looked through the photographs of the accident. Blood. Twisted metal. Lumps of flesh, scattered limbs sticking out from the bodywork. He went on rapidly. It was more than he could take. Then he came across the death certificate, the doctor's description, which confirmed that the characteristics of the body were highly abstract.

Feeling dizzy, Karim leant back against the wall. Then he looked at his watch. He had now thoroughly killed his two hours.

And they had killed him, too.

He forced himself to take a last look at the pages in the file. Some fingerprints were stuck in blue ink on a sheet of cardboard. He gazed at these prints for a few seconds, then asked:

"These are his prints?"

"What do you mean?"

"These are the child's fingerprints?"

"I don't see what you're driving at ... But, yes, of course they are ... I was the one who held the inkpad. The rest of the body was under the blankets. The doctor pressed down on the little hand. It was covered in blood. Jesus! We were all in a hurry to get it over with. Look, I still get nightmares about it even today ..."

Karim stuck the file under his leather jacket.

"OK. I'm going to hang on to this."

"Do. And good luck to you."

The lieutenant set off again. He was feeling all in. Stars were dancing under his eyelids. When he was on the steps outside, the old man called after him:

"Watch out for yourself."

Karim turned round. In the salt wind, propping open the glass door with his shoulder, the man was observing him. His figure was duplicated in a golden brown reflection in the pane.

"What?" the cop asked.

"I said, watch out for yourself. And never mistake someone else for your own shadow."

Karim tried to smile.

"Why not?"

The man pulled down his balaclava.

"Because, from what I can sense, you're walking among the dead."

CHAPTER 35

"The things you have me do, lieutenant . . . I went to see the person I know at the education board . . ."

The woman's voice was trembling with glee. Karim had stopped at another phone box to call the headmistress on her mobile. She went on:

"The janitor was good enough to . . ."

"What did you find?"

"All the records relating to Fabienne Hérault, née Pascaud. But it's another blind alley. After her two years in Sarzac, she seems to have vanished. She must have given up teaching."

"There's no way to find out where she went?"

"None. Apparently, she worked out her contract with the educational authorities that year, then did not request a further post. That's all. The board never heard from her again."

Karim was on the edge of a residential estate in the suburbs of Sète. Through the glass panes of the phone box, he could see a number of parked cars, their bodywork glistening under the streetlamps. He did not find this piece of information particularly surprising. Fabienne Pascaud had disappeared without a trace. Into her mystery. Her tragedy. Her demons.

"And where had she been before Sarzac?"

"Guernon. It's a university town in the Isère, just above Grenoble. She taught there only for a few months. Before that, she had been head of a tiny primary school in Taverlay, a village on the slopes of the Pelvoux, one of the mountains in that region."

"Did you get her personal details?"

In a mechanical voice, she read out:

"Fabienne Pascaud was born in 1945, in Corivier, in one of the valleys in the Isère. In 1970, she married Sylvain Hérault and that same year won first prize in the Grenoble Conservatoire piano competition. She could, in fact, have become a music teacher and . . ."

"Go on, please."

"In 1972, she went to the teacher training college. Then, two years later, she started running the Taverlay primary school, still in the Isère. She taught there for six years. In 1980, the Taverlay school was closed down – a new road allowed the children to attend a larger school in a nearby village, even during the winter. Fabienne was then transferred to Guernon. Quite a stroke of luck – it's only thirty-two miles from Taverlay, and a famous place in educational circles. A university town. Very nice. Very intellectual."

"You told me that she was a widow. Do you know when her husband died?"

"I'm coming to that, young man! When she arrived in Guernon in 1980, Fabienne gave her married name – there seems to have been no problem about that. But then, six months later, she presented herself as a widow in Sarzac. So her husband presumably died during her stay in Guernon."

"Your file doesn't say anything about him, does it? His age? Or his occupation?"

"This is an education authority, not a detective agency."

Karim sighed.

"Go on."

"Soon after arriving in Guernon, she asked to be transferred – anywhere, just so long as it was far away from that town. Strange, don't you think? She quickly obtained a post in Sarzac, which isn't particularly surprising – nobody wants to come and work in our beautiful region. Once there, she started using her maiden name again. As though she badly wanted to turn over a new leaf."

"You haven't mentioned her child."

"True enough. She had a child who was born in 1972. A little girl . . ."

"That's what it says?"

"Um, yes . . ."

"What name does it give?"

"Judith Hérault. But no mention is made of her in Sarzac."

Each fact precisely confirmed the version Karim had suspected. He went on:

"Have you found anybody who knew her in Sarzac?"

"I have. I spoke to the then headmistress, Mathilde Sarman. She clearly remembers Fabienne. A strange woman, apparently. Mysterious. Kept herself to herself. Very beautiful. And very tall. Over six feet. With massive shoulders . . . She often used to play the piano. A real virtuoso. I'm just repeating what I've been told . . ."

"Did Fabienne Pascaud live alone when she was in Sarzac?"

"Yes she did, at least according to Mathilde. In an isolated valley, about six miles outside town."

"And no one knows why she left Sarzac so suddenly?"

"No, no one."

"Or Guernon, two years before?"

"No. I suppose we would have to ask there, I . . ." The woman hesitated, then dared ask her question. "Now listen, lieutenant . . . You could at least tell me what the connection is between this investigation and the robbery in my school, I . . ."

"Later. Are you going home now?"

"Um ... yes, of course ..."

"Take everything that concerns Fabienne Pascaud with you, and wait for my call."

"I ... All right. When do you think you can call?"

"I don't know. Soon. I'll explain everything then."

Karim hung up and took another long look at the cars in the car park. There were some Audis, BMWs, Mercedes, shiny, fast – and chock-full of alarms. He looked at his watch. It was just after half-past eight. And time to confront the old lion. The lieutenant dialled Henri Crozier's personal number. A voice immediately roared:

"For fuck's sake, WHERE ARE YOU?"

"I'm pursuing my enquiries."

"I hope you're on your way back to the station."

"No. I have to pay one last call. In the mountains."

"The mountains?"

"Yes, to a small university town near Grenoble. Called Guernon."

There was a moment's silence, then Crozier said:

"You'd better have a good reason for ..."

"An excellent one, superintendent. The lead I've got points that way. I reckon that's where I'll find the desecrators."

Crozier did not respond. Karim's nerve seemed to have left him speechless. Taking advantage of the silence, the lieutenant pressed on:

"Do you have any news about the vehicle?"

The superintendent hesitated. Karim raised his voice:

"Do you have any news, yes or no?"

"We've found the vehicle and its owner."

"How?"

"A witness on the D143 road. A farmer who was going home on his tractor. He saw a white Lada go by, at around two o'clock. All he could remember was the code of the *département*. So we checked it out. A Lada has just been registered over there. And, during its test, it still had its original East European tires. You can be about eighty per cent certain that she's our car."

Karim thought it over. This piece of information seemed too convenient, and hence suspect.

"Why did the witness come forward?"

Crozier chuckled.

"Because Sarzac's in a frenzy. The regional squad's arrived, with its usual absolute damn discretion. They're playing it as if it was a full-scale profanation, like at Carpentras." Crozier cursed. "The press has turned up too. It's a fucking mess."

Karim clenched his teeth.

"Give me the name and the town, quick!"

"Don't talk to me like that, Karim, I'll . . ."

"The name, superintendent. Don't you realise yet that this is my enquiry? That I'm the only person who knows the real reason for this mayhem?"

Crozier paused for a moment, the time he needed to recover his calm. When he spoke again, his voice was impassive:

"Karim, in all my years on the force, nobody has ever spoken to me like that. So, I want an update on 'your' enquiry. And be snappy about it. If not, I'll put out an APB on your ass."

The tone of his voice made it clear that this was no time to try and negotiate. Karim briefly told him what he had found out. He recounted the story of Fabienne and Judith Hérault, the two loners on the run. He described the crazy path they had taken, the changes of identity, the car accident that had killed the child. At the end, Crozier sounded perplexed:

"Quite a story you've got there."

"Death is a story, superintendent."

"Yeah . . . if you say so. Anyway, I don't see the connection between your yarn and our business of last night . . ."

"This is what I think, superintendent. Fabienne Hérault was not mad. Some people really were pursuing her. And I think the same ones came back to Sarzac last night."

"What?"

Karim took a deep breath.

"I think they came back to check something. Something that they knew, but which a recent event had given them cause to doubt."

"What are you on about? And who are these people supposed to be?"

"No idea. But I reckon that the demons are back, superintendent."

"That's bullshit."

"Maybe it is, but just look at the facts: Jean-Jaurès School was definitely burgled and Jude Ithero's grave was definitely desecrated. So, superintendent, would you please give me the desecrator's name and where he lives? I'd like to know if it's in Guernon, because that's where I think the key to this nightmare lies . . ."

"Got a pen? His name is: Philippe Sertys. 7, Rue Maurice-Blasch."

Karim's voiced quavered:

"And the town, superintendent? Is it Guernon?"

Crozier let him sweat for a moment.

"Yes, it's Guernon. Christ knows how you managed to work that one out, but you're certainly the one who's onto the hottest lead."

VII

CHAPTER 36

The German photographer's pictures had taken on flesh.

Athletes with shaven heads were running in the pre-war Berlin stadium. Nimble. Powerful. The race had fallen into the rhythm of an old flickering movie, with grainy images, colored like the covering of a tomb. He watched the men run. He heard their heels on the track. He sensed their hoarse breathing, beating in counterpoint to their strides.

But soon other confusing details appeared. Their faces were too somber, too rigid. Their brows were too strong, too prominent. What lay behind their staring eyes? As a deep, hysterical cheering started up among the spectators, the athlete's eyes suddenly seemed to have been ripped out, their sockets were empty, but this did not stop them from seeing, or from running on. Instead, within those gaping wounds, things were apparently swarming around . . . tongues clicked . . . scales gleamed . . .

Niémans woke up covered in icy sweat. He was immediately dazzled by the white light from the computer, as though it was playing at interrogating him. He quietly pulled himself together and looked round: nobody had noticed that he had nodded off and that terror had ripped into his dreams in the form of those photos he had noticed in Sophie Caillois's flat. The pictures taken by that Nazi film director, whose name he had now forgotten.

Half past nine.

He had slept for only forty-five minutes. After his visit to the warehouse, Niémans had immediately sent everything he had found (the exercise book, the wire meshes, the packets of white powder) to Patrick Astier, the scientist in Grenoble, by way of Marc Costes, who was still awaiting the arrival of the frozen corpse in the hospital.

Then Niémans had come here, to the library, to start a word search using the terms "blood-red" and "rivers". His first thought had been to check the maps of the area to see if there was not a network of waterways that bore this name. After that, he had consulted the computer index in search of a book, a catalog or a document which contained this expression. But he had found nothing and, while reading, had suddenly dozed off. Almost forty hours without sleep and his nerves had abruptly dumped him, like a puppet with its strings cut.

The superintendent glanced round the main reading-room again. Around the tables and carrels, ten policemen were continuing their research, picking their way through books which contained references to evil, purity or eyes ... Two of them were drawing up a list of those students who had regularly consulted some of these, supposedly suspect, titles. Another one was still reading Rémy Caillois's thesis.

But Niémans no longer believed in a literary connection. And neither did those police officers, who were waiting to be relieved. For the last two hours, everybody knew that, because of the lack of results of the Niémans/Barnes/Vermont team, the Grenoble regional crime squad was going to take over the investigation.

It was true: their enquiries had not progressed one inch, despite all of the means put at their disposal. Three hundred soldiers had been requisitioned from the Romans military base to help Captain Vermont's units search the area around the Pointe du Muret, then the western slopes of the Belledonne. They had arrived by truck at about seven o'clock and had at once begun their nocturnal explorations. Apart from these soldiers, the captain had also called in two companies of CRS riot police, based in Valence. Over three hundred hectares had now been examined. For the moment, this close search had revealed nothing and, Niémans was convinced, would reveal nothing. If the killer had left any clues behind, then they would already have been discovered. And yet, the superintendent remained in radio contact with Vermont and had personally traced out, on an ordnance survey map, the crucial points of the investigation: the places where the first and second bodies had been found, the position of the university, Sertys's warehouse, the location of the various refuges, and so on.

The roads were also being more and more closely watched. The number of road-blocks had risen from eight to twenty-four. They now covered a large circumference around Guernon. All the towns and villages, the autoroute exits and entrances, and the A- and B-roads were all sealed off. The paperwork was piling up, too. Under the responsibility of Captain Barnes, the general requests for information continued. Faxes poured into his office: statements, answers to questionnaires, commentaries ... Other forms were then dispatched to the nearby ski resorts. Messages and circulars were sent off. The brigade's switchboard had been equipped with four extra fax machines.

That afternoon, they had also begun to question everybody who had been in contact with the first victim over the previous few weeks. One team was still questioning the region's top mountain climbers, in particular those who had already gone up the Vallernes glacier. Wild men, who did not live in Guernon, but in the villages high up the slopes, on the rocky flanks that overlooked the university. The *gendarmerie* station was constantly crammed with people.

A further team, made up of Vermont's men, was slowly piecing together the probable itinerary Rémy Caillois took during his last expedition, while others still were already beginning to work on the second victim's journey, as well as that of the murderer, up to the summit of the glacier. Their paths were entered into the computer, memorised and compared. In the midst of this tumult, of these rumors of war, Niémans obstinately clung to the personal angle. More than ever, he was convinced that if he could discover the motive, then he would find the murderer. And the motive was, perhaps, revenge. But he was going to have to be very careful about this hypothesis. Neither the authorities nor the general public approved of paradoxes when it came to murder. Officially, a murderer killed innocent people. But Niémans was now trying to show that the victims, too, had been guilty.

But where could he look? Caillois and Sertys had both died with their secrets intact. Sophie Caillois was not going to say a word, and having her followed had not, for the moment, produced anything of interest. As for Sertys's mother, or his colleagues at work, they had been questioned and clearly knew only the public face of Philippe Sertys. His mother had not even been aware of the warehouse's existence, despite the fact of its having belonged to her husband, René Sertys.

So?

So, Niémans's mind was now locked on another mystery, which had begun to swamp all of the others. He switched on his phone and called Barnes:

"Any news of Joisneau?"

The young lieutenant, that enthusiastic officer who was dying to acquire the "master's" art, had still not reappeared.

"Yeah," Barnes growled. "I sent one of my boys to the home for the blind, to find out where he went next."

"And?"

The captain's voice sounded tired and strained.

"And, Joisneau left the home at about five o'clock. Apparently, he was on his way to Annecy, to see an oculist there. A professor at the University of Guernon, who looks after the patients in the home."

"Have you called him?"

"Of course. We've tried his business and personal lines. No answer."

"Have you got his address?"

Barnes dictated the name of one street: the doctor lived in a house which also contained his surgery.

"I'll drop in and see," Niémans said.

"Why? Sooner or later, Joisneau's bound to . . ."

"I feel responsible."

"Responsible?"

"If the kid's done anything crazy, if he's taken any unnecessary risks, then I'm sure that it was to impress me. See what I mean?"

The gendarme adopted a soothing tone.

"Joisneau will turn up. He's young. He's probably set off on some wild goose chase."

"Yes, probably. But he might also be in danger. Without knowing it."

"In . . . danger?"

Niémans did not reply. A few seconds of silence ensued. Barnes seemed not to grasp the meaning of the superintendent's words. Then he suddenly added:

"Oh yes, I was forgetting. Joisneau also phoned the hospital. He wanted to take a look at the archives."

"The archives?"

"Those huge underground galleries beneath the university hospital. They contain the entire history of the region, in terms of its births, illnesses and deaths."

The policeman felt his chest go tight: so, the kid was off following up a lead on his own. A lead which had started at the blind home, continued to that oculist and then to the hospital archives. He concluded:

"But he hasn't been seen at the hospital?"

Barnes replied that he had not. Niémans hung up. Then his phone immediately rang again. This was no time for pagers, secret codes and precautions. All the investigators were now working flat out. Costes's voice was quavering:

"I've just been given the body."

"Is it Sertys?"

"Yes, it is. No doubt about it."

The superintendent whistled. So, all the pieces of information he had picked up during the last three hours did fit into the frame. And now he was going to be able to send a special team to conduct a systematic search of the warehouse. Costes went on:

"There's one very important difference from the first set of mutilations."

"What's that?"

"The murderer removed the eyes, but also the hands. He cut them off at the wrists. You didn't notice this because of the foetal position of the body. The stumps were stuck between his knees."

The eyes. The hands. Niémans glimpsed an occult link between those parts of the anatomy. But he was incapable of deciphering the infernal logic which lay behind these mutilations.

"Is that all?" he asked.

"Yes, that's all for now. I'm just beginning the autopsy."

"How long will it take?"

"Two hours, at least."

"Start with the eye-sockets and call me as soon as you find anything. I'm sure there's going to be a clue for us."

"I feel like I'm a messenger from hell, superintendent."

Niémans crossed the reading-room. Near the door, he noticed the officer hunched over Rémy Caillois's thesis. He allowed himself a little detour and sat down in front of him, in one of the carrels.

"How's it going?"

The officer looked up.

"I'm sinking fast."

The superintendent smiled and pointed at the wad of paper.

"Anything of interest?"

The man shrugged.

"We're still in ancient Greece and the Olympiads, sports events and all that sort of thing: running races, the javelin, wrestling . . . Caillois goes on about the sacred nature of physical competition, of breaking records . . ." The officer curled up his lips in disbelief. "As a kind of . . . of communion with higher forces. According to him, a broken record was, at that time, considered to be a real way of communicating with the gods . . . For example, the *athlon*, the ideal athlete, could unleash the hidden powers of the earth by surpassing his own physical limitations. Mind you, when you see the hysteria at some football matches, it really does seem as though sport sets off strange forces ..."

"What else have you picked up?"

"Caillois says that, in ancient times, athletes were also poets, musicians and philosophers. Our little librarian was very insistent about that point. He seems to miss the days when the mind and the body were bound together within one single human being. Which also explains the title: 'Nostalgia for Olympia'. It's nostalgia for a time of supermen, who were at once cerebral and muscular, intellectuals and sportsmen. Caillois sets that rigorous period against our own century, in which the brainy ones can't lift a pea and the athletes are pea-brains. He considers it to be a sign of decadence, of a separation between the mind and the body."

Niémans glimpsed once more the athletes in his nightmare. Those blind men in their stony reality. Sophie Caillois had explained how her husband believed that those sportsmen in Berlin had re-established that profound communion between the physical and the intellectual.

The policeman also thought of this university's champions: the lecturers' children who, in the words of Joisneau, won all the prizes, including the sporting ones. In a way, these gifted youngsters were also acting out the part of the ideal athlete. When Niémans had looked at those photographs of medal winners in the ante-chamber to the vice-chancellor's office, he had noticed a terrible youthful vitality in their faces. As though it were the incarnation of some physical force, but also of a separate way of thinking. Of some philosophy, perhaps? He smiled at the young officer, who was now staring at him with a worried expression.

"Well, you seem to have grasped the essential," he concluded.

"I'm completely out of my depth. I understand about every other sentence." He tapped his index finger against the tip of his nose. "But I'm relying on my flair. I can smell out a fascist from miles away."

"You reckon Caillois was a Nazi?"

"I wouldn't put it that way ... It seems more complicated than that ... But, his myth of the superman, the athlete with the pure spirit, does sound like the usual claptrap about racial superiority and all that bullshit."

In his mind's eye, Niémans saw those pictures of the Berlin Olympics again, in the corridor of the Caillois's flat. A secret lay behind those images, and behind the sporting records at Guernon. They were perhaps connected. But how?

"He doesn't mention any rivers?" he asked at last. "Blood-red rivers?"

"What?"

Pierre Niémans stood up.

"Forget it."

The officer watched the tall man in the blue coat as he started to leave.

"Really, superintendent, you could have got a student on this job, someone more qualified than me to . . ."

"I wanted a professional opinion. An interpretation which would fit into our frame of reference."

The officer pursed his lips once more.

"And you really think that all this crap has something to do with the murders?"

Niémans put his hand on the glass partition and leant over.

"In this sort of business, every element is important. Coincidences don't exist. And neither do irrelevancies. It all works like an atomic structure, do you see that? So, keep reading."

Niémans left the officer, who was looking decidedly dubious. Outside, on the campus, he noticed distant flashes coming from the projectors of television crews. He screwed up his eyes and distinguished the far-away figure of Vincent Luyse, the vice-chancellor, who was stammering out some reassuring declaration on the steps of the main building. He also made out the distinctive logos of the local, national and even Swiss television channels . . . A seething crowd of journalists, questions from all directions. The process had started. The lenses of the media were now focused on Guernon. News of the murders was about to spread across France, and panic had gripped the little town.

And it was just the beginning.

CHAPTER 37

As he walked on, Niémans phoned Antoine Rheims.

"Any news of our Englishman?"

"I'm at Hôtel-Dieu now. He still hasn't regained consciousness and the medics are sounding pessimistic. The British Ambassador has just let loose a pack of lawyers. They've come straight over from London. The journalists are here, too. Imagine the worst, then double it."

The satellite connection was perfect; Rheims's voice crystal clear.

Niémans pictured his boss on the Ile de la Cité, then saw himself once more in those hospitals, questioning prostitutes who had been beaten up by their pimps – their faces swollen, flesh torn by signet rings. He could also see the bloodied features of suspects he himself had shaken up a bit. Their hands cuffed to the bed, with a whole array of flashing lights and other gadgets, in the ghostly pallor of the room.

He saw the square outside Notre Dame, when he used to leave Hôtel-Dieu at three o'clock in the morning, weary, his mind in a whirl, in the bright silence of the night. Pierre Niémans was a warrior. And his memories had a metallic gleam, of ammunition belts, of the fires of combat. He felt a strong pang of regret for that strange existence, which few people would have wanted, but which was his sole reason for carrying on.

"How are your enquiries going?" Rheims asked.

His voice sounded less aggressive than it had during the last phone call. Solidarity between colleagues, their shared experiences and old intimacy were beginning to take control once again.

"We now have two murders. And not the slightest lead. But I'm keeping at it. And I know that I'm on the right track."

Rheims added nothing, but Niémans sensed that his silence indicated trust. He asked:

"And what about me?"

"What about you?"

"I mean, in the service. Is anyone looking into this hooligan business?"

Rheims laughed sardonically.

"You mean the disciplinary board? They've been waiting for this moment for ages. And they can wait a while longer."

"For what?"

"For the Brit to die. So they can do you for murder."

Niémans reached Annecy at about eleven o'clock. He drove down the town's large clear avenues, under the boughs of the trees. The leaves, lit up by the streetlamps, gleamed like pieces of gold. At the end of each street, Niémans encountered some small constructions that seemed to rise up from a well of light: newsstands, fountains and statues. At a distance of several hundred yards, these tiny objects looked like figurines in music boxes, or Christmas cribs. As though the town were hiding its treasures in cases of stone, marble or wood, along its squares and crossroads.

He went alongside the canals of Annecy, with their fake Amsterdam look, opening out in the distance onto the lake. The policeman could hardly believe that he was only a few miles away from Guernon, from his corpses, from his savage killer. He reached the town's residential area. Avenue des Ormes. Boulevard Vauvert. Impasse des Hautes-Brises. Names which, to the inhabitants of Annecy, were presumably impregnated with dreams of white stone, with symbols of power.

He parked his saloon at the end of the cul-de-sac, which sloped downwards. The tall houses were crammed in, one against the other, at once affected and overpowering, divided by gardens concealed behind verdigris walls. The number he was looking for corresponded to a large town house in cut stone, with an oblong glass porch. The policeman pressed twice on the diamond-shaped doorbell, the button of which was made to look like an eye. Beneath it, the plaque of black marble indicated: "Dr Edmond Chernecé. Ophthalmology. Eye Surgery".

No answer. Niémans looked down. The lock presented no difficulties and one more break-in would not now make any difference. He skilfully forced open the latch, and found himself in a marble-tiled corridor. Arrows indicated the direction of the waiting-room, down the corridor on the left, but the policeman was more interested in a leather-covered door to the right. The surgery itself. He turned the handle and discovered a long room, which was in fact a large veranda, its roof and two of its walls being entirely made of panes of glass. In the darkness, water could be heard trickling. It took Niémans a few seconds to distinguish a human form at the end of the room, standing in front of a sink.

"Doctor Chernecé?"

The man stared round at him. Niémans approached. The first detail he noticed with any precision were the doctor's hands, tanned and shining in the flowing water. Old roots, mottled with brown stains, the veins reaching up in a tangle toward the powerful wrists.

"Who are you?"

The voice was deep, and calm. The man was short, but extremely stocky, and he looked over sixty. White hair flowed out in luxuriant waves from his high sunburnt forehead, which was mottled with liver spots, too. A profile like a rock face, the build of a dolmen. The man looked like a monolith. A mysterious block of stone, made all the stranger because the doctor was wearing only a white tee-shirt and boxer shorts.

"Superintendent Pierre Niémans. I rang the bell, but nobody answered."

"How did you get in?"

Niémans flicked his fingers, like a circus conjurer.

"I improvised."

Without seeming at all put out by the policeman's lack of decorum, the doctor smiled elegantly. With his elbow, he turned off the long arm of the tap and walked across the transparent room, his forearms raised, in search of a towel. Oculist's instruments, microscopes, anatomical plates illustrating eyeballs, entire and cut open, appeared in the half-light. In a neutral tone of voice, Chernecé declared:

"I've already had one visit from a police officer this afternoon. What do you want?"

Niémans was now only a few feet away from him. And he realised that he had not yet noticed the man's main distinguishing mark, the one that set him apart from thousands of other people: his eyes. Chernecé's stare was colorless. Gray irises which gave him a look of snake-like vigilance. Pupils which resembled minia-ture aquariums, containing killer fish, protected by scales of steel. Niémans said:

"I'm here to ask you a few questions about him."

The man smiled indulgently.

"How original. Are the police now investigating one another?"

"What time did he come here?"

"About six this evening, I should think."

"That late? Do you remember what he asked you?"

"Of course I do. He questioned me about the inmates of a home near Guernon. A home for children suffering from eye problems, whom I regularly treat."

"What did he want to know?"

Chernecé opened a cupboard with mahogany doors. He picked out a light-colored shirt, with baggy sleeves, and rapidly slipped it on.

"He wanted to know the reasons for the children's conditions. I told him that they were hereditary diseases. He also asked if there might be another explanation for such problems, such as poisoning, or a wrongly administered drug."

"And what was your answer?"

"That the idea was preposterous. These genetic conditions arise from the town's isolation, and from interbreeding. Marriages between closely related people mean that the diseases are passed on, in the blood. This sort of phenomenon is well attested in communities that are cut off from the outside world. The region around the Lac Saint-Jean in Quebec, for instance, or the groups of Amish in the USA. And it also applies to Guernon. People from that valley do not mix with outsiders ... Why look for another explanation to the phenomenon?"

Without the slightest sign of embarrassment at Niémans's presence, the doctor was now pulling on some navy blue trousers, made of a slightly moiré material. Chernecé was clearly quite a snappy dresser. The policeman went on:

"Did he ask you anything else?"

"Yes. About grafts."

"What about grafts?"

He was buttoning up his shirt.

"Eye grafts. I had no idea what he was on about."

"He didn't tell you the reason for his enquiries?"

"No. But I answered as best I could. He wanted to know if there was any point removing people's eyes, with a view to performing a graft of the cornea, for example."

So, Joisneau had thought of the surgery angle.

"And?"

Chernecé went stock still, and wiped the back of his hand over his chin, as though testing the harshness of his stubble. The shadows of trees were dancing outside the panes of glass.

"I told him that such practices were now unnecessary. It is very easy to find substitute corneas these days. And much progress has been made in the production of artificial ones. As for the retinas, we still do not know how to preserve them, so grafts are out of the question ..." The doctor gave a slight chuckle. "You know, all those stories about the smuggling of organs are just urban myths."

"Did he ask you anything else?"

"No. And he looked disappointed."

"Did you advise him to go anywhere? Did you give him another address?"

Chernecé laughed affably.

"Goodness me. It rather sounds as though you have lost your fellow officer."

"Answer my question. Do you have any idea where he went after leaving here? Did he mention anything?"

"No. Absolutely not." His face hardened. "Now, would you mind telling me what all this is about?"

Niémans took the Polaroids of Caillois's corpse out of his coat pocket and laid them down on the desk.

"That's what it's about."

Chernecé put on his glasses, lit a small desk lamp and examined the photographs. The gaping eyelids. The empty sockets.

"Good Lord . . ." he murmured.

He seemed horrified and at the same time fascinated by the images. Niémans spotted a collection of chrome-plated probes in a Chinese pencil-case at the end of the desk. He decided to adopt a different line of approach. He had a specialist in front of him, so why not ask specialist questions?

"I now have two victims in this state. Do you think that it was a professional who mutilated them in this way?"

Chernecé looked up. His face was beaded with drops of sweat. He remained silent for some time, then asked:

"My God, what the hell do you mean?"

"I'm talking about the excision of the eyes. I've got some close-ups." Niémans handed him the photographs of the sockets. "Does it at all look like the work of a professional surgeon? Are there any specific signs? The killer carefully avoided cutting the eyelids. Is that easily done? Or does it require any special anatomical knowledge?"

Chernecé stared again at the images.

"Who could have done such a thing? What sort of . . . monster? Where did this happen?"

"Near Guernon. Doctor, would you answer my question? Do you think that this operation was carried out by a professional?"

The oculist stood up.

"I'm sorry. I . . . I don't know."

"What technique do you suppose he used?"

The doctor took another look.

"I think he slid a blade under the eyeballs . . . that he managed to slice through the optical nerves and oculomotor muscles thanks to the suppleness of the eyelid. I think that he then rotated the eye, using the flat of the blade as leverage. Rather as if with a coin, do you follow me?"

Niémans pocketed his Polaroids. The sunburnt medic watched his every move, as if he could still see the images through the material of the coat. On the bulwark of his chest, his shirt was stained with sweat.

"I'd like to ask you a general question," Niémans said. "Think carefully before answering it."

The doctor pulled back. The veranda seemed haunted by the dancing reflections of the trees. He gestured to the policeman to go on.

"What do you think eyes and hands have in common? What connection could there be between those two parts of the body?"

The oculist paced up and down for a moment. He had recovered his calm, the coolness of the man of science.

"The connection is obvious," he said at last. "Our eyes and our hands are the only two unique parts of our anatomy."

Niémans shivered. Since hearing the news from Costes, he had sensed this, but had been incapable of putting his finger on the reason. Now it was his turn to sweat.

"What do you mean?"

"Our irises are unique. They are made of thousands of fibrillae, which form a pattern which is distinct to each of us. A biological marker, created by our genes. The iris is as good a distinguishing mark as our fingerprints. So that is what our eyes and hands have in common. They are the only parts of our bodies to have a bio-logical, or biometric signature, as the specialists put it. Deprive a body of its eyes and hands, and you take away its external markers. Now, what is a man who dies without such markers? Nobody. An anonymous corpse, which has lost its personal identity. Even its soul, perhaps. Who knows? In some ways, it is the worst possible end. An unmarked, common grave of dead flesh."

The panes of glass were setting off reflected glints in Chernecé's colorless eyes, making them look even more translucent. The entire room now resembled a glass iris. The anatomical plates, the figure in the shadows, the claws of the trees – everything was dancing as though in the deepest reaches of a mirror.

An idea flashed into the superintendent's mind. Caillois's hands, which had lost their fingerprints, and which the killer had not removed. The murderer had clearly let them alone because they were already anonymous.

The killer was stealing his victims' biological signatures.

"In fact," the doctor went on, "I would say that the irises are a more certain means of identification than the fingerprints. Your specialists ought to look into the matter."

"Why do you say that?"

In the half-light, Chernecé smiled. He had recovered his professorial poise.

"Some scientists believe that it is possible to read in the irises not only a person's state of health, but also his entire history. Those little circles which glimmer around our pupils carry our very genesis ... Have you never heard of iridology?"

For some inexplicable reason, Niémans felt sure that this information was casting a new, transversal beam of light across the case. He did not yet know where it might lead, but he sensed that the killer shared the oculist's point of view. Chernecé went on:

"It is a study which was first started at the end of the nineteenth century. A German eagle-trainer noticed a curious phenomenon. One of his birds broke its foot. The man then observed that a new mark, like a golden scratch, had appeared in its iris. As though the accident had had an effect on the bird's eye. Such physical echoes exist, superintendent. I am sure about that. So, who knows? Maybe your killer removed his victims' eyes so as to wipe out the trace of some past event, which could be read in their irises."

Niémans backed off, letting the doctor's shadow fill up the space he left. He asked one final question:

"Why didn't you answer the phone this afternoon?"

"Because I unplugged it," he smiled. "I don't consult on Mondays. I wanted to spend my afternoon and evening tidying up my surgery."

Chernecé went back to the wardrobe and removed a jacket. He put it on with a broad, exact gesture. It was dark blue, airy and square-cut. As though finally grasping the reason for Niémans's visit, he said:

"So you tried to contact me this afternoon? I am sorry. I could have told you all this by telephone. Please forgive me for having you waste your precious time."

The words rang false. The man oozed egoism and indifference from every pore of his sun-tanned forehead. He had probably even forgotten about Rémy Caillois's stolen eyes by then.

Niémans gazed at the engravings of sliced-up eyeballs, the blood vessels dancing across the whites, as though mimicking the shadows of the trees through the thick panes of the ceiling and walls.

"I haven't wasted my time," he murmured.

Outside, Superintendent Niémans was in for another surprise. A man was apparently waiting for him, with his back to the light from the streetlamp, leaning on his saloon. He was as tall as Niémans, looked North African, with long dreadlocks, a colored woolly hat and a devil's beard. An experienced policeman can always spot a dangerous man when he sees one. And, despite his nonchalant pose, this bean-pole was certainly in that category. He reminded him of the drug pushers he had so often hunted down through the shadows of the Parisian nights. Niémans also reckoned that he probably had a gun hidden somewhere on his person. His hand clutching his MR73, he approached him and could not believe his eyes. The Arab was smiling at him.

"Superintendent Niémans?" he asked, when the policeman was just a few yards away from him.

The North African slid one hand into his jacket. Niémans immediately drew and aimed his gun.

"Don't move!"

The man with the sphinx face grinned, with a mixture of self-assurance and irony that was blown up to a degree that Niémans had rarely encountered before, even on the faces of the hardest suspects.

The Arab said, calmly:

"Easy does it, superintendent. My name's Karim Abdouf. I'm a police lieutenant. Captain Barnes told me that I would find you here."

He then rapidly completed his hand movement, waving his tricolor police card in front of him. Niémans cautiously put his gun away. He drank in the young Arab's extraordinary appearance. He could now make out the glinting of assorted ear-rings amid the dreadlocks.

"You're not from the Annecy brigade?" he asked incredulously.

"No. I'm here from Sarzac. In the Lot."

"Never heard of it."

Karim pocketed his card.

"We keep ourselves pretty much to ourselves."

Niémans smiled and peered once more at this apparition.

"So, what sort of a cop are you?"

The sphinx slapped his hand on the bonnet of the saloon.

"The sort of cop you need."

CHAPTER 38

The two officers drank a coffee in a small lorry drivers' café on the way back. In the distance could be seen the lights from a road-block and the glittering of cars braking in front of the barriers.

Niémans listened attentively to Abdouf's hastily told story, this cop who had sprung out of nowhere and whose investigations had quite suddenly become linked to the murders in Guernon. But his tale seemed incomprehensible. He told of a mysterious mother and her life on the run, of a little girl transformed into a little boy, of demons trying to destroy the child's face, because they considered it to be a piece of incriminating evidence ... It would all have sounded like the ravings of a madman, had the lieutenant from Sarzac not produced, amidst this deluge of information, formal proof that Philippe Sertys had desecrated a grave in a small town in the Lot, on Sunday night.

And this was vital evidence.

Philippe Sertys was, clearly, the desecrator of the tomb. Of course, it would still be necessary to compare the scraps of rubber found near the cemetery of Sarzac with the tires on his Lada. But, if this did check out, then it would mean that Niémans now had proof of the guilt of his second victim.

On the other hand, the superintendent could not see how to fit the other elements Karim Abdouf produced into his own investigations. All that nonsense about a mother and her little girl being pursued by "demons".

Niémans asked Karim:

"What's your conclusion?"

The young Arab fiddled nervously with a lump of sugar.

"I think that the demons were reawoken last night, for a reason that is unknown to me, and that Sertys went to the school and the cemetery in Sarzac to check something. Something to do with what happened in 1982."

"So, Sertys was one of your demons?"

"Exactly."

"But that's ridiculous," Niémans riposted. "In 1982, Philippe Sertys was only twelve. Do you really reckon a little kid like that terrified some mother and then chased her halfway across France?"

Karim Abdouf frowned.

"Yeah, I know. It doesn't all quite fit together yet."

Niémans smiled and ordered another coffee. He was not yet sure whether or not to believe everything Karim Abdouf had told him. Nor was he sure whether or not to trust an Arab who measured six foot two, had dreadlocks, carried an unauthorised automatic weapon, and was driving what was clearly a stolen Audi. But this tale was no crazier than his own hypothesis: the guilt of the victims. And the gutsy enthusiasm of this young Arab was highly contagious.

He finally decided to trust him. He gave him the key to his personal office, in the university, where Karim could take a look at the entire case and explain its arcane sides to him.

In hushed tones, the superintendent revealed his own deeply rooted convictions: the victims were guilty; the murderer was revenging one, or several criminal acts. He summed up the flimsy evidence at his disposal. Rémy Caillois's schizophrenia and brutality. Philippe Sertys's isolated warehouse and exercise book. Niémans also spoke of the "blood-red rivers", but without being able to explain this curious expression. Then he filled him in concerning the current situation: they were waiting for the results of the autopsy. Perhaps the body contained another message.

There was also the vague hope that all the enquiries being conducted in the region might produce something concrete. Finally, his voice dropped a tone. He mentioned Eric Joisneau, and how worried he was.

Abdouf asked several precise questions about the lieutenant's disappearance, which he seemed to find extremely interesting. So, Niémans asked him:

"What's your opinion about all this?"

The young cop smiled wearily.

"The same as yours, superintendent. I think your kid's in trouble. He must have turned up something important, then tried to go it alone so as to prove himself to you. I reckon he discovered something vital, then that vital something exploded on him. I hope I'm wrong, but your Joisneau may well have unmasked the murderer and this may well have cost him his life."

There was a pause. Niémans observed the lights from the distant road-block. He had not wanted to admit it to himself but, since waking up in the library, that was precisely what he had suspected. Karim went on:

"Don't think I'm a cynic, or anything, superintendent. Since this morning, I've been going from one nightmare to another. Now here I am in Guernon, up against a killer who rips his victims' eyes out. And sitting in front of you, Pierre Niémans, one of the stars of the French police force, who seems about as lost as I am in this dump of a town ... So, I'm not going to be surprised by anything any more. I reckon these murders are directly related to my own investigations and I'm ready to see it all through to the end."

The two policemen left.

It was midnight. A slight drizzle was filling the air. In the distance, the *gendarmerie* road-blocks lingered there in the rain. The drivers were waiting patiently to go through. Some of them were looking out through their wound-down windows, staring cautiously at the officers' machine-guns, which glistened in the damp air.

The superintendent instinctively glanced at his pager. There was a message from Costes. He called him at once.

"What is it? Have you finished the autopsy?"

"Not quite. But there's something I'd like to show you. Here at the hospital."

"Can't you tell me on the phone?"

"No, not really. Also, I'm waiting for the results of some tests. They should be here any minute. I'll be ready by the time you get here."

Niémans hung up.

"Anything new?" Karim asked him.

"Maybe. I've got to go and see the forensic pathologist. What about you?"

"I came here to question Philippe Sertys. Sertys is dead. So, I'll go on to the next stage."

"Which is?"

"To find out the circumstances of Judith's father's death. He died here in Guernon, and I'm pretty sure that my demons had a hand in it."

"What? You think they murdered him?"

"Yes, maybe."

Niémans shook his head.

"I've been all through the records in the *gendarmerie* and all the local police stations covering the last twenty-five years. There's no trace of anything like that happening . . . And, as I just said, Philippe Sertys was only a kid at the time."

"We'll see. Anyway, I'm certain I'll find a link between that death and the name of one or other of your victims."

"Where are you going to start?"

"In the cemetery." Karim smiled. "It's becoming my specialty. A second nature. I want to be sure that Sylvain Hérault was really buried in Guernon. I've already contacted Taverlay and traced Judith Hérault's birth certificate. The only child of Fabienne and Sylvain Hérault, born in 1972, here in the University Hospital of Guernon. Now what I need is the father's death certificate."

Niémans handed him the numbers of his cell phone and pager.

"For confidential messages, use the pager."

Karim Abdouf pocketed the scrap of paper and declared, in a semi-professorial, semi-ironic tone:

"'In an investigation, each fact, each witness is a mirror, in which part of the truth behind a crime is reflected' . . ."

"What?"

"I attended one of your lectures, superintendent, while I was at the police academy."

"And?"

Karim turned up the collar of his jacket.

"And, as far as mirrors are concerned, our two investigations go together like this."

He put out his two palms and pointed them slowly toward each other.

"They're mirror reflections, get me? And in one of the dead angles, Jesus, I'll bet on it, the murderer is lurking."

"And how can I get in touch with you?"

"I'll call you. I asked for a cell phone, but the 1997 Sarzac budget wouldn't run to that."

The cop bowed an Arabian farewell and disappeared into the night. Niémans, too, went back to his car. He took a last look at the brand-new Audi as it pulled off into the drizzle. He suddenly felt older, wearier, as though oppressed by the night, the years, the uncertainty. A taste of oblivion rose up in his throat. But he also felt stronger. He now had an ally.

One hell of an ally.

CHAPTER 39

The crystals glittered with a rainbow profusion of pinks, blues, greens and yellows. Multi-colored prisms. Shattered light, kaleidoscopic, under the transparent slides. Niémans raised his eye from the microscope and asked Costes:

"What are they?"

The doctor replied incredulously:

"It's glass, superintendent. This time, the killer left behind some pieces of glass."

"In which part of the body?"

"In the eye-sockets again. Just under the lids. They were stuck there, like little petrified tears."

The two men were in the hospital morgue. The doctor was wearing a blood-stained white coat. It was the first time that Niémans had seen him dressed like that, standing stock still like a porcelain statue. The clothes and the place gave him a sort of icy authority. Behind his glasses, the forensic pathologist was smiling.

"Water, ice, glass. There's an obvious link between these substances."

"I can still spot the obvious, thank you," Niémans grumbled, as he went over to the body, which was laid out under a sheet in the center of the room. "But what does it mean? Or rather, where does it point us next? Is there anything special about this glass?"

"I'm still waiting for Astier's results. He rushed off back to his lab to carry out an in-depth study of the glass and try to work out where it comes from. He should also be bringing the results of the tests on the wire meshes and white powder you found in the warehouse. He's already analysed the ink in the exercise book, and his findings are disappointing. It's just common-or-garden stuff. Nothing more. As for the pages of figures, we can do nothing until we have something more to go on. But we did check the handwriting, and it certainly belongs to Sertys."

Niémans ran his hand through his brush of hair; he had almost forgotten about the evidence found in the warehouse. Silence descended. The policeman glanced up and noticed how Costes's face was sparkling with intelligence, as if a solved mathematical equation was gleaming in the pupils of his eyes. Irritated, the superintendent asked:

"What's up?"

"Nothing . . . It's just . . . Water, ice, glass. Each time, it's a crystal."

"As I just told you, that much is obvious, but . . ."

" . . . but one that corresponds to a different temperature."

"I'm sorry?"

Costes slapped his hands together.

"The structures of these substances exist at different levels of temperature, superintendent. The coldness of ice, the room temperature of water, and the burning of sand at an extreme heat to turn it into glass."

Niémans dismissed the idea with an angry gesture.

"So what? What can that tell us about the murders?"

Costes hunched his shoulders, as though drawing back into his shell.

"Nothing. I was just thinking aloud . . ."

"I'd rather you told me about the mutilations on the body."

"Apart from the fact that the hands have been amputated, the body is identical to Caillois's. Minus the signs of torture."

"Sertys wasn't tortured?"

"No. I suppose the killer already knew what he wanted to know. And so got straight down to business. Mutilation of the eyes and hands. Then strangulation. But the pain must still have been intolerable. Because it looks as if he started with the mutilations. He cut off the hands, extracted the eyes and only then finished off his prey."

"How was he strangled?"

"In the same way. The killer used a metal wire. First he strapped him up with it, just like last time. The weals on the limbs are identical."

"What about the hands? How were they amputated?"

"Hard to say. It looks to me as if the same cable was used. Something like a cheese wire, which the killer must have tied round the wrists, then tightened with extraordinary force. We're looking for a monster, superintendent. Someone with almost superhuman strength."

Niémans thought for a moment. Despite these new details, he just could not picture the murderer. Not even his physique. Something was holding him back. All he could see was an entity, a force, a field of energy.

"And the time of death?" he asked.

"Forget it. He was frozen into the ice. There's absolutely no chance of drawing even the vaguest conclusion about that."

The door of the morgue flew open. A bean-pole with an anaemic face, squashed nose and a bright stare burst through it. His eyes were like saucers. Costes took care of the introductions. Patrick Astier, Pierre Niémans. The chemist put down a small plastic bag onto the bench, and went straight to the heart of the matter:

"I've got the composition of the glass. Fontainebleau sand, soda, lead, potassium and borax. The exact composition allows us to deduce where it comes from. It is the sort used for sculpted blocks of glass. You know, like in swimming pools, or in houses from the 1930s. The killer must be pointing us toward some place of that sort, covered with thick panes of glass . . ."

219

Niémans turned on his heels. An image had flashed into his mind of the walls and ceiling in that oculist's surgery. He swore to himself. This could not just be a coincidence. Edmond Chernecé must be the third victim.

Marc Costes called him back when he was already half out of the door.

"Where are you going?"

Niémans answered over his shoulder:

"I might have worked out where the killer's going to strike next. If it's not already too late."

The policeman set off down the corridor. Astier ran after him and grabbed him by the sleeve.

"Superintendent, I also have the composition of that white dust in the warehouse . . ."

Pierre Niémans peered at the chemist through his glasses, which were beaded with sweat.

"What?"

"You know, the samples you picked up in that warehouse."

"And?"

"They're bones, superintendent. Animal bones."

"What sort of animal?"

"Probably rats. I know it sounds crazy, but Sertys must have been breeding rats and . . ."

Another shiver. More pinpricks.

"Later," Niémans panted. "Later. I'll be back."

Niémans wrenched convulsively at his steering wheel. He was driving at more than ninety miles per hour.

If Dr Edmond Chernecé was the third victim, then he was also a culprit.

After Rémy Caillois.

After Philippe Sertys.

And if Chernecé was guilty, then it also meant that he had murdered young Eric Joisneau.

Jesus fucking Christ. The superintendent bit his lips to stop himself from screaming out loud. He ran through all the mistakes he had made since the outset. And drew up a report of his own incompetence. He had not wanted to go to that home for the blind because of all that crap about dogs. And so he had missed out on the first real lead.

After that, he had gone right off the rails.

While he had been inching forward in his investigations, playing the apprentice mountaineer in the glaciers, or questioning Sertys's mother, Eric Joisneau had gone straight to the home for the blind and found out something important. Something which had then led him to Dr Chernecé. But the young lieutenant was now over-extending himself. He had been incapable of evaluating the gravity of his own discoveries. The kid had not been sufficiently wary of the doctor, had questioned him about some vital aspect of the case, some element of the truth which personally threatened the oculist. So, Chernecé must have killed him.

In Niémans's mind, another terrifying certainty began to crystallise itself, even though he had not a scrap of supporting evidence, apart from his own instinct: Caillois, Sertys and Chernecé had committed some crime together. They shared a common responsibility.

A deadly one.

> WE ARE THE MASTERS, WE ARE THE SLAVES.
> WE ARE EVERYWHERE, WE ARE NOWHERE.
> WE ARE THE SURVEYORS.
> WE CONTROL THE BLOOD-RED RIVERS.

Could that *we* refer to those three men? Was it possible that Caillois, Sertys and Chernecé controlled the "blood-red rivers"? That they had been behind some plot against the entire town, and that this conspiracy was the motive for the murders?

CHAPTER 40

This time, the front door was ajar. Niémans forked straight off to his right and entered the glass veranda. Shadows. Silence. Optical instruments glinting arrogantly. The policeman drew his revolver and walked round the room, gun in hand. Nobody. Only the patterns of the trees, still dancing on the floor, filtered through the thick panes of glass.

He went back into the house. He glanced round the darkened waiting-room then paced across the marble hall, where walking sticks with ivory or horn handles stood in an umbrella rack. He found a sitting-room crammed with cumbersome furnishings and hung with tapestries, then some old-fashioned bedrooms with large beds made of varnished wood. Nobody. No trace of a struggle. No trace of a sudden departure.

Still holding his MR73, Niémans went up the staircase to the first floor. He entered a small office, which smelt of bees' wax and cigars. He found some luggage made of fine leather, with gold-plated locks, laid out on a worn Turkish rug.

He explored further. The entire place stank of danger. Of death. Through an oval window he saw the high tips of the trees, still being shaken by the wind. After a second's thought, he realised that this window looked down over the glass ceiling of the veranda. He shoved it open and gazed down at that transparent covering.

His blood froze in his veins. In the panes, splattered with rain, could be seen the reflection of Chernecé's body, rippling in the sculpted glass. Arms open, feet together, he had been crucified. A martyr reflected in a lake of greenish waters.

Swallowing back a scream of rage, Niémans looked again at this mirror image and worked out the exact position of the real body. He pushed the window fully open and leant out, gazing up at the top of the façade. The body was suspended just above his head.

In the blustering rain, Edmond Chernecé had been fixed up against the outer wall, like a ghastly figurehead.

The superintendent pulled himself back inside, rushed out of that tiny office and leapt up a second staircase of narrow wooden steps, stumbling as he went, until he had reached the attic.

Another window, another sill, and he was now perched on the gutter, with the closest possible view of the corpse of Dr Edmond Chernecé, deceased. The eyes had gone from the face. The empty sockets were exposed to the rain and the wind. Both arms were wide open and finished in bloody stumps. The body was being maintained in this position by a network of gleaming, twisted wires, which sliced into the chubby sunburnt flesh. Beaten by the deluge, Niémans took stock.

Rémy Caillois.

Philippe Sertys.

Edmond Chernecé.

All the things he was certain about ran through his mind. NO: the murders had not been committed by a sexual pervert attracted to some particular type of face, or anatomy. NO: this was not a serial killer, massacring innocent victims according to his crazy whims. This was a rational murderer, someone who stole his victim's biological identity, and who had a precise motive: revenge.

Niémans let himself drop back down into the attic. The only sound in that house of death was the beating of his heart. He knew that his mission was not over. He realised what the last episode of this nightmare would be. Eric Joisneau's body was somewhere, hidden in that building.

A few hours before being a victim, Chernecé had been a killer.

Niémans went through each room, each piece of furniture, each recess. He tore apart the kitchen, the living-room, the bedrooms. He dug up the garden, emptied out a shed that stood under the trees. Then, on the ground floor, he discovered a door that had been covered over with wallpaper. He frantically yanked it off its hinges. The cellar.

As he rushed down the stairs, he thought over the sequence of events. If, at eleven o'clock, he had found the doctor in a tee-shirt and shorts, then he must just have finished his ghastly operation – Joisneau's murder. That was why he had unplugged his phone. That was why he had so neatly tidied up his surgery, after having stabbed the young lieutenant, probably with one of those chrome-plated probes which Niémans had spotted in the Chinese pencil-case. That was also why he had put on a clean suit and packed his bags.

Stupidly, blindly, Niémans had questioned a murderer who was just fresh from his bloody crime.

In the cellar, the superintendent discovered a set of metal racks, swamped over with cobwebs, containing hundreds of bottles of wine. Dark glass, red wax, yellow labels. He examined every nook and cranny in the cellar, moving aside the barrels, pulling at the metal racks, and sending the bottles crashing onto the floor. The pools of wine started to give off a heady stench.

Bathed in sweat, screaming and spitting, Niémans at last found a trench, concealed by two iron flaps. He broke open the lock.

Under these trap doors lay the body of Eric Joisneau, half submerged in some dark corrosive liquid. Around him floated various bottles of acid for unblocking drains. The chemicals had already started their terrible work, soaking up the gases of the body, eating into its flesh, transforming it into flurries of steam, gradually annihilating the biological entity that had once been Eric Joisneau, a lieutenant with the Grenoble brigade. The kid's open eyes seemed to be staring up at the superintendent from the bottom of that terrifying grave.

Niémans backed off and screamed crazily. He felt his ribs rising up, opening like the struts of an umbrella. He spewed up his guts, his fury, his remorse, grabbing hold of the bottle racks, in a shower of broken glass and rivers of wine.

He did not know exactly how long he stayed like that. In the fumes of the alcohol. In the rising smoke from the acid bath. But, little by little, the last part of the truth began to form in his mind, like a dark stagnant pond. It had nothing to do with the death of Eric Joisneau. But it cast new light on the murders in Guernon.

Marc Costes had mentioned the link between the substances associated with each murder: water, ice and glass. Niémans now realised that this was not relevant. What was relevant was how each body had been discovered.

Rémy Caillois had been found thanks to a reflection in the river.

Philippe Sertys to a reflection in the glacier.

Edmond Chernecé to a reflection in the glass roof.

The killer had so arranged his victims that their mirror-images were discovered before the real bodies.

What did that mean?

Why did the killer put himself out so as to set up this multiplication of appearances?

Niémans did not know what lay behind this strategy, but he sensed there was a connection between these reflections and the thefts of the eyes and hands, which robbed the bodies of their unique, biological identities. He sensed that all this was part of the same sentence, proclaimed by an implacable judge: the destruction of the entire BEING of the condemned. What, then, had these men done to deserve being reduced to mirror-images, to being deprived of their biological signatures?

VIII

CHAPTER 41

The cemetery in Guernon was unlike the one in Sarzac. White tombstones jutted up like tiny symmetrical icebergs across the dark lawns. The crosses stood out as though they were strange figures, stretched up onto the tips of their toes. The only vague sign of disorder was the dead leaves – yellow blotches on the immaculate grass. With methodical patience, Karim Abdouf was making his way around each alley, reading the names and epitaphs that were engraved in the marble, stone or metal.

So far, he had not found Sylvain Hérault's tomb.

As he walked on, he thought over the case, and the extraordinary developments of the last few hours. He had rushed as quickly as he could to this town, and had had no qualms about "borrowing" a superb Audi for transport. He had imagined that he would then arrest a desecrator of graves and now he found himself after a serial killer. Now that he had read and memorised the entire file in Niémans's office, he was forcing himself to believe that it truly tied in with his own investigations. The burglary at the school and the violation of the tomb in Sarzac had revealed the tragic destiny of a family. And that destiny had now led to this series of murders in Guernon. Sertys was the link between the two cases and Karim had decided to follow his own nose until he had turned up other common points, other connections.

But it was not this terrible spiral which fascinated him most. It was the fact that he was now working alongside Pierre Niémans, the superintendent who had made such a strong impression on him during his time at the police academy. The cop with the reflecting mirrors and atomic theories. A violent, short-tempered, obstinate man of action. A brilliant detective, who had carved out a superb place for himself in the world of criminal investigation, but who had finally been put out to grass because of his uncontrollable temper and his fits of psychotic violence. Karim could not stop thinking about his new partner. Naturally, he felt proud. And thrilled. But also disturbed at the uncanny way he had been thinking of the man only that day, a few hours before meeting him.

Karim had just completed the last alleyway in the cemetery. No Sylvain Hérault. All he had to do now was to pay a call on a building which rather resembled a chapel, propped up by cracked columns: the crematorium. He rapidly strode over toward it. Explore every avenue. Always. A corridor opened out in front of him, dotted with small plaques bearing names and dates. He walked on into the mausoleum, glancing from left to right as he advanced. Little containers, like pigeon holes, were piled up covered with a variety of different lettering and designs. Sometimes, a wilting, multi-colored wreath lay at the bottom of a niche. Then the old monochrome dullness started all over again. At the end, a wall of sculpted marble bore the words of a prayer.

Karim walked on. A damp breeze, little more than a draught, whistled between the walls. Slender columns of plaster rose up from the floor, over a carpet of dried petals.

It was then that he found it.

The commemorative plaque. He went up to it and read: "Sylvain Hérault. Born February 1951. Died August 1980." Karim had not been expecting Judith's father to have been cremated. It just did not fit in with Fabienne's religious beliefs.

But it was not this which astonished him most. It was the fresh red flowers, dripping with sap and dew, that were lying just beneath the opening. He fingered the petals. The wreath was extremely recent. It must have been laid there that day. The policeman spun round, stopped and clicked his fingers.

The chase was still on.

Abdouf left the cemetery and walked all round its walls, looking for a house or building that might be occupied by a keeper. He discovered a grim, tiny dwelling which abutted the left side of the sanctuary. A pale light shone from one of its windows.

He silently opened the gate and entered a garden, which was roofed off by a sort of enormous cage. A sound of cooing could be heard. Where the hell had he ended up this time?

Karim took another few steps – the cooing grew louder and a flapping of wings broke through the silence. He screwed up his eyes and examined a wall of niches, rather reminiscent of the inside of the crematorium. Pigeons. Hundreds of gray pigeons were dozing in small dark green compartments. The policeman climbed up the three steps and rang the doorbell. It opened at once.

"What do you want, you bastard?"

The man was pointing a pump-action shotgun at him.

"I'm from the police," Karim calmly declared. "Just let me show you my card and . . ."

"Course you are, you fucking A-rab. And I'm the Queen of fucking England. Don't move!"

The cop backed down the steps. The insult had electrified him. The murderous fury which had been lying dormant inside him woke up.

"I told you not to move!" the gravedigger yelled, aiming his gun at the cop's face.

Saliva foamed from the corners of his mouth.

Karim continued to back off slowly. The man was shaking. He, too, started coming down the steps. He was brandishing his weapon like a hardy peasant with a pitchfork confronting a vampire in a B-movie. Behind them, the pigeons were fluttering their wings, as though stricken with the tension.

"I'll blow your fucking brains out, I'll . . ."

"I don't think so, grandpa. Your piece's empty."

The man grinned.

"It is, is it? I loaded it last night, dick-head."

"Maybe you did. But you didn't put the bullet in the breech."

The man glanced down rapidly at his gun. And Karim was in. He leapt up the two steps, pushed the oily barrel away with his left hand, while drawing his Glock with his right hand. He threw the man back against the door frame and crushed his wrist against the corner.

The gravedigger screamed and dropped his gun. When he opened his eyes, it was to see the black orifice of the automatic, poised a few inches away from his forehead.

"Now you listen to me, fuck-face," Karim whispered. "I need some information. You answer my questions, then I go. Nice and easy. You fuck me about, and things will start getting nasty. Very nasty. Specially for you. Clear?"

The cemetery keeper nodded, his eyes bulging. All sign of aggression had vanished from his features, to be replaced by a fiery redness. It was the "red panic" that Karim knew so well. He gave the wrinkled throat another squeeze.

"Sylvain Hérault. August 1980. Cremated. I'm listening."

"Hérault?" the gravedigger stammered. "Never heard of him."

Karim dragged him forward then slammed him back against the wall. The man grimaced. Blood splattered the stone, just behind his neck. The panic had even infected the niches. The pigeons, imprisoned by the wire mesh, were now flapping around in every direction. The cop murmured:

"Sylvain Hérault. His wife's very tall. A brunette. Curly hair. Glasses. And very beautiful. Just like his daughter. Think."

The man's head started nodding up and down convulsively.

"All right, all right, I remember ... It was a really strange funeral ... There was nobody there ..."

"Nobody there?"

"Just like I said, nobody, not even his missus. She paid me in advance for the cremation, and was never seen again in Guernon. I burnt the body. I ... I was all on my own."

"So what did he die of?"

"An ... an accident ... A car accident."

The Arab remembered the autoroute and those awful photographs of the child's body. So tragic car accidents had now become another leitmotif, another recurring factor. Abdouf released his grip. The pigeons were now zooming around crazily, smashing themselves into the caged roof.

"Give me some details. What happened exactly?"

"He ... he got himself run over by a hit-and-run driver on the road that goes to the Belledonne. He had a bike ... He was going to work ... The driver must have been blotto ... I ..."

"Was there an inquest?"

"I dunno ... Anyway, they never found out who did it ... They just found his body on the road ... It was completely crushed."

Karim shivered.

"You said he was going to work. What was his job?"

"He worked in the villages up the mountains. He was a crystaller."

"What's that?"

"Someone who goes up to the highest peaks and digs out precious stones ... Apparently, he was the best of the bunch. But he used to take terrible risks ..."

Karim changed the subject.

"Why didn't anyone in Guernon come to his funeral?"

The man was massaging his neck, which was burnt as if he had just been hanged. He peered round in terror at his wounded pigeons.

"They were newcomers ... From another place ... Taverlay ... In the mountains ... Nobody was interested in coming to the funeral. So there wasn't anyone, just like I told you."

Karim asked a final question:

"There's a wreath of flowers just by his urn. Who laid it there?"

The keeper rolled his eyes in panic. A dying bird flopped down onto his shoulders. He choked back a cry, then stammered:

"There's always flowers by it . . ."

"So who puts them there?" Karim repeated. "Is it a tall woman? A woman with a flowing head of brown hair? Is it Fabienne Hérault?"

The old man shook his head vigorously.

"Who then?"

He hesitated, as though afraid to pronounce that name which was trembling on his lips in a foam of saliva. Feathers floated down like flocks of gray snow. At last, he whispered:

"It's . . . it's Sophie . . . Sophie Caillois."

Karim was dumbstruck. Suddenly, another link had been established between the two cases. A chain that was now encircling his neck. He pushed his face right up into the man's ear and barked: "WHO?"

"It's . . ." he stuttered. "Rémy Caillois's wife. She comes here every week. And sometimes more often than that . . . When I heard about the murder on the radio, I meant to call the police . . . Really I did . . . I was going to tell them what I knew . . . It might be relevant . . . I . . ."

Karim threw the old man back against the dovecot. He pushed open the iron gate and ran to his car. His heart was beating fit to bust.

CHAPTER 42

Karim made his way to the university's main building. He immediately picked out the officer stationed at the front entrance; presumably the one whose job it was to keep an eye on Sophie Caillois. He casually continued on his way, drove round the block, and discovered a side door made of two dark panes of glass, under a cracked concrete porch, partly covered over with a plastic sheet. He parked his car one hundred yards away and looked at the map of the university, which he had collected from Niémans's HQ, and which indicated Sophie Caillois's flat: number 34.

He went out into the rain and strolled over to the door. He formed his hands into a telescope and placed them against the glass, in order to see what was inside. The two doors were bolted together with an ancient motorbike wheel lock, in the shape of a hoop. The rain began to pour down, beating against the plastic sheeting in a crazed techno rhythm. It was making a loud enough din to drown out any noise of a break-in. Karim stepped back and smashed the glass with one kick.

He dived down the narrow corridor, then found himself in a huge dark hall. A glance through the windows revealed that the shivering officer was still at his post. He took the staircase to his right, leaping up the steps four at a time. The lamps on the emergency exits allowed him to find his way without having to switch on the neon lighting. Karim did his best not to make the hanging staircase resonate under his steps, nor the vertical metal slats which rose up at the center.

The eighth floor, where the boarders lived, was plunged into silence. Still following Niémans's annotated map, he advanced down the corridor and examined the names written above the doorbells. Under his feet, he felt the cold cushioning of the linoleum.

Even at two o'clock in the morning, he had been expecting to hear some music, a radio, anything resembling the usual noises that went with student life. But here, there was no sound. Perhaps they were all barricaded into their rooms, terrified of having their eyes ripped out by the killer. Karim continued on his way and finally found the door he was looking for. He decided not to ring the bell and instead knocked lightly.

No answer.

He gave it another gentle knock. Still no answer. And no sound from inside. Not the slightest murmur. Odd. The presence of the sentry man downstairs meant that Sophie Caillois was at home.

Instinctively, Karim drew his gun and peered at the lock. The door was not bolted. He slipped on his latex gloves and took out a set of polymer rods. He slipped one of them under the latch and pushed against the door, heaving the rod upwards at the same time. It opened almost at once. Karim went in as noiselessly as a whisper.

He went through each room. Nobody. His sixth sense told him that she had taken off. For good. He started to search the place more thoroughly. He examined the strange pictures on the walls – black-and-white photos hung up on hooks depicting Nazi athletes running round a stadium. He went through the furniture, pulled out the drawers. Nothing. Sophie Caillois had left no message, no clear sign that she had gone – yet Karim sensed that she was gone for good. And also that he could not yet leave. Some mysterious detail was holding him back. He paced around, staring up and down in an attempt to identify what was bugging him.

At last, he found it.

There was a strong smell of glue in the air. Wallpaper paste, only just dry. Karim hurriedly examined each of the walls. Had both the Caillois simply been redecorating a few days before all this violence had broken out? Was this just a coincidence? Karim rejected that hypothesis. In this case, there were no coincidences. Every single element was a part of the overall nightmare.

Impulsively, he pushed aside some of the furniture and stripped away a section of the wallpaper. Nothing. He stopped for a moment. He was outside his jurisdiction. He had no search warrant. And here he was vandalising the flat of a woman who was about to become a prime suspect. He hesitated, swallowed hard, then ripped away a second section. Nothing. Karim spun round and attacked a different part of the wall. As he pulled, the paper peeled off easily, revealing a large area of the previous layer.

On the wall, he could make out the end of an inscription written in brown. The only word he could read was "RIVERS". He stripped away the section that lay to the left. Under the smeared paste, the message appeared in its entirety:

I SHALL REACH THE SOURCE
OF THE BLOOD-RED RIVERS

JUDITH

The handwriting belonged to a child, and it was written in

blood. The inscription was engraved into the plaster, as if it had been dug out with a knife. Rémy Caillois's murder. The "blood-red rivers". Judith. It was no longer a matter of connections, of vague relationships, of echoes. The two cases had now become one.

Suddenly, he heard a slight shuffling behind him. In a reflex action, Karim wheeled round holding his Glock in both hands. He just had time to see a figure disappear through the half-open door. He cursed and dived after it.

The form had just vanished round a corner of the corridor. The sound of running had already roused the neighbors, as though they had been on the qui vive, ready for the slightest sign of danger. Doors were opening to reveal frightened faces.

The cop sped along to the first turning, then leapt forward, sprinting down the next straight. He could already hear footsteps echoing down the hanging staircase.

He, too, started down the well. The metal slats quivered as the shadow rapidly descended the granite steps. Karim was in full pursuit. His metal-studded shoes touched down only once per flight.

The floors shot by. Karim was gaining. He was now only a few paces from his prey. They were going down the same storey, on either side of the barrier of metal slats. In the darkness, the cop could just make out the gleaming black of an oil-skin jacket. He shot one of his hands in between the symmetrical iron blades and seized a shadowy sleeve, just under the shoulder. Not firmly enough. His arm was thrown away, becoming stuck in among the metal slats. The figure made off. Karim accelerated again. He had lost a few seconds.

He reached the massive hall. It was completely deserted. Utterly silent. Karim noticed the guard who was still outside. He sprinted toward the side entrance, through which he had come in. Nobody. A sheet of rain obscured the exterior scene.

Karim swore. He went out through the smashed pane and stared across the campus, hazed over by the gray glints of the downpour. Not a sign of life. No cars. Only the din from the plastic sheeting, which was making a furious slapping noise. Karim lowered his gun and turned back. There was now one hope left: the shadow might still be inside.

Suddenly, a tidal wave hit the glass panes of the door. In a moment of confusion, he dropped his weapon. An icy torrent had engulfed him. Crouching on the ground, Karim glanced upwards and realised that the plastic sheeting over the porch had just given way under the weight of the rain.

A simple accident.

But then, behind the plastic sheet, still suspended from the roof by two cords, he saw a gleaming dark shape. A black oil-skin, polycarbonate leggings, a face masked by a balaclava and topped by a cyclist's helmet, gleaming like the head of a massive bumble bee, the shadow was holding Karim's Glock in both hands, and aiming it toward his face.

The cop opened his mouth, but not a word emerged.

The shadow abruptly pressed the trigger, emptying the magazine with a cascade of breaking glass. Karim curled into a ball, protecting his face with his hands. He screamed out in a cracked voice, as the din from the shots mingled with the smashing of glass and the thundering downpour. Karim mechanically counted the sixteen bullets and dared to look up only when the last cartridge cases had flopped out onto the ground. He just had time to see a naked hand drop the gun, before vanishing behind the curtain of rain. It was a dark hand, with knotted muscles, scratched and covered with plasters, and with short clipped nails.

A woman's hand.

The cop looked down for a few seconds at his Glock, which was still smoking through its breech. Then he stared at its grip, crisscrossed with tiny diamond shapes. His mind was still jolting in time with the gun blasts. His nostrils were full of the pungent smell of cordite. A few seconds later, the policeman who was guarding the main entrance arrived, gun in hand.

But Karim was oblivious to his warnings and panic-stricken yells. Amid this apocalypse, he had acquired two vital pieces of evidence.

First: the murderer was a woman and she had spared his life.

Second: he had her fingerprints.

CHAPTER 43

"What were you doing in Sophie Caillois's flat? You're outside your jurisdiction, you've infringed the most basic rules, we could . . ."

Karim watched Captain Vermont as he worked himself up. Head bare, his face was going puce. Karim nodded and did his best to look contrite. He said:

"I've already explained everything to Captain Barnes. The Guernon murders are linked to a case I'm investigating . . . Crimes that were committed in my town, Sarzac, in the Lot."

"Very interesting. But it doesn't explain your presence in the flat belonging to one of our principal witnesses, nor the violation of property."

"I had an agreement with Superintendent Niémans to . . ."

"Forget Niémans. He's been taken off the case." Vermont flung the official mandate down onto the desk. "The boys from the Grenoble brigade have just arrived."

"Really?"

"Superintendent Niémans is in a lot of trouble. The other night, he beat up an English football hooligan after the match at the Parc des Princes. Things are starting to look nasty. He's been called back to Paris."

Karim now understood why Niémans was working in this little town. He must have been trying to lie low, after an umpteenth piece of brutality. One of his trademarks. But he could not imagine him going back to Paris that night. Not at all. And he could not imagine him dropping this case – and certainly not if it was to go and stand before a disciplinary board. Pierre Niémans would unmask the killer, having first uncovered a motive. And Karim would be there by his side. However, he played at following the gendarme's drift:

"So are the Grenoble boys on the case already?"

"Not yet," Vermont replied. "We'll have to give them the low-down first."

"It doesn't sound as though you're going to miss Niémans."

"Oh yes I am. He might be a headcase, but at least he knows the world of crime. It's his backyard. With the Grenoble brigade, we're going to have to start all over again from scratch. And where will that get us, I wonder?" Karim stuck his fists down onto the desk and leant across toward Vermont.

"Give Superintendent Henri Crozier a ring, at the Sarzac police station. He'll confirm my story. Jurisdiction, or no jurisdiction, my enquiries are linked to the Guernon murders. Philippe Sertys, one of the victims, desecrated a cemetery on my patch. Last night. Just before he was murdered."

Vermont pouted skeptically.

"Then write up a report. Victims desecrating a cemetery. Policemen cropping up from nowhere. Don't you reckon this story is already complicated enough as it is . . ."

"I, uh, . . ."

"The murderer has struck again."

Karim turned round. Niémans was standing in the door frame. His face was livid and strained. It reminded the Arab of the grave-yard sculptures he had encountered in the last few hours.

"Edmond Chernecé," Niémans went on. "An ophthalmologist in Annecy." He walked over to the desk, staring at Karim, then at Vermont. "Strangled with a cable. Eyes gone. Hands gone. The series has only just begun."

Vermont pushed his chair back against the wall. After a moment's pause, he murmured plaintively:

"I told you so . . . Everyone told you so . . ."

"What? What did you tell me?" Niémans yelled.

"That it's a serial killer. A psychopath. Like in the States! We'll have to use the same methods as they do. Call in some specialists. Draw up a psychological profile . . . That sort of thing . . . Even a provincial cop like me knows that . . ."

Niémans bellowed:

"This is a series, but not with a serial killer! Our murderer's no madman. This is revenge. He has a perfectly rational motive for killing his victims. There is a link between those three men, which explains their deaths. That's what we should be looking for, for fuck's sake!"

Vermont was silent. He gestured wearily. Karim butted in:

"Superintendent, may I . . ."

"Not now."

Niémans stretched and, with twitching hands, pressed out the creases in his coat. This concern for his appearance sat uneasily with the cop's inscrutable expression. Karim tried again:

"Sophie Caillois's taken off."

The metal-framed eyes turned round toward him.

"What? Wasn't someone watching her?"

"He didn't see anything. And, if you want my opinion, she's already long gone."

Niémans weighed up Karim, as though he was a strange, genetically improbable animal.

"What the fuck's all this about now?" he asked. "Why would she have run away?"

"Because you've been right all along." Karim was speaking to the superintendent, but staring at Vermont. "The victims share a secret. And this secret is linked to the murders. Sophie Caillois has split because she knows that secret. She might even be the murderer's next victim."

"Jesus Christ . . ."

Niémans readjusted his glasses. He stopped to think for a few seconds, then motioned with his chin, like a boxer, for Karim to go on.

"I've got something new, superintendent. In the Caillois's flat, I discovered an inscription scratched into one of the walls. It's signed 'Judith' and mentions 'the blood-red rivers'. You were looking for a common factor between the victims. I can at least suggest one between Caillois and Sertys: Judith. My little girl. My missing face. Sertys desecrated her tomb. And Caillois received a message signed with her name."

The superintendent headed for the door.

"Come with me."

Vermont stood up in anger.

"That's right, get lost, both of you! You and your mysteries!"

Niémans was already pushing Karim out into the corridor. The captain's voice roared on:

"You're off the case, Niémans! It's official! Don't you understand that? You're nothing any more ... Nothing! You don't count for shit! So go and listen to your darky's ranting ... A bent cop and a thug! The two of you are made for each other! I'll ..."

Niémans burst into an empty office, a few doors down the corridor. He shoved Karim inside, turned on the light and closed the door, cutting short the gendarme's speech. He grabbed a chair, handed it to the Arab, then whispered simply:

"I'm listening."

CHAPTER 44

Still standing, Karim launched into his explanations:

"The inscription on the wall reads: 'I shall reach the source of the blood-red rivers'. It's written in blood and was scratched into the plaster with a blade. It's enough to scare the shit right out of you. Specially since the message is signed 'Judith', in other words, 'Judith Hérault'. Who's dead, superintendent. She died in 1982."

"I don't get it."

"Neither do I," Karim sighed. "But I can imagine some of the events of that weekend."

Niémans, too, remained on his feet. He slowly nodded his head. The Arab went on:

"Right. So the killer starts by knocking off Rémy Caillois, probably some time on Saturday, then mutilates the body and wedges it up into that rock face. But Christ knows what lies behind all that elaborate staging. The next day, our murderer goes on the look-out somewhere on the campus so as to keep an eye on Sophie

239

Caillois. At first, she stays put. But she finally makes a move, let's say around mid-morning. Perhaps she goes up into the mountains to look for her husband, for example. Meanwhile, the killer breaks into the flat and inscribes a signed confession into the wall: 'I shall reach the source of the blood-red rivers'."

"Go on."

"Later, Sophie Caillois comes back home and finds the message. She immediately understands what it means. The past has come back to haunt them, and her husband has obviously been murdered. She panics, breaks the code of secrecy and phones up Philippe Sertys who is, or was, Rémy Caillois's accomplice."

"What's your evidence for all this?"

Karim leant over and whispered:

"My notion is that the Caillois couple and Sertys were childhood friends and that they committed some crime or other together when they were kids. A crime that is linked to the expression 'blood-red rivers', and Judith's family."

"Karim, I've already told you that in the early 1980s, Caillois and Sertys were about ten, how can you imagine that they . . . ?"

"Let me finish. Philippe Sertys arrives at the Caillois's flat. He, too, reads the inscription and understands the reference to "the blood-red rivers". It's now total panic stations. But the first thing to do is hide the inscription which refers to some secret that they absolutely have to conceal. That much I'm sure of – despite Caillois's death and the threat of a killer who's using the name 'Judith', Sertys and Sophie Caillois's initial reaction is to cover up this message which reveals their own guilt. The auxiliary nurse then rushes off to get some wallpaper, which he pastes over the words. Which is why there's a strong smell of glue in the place."

Niémans's eyes were shining. Karim realised that the superintendent had obviously noticed that detail, too, presumably while questioning the woman. He went on:

"They spend all Sunday waiting, or perhaps search for Rémy again. I don't know. Finally, at the end of the afternoon, Sophie Caillois decides to inform the police. At that very moment, the body is discovered in the cliff."

"And then?"

"Then, that night, Philippe Sertys heads off for Sarzac."

"Why?"

"Because Rémy Caillois's murder was signed 'Judith', and Sertys knows that Judith has been dead and buried in Sarzac for the last fifteen years."

"Sounds a bit far-fetched."

"Maybe it is. But Sertys was certainly in my town last night, with an accomplice who might well be our third victim, Edmond Chernecé. They searched through the archives of the primary school. They went to the cemetery and opened Judith's tomb. Where do you look for a dead person? In the grave."

"Go on."

"Now, I don't know what Sertys and his friend find out in Sarzac. I don't know if they open the coffin. I wasn't allowed to carry out a thorough search of the tomb. But I figure that they were not particularly reassured by their discoveries. So, with panic in their guts, they go back to Guernon. Jesus, can you just imagine it? A ghost is on the prowl, who's all set to wipe out the people who once harmed it . . ."

"You haven't got a shred of evidence for all this."

Karim ignored this remark.

"It's now dawn on Monday, Niémans. As he goes home, Sertys gets jumped by our ghost. No torture session, no third degree. The killer already knows the truth and is simply carrying out a program of revenge. So the phantom takes a cable car and places the body up in the mountains. Everything has been pre-meditated: a first clue was left on the first victim and a second one will be left on the second victim. And so on. Your vengeance hypothesis is starting to take off, Niémans."

The superintendent slumped down onto the chair. He was glistening with sweat.

"But vengeance for what? Who is the killer?"

"Judith Hérault. Or, rather, someone who's acting on her behalf."

241

Head down, the superintendent remained silent. Karim leant over further:

"I found Sylvain Hérault's memorial in the town crematorium, Niémans. There's nothing particularly suspicious about his death. He was killed by a hit-and-run driver. Though maybe that is worth looking into, I don't know . . . But it was the urn itself which taught me something of interest. There was a wreath of fresh flowers in front of it. So I asked who put them there. And who do you think has been bringing flowers for the last few years? Sophie Caillois."

Niémans was now shaking his head, as though in a fit of dizziness.

"And what's your theory about that?"

"I reckon it's because she feels guilty."

The superintendent did not bother to respond. Abdouf raised himself up and yelled:

"But it all fits, for Christ's sake! I can't imagine Sophie Caillois as a real criminal, but she shared her husband's secret and kept quiet about it, because she loved him, or was frightened of him, one or the other. Meanwhile, she discreetly carried on putting flowers in front of Sylvain Hérault's urn, out of respect for the family which her guy had persecuted."

Karim knelt down. His dreadlocks were almost brushing against the superintendent.

"Just think it through," he pleaded. "Her husband's body has just been discovered. The murder has been signed by 'Judith', and so is clearly the vengeance of a little girl from the past. And even then, she goes and puts a fresh wreath on the father's tomb the next day. These murders have not provoked hatred in Sophie Caillois. They've revived her memories. And her regrets. Shit, Niémans, I'm sure I'm right. Before vanishing, she wanted to pay her last respects to the Hérault family."

The superintendent remained silent. His face had become so strained that its wrinkles were deepening out into dark crevices. Seconds ticked by. At last, Karim got to his feet and continued hoarsely:

"Niémans, I've carefully read through your findings. They contain other indications, more evidence which points toward Judith Hérault."

The old cop sighed.

"I'm listening. Christ knows why, but I'm still listening."

The lieutenant was now pacing up and down, like a caged lion.

"In the file, you say that the only sure thing about the killer is that he is an experienced mountain climber. And what was Sylvain Hérault's profession? A crystaller. Someone who climbs the highest peaks to dig the crystals out of the rock. He was a brilliant mountaineer. He spent all his life on rock faces and in glaciers. The very places where the first two bodies were found."

"Him and hundreds of other qualified climbers in the region. Is that all?"

"No. There's also fire."

"What fire?"

"I noticed a detail in the report of the first autopsy. And it's been bugging me ever since. Rémy Caillois's body had traces of burns. Costes says that the murderer sprayed gasoline over his victim's wounds. He mentions some sort of adapted aerosol."

"And?"

"And, there could be another explanation. The killer might have been a fire-eater, who spat flames out of her mouth."

"I'm sorry?"

"There's something you don't know: Judith Hérault once learnt to be a fire-eater. It sounds incredible, but it's true. I met the performer who taught her his technique, just a few weeks before she died. Apparently, it fascinated her. She told him that she wanted to use it as a weapon, to protect her 'mum'."

Niémans was massaging the nape of his neck.

"For fuck's sake, Karim. Judith's dead!"

"There's one other thing, superintendent. It's just a vague indication, but it might fit into the overall scheme. In the report of the first autopsy, the forensic pathologist noted that the victim had been strangled with 'a metal cord, perhaps a brake cable or a piano wire'. Was Sertys killed the same way?"

The superintendent nodded. Karim went on:

"Maybe it doesn't mean anything, but Fabienne Hérault was a pianist. A virtuoso. If we suppose that it really was a piano wire which was used to kill the three victims, then this could be another symbolic link. A wire plugged into the past."

Pierre Niémans finally got to his feet and shouted:

"Where the hell are you headed, Karim? What are we supposed to be doing? Ghost hunting?"

Karim shuffled around nervously in his leather jacket, like a guilty child.

"I dunno."

It was Niémans's turn to start pacing up and down.

"What if it's the mother?"

"No," Karim replied. "It can't be her." He lowered his voice. "Keep listening, superintendent. I've kept the best bit for the end. When I was in the Caillois's flat, I caught a glimpse of the ghost. I ran after it, but it escaped."

"What?"

Karim grinned apologetically.

"Shame on me."

"What did he look like?" Niémans asked at once.

"What did *she* look like? A woman. I saw her hands. I heard her breathing. There's no doubt about it. She's about five feet nine inches tall. She looked pretty powerful, but she was not Judith's mother. The mother was a colossus, six feet tall and with the shoulders of a shot-putter. All the eye-witnesses agree on that point."

"So who was it?"

"I don't know. She was wearing a black oil-skin, a cyclist's helmet and a balaclava. That's all I can tell you."

Niémans came to a stop.

"Let's put out her description."

Karim grabbed his arm.

"What description? A cyclist in the night?" Karim smiled. "But I might have something better than that."

From his pocket, he removed his Glock, which was wrapped up in a plastic bag.

"Her fingerprints are on it."

"She held your gun?"

"She even emptied it over my head. She's quite an original murderess, superintendent. She's carrying out a psychopathic vengeance, but I'm sure she doesn't mean any harm to the rest of humanity."

Niémans threw open the door.

"Go up to the first floor. The Grenoble brigade have brought round a fingerprint analyser. A brand new computer plugged straight into MORPHO. But they can't make it work. So Patrick Astier, one of our technical guys, is helping them. Go and see him – Marc Costes, the forensic pathologist, should be there with him. Take them to one side, tell them your story and ask them to compare the prints with the records on MORPHO."

"What if they don't tell us anything?"

"Then look for the mother. Her evidence is going to be vital."

"I've been looking for her for the last twenty hours, Niémans. She's well hidden somewhere."

"Start all over again. You might have missed something important."

Karim bridled.

"I haven't missed anything at all."

"Yes you have. Didn't you say that the little girl's tomb, in your town, has been well looked after? So, someone must go there on a regular basis. Who? Surely not Sophie Caillois. Get an answer to that question, and you'll find the mother."

"I asked the cemetery keeper. He's never seen anybody . . ."

"Perhaps she doesn't go there herself. Maybe she pays a company of undertakers to do it, I don't know. Find who it is, Karim. Anyway, you're going back there to open the coffin."

The Arab shuddered.

"Open the . . ."

"We have to know what the desecrators were looking for. Or what they found. In it, you'll also find the address of the funeral parlor." He winked in a sinister fashion. "Coffins are like pullovers. The label's on the inside."

Karim swallowed hard. The idea of returning to Sarzac cemetery, of plunging back into that darkness and of descending into that vault was turning his legs to jelly. But Niémans rounded off imperiously:

"First the fingerprints. Then the cemetery. We've got until dawn to find the answers, Karim. Just you and me. And no one else. Then we'll have to go back home and face the music."

The Arab raised his collar.

"What about you?"

"Me? I'm going to try to reach the source of the blood-red rivers. I'll follow up the lead young Eric Joisneau discovered. He found out part of the truth all on his own, before . . ."

"Before what?"

Niémans's face became ravaged.

"Before Chernecé killed him, just prior to being murdered himself. I found his body in a vat of chemicals in the doctor's cellar. Chernecé, Caillois and Sertys were pieces of shit, Karim. That much I'm sure of. And I reckon Joisneau found out something which pointed in that direction. And it cost him his life. Find the identity of the murderer, and we'll find the motive. You find out who's acting as Judith's ghost. And I'll find out the meaning of 'the blood-red rivers'."

Without a glance at the other gendarmes, the two men vanished down the corridor.

CHAPTER 45

"Nothing doing, guys, nothing doing . . ."

"Anyway, we haven't got any prints to go on, so why bother . . . ?"

At the threshold of a tiny room on the first floor, a group of cops was staring in desperation at a computer, topped by a mobile magnifying glass, and connected to a scanner by a network of cables.

Inside the compartment, a tall fair-haired young man, his eyes like saucers, was struggling to fix the parameters of some software. Karim was told that this was Patrick Astier, in person. By his side stood Marc Costes – dark-haired, stooping, with large misted-up specs.

The cops bustled off down the narrow corridor, muttering an assortment of philosophical reflections concerning modern technology's lack of reliability. They paid no attention to Karim.

He went over and introduced himself to Costes and Astier. The three men immediately sensed that they were on the same wavelength. Young and keen, they were so absorbed in this investigation that they were suppressing their own fears. When the Arab had explained what he wanted, Astier could hardly restrain his excitement. He cried out:

"Shit! The killer's fingerprints? Really? We'll get them on the computer straight away."

Karim exclaimed:

"Does it work, then?"

The scientist grinned. A tiny crack in his china-white face.

"Course it does." He waved over at the cops, who were already otherwise occupied. "They're the ones that don't compute."

Astier rapidly opened one of the nickel-plated cases which Karim had noticed in a corner of the room. Kits for revealing latent fingerprints and taking moulds of their traces. The scientist removed a magnetic brush. He slipped on some latex gloves, then dipped the bristles into a box containing ferrous oxide powder. The tiny particles immediately grouped themselves together into a pink ball at the tip of the magnetic brush. Astier grabbed the Glock and ran the instrument over its grip. He then applied a strip of transparent adhesive across it, which was in turn glued onto a sheet of cardboard. The silvery whirls of the fingerprints promptly started to shine out below the translucent plastic.

"Brilliant," Astier exhaled.

He slipped the kit into the scanner, then sat down again in

front of the screen. He pushed aside the rectangular magnifying glass and worked on the keyboard. Almost at once, the prints flashed up onto the screen. Astier observed:

"First-class quality prints. We can make a twenty-one point digital analysis. The highest one possible . . ."

Bright red dots, linked up by sloping lines, appeared above the hills and valleys. The apparatus bleeped like a hospital monitor. As though talking to himself, Astier went on:

"Now let's see what MORPHO comes up with."

It was the first time Karim had seen the system in operation. In professorial tones, Astier explained how MORPHO was a massive computer file containing the fingerprints of criminals from most of the countries of Europe. Via a modem, the software was able to compare any new set of prints with the records almost instantaneously. The hard disc was crackling with activity.

Finally, the computer delivered its answer: negative. The ghost's prints did not match any known delinquents. Karim stood up and sighed. It was what he had been expecting. The murderer was certainly no common criminal. Suddenly, he had another idea. His wild card. From his leather jacket, he produced the cardboard strip which bore the fingerprints of Judith Hérault, taken just after that fatal car accident fourteen years before. He asked Astier:

"Could you scan these prints, too, and make a comparison?"

Astier spun round on his chair and grabbed the card.

"No problem."

The scientist was now sitting bolt upright. He glanced briefly at the new set of prints. He stopped to think for a moment, then raised his hyacinth blue eyes to Karim.

"Where did you get this lot from?"

"From a autoroute station. They belong to a little girl, who was killed in a car accident back in 1982. Who knows? They might be similar, or . . ."

The scientist cut him off:

"She can't have been killed."

"What?"

Astier slid the card under the glass. The loops and whirls loomed up, glistening, hugely magnified.

"I don't even have to analyse these prints to be able to tell you that they're the same as the ones on the gun. Same transversal peaks, same whirls just below the peaks."

Karim was utterly amazed. Astier moved the magnifying glass on the computer over, so that the two sets of prints were now juxtaposed.

"They're the same," he repeated. "But at two different ages. The ones on your card belong to a child, the ones on the grip to an adult."

Karim stared at the two images and drank in the impossible.

Judith Hérault had died in 1982, in the shattered wreck of a car.

Judith Hérault, dressed in an oil-skin and a cyclist's helmet, had just emptied his Glock over his head.

Judith Hérault was both dead and alive.

CHAPTER 46

It was time to call up one of his former colleagues.

Fabrice Mosset, one of Paris's finest fingerprint experts, whom Karim had got to know while solving a particularly sordid crime during his training period in the fourteenth *arrondissement* police station on Avenue du Maine. A brilliant man, who claimed he could spot twins just by glancing at their prints. According to him, the method was as reliable as genetic sampling.

"Mosset? It's Abdouf. Karim Abdouf."

"How's it going? Still buried in your hole?"

A sing-song voice. Light years away from this nightmare.

"Yup," Karim murmured. "Except that I've been traveling from one hole to another."

The scientist chuckled.

"Like a mole?"

"Like a mole. Mosset, I've got an apparently insoluble problem for you. Can you give me your opinion? Off the record, and straight away. OK?"

"You're on a case? No problem. Fire away."

"I've got two sets of identical prints. One lot belong to a little girl who died fourteen years ago. The others come from an unknown suspect and were taken today. What do you reckon?"

"You're sure the little girl's dead?"

"Definitely. I questioned the man who held the corpse's arm over the inkpad."

"Then all I can say is that someone made a mistake. You or your colleagues must have slipped up when taking the prints on the scene of the crime. It's impossible for two different people to have the same fingerprints. Ab-so-lu-tely impossible."

"Can't they be members of the same family? Twins? I remember your program and . . ."

"Only prints belonging to homozygous twins have points in common. And the genetic laws are extremely complex. Millions of different parameters determine the final patterns of the dactylic spirals. It would require an incredible coincidence for two distinct sets to be that similar . . ."

Karim broke in.

"You got a fax in your place?"

"I haven't gone home yet. I'm still in the lab." He sighed. "There's no peace for the scientific."

"Can I send you my files?"

"Honestly, there's nothing more I can tell you."

The lieutenant remained silent. Mosset sighed again:

"OK. I'll go to the fax. Call me straight back afterward."

Karim left the tiny office where he had taken refuge, sent the two faxes, returned to his den and pressed redial on his phone. Gendarmes were toing and froing. In the general confusion, nobody paid any attention to him.

"Very impressive," Mosset mumbled. "And you're certain that

the first card belongs to a dead girl?"

The black-and-white photographs of the accident flashed across Karim's mind. The child's frail limbs emerging from the crushed bodywork. Once again, he saw the face of the old officer who had kept the file.

"Definitely," he replied.

"Then there's been some mix up with the ID mentioned on the file. It happens, you know, we . . ."

"You don't seem to get it," Karim murmured. "Who cares about the ID? Who cares about the names and the spelling? What I'm telling you is that the hand of a dead child bore the same spirals as the hand that seized my gun tonight. That's all. I don't give a toss about the goddam identity. It's the same hand, I'm telling you!"

There was a pause. A moment of suspense in that electric night, then Mosset burst out laughing.

"Your story's impossible, bud. That's all I can say."

"You used to come up with better ideas than that. There must be an answer!"

"There always is. You know that as well as I do. And I'm sure you'll find out what it is. Ring me back when you do. I like stories with a happy ending. And a rational explanation."

Karim promised to do so, then hung up. Cogs were whirring crazily in his mind.

He bumped into Marc Costes and Patrick Astier again in the corridors of the police station. The forensic pathologist was carrying a leather bag, with diamond stitching, and was looking wan.

"I'm off to the Annecy University Hospital," he explained. He glanced round incredulously at his companion. "We . . . we've just heard that there are two bodies. Shit! That young cop . . . Eric Joisneau . . . he bought it as well. This isn't an investigation any more, it's a goddam massacre."

"I know. I've heard. How long will you need?"

"Till dawn, at the earliest. But another pathologist is already there. Things are hotting up."

Karim stared at the doctor whose sharp features made him look both boyish and haughty. He looked frightened, but Abdouf sensed that his own presence reassured him.

"Costes, I've just thought of something ... Can I ask you a question?"

"Sure."

"In your first report you talk about the metal cord used by the killer and say it was perhaps a brake cable or a piano wire. Do you think Sertys was killed with the same one?"

"Yes, it was the same. The same texture. The same diameter."

"If it was a piano wire, could you work out which note it was?"

"Which note?"

"Yeah. The note. By measuring the diameter, could you decide which pitch it corresponded to in the musical scale?"

Costes smiled in astonishment.

"I see what you mean. I calculated the diameter. Do you want me to ... ?"

"You or your assistant. But the note interests me."

"You've got a lead?"

"I don't know."

The forensic pathologist fiddled with his glasses.

"Where can I contact you? Do you have a cell phone?"

"No."

"Now you do."

Astier had just thrust a tiny black, chrome-plated mobile into Karim's hand. The Arab blinked. The scientist smiled.

"I've got two. And I think you'll be needing one in the next few hours."

They exchanged numbers. Marc Costes hurried off. Karim turned toward Astier.

"And what are you going to do now?"

"Not a lot." He opened both of his large empty hands. "I've got nothing for my machines to work on any more."

Karim promptly asked the scientist to help in his own investigation and undertake two missions on his behalf.

"Two missions?" Astier repeated enthusiastically. "As many as you want!"

"First, go and check the list of births in the Guernon University Hospital."

"What are we after?"

"For 23 May 1972, you should find the name of Judith Hérault. See whether she didn't have a twin brother or sister."

"That's the girl with the fingerprints?"

Karim nodded. Astier went on:

"You're wondering if another kid might have exactly the same prints?"

The cop smiled in embarrassment.

"I know. It doesn't hold water. Just do it, anyway."

"And the second mission?"

"The girl's father was killed in a car accident."

"Him too?"

"Yeah, him too. Except that he was on a push-bike and he got run over. It was in August 1980. His name's Sylvain Hérault. Check it out, here in the police station. I'm sure there must be a record of it."

"What are you looking for?"

"The precise circumstances of the accident. He was knocked over by a hit-and-run driver. Go through every detail. There may be something odd about it."

"Meaning . . . he was killed accidentally on purpose?"

"Yeah, that sort of thing."

Karim turned on his heel. Astier called him back:

"And where are you going?"

He spun round nimbly, looking almost jovial in the face of the coming terror.

"I'm going back to square one."

IX

CHAPTER 47

The home for the blind was a bright building. Not like the fake brightness of the houses in Guernon, but a splendid edifice standing in the pouring rain, at the foot of Les Sept-Laux. Niémans approached the main entrance.

It was three o'clock in the morning. All the lights were out. Peering across the long sloping lawns that surrounded the structure, the superintendent rang the bell. He then noticed some photoelectric cells on the small posts around the perimeter. This invisible network was thus a system of alarms, presumably for warning the inmates when they had strayed too far from home, rather than for warning off potential burglars.

Niémans rang once more.

An astonished janitor finally opened the door and listened to his explanations without once batting an eyelid. He then showed the superintendent into a large room, before departing to wake up the director.

Niémans waited. The room was lit solely by the lamp in the hall. Four white concrete walls, a bare floor, which was also white. A double staircase at the end, which rose up into a triangle, with banisters of pale, undressed timber. Lamps that were sunk into the ceiling of taut cloth. Bay windows, with no handles, through which the adjacent mountains could be seen. It felt like a new-age sanatorium, clean and invigorating, designed by some architect with rapidly changing moods.

Niémans spotted some more photoelectric detectors. The partially

254

sighted residents were thus constantly cordoned off. The rain poured endlessly down the panes, casting shadows across the partitions. A scent of wax and of cement hung in the air. The place was not quite dry yet and totally lacked any human warmth.

He walked on. One detail puzzled him: the room was dotted with easels, with drawings made up of strange symbols. From a distance, they looked like a mathematician's equations. From closer up, he made out thin primitive bodies, topped by faces with haunted expressions. Astounded, Niémans realised that he was in an art studio in a home for unsighted children. But, most of all, he was feeling deeply relieved. So much so, that he could feel the fibers of his skin relaxing. Since his arrival, he had not heard a single bark or rustling of fur. Were there really no dogs in this home for the blind?

Suddenly, footsteps echoed on the marble. The policeman then realised why the floors were all bare. The building had been made for people who used their ears to see. He turned round to discover a strapping man with a white beard. A sort of patriarch, with red cheeks, sleepy eyes, and a yellow cardigan. He immediately sensed that this was someone he could trust.

"I'm Dr Champelaz. I run this home," the big man declared in a bass voice. "What the hell do you want at this time of night?"

Niémans handed him his tricolor card.

"Superintendent Pierre Niémans. I'm here in connection with the murders in Guernon."

"Another visit?"

"Yes, another one. The first visit you received, that of Lieutenant Eric Joisneau, is in fact precisely what I want to ask you about. I think that you must have given him some vital information."

Champelaz looked worried. The reflected raindrops made tiny rivers across his immaculate white hair. He gazed down at the handcuffs and gun on Niémans's belt. Then he raised his head.

"My God . . . all I did was answer his questions."

"And your answers led him to Edmond Chernecé's residence."

"Yes, of course they did. And?"

"And, they're both now dead."

"Dead? But, they can't be ... That's ..."

"I'm sorry, I don't have time to explain it all now. What I'd like you to do is to repeat exactly what you told him. Without knowing it, you are in possession of some very important evidence."

"But, I don't understand ..."

The man stopped in his tracks. He rubbed his hands together energetically, with a mingled feeling of cold and apprehension.

"Well, in that case ... I'd better wake myself up properly, hadn't I?"

"I rather think so, yes."

"Would you like some coffee?"

Niémans nodded. He followed where the patriarch led, down a corridor of high windows. Flashes of lightning momentarily lit up the air, followed by renewed semi-darkness, broken only by the serpentine pathways of the rain. The superintendent felt as though he were walking through a forest of phosphorescent creepers. On the walls facing the windows, he noticed some more drawings. This time, of landscapes. Mountains with chaotic skylines. Streams sketched in with pastels. Huge animals, with coarse scales and overly numerous vertebrae, which seemed to come from an age of stone, an age of monsters when mankind was the size of a mouse.

"I thought that your center was only for blind children."

The director turned round and joined him.

"Not only. We treat all sorts of different eye conditions."

"For example?"

"Pigmentary retinitis. Color blindness ..."

The man pointed a powerful finger at the pictures.

"These images are peculiar. The children here do not see reality in the same way we do, nor even their own drawings, for that matter. The truth – their truth – lies neither in the real landscape, nor on the paper. It is in their minds. They alone know what they wanted to express, and we can get but a glimpse of it, through their artwork and through our normal vision. Rather disturbing, don't you think?"

Niémans gestured vaguely. He could not take his eyes off those strange drawings. With their broken contours, as though crushed by some heavier matter. Their shrill, vivid colors. Like a battlefield of lines and shades, but which also gave off a feeling of gentleness, an echo of ancient nursery rhymes.

The man slapped him on the back.

"Come on. Some coffee will do you good. You look all in."

They entered a large kitchen. The furnishings and utensils were all made of stainless steel. The gleaming walls reminded Niémans of a morgue or a death chamber.

The director poured out two mugs of coffee from a round shiny pot, which was heated permanently. He handed one to the policeman then sat down at a stainless steel table. Once again, Niémans thought of bodies during an autopsy, the faces of Caillois and of Sertys. Their dark, empty eye-sockets, like black holes in space-time.

Champelaz declared in astonishment:

"I just cannot believe what you told me . . . Those two men are both dead? But how?"

Pierre Niémans ducked the question.

"What did you tell Joisneau?"

Stirring the coffee in his mug, the doctor shrugged.

"He asked me about the conditions we treat here. I explained that they are generally hereditary diseases, and that most of my patients come from the families in Guernon."

"Did he ask you anything in particular?"

"Yes. He wanted to know how such diseases are contracted. I gave him a brief explanation of how recessive genes work."

"Which is?"

The director sighed, then calmly went on:

"It's quite simple. Certain genes carry diseases. They are defects, spelling mistakes in the system. We all have them, but fortunately not in sufficient quantity to trigger off such a condition. But, if both parents have the same gene, then things can start to go wrong and their children can contract the affliction. The genes merge together and transmit the disease, rather like a plug and a socket which allow the current to flow through, you follow me? That is why we say that inbreeding weakens the blood. It's an expression which means that two closely related parents have a high chance of passing a latent disease, which they both carry, on to their children."

Chernecé had already mentioned that fact. Niémans pressed on:

"So the hereditary diseases in Guernon are down to inbreeding?"

"Definitely. Many of the children we look after here, either as in-patients or out-patients, come from that town. And in particular from the families of lecturers and researchers at the university. It's an elite society, and hence extremely isolated."

"Sorry, could you be more precise?"

Champelaz crossed his arms and held forth.

"There is an extremely ancient university tradition in Guernon. The college dates back to the eighteenth century, I believe, and was set up in conjunction with the Swiss. In the past, it was in what is now the hospital ... Anyway, for almost three centuries, the university teachers and researchers have been living on the campus and marrying one another. They produced several lines of highly gifted thinkers, but now their inheritance is genetically exhausted. Guernon was already cut off, like all towns lost in the bottoms of valleys. But the university created a sort of isolation within that isolation, you follow me? A true microcosm."

"And that isolation is enough to explain the outbreak of genetic diseases?"

"Yes, I think so."

Niémans failed to see how this information might be of importance. "What else did you tell Joisneau?"

Champelaz tilted his head, then declared in his booming voice:

"I also told him about a particular point of interest. Something rather odd."

"What's that?"

"Over the last generation, families with this weakened blood have been producing radically different children. They are intellectually brilliant, but they are also possessed of an inexplicable

258

physical strength. Most of them win all the sports competitions while at the same time gaining the highest academic distinctions."

Niémans remembered the portraits in the vice-chancellor's antechamber, young radiant champions carrying off all the cups and medals. He also recalled the photographs of the Berlin Olympics and Caillois's door-stopper about the good old days of Olympia. Could all of these elements really fit together into the overall design?

Playing dumb, the policeman asked again:

"You mean, all of those children should really be sick?"

"It's not that straightforward, but it must be said that they should have weak constitutions and suffer from recursive conditions, like the children in this home. But they don't. On the contrary, it is as if these little supermen had made off with the entire community's genetic wealth and left all its genetic poverty to the others." Champelaz glanced awkwardly at Niémans. "You're not drinking your coffee."

Niémans remembered that he had a mug in his hands. He took a scalding sip. He barely felt the heat. It was as if his entire being was tensed up, ready to pounce on the slightest sign, the slightest glimpse of the truth. He asked:

"Have you made an in-depth study of this phenomenon?"

"About two years ago I did look into it, yes. I started by checking to see if the champions really did come from the same families, and same blood-lines. I went to the local registry office and . . . All the children in question are of the same stock. After that, I took a closer look at their family trees. I checked their medical records at the maternity clinic. I even went through their parents' records and their grandparents', too, in the hope of digging out some sort of explanation. But I found nothing conclusive. Some of their ancestors were even carriers of the same hereditary diseases as the ones I now treat . . . It was all decidedly odd."

Niémans drank in every detail. Without knowing why, he once again sensed that this information was going to be of vital importance.

Champelaz was now pacing up and down the kitchen, making the stainless steel echo icily.

"I questioned the doctors and obstetricians at the university hospital, who informed me of another fact which astounded me. Apparently, over the last fifty years, the families in the villages, up on the slopes of the mountains around the valley, have experienced an abnormally high rate of infant mortality. Cot deaths, immediately after delivery. But such children are, generally, extremely healthy. We seem to be witnessing a sort of inversion, you see? The children of the university families have magically become extremely strong, while the offspring of the country folk have become corrupted ... So I examined the medical records of those farmers' and crystallers' children who had suddenly died. I discovered nothing of interest. I discussed the matter with the hospital staff and some of the medical researchers who specialised in genetics. Nobody could come up with a reasonable explanation. So I let the subject drop, but remain dissatisfied. How can I put it? It is as if the children of the university were robbing their little neighbors of their life force."

"My God, what do you mean?"

Champelaz immediately drew back from this dangerous territory.

"Forget I said that. It's hardly scientific. And totally irrational."

Irrational maybe, but Niémans now felt certain that the mystery of those highly gifted children was not a matter of chance. It was one of the links in the nightmare. He asked hoarsely:

"Is that all?"

The doctor hesitated. The superintendent's voice went up a tone:

"Is that really all?"

"No," Champelaz winced. "There is something else. Last summer, this story took a strange turn, which was at once trivial and disturbing ... In the month of July, the Guernon hospital was totally refurbished, which also meant computerising its archives. Specialists went through the basement, which is brimming over with old dusty files, in order to estimate how long the job would take. Their task also led them to investigate the cellars of the original university building, and in particular the pre-1970s library."

Niémans froze. Champelaz went on:

"And the experts made a curious discovery during their investigations. They found some birth papers, that is to say the first pages of the newly-born babies' medical records, covering a period of about fifty years. But these pages were on their own, without the rest of the files, as though . . . as though they had been stolen."

"Where were these papers found? I mean, where exactly?"

Champelaz paced back across the kitchen. He was struggling to maintain a detached tone, but agitation was breaking into his voice.

"That's the strangest part of all . . . They were all stacked together in files belonging to one man, a member of the library staff."

Niémans felt the blood accelerating in his veins.

"And his name was?"

Champelaz glanced nervously at the superintendent. His lips were trembling.

"Caillois. Etienne Caillois."

"Rémy's father?"

"Exactly."

The policeman sat up.

"And it's only now you tell me that? With the body we found yesterday?"

The director bridled.

"I do not like your tone of voice, superintendent. Please do not mistake me for one of your suspects. In any case, this was a mere slip-up in the paperwork. What on earth could it have to do with the Guernon murders?"

"I'm the one who'll decide that."

"So be it. Anyway, I already told all of this to your lieutenant. So calm down. What is more, this whole story is certainly no secret. Everyone in town knows about it. It is public knowledge. It was even in the local press."

At that precise moment, Niémans would not have liked to see

his face in a mirror. He knew that his expression was so harsh, so tense, that the mirror itself would not have recognised him. He wiped his forehead with his sleeve and said, more coolly:

"I'm sorry. This case gives me the creeps. The killer has already struck three times and will again. Every minute, every scrap of information counts. Where are those old records now?"

The director raised his eyebrows, relaxed slightly and leant once more on the stainless steel table.

"They were put back in the hospital basement. The archives are to be kept together until they have been fully computerised."

"And I suppose that those papers included records of our little supermen . . . ?"

"Not directly – they date back to before the 1970s. But some of them did include their parents or grandparents. That was what I found strange. Because I had already examined their records myself, during my research. And the official files were all complete, you follow me?"

"Had Caillois simply made some copies?"

Champelaz started shifting around again. The weirdness of his story seemed to electrify him.

"Copies . . . or else the originals. Caillois had perhaps replaced the genuine notifications of birth in the records with false ones. Which is to say that the real ones were discovered in his files."

"Nobody mentioned this to me. Did the gendarmes look into it?"

"No. There was no big scandal. It was just an administrative slip-up. What is more, the only possible suspect, Etienne Caillois, had died three years before. In fact, I'm the only person who seems interested in all this."

"Exactly. And did you try to consult these newly discovered records? To compare them with the official versions?"

Champelaz forced himself to smile.

"I meant to. But finally I didn't have time. You don't seem to grasp what these documents are. Just a few columns photocopied onto a loose sheet, giving the weight, height and blood group of the baby . . .

"This information is then copied out the next day onto the child's personal medical records. They are just the first link in the chain."

Niémans recalled how Joisneau had wanted to see the hospital archives. These papers might sound irrelevant, but he had clearly thought they would be of interest. The superintendent suddenly changed the subject:

"What brought Edmond Chernecé into all this? Why did Joisneau go to see him immediately after leaving you?"

At once, the director looked hunted again.

"Edmond Chernecé was extremely interested in the children I just mentioned."

"Why?"

"Chernecé is ... or, rather, was this home's official doctor. He knew all about our patients' genetic conditions. So he was well-placed to find it odd that other children, their first or second cousins, should be so different from the ones we treat. What is more, genetics fascinated him. He thought that a person's genetic history could be read in his irises. In some respects, he was a rather eccentric practitioner ..."

The superintendent pictured that man with his speckled forehead. "Eccentric" he certainly was. He also recalled Joisneau's body as it was being eaten up in the acid bath. He asked:

"Did you ask his professional opinion?"

Champelaz wriggled strangely, as though his cardigan were irritating his skin.

"No. I ... I didn't dare to. You don't know what this town is like. Chernecé belonged to the university elite, you understand? He was one of the region's most eminent ophthalmologists. A prestigious professor. As for me, I just look after this little place ..."

"Do you think Chernecé might have examined the same records as you did – the official notifications of birth?"

"Yes."

"Do you think he might have looked at them even before you did?"

"That is possible, yes."

The director lowered his eyes. His face was scarlet, running with sweat.

Niémans pressed the point:

"Do you think that he also found out that the records had been falsified?"

"I ... How do I know? What are you trying to suggest?"

Niémans let it drop. He had just understood another part of the story: Champelaz had not been back to examine the papers Caillois had stolen because he was afraid of discovering something about the university lecturers. Those lecturers who lorded it over the town, and who controlled the destiny of people like him.

The superintendent stood up.

"What else did you tell Joisneau?"

"Nothing. I told him exactly what I have just told you."

"Think about it."

"That's all. Honestly it is."

Niémans stood in front of the doctor. "Does the name Judith Hérault mean anything to you?"

"No."

"And Philippe Sertys?"

"The second victim?"

"You had never heard of him before?"

"No."

"Does the term 'blood-red rivers' ring any bells?"

"No, none. I ..."

"Thank you, doctor."

Niémans saluted the terrified medic and turned on his heel. He was on his way through the door, when he looked back over his shoulder.

"One last thing, doctor. I have neither heard nor seen any dogs. Aren't there any in the home?"

Champelaz was wan.

"D ... dogs?"

"Yes. Guide dogs for the blind."

The penny dropped and he found the energy to reply:

"Dogs are of use to blind people who live on their own, and who do not have any other assistance. Our home is equipped with the latest technology. The patients are guided and warned of the slightest obstacle, there's no need for dogs."

Outside, Niémans turned back toward that bright building, which was glistening in the rain. Since yesterday morning, he had been avoiding this home because of some non-existent dogs. His phobia had made him send Joisneau there. Those phantoms baying in the darkness of his dreams. He opened his car door and spat on the ground.

His ghosts had cost that young lieutenant his life.

CHAPTER 48

Niémans drove down the rolling slopes of Les Sept-Laux. The downpour doubled in intensity. Rising from the asphalt, a bright mist was shining in his headlamps. From time to time, a puddle of mud had formed which swished under his tires with the din of a waterfall. Niémans clutched his steering wheel and fought to control his car which was constantly skidding dangerously close to the edge of the precipice.

Suddenly, his pager rang in his pocket. With one hand, he flicked on the screen. A message from Antoine Rheims in Paris. With the same hand, he grabbed his cell phone and picked Rheims's number from its memory. As soon as he heard Niémans's voice, his superior said:

"The hooligan's dead, Pierre."

Totally submerged in his case, Niémans struggled to concentrate on the possible consequences of this news. But he could not. His boss went on:

"Where are you?"

"Near Guernon."

"You're under arrest. In theory, you should now give yourself up, hand over your gun and limit the damage."

"In theory?"

"I've spoken to Terpentes. He says that your enquiries haven't led anywhere and that things are starting to look nasty. The media have also turned up in the place. Tomorrow morning, Guernon's going to be the most famous town in France." Rheims paused. "And everyone's looking for you."

Niémans did not respond. He was keeping his eyes on the road, which continued to corkscrew through the sheets of rain that seemed to be spiralling in a reverse motion. Rheims continued:

"Pierre, are you about to arrest the murderer?"

"I don't know. But, I'll say it again, I'm definitely on the right track."

"In that case, we'll sort the other business out later. I haven't spoken to you. No one can find you. No one can contact you. You've still got an hour or two left to stop this slaughter. After that, there's nothing more I can do for you. Except find you a good lawyer."

Niémans grunted something in reply and hung up.

At that moment, a car appeared in his headlamps and bounced toward his right. The superintendent reacted a second too late. The vehicle smashed straight into his right wing. The steering wheel flew out of his hands. His saloon hit the boulders at the foot of the rock face. He swore and tried to straighten up. In a flash, he was back in control and glancing in panic at the other car. A dark Range Rover, with its headlamps off, which was coming back for the kill.

Niémans reversed. The bulky vehicle rebounded slightly and swerved to the left, forcing him to brake suddenly. He then accelerated forward again. The Range Rover was now in front of him and driving flat out, systematically stopping him from overtaking. Its number plate was covered with lumps of mud. His mind empty, the superintendent put his foot down once more and tried to pass the Range Rover on the outside curve. In vain. That black mass was eating up the slightest gap, shoving into the saloon's left wing as it approached and pushing it toward the edge of the precipice.

What was this lunatic after? Niémans abruptly slowed down, giving the killer car a lead of a good fifty yards. The Range Rover immediately slowed down as well, closing the gap between them. The superintendent seized his chance. Slamming his foot right down, he managed to slip past it on the left. A close call.

The superintendent was now giving it all he could, foot flat on the floor. In his rear-view mirror, he saw the four-wheel drive slowly vanish into the darkness. Without a moment's thought, he drove on at the same speed for a couple of miles.

He was once again all alone on the road.

Following the dark twisting trace of the asphalt, he sped forward through the dense rain, between the conifers. What had happened? Who had attacked him? And why? What had he found out which would now cost him his life? It had all happened so quickly that he had not even had time to make out the figure behind the Range Rover's steering wheel.

As he came out of a bend, Niémans could see the Jasse suspension bridge: three and a half miles of concrete, balanced on steel towers that were over three hundred feet tall. This meant that he was now only six miles away from Guernon, and safety.

He accelerated once more.

He was starting to cross the bridge when a white light blinded him, suddenly engulfing his rear windscreen. Headlamps full on, the Range Rover was back against his bumper. Niémans lowered his gaze from the dazzling rear-view mirror and stared at the concrete strip, hanging in the darkness. He said to himself: "I can't die. Not like this." Then he slammed his foot down once more.

The headlamps were still behind him. Bent over his steering wheel, he kept his eyes on the safety railings, which glimmered in his own lights, surrounding the road in a sort of fiery embrace, a glittering halo, steaming as the rain poured down.

Yards snatched from time.

Seconds stolen from the earth.

A strange idea crossed Niémans's mind, a sort of inexplicable conviction: while he was still driving on this bridge, still heading through this storm, nothing could happen to him. He was alive. He was light. He was invulnerable.

The collision took his breath away.

His head snapped forward into the windscreen. The rear-view mirror smashed into pieces. Its composite support ripped into Niémans's forehead like a hook. He groaned and rolled up, hands locked together over his head. He felt his car pulling over to the left, then to the right, wobbling on its axis . . . Blood poured down half of his face.

Another jolt, then suddenly the icy slap of the rain. The cold reaches of the night.

There was silence. Darkness. Seconds.

When Niémans next opened his eyes, he could not believe what he was seeing: the sky and the stars, upside down. He was alone, flying through the wind and the rain.

His car had hit the parapet, throwing him out, off the bridge, into the void. He was diving down, slowly, silently, aimlessly beating his arms and his legs, wondering absurdly what death was going to feel like.

A varied succession of pain was the answer. The whipping of pine needles. Branches cracking. His flesh torn apart into a thousand shards of agony, through forests of spruce and larch.

There were two almost simultaneous shocks.

Firstly, he hit the ground, his fall broken by the countless boughs of the trees. Then an apocalyptic crash. An ear-splitting din. As though a massive lid had just been brought down onto his body. The moment exploded into a riot of contradictory sensations. Biting cold. Scalding steam. Water. Rock. Darkness.

Time passed. An eclipse.

Niémans opened his eyes again. In front of his eyelids, a second set welcomed him – the blackness of the forest. Little by little, like a glimmer of the living dead, light returned. His numbed brain slowly formed the following conclusion: he was alive, still alive.

He had fallen down between the trees and, by pure chance, landed in a water drainage channel at the foot of one of the supporting pylons. Following exactly the same trajectory, his car had flown off the bridge and, like a huge army tank, had crashed down on top of him. But without touching him. The broad chassis of the saloon had been stopped by the banks of the drainage canal.

A miracle.

Niémans closed his eyes. Multiple wounds tortured his body, then a stronger, burning sensation – like a lance of fire – beat into his right temple. The superintendent guessed that the strut of the rear-view mirror had gouged its way into his flesh, just above his ear. On the other hand, he felt as if the rest of him had escaped relatively unscathed.

His chin stuck down on his chest, he stared up at the steaming wreck of his car. He was imprisoned beneath a roof of red-hot metal, in a concrete coffin. He turned his head to the right, then to the left and noticed that a section of one of the bumpers was pinning him down into the canal.

In desperation, he made a violent lateral movement. The various pains that were prickling across his body now turned out to be an advantage: they canceled one another out, leaving his flesh in a kind of agonised indifference.

He managed to slide beneath the bumper and extricate himself from his death bed. Once his arms were free, his hand instinctively shot to his temple and felt a thick flow of blood oozing out from the torn flesh. He groaned as he felt it stream slowly between his aching fingers. It made him think of the beak of an oily bird, spewing out gasoline. Tears came to his eyes. He straightened up, leaning one arm on the edge of the canal, then rolling over onto the ground. Meanwhile, another thought crossed his addled brain.

The killer was coming back. To finish him off.

Grabbing hold of the bodywork, he managed to get to his feet.

He punched at the dented boot; it flew open, allowing him to retrieve his pump-action shotgun, as well as a handful of cartridges which had spilled out inside. He stuck the weapon under his left arm – his left hand was still clamped on his wound – and succeeded in loading it with his right hand. The process was carried out by touch. He could scarcely see a thing. His glasses were broken and the night was still pitch black.

His face splattered with blood and dirt, his body wracked with pain, the superintendent turned round, sweeping all before him with his gun. Not a sound. Not a movement. His head went dizzy. He slid down the side of his car and fell once more into the drainage canal. This time, he felt the chill of its waters and woke up. He was now bouncing against the concrete edges as they funnelled him down toward the river.

Why not, after all?

He clutched his gun against his body and let himself float on the rainwater, like a pharaoh on his way down the river of the dead.

CHAPTER 49

Niémans floated for a long time. His eyes open, he could see the dark mass of the starless sky through the gaps in the trees. To his right and to his left, he made out landslides of red clay, heaps of branches and leaves, forming an inextricable mangrove swamp.

Soon, the stream swelled, becoming stronger and louder. Head back, he let himself be borne away. The icy water caused a vaso-constriction in his temple, thus preventing him from losing too much blood. As he drifted onwards, he began to hope that the course of the water would take him back to Guernon and the university.

Before long, he realised that his hopes were groundless. The stream was a dead end; it did not flow down in the direction of the campus. It meandered round in increasingly tight bends within the forest, once more losing its strength and speed.

The current stopped.

Niémans swam to the bank and, gasping for breath, pulled himself out of the water. The stream was so full of debris and loaded down with mud, that it gave off no reflection at all. He slumped down onto the damp earth, carpeted with dead leaves. His nostrils filled with the scent of mould, that characteristic, slightly smoky smell of the soil, mingled with fibers and shoots, humus and insects.

He rolled onto his back and glanced up at the boughs of the forest. The wood was not twisted and overgrown, but instead formed a spacious airy grove, in which reigned an atmosphere of vegetative freedom. It was so dark, however, that he could not even see the black forms of the mountains that towered above him. And he did not know how long he had been drifting, nor in which direction.

Despite the pain and the cold, he dragged himself over to a tree and leant against its trunk. Forcing himself to think, he tried to picture in his mind the map of the region on which he had marked the important places in the case. He remembered in particular that the University of Guernon lay to the north of Les Sept-Laux.

The north.

Since he had no idea where he was, how could he find the north? He had no compass, nor other magnetic device. During the day he could have used the sun as a guide, but during the night?

He thought again. The blood started to seep back down his face and the cold was already numbing the extremities of his limbs. He realised that he had only a few hours left.

Suddenly, he had a flash of inspiration. Even at that time of the night, he could still work out the diurnal path of the sun. Thanks to the plant life. The superintendent knew nothing about flora, but he knew what everyone else knows: certain varieties of moss and lichen love damp climates, and avoid all contact with the sun. Such plants must then grow only at the foot of trees, facing north.

Niémans knelt down and searched through his coat to find the shock-proof case in which he always kept a spare pair of glasses. They were intact. Thanks to these fresh lenses, he was now able to discern his immediate surroundings.

He then started to search around the trunks of the conifers and the edges of the hillocks. A few minutes later, his fingers frozen and black with soil, he realised that he had been right. Near the roots, little emerald clumps of tiny fresh mosses always grew according to the same orientation. The superintendent fingered these minuscule canopies, stringy textures, soft surfaces – a miniature jungle that was now pointing him toward the north.

Niémans eased himself to his feet and followed the moss trail.

He staggered, stumbling over the clods, feeling his heart beating in his throat. Puddles, bark, boughs full of needles crashed past him. His feet slid over pebbles, flint sanctuaries, holes full of spines, mattings of light vegetation. He went on following the lichen. On other occasions he plunged into swamps of crackling ice, which dug out brackish furrows on the slopes of the hills. Despite the fatigue, despite his injuries, he was gaining speed, gasping in strength from the drifting scents on the air. He seemed to be walking in the very breath of the downpour, which had just stopped to draw in another breath.

At last, he stumbled across a road.

Gleaming tarmac. The road to freedom. Once again, he examined the snug growths along the side of the track in order to ascertain the correct direction. Then, suddenly, a *gendarmerie* van appeared round the bend, its headlamps full on.

It braked immediately. Men leapt out to help Niémans who, still clutching his gun, slowly collapsed.

He felt the grip of the gendarmes. He heard their murmurs, their shouts, the rustling of their oil-skins. The headlamps danced obliquely. Once inside the truck, a man yelled at the driver:

"The hospital! And fast!"

Semi-conscious, Niémans stammered:

"No, the university."

"What? Haven't you seen the state you're in?"

"The university. I . . . I have a date there."

CHAPTER 50

The door opened to reveal a smile.

Pierre Niémans lowered his eyes. He saw the woman's powerful, muscular wrists. Just above them, he noticed the close stitch
of her heavy pullover, then he followed it up to the collar and her
neck, where her hair was so fine that it formed a sort of misty halo.
He thought of her marvelous skin, so beautiful and so immaculate
that it magically transformed each material, each garment that it
touched. Fanny yawned:

"You're late, superintendent."

Niémans attempted a smile.

"You . . . you weren't asleep?"

The young woman shook her head and stood aside to let him
in. As he advanced into the light, her expression froze. She had
just noticed his blood-covered face. She pulled back to get a good
view of the damage, his shattered body, blue coat in ribbons, torn
tie, singed cloth.

"What happened? Did you have an accident?"

Niémans nodded curtly.

He glanced round the living-room. Despite the temperature he
was running, and the blood that was pounding through his veins,
he was pleased to be in her little flat. With its spotless walls and
pastel shades. A desk buried beneath a computer, books and papers.
Stones and crystals lined up on the shelves. Climbing equipment,
piles of day-glo clothing. The flat of a young woman who was at

once sedentary and sporty, home-loving and adventurous. The memory of that expedition into the glacier flashed through his blood vessels like a shower of sparkling ice.

Niémans slumped down onto a chair. Outside, it had started to rain again. He could hear drops hammering on the roof somewhere above them and the hushed noises of the neighbors. A creaking door. Footsteps. A hall of residence full of worried, cramped students.

Fanny pulled off the superintendent's coat, then carefully examined the open wound on the side of his head. She did not seem the slightest bit put out at the sight of caked-up blood and dark, gaping flesh. She whistled between her teeth:

"Quite a nasty cut! I hope that the temporal artery hasn't been severed. It's rather hard to tell. The head always gushes blood like that and . . . How did it happen?"

"It was an accident," Niémans repeated brusquely. "A car accident."

"I'm going to have to take you to hospital."

"No way. I've got work to do."

Fanny disappeared into the other room, then came back laden down with lint, drugs and vacuum packs containing needles and serum. She ripped several of them open with her teeth. Then she screwed a needle into the body of a plastic syringe. He tensed and grabbed the packaging:

"What is this?"

"An anesthetic. It'll kill the pain. Don't panic."

Niémans seized her wrist.

"Wait."

He read through the description of the product. Xylocain. An adrenaline-laced painkiller which should reduce the aches without knocking him out. With a gesture of agreement, Niémans dropped his arm.

"Don't worry," Fanny whispered. "This stuff will also help stop the bleeding."

With his head down, he could not see exactly what she was doing. But it felt as if she was making several injections around the wound. A few seconds later, the pain had already diminished.

"Can you stitch me up?" he murmured.

"Of course I can't. You'll have to go to hospital. You'll start bleeding again soon and ..."

"Tie a tourniquet, or something. I've got to stay on the case, and keep my wits about me."

Fanny shrugged, then sprayed an aerosol onto some pieces of lint. Niémans looked over at her. In her tight jeans, her thighs formed two curves of force which he found vaguely arousing, despite the state he was in. He wondered at her contrasting qualities. How could she be so nymph-like and so concrete? So sweet and so hard? So near and so distant? He found the same contradiction in her stare: the aggressive flash of her eyes and the incredible gentleness of her brows. Breathing in the acrid smell of the antiseptic, he asked:

"Do you live alone?"

Fanny was cleaning his wound in short, precise dabs. The painkiller was now flowing, so he scarcely felt any sensation of burning. She grinned:

"You really don't miss a trick, do you?"

"Sorry, um ... Am I being nosy?"

Close beside him, Fanny concentrated on the job in hand. Then she whispered into his ear:

"Yes, I live alone. And I don't have a boyfriend, if that's what you mean."

"I ... um ... But why in the university?"

"I'm near the lecture halls, the labs ..."

Niémans turned his head. Tutting, she at once shifted it back into position. Then, his face tilted down, he remarked:

"That's right, I remember ... the youngest PhD in France. Daughter and granddaughter of emeritus professors. Which means you're one of those children who ..."

Fanny butted in:

"One of those children who what?"

Niémans swivelled round slightly.

"Nothing . . . What I meant was . . . one of the campus's super-heroes who's also a sports champion . . ."

The woman's expression hardened. A sudden note of suspicion broke into her voice.

"What are you insinuating?"

Despite his burning desire to question Fanny about her family background, the superintendent did not answer. Was it done to ask a woman where she got her genetic riches from or what was the source of her chromosomes? It was Fanny who spoke next:

"Superintendent, I have no idea why you dragged yourself along to my flat in this sorry state. But if you have something to ask me, then please come out with it."

The tone of this command was biting. Niémans was now no longer in pain, but he would have preferred that gnawing agony to the lashing of her voice. He smiled in embarrassment:

"I just wanted to talk to you about that university magazine you write for . . ."

"*Tempo*?"

"That's right."

"And?"

Niémans paused. Fanny put the lint back into one of the plastic packets, then strapped a bandage around his head. Feeling the pressure rising round his skull, the superintendent went on:

"I was wondering if you had written anything about a strange occurrence in the university basement last July . . ."

"What do you mean?"

"Some birth papers were discovered in a file belonging to Etienne Caillois, Rémy's father."

Fanny shrugged.

"Oh, that?"

"So did you write an article about it?"

"A couple of lines, perhaps."

"Why didn't you mention it to me?"

"You mean . . . It might be connected to the murders?"

Niémans raised his head and hardened his tone of voice:

"Why didn't you tell me about that theft?"

Fanny replied with another slight shrug of her shoulders; she was still wrapping the bandage round Niémans's temples.

"There's no proof it was really a theft ... Those archives are an absolute mess. Papers go missing here, then turn up there. Do you really think it matters?"

"Have you seen those papers yourself?"

"Yes, I went to the archives to have a look."

"And you didn't notice anything odd?"

"What, for example?"

"I don't know. You didn't compare them with the original files?"

Fanny pulled back. The dressing was finished. She declared:

"They were just some loose leaves, with nurses' notes on them. Nothing very exciting."

"How many of them were there?"

"Several hundred. But I don't see what you ..."

"Did you name any of the people concerned in your article?"

"I told you, I just wrote a couple of lines."

"Can I see your piece?"

"I never keep what I write."

She was standing stock upright, her arms crossed. Niémans went on:

"Do you think somebody else might have taken a look at those records? Somebody who might have found their name or their parents' names among them?"

"I've already told you, I didn't mention any names."

"Do you think it's possible that somebody else had a look?"

"No, I don't think so. They're all locked up now ... Anyway, who cares? What's all that got to do with the case?"

Niémans took his time. Avoiding her eyes, he hit her with another question, like a punch in the guts.

"You went through those records in detail, didn't you?"

No reply. The policeman raised his eyes. Fanny had not moved, but suddenly she seemed far away from him. She finally answered:

"I've just told you that I did. What do you want to know?"

A moment's hesitation, then Niémans asked:

"I want to know if you found your parents' names among those records. Or your grandparents'."

"No, not at all. Why?"

Without responding, the superintendent got to his feet. They were now both standing, two enemies, like opposite poles. Niémans noticed his bandaged head reflected in a mirror at the other end of the room. He turned toward the young woman and whispered apologetically:

"Thank you. And sorry about the questions."

He picked up his coat and said:

"I know it sounds incredible, but I think those records have already cost one of our officers his life. A young lieutenant, at the beginning of his career. He wanted to look through them. Which is why I think he was killed."

"But that's ridiculous."

"We'll see about that. I'm off to the archives now to compare those papers and the files they belong to."

He was slipping on his soaked rags, when the young woman stopped him.

"You're not going to put those tatters back on!"

Fanny dived off and returned a few seconds later with a tee-shirt, a pullover, a fur-lined jacket and waterproof leggings.

"They won't fit you," she explained. "But at least they're warm and dry. And this is essential . . ."

She smoothly slipped a polyester balaclava over his bandaged head, then folded it up over his ears. When he had recovered from his surprise, Niémans rolled his eyes comically behind his mask. Suddenly, they both burst out laughing.

Their complicity momentarily returned, as though blown back from the past. But the superintendent gravely announced:

"I really must get going. To the archives. To continue my enquiries."

Niémans did not have time to react. Fanny had already wrapped her arms round him and was kissing him. He stiffened. A new warmth flowed through him. He did not know if it was his fever coming back, or the sweetness of that little tongue which was working its way in between his lips, burning him up with its heat. He closed his eyes and mumbled:

"The case. I've got to get back onto the case."

But his shoulders were already pinned down against the floor.

X

CHAPTER 51

Karim tore down the yellow no-entry cordon and knelt in front of the door of the tomb, which was still ajar. He slipped on his gloves, stuck his fingers into the gap and pulled violently. It gave way. Without a moment's hesitation, he switched on his torch and slid inside the vault. Bent double, he edged down the steps. The beam of light bounced back off a mass of dark water – a veritable underground lake. The rain had got in through the door and half filled the vault.

He said to himself: "There's no other choice." He held his breath and dropped into the water. Holding his torch in his left hand, he advanced, Indian-style, in a sort of breast-stroke. The ray of light cut through the darkness. As he entered further into the vault, the trickling of the rain rang deeper and the smell of mould and decay grew heavier. With his face turned up toward the ceiling, he spat out the water and paddled onwards, caught between the lake and the arched roof.

Suddenly, his head hit the coffin. In a panic, he screamed, span round and slowed his movements, in an attempt to calm himself down. He then looked at the little casket that was floating on the waters like a boat.

He repeated to himself: "There's no other choice." Then he swam round the coffin, examining each of its sides. The lid was still screwed down, but he noticed something which he had not had time to spot that morning, when the keeper had caught him trespassing. Around the screws, the pale wood was coming away in darker splinters. The paint had cracked. Someone had – perhaps – opened the coffin. "There's no other choice." From his jacket pocket, Karim produced a pair of folding pliers, the two ends of which formed the blade of a screwdriver, and tried to prise open the lid. Little by little, the wood started to give way. At last, the final screw loosened. Banging his head against the ceiling – the water was still rising and was now up to his shoulders – Karim managed to pull away the lid. He wiped his eyes with his sleeve then, telling himself to hold his breath, he peered inside.

He need not have bothered. He felt as though he were already dead himself.

The coffin did not contain a child's skeleton. Nor had there been a hoax, or any sign of desecration. It was filled to the brim with tiny sharp white bones. A sort of rodents' burial ground. Thousands of dried out skeletons. Chalky snouts, as pointed as daggers. Rib-cages, as vivid as claws. Countless scraps, as thin as matchsticks, coming from tiny femurs, tibias and humeruses.

Still leaning against the edge, Karim's muscles started to give way and he reached out a hand toward that charnel-house. Those myriads of skeletons, reflecting the beam of his torch, looked like a mass prehistoric grave. It was then that he heard a voice coming from behind him, breaking through the din of the rain.

"You shouldn't have come back, Karim."

He did not need to turn round to know who had spoken. He clenched his fists and lowered his head until it was resting on the bones, then murmured:

"Crozier, don't tell me you're involved in this business . . ."

The voice answered:

"I should never have let you loose on this case."

Karim glanced rapidly at the doorway of the vault. Henri Crozier's figure was clearly outlined. He was holding an MR73 model Manhurin – the same gun as Niémans used. Six bullets in the cylinder. Fast-loading magazines in his pocket. A few seconds to empty it, then reload it, without any risk of it jamming. A precision piece. The lieutenant asked:

"What the fucking hell's your role in all this?"

The man did not reply. Lifting up his soaked elbows, Karim tried again:

"Can I at least get out of this shit-hole?"

Crozier gestured briefly with his gun.

"Come toward me. Only slowly. Nice and slowly."

Letting go of the desecrated coffin, Karim slipped through the water and headed for the steps. His torch, which he had put back between his teeth, flickered up crazily at the stone ceiling. Whirling flashes, like stabs of lightning.

The lieutenant reached the staircase and heaved himself up it. As he ascended, Crozier pulled back, keeping his gun on him. The rain was beating down in gusts. Soaked to the skin, the Arab got to his feet and faced the superintendent. He asked again:

"What's your part in all this? What do you know?"

Crozier replied at last:

"It was in 1980. I spotted her as soon as she arrived. This is my town. And it's small. My patch. What's more, I was practically the only cop in Sarzac at the time. That woman who'd come to work as a primary school teacher, she was too beautiful, too powerful ... I immediately sensed there was something wrong about her."

The Arab whispered:

"Crozier, the Guardian of Sarzac."

"Yeah. So I looked into things. I found out that she had a child with her ... And I got her to confide in me. She told me everything. She said that the demons wanted to kill her child."

"I know all that already."

"What you don't know is that I decided to protect that family. I had false papers made for them, I ..."

Karim felt as if he was on the edge of a precipice.

"Who were these demons?"

"One day, two men came to town. They said they were collecting old school books. They'd come from Guernon, the same town as Fabienne. So I guessed at once that they were the demons ..."

"What were their names?"

"Caillois and Sertys."

"Don't fuck me about. At that time, Rémy Caillois and Philippe Sertys were only about ten years old!"

"Those weren't their names. They were called Etienne Caillois and René Sertys. They must have been about forty. With bony faces, and wild staring eyes like fanatics."

A taste of acid rose up into Karim's throat. Why had he not thought of that? The "crime" of the blood-red rivers went back several generations. Before Rémy Caillois there had been Etienne Caillois; before Philippe Sertys, René Sertys. He murmured:

"And then?"

"I acted the inquisitorial cop. ID check, the works. But they were clean. As straight as dies. Still, they left again without having been able to identify Fabienne and her child. At least, that's what I thought. But, as soon as she heard that they'd been nosing around Sarzac, Fabienne wanted to beat it. So, I didn't ask her any questions. We just destroyed all the records, tore pages out of registers, wiped out every trace ... Fabienne had changed her child's identity, but ..."

Karim interrupted him. A curtain of rain lay between the two men.

"Young Sertys came back here on Sunday night. Do you have any idea what he was looking for in this vault?"

"No."

Abdouf pointed back at the tomb.

"That fucking coffin's full of rats' bones. It's a goddam nightmare. What does it all mean?"

"I don't know. You shouldn't have opened that coffin. You should respect the dead ..."

"Who? Where's Judith Hérault's body? Is she really dead?"

"Dead and buried, my boy. I was the one who arranged her funeral."

The Arab shivered.

"And you tend the grave?"

"Yes, at night."

Walking up to the barrel of the gun, Karim suddenly roared:

"Where is she? Where is Fabienne Hérault now?"

"You mustn't harm her."

"Superintendent, this case goes far deeper than a simple profanation of a cemetery. There have been murders."

"I know."

"You know?"

"It was all over the TV. On the late night news."

"So you know that there's a series of murders, the bodies mutilated and set in macabre positions, the works! ... Crozier, tell me where I can find Fabienne Hérault!"

In the darkness, Crozier's face was knotted with tension. His gun was still pressing against the Arab's torso.

"You mustn't harm her."

"No one's going to harm her, Crozier. But now Fabienne Hérault's the only person who can shed a bit of light on this chaos! Everything points to her daughter, right? Everything points to Judith Hérault, who should be there in that tomb!"

A few seconds more under that overpowering deluge then, slowly, Crozier lowered his gun. The Arab knew that if he was going to solve a case once in his life, then this was the one. Finally, the superintendent said:

"Fabienne lives about twelve miles from here, on the Herzine hill. I'm coming with you. If you harm her, I'll kill you."

Karim smiled and pulled back. Then he swung round and kicked the superintendent full in the throat. Crozier was thrown back against the marble monument.

The Arab leant down over the unconscious old man. He did up his hood and pulled him under the shelter of a granite tombstone. Then he silently apologised.

But what he needed right now was a free hand.

CHAPTER 52

"It's hot stuff, Abdouf. Very hot stuff."

Patrick Astier's voice broke through a whirlwind of interferences. The cell phone had rung while Karim had been driving across a veritable steppe of gray rock. The cop had leapt out of his skin and narrowly avoided skidding off the road. Astier went on enthusiastically:

"Your two missions were time bombs waiting to go off. And they both blew up on me."

Karim felt his nerves harden into steel beneath his skin.

"Go on," he declared, pulling onto the side of the road and switching off his headlights.

"Firstly, Sylvain Hérault's accident. I found the police records. And got confirmation of what you'd been told. Sylvain Hérault was killed on his bicycle, on the D17, by an unidentified car. A shifty case. And left unsolved. At the time, the *gendarmerie* conducted a routine enquiry. No witnesses. No motive that could have suggested another explanation . . ."

His intonation indicated that he was waiting for a question. So Karim dutifully asked it:

"But?"

"But," the chemist went on, "Since that distant period, we have made giant strides in the treatment of photographs."

Karim sensed that another science lecture was about to start. He butted in:

"Please, Astier, just get to the point, will you?"

"OK. So I found some photos in the file. Black-and-white prints taken by a local hack. In them, you can make out the tyre-tracks of the bike, mixed in with the traces left by the car. They're all so small and out of focus that you wonder why they bothered to keep them."

"And?"

The scientist paused, for dramatic effect.

"And, Grenoble University boasts a state-of-the-art optical laboratory."

"For fuck's sake, Astier, get on with it!"

"Hang on a sec. Those guys can do things to a photograph that you would just not believe! They make a digital analysis, blow it up, contrast it, get rid of any imperfections, change the angles ... to cut a long story short, they can dig out things that are invisible to the naked eye. They're good friends of mine. So I thought it might be a good idea to wake them up and get them onto the case. I used the fingerprint analyser as a scanner and sent them the photos. Even when woken up in the middle of the night, those guys are still absolute geniuses. They treated the film straight away and ..."

"AND WHAT?"

Another one of Astier's pregnant pauses.

"Their analysis tells quite a different tale from the official version. They blew up the tyre-tracks of the bike and the car. By heightening the contrast, they were able to examine the direction of the prints on the tarmac. Their first conclusion is that Sylvain Hérault was not on his way to work, up in the mountains, as it says in the file. The tyre-prints run the other way round. Hérault was cycling toward the university. I've checked that on a map."

"But ... What about his wife Fabienne's testimony?"

"Fabienne Hérault lied. I've read her statement. She just confirmed what the *gendarmerie* suspected, that the crystaller was going to work on the Belledonne. Which is totally untrue."

Karim clenched his teeth. Another lie. Another mystery. Astier went on:

"But that's not all. My experts also took a look at the tire-prints made by the car." Another pause, and then: "They go in both directions, Abdouf. The driver ran over the body once, then reversed over it a second time. It's a fucking murder. As cold-blooded as a snake in its egg."

Karim was no longer listening. His heart was now beating against his chest. This, then, was the motive for the Hérault family's vengeance. Apart from the escapades of the mother and daughter, that life spent in fear of pursuit, which had indirectly brought about Judith's death, there had first been a murder. Sylvain Hérault. The demons had begun by wiping out the "strong man" of the family, and had then pursued the women.

Fabienne Hérault. Judith Hérault. Abdouf's thoughts were sparking wildly.

"What about the hospital?" he asked.

"That's time bomb number two. I looked at the list of births for 1972. The page corresponding to 23 May has been torn out."

This story sounded rather too familiar to Karim – a déjà vu from another life that he had lived out in a mere few hours.

"But that's not the strangest part," Astier continued. "I also looked through the archives, in the section where children's medical records are kept. It's a real labyrinth and it's starting to get damp. This time, I found Judith's file easily enough. So you see what that means, don't you? Something else happened that night. Something which was noted down in the main register, but not in the child's personal records. That page has been torn out to hide this mysterious event, not to conceal the birth of your Judith. I asked a few nurses about it, but they were all dropping off to sleep. What's more they were too young to bother with Uncle Astier's stories . . ."

Karim realised that the chemist was playing the fool to chase away his own fears. He could sense it, despite the interference on the line. He thanked him and hung up.

He could already see the large, grassy Herzine hill jutting up four hundred yards away from him.

On those shadowy slopes, the truth was waiting for him.

CHAPTER 53

Fabienne Hérault's house.

The top of a hill. Stone walls. Dark windows.

Pale clouds fluttered across the thick sky. The rain had stopped. Flurries of mist floated slowly along the emerald slopes. All around, the lonely horizon drew away. A heap of stones. Nothing and no one in a radius of twelve miles.

Karim parked his car and clambered up the grassy flank. The house reminded him of the place she had lived in near Sarzac – those fat stones gave it the look of a Celtic burial mound. Near the building, he spotted a huge white satellite dish. He drew his gun. And noticed that a bullet was already in its breech. He found that fact reassuring.

Before going up to the front door, he checked the garage, which contained a five-door Volvo under a pale tarpaulin. It was not locked. He opened the bonnet and, in a series of rapid gestures, demolished the fuse box. Now, whatever happened, if things went wrong, Fabienne Hérault was not going anywhere.

He strode up to the door and knocked lightly. Gun in hand, he stepped back from the threshold. A few seconds of silence, then the door opened. Noiselessly. Without any click of a lock. Fabienne Hérault evidently no longer felt in danger.

Karim stood in the light and concealed his weapon.

He was confronted with a figure as tall as he was, whose eyes were drilling into him. Shoulders like cliffs, a translucent perfectly-formed face, ringed by a brown head of curls, that were almost fuzzy. Glasses with frames as thick as walking sticks. Karim would have been incapable of describing that dreamy, almost absent face.

He controlled his voice:

"Police. Lieutenant Karim Abdouf."

No sign of astonishment from the woman. She was looking at Karim over her glasses, her head gently swaying. Then she lowered her gaze to the hand which was concealing the Glock. Through those lenses, Abdouf thought he detected a wicked gleam.

"What can I do for you?" she asked warmly.

Karim remained motionless, petrified in the nocturnal silence of the countryside.

"Come in. For a start."

The shutters were down, most of the furniture was covered with striped cloths. A television screen gleamed darkly, and the lacquered notes of a piano glinted. Karim noticed the score which was open above the keyboard: Frederick Chopin's Sonata in B-flat minor. The whole room was plunged into the darkness of ten fluttering candles.

Following the lieutenant's eyes, Fabienne Hérault murmured:

"I have left behind the world and time. This house is in my image."

It reminded Karim of Sister Andrée and her retreat into the shadows.

"What about the satellite dish?"

"I have to keep contact. I have to know when the truth will come out."

"It's on its way out right now, madame."

Without any change of expression, she nodded. The policeman had not been expecting this calm, smiling woman, with her comforting voice. He raised his gun and felt ashamed as he threatened her.

"Listen, lady," he panted. "I don't have much time. I need to see the photos of Judith, your daughter."

"The photos of . . ."

"Please. I've been looking for you for more than twenty hours. I've been reconstructing your story, and trying to understand. Why did you organise that scheme? Why did you obliterate the face of your child? For the moment, I'm sure of only two things. First, that Judith was no monster, as I first suspected. In fact, I reckon she was a real beauty. But the second fact is that her face somehow gave away the keys to a nightmare. A nightmare which, long ago, forced you to run away and which has just reawoken like a dormant volcano. So, show me the photos and tell me your

289

story. I want dates, details, explanations, the lot! I want to know how and why a little girl who died fourteen years ago is now massacring people in a university town in the Alps!"

The woman remained motionless for a few seconds, then strode down a corridor with her giantess's gait. Clutching his gun, Karim followed her. Other rooms, other sheets, other colors. The house was a mixture of a morgue and a carnival.

At the far end of a small bedroom, Fabienne Hérault opened a wardrobe and removed a metal box. Karim stopped her hand, and opened it himself. Photographs. Just photographs.

The woman gave Karim a questioning look, then turned it over, making it shine in the light, as if she were plunging her hand into a stream of clear water. Finally, she lifted a photo up in front of him.

He could not help smiling.

A little girl was staring out at him, her dark face was oval, ringed with brown short-cropped curls. Bright blue eyes shone from beneath the shadows of her brows, emphasised by her long lashes, which were almost too luxuriant. That slightly masculine touch went with her slightly over-aggressive gaze.

Karim examined the picture. He felt as if he had known that face for a long time, a very long time, for ever.

But the miracle refused to happen. He had been hoping that her face would, somehow or other, reveal the path of truth to him. Fabienne whispered in her warm tones:

"It was taken a few days before she died. In Sarzac. She had short hair, we were ..."

Karim looked up.

"That doesn't wash. This picture, her face, ought to tell me something. Act as a clue. All I can see is a pretty little girl."

"It's because this photograph is incomplete."

He started. The woman now handed him a second picture.

"This is the last school photograph taken in Guernon, at Lamartine School, in CE2. Just before we left for Sarzac."

The cop examined the children's smiling faces. He spotted Judith, then grasped the unbelievable truth. He had been expecting this. It was the only possible explanation. But still he did not fully understand. He whispered:

"So Judith wasn't an only child?"

"Yes and no."

"Yes and no? What ... what the hell's that supposed to mean? Explain yourself."

"I can't explain anything, young man. All I can do is tell you how something inexplicable destroyed my life."

XI

CHAPTER 54

The basement contained a veritable sea of paper. A tidal wave of bulging files tied up in bundles was splashed crazily all over the walls. On the floor, heaps of cardboard boxes blocked most of the aisles. Further on, the neon lighting revealed more shelves weighed down with documents, fading away into the distance.

Niémans clambered over the stacks and headed down the first corridor. The endless files were being held in place by long pieces of netting, of the sort used to stop cliffs from crumbling. As he wandered past these registers, he could not help thinking about Fanny, and the dream-like hour he had just spent with her. The young woman's smiling face in the half-light. Her wounded hand putting out the lamp. The contact of dark skin. Two tiny bluish flames gleaming in the shadows – Fanny's eyes. It had been an intimate, discreet tableau, with soft motion, gestures and murmurs, instants and eternities.

How long had he spent in her arms? Niémans had no idea. But, on his lips, on his bruised flesh, he still felt a sort of mark, a lingering presence that astonished him. Fanny had rearoused forgotten passions in him, ancient secrets whose reawakening he now found disturbing. Had he, in the midst of all that horror, at the end of his enquiries, sipped from a loving cup, been caressed by a flame?

He tried to concentrate. He knew where the pile of rediscovered papers had been placed – he had contacted the records clerk who, despite being half asleep, had given him a set of extremely precise directions. Niémans walked on, turned, and walked on again. At last, he came across a closed box, caged off behind some chicken wire and protected by a solid padlock. The hospital porter had given him the key. If these papers were really "so unimportant", why were they being so carefully looked after?

Niémans went inside the alcove and sat down on some old bundles which were lying on the floor. He opened the box, grabbed a handful of papers and started to read them. Names. Dates. Nurses' reports concerning new-born babies. The records contained the surname, weight, height and blood group of each child. The number of feeds and the names of what sounded like medicines, perhaps vitamins or something of that sort.

He flicked through the sheets – there were several hundred of them, covering more than fifty years. Not one name that meant anything to him. Not one date that seemed promising.

Niémans got to his feet and decided to compare these papers with the original files of newly-born babies, which had to be somewhere among the archives. He examined the shelves and picked out about fifty files. His face was dripping with sweat. He felt the heat from his arctic jacket radiate onto his flesh. Laying the files down on a metal table, he spread them out so as to be able to see the surnames on the covers. He started to open each file and compare the first page with the other sheets. They were fakes.

From a rapid examination it was obvious that the sheets contained in the official files had been falsified. Etienne Caillois had imitated the nurses' handwriting fairly convincingly, but not well enough to stand up against a direct comparison with the originals.

Why?

The policeman laid the two pages side by side. He compared each column and each line, but found nothing. They were identical copies. He tried other pages. Still he found no difference. He readjusted his glasses, wiped the rivulets of sweat off the lenses, then examined a few more with greater attention.

Then, at last, he saw what he was looking for.

One tiny detail differentiated the genuine papers from the fakes. THE DIFFERENCE. Niémans did not yet know what it meant, but he sensed that he had unearthed another key. His face was burning like a cauldron and yet – at the same time – an icy sensation ran through him. He checked others to see if they, too, were different in the same way, then stuffed all the documents, the official files plus the sheets Caillois had stolen, into a cardboard box.

He made off with his prize and left the records office.

He dumped the box into the boot of his new car – a gendarme's blue Peugeot – then went back inside the hospital, this time to the maternity clinic.

It was six in the morning and, despite the bright neons which glittered down onto the floor, the place seemed heavy with sleep and silence. He went down to the delivery rooms, passing by nurses and midwives, all dressed in pale coats, hats and little paper over-shoes. Some of them tried to stop him, as he was not wearing the standard surgical outfit. But his tricolor card and fraught expression were a highly effective deterrent.

He finally managed to find an obstetrician, who was just emerging from an operating theater. His face seemed weighed down with all the fatigue of the world. Niémans rapidly introduced himself and asked his sole and unique question:

"Doctor, is there any logical reason why a newly-born baby should change weight during its first night of existence?"

"What do you mean?"

"Do babies commonly lose or gain several hundred grams shortly after being born?"

Staring at the policeman's balaclava and the clothes that were too short for him, the doctor replied:

"No. If a child loses a lot of weight, then we have to undertake detailed tests immediately, because there is obviously some problem and . . ."

"And what if he puts some on? What if he suddenly gains weight during the first night?"

In his paper hat, the obstetrician looked bewildered.

"But that never happens. I don't understand."

Niémans smiled.

"Thank you, doctor."

He left, closing his eyes as he walked. Under his seething eyelids, he now at last glimpsed the motive for the Guernon murders.

The incredible machination of the blood-red rivers.

There was just one more detail he had to check.

In the university library.

CHAPTER 55

"Out! Everybody out!"

The library reading-room was brightly lit. The police officers lifted their noses from their books. Six of them were still going through works more or less closely associated with evil and purity. Others were examining the lists of students who had used the library during the summer or early fall. They looked like forgotten soldiers, fighting a war that had, unbeknown to them, shifted onto a different front.

"Out!" Niémans repeated. "It's all over here!"

The policemen glanced warily at one another. They had presumably been told that Superintendent Niémans was no longer in charge of the case. They were certainly also surprised to see the famous detective with his head stuck in some sort of a sock, and with a damp brown cardboard box under his arm. But who could stand up to Niémans? Especially when he had that expression on his face.

They stood up and slipped on their jackets.

One of them, passing by the superintendent on his way to the door, called softly to him. The superintendent recognised the broad-backed lieutenant who had been studying Rémy Caillois's thesis.

"I've got to the end of the thing, superintendent. And, maybe it doesn't mean anything, but ... how can I put it? Caillois's conclusion is really weird. You remember the *athlon*, the ancient man who brought together strength and intelligence, the mind and the body? Well, Caillois talks of some kind of project to achieve exactly that. A totally crazy idea. The point isn't to set up a new program of education at school or university. Nor is it to retrain the teachers, or anything like that. The solution he had in mind was . . ."

"Genetic."

"So you've read it, too, have you? It's crazy. He seemed to think that intelligence is a biological fact. A genetic trait which must be associated with other genes, which control physical strength, and so recover the perfection of the *athlon* . . ."

His words whirled round Niémans's mind. He now knew the nature of the blood-red rivers conspiracy. And he did not need this half-witted cop's explanation. He wanted the horror to remain latent, implicit, unspoken. Written on his soul in letters of fire.

"Off with you now," he grunted.

But the officer was now flying:

"In the last pages, Caillois talks of selected births and rationally chosen couples. A sort of totalitarian system. A load of gibberish, superintendent, like in science fiction books of the sixties. Jesus, if the guy hadn't died the way he did, the whole thing would be a real scream!"

"Get lost."

The stocky lieutenant stared at Niémans, hesitated, then went his way. The superintendent crossed the totally deserted reading-room. He felt his fever mounting again, like roots of fire, encircling his skull as though with burning electrodes. He reached the office on the central rostrum. The office belonging to Rémy Caillois, the university's chief librarian. He tapped on the keyboard of the computer. The screen lit up at once. Suddenly, he changed his mind: the information he was looking for dated back to the 1970s, so it was not to be found on the data bank. Niémans frantically rummaged through the desk drawers in search of the registers containing the lists he wanted to consult.

Not the lists of books.

Nor the lists of students.

Just the list of boxed-in carrels, which had been occupied by thousands of readers over the last few years.

Strangely enough, it was in the inner logic of those compartments, which Etienne then Rémy Caillois had so carefully organised, that Niémans hoped to unearth a link with what he had discovered at the maternity clinic.

At last, he found the registers of seating arrangements. He opened his box and once more laid out the files dealing with new-born babies. He calculated the years when these children had become students, spending their evenings in the library, then he looked for their names among the lists of carrels which the two chief librarians had kept so accurately.

Before long, he found some plans of the compartments, with the names of the students written into each space. He could not have imagined a system that was more logical, more rigorous, more suited to the conspiracy he suspected. All of the children named on the original sheets had, when studying twenty years later, not only been placed in the library in the same carrel, day in day out, year in year out, but also facing the same student of the opposite sex.

Niémans was now certain that he was right.

He went through the same procedure for a few other students, intentionally picking them out over a time span of several decades. Each time, he found that they had been seated facing the same person of the same age, but opposite sex, during their daily work in Guernon University Library.

His hands shaking, the superintendent switched off the computer. The huge reading-room was resonant with stuffy silence. Still sitting at Caillois's desk, he turned on his phone and called the night watchman at the Guernon town hall. He had quite a job persuading him to go down at once into the archives in order to consult the registry books of marriages in Guernon. The night watchman finally agreed and Niémans was able, via his mobile, to direct the investigations he wanted him to carry out. He dictated the names, and the watchman checked them. What he wanted to know was if the names he read out belonged to people who had married each other. He was right seventy per cent of the time.

"Is this a bet, or what?" the watchman grumbled.

When they had been through about twenty examples, the superintendent stopped and hung up.

He tied his papers together and rushed off.

Niémans trudged across the campus. Despite himself, he kept looking for Fanny's window, but failed to locate it. On the steps outside one of the buildings, a group of journalists seemed to be waiting expectantly. Everywhere else, uniformed policemen and gendarmes patrolled the lawns and entrances to the buildings.

Faced with a choice between cops and hacks, the superintendent opted for his own people. Flashing his card, he crossed several road-blocks. None of the faces meant anything to him. They were presumably the reinforcements from Grenoble.

He entered the administrative building and found himself in the large over-lit hall, where a group of pale-faced people, old for the most part, was idling around. Probably the professors, doctors and academics. Everybody was on the alert. Niémans strode straight past them, ignoring their questioning stares.

He went up to the first floor and headed for the office of Vincent Luyse, the university vice-chancellor. The superintendent crossed the antechamber and tore some of the photographs of students sporting blues off the walls. He opened the door without knocking.

"What the . . . ?"

The vice-chancellor calmed down as soon as he saw that it was Niémans. With a curt nod of his head, he gave his other visitors their leave, then said to the superintendent:

"I hope you have a lead! We are all . . ."

The policeman laid the pictures down onto the desk, then produced the files and the register. Luyse looked uneasy.

"Really, I . . ."

"Wait."

Niémans finished laying out the photos and the papers in front of the vice-chancellor. Then he leant over the desk and asked:

"Compare these records with the names of your champions, are they from the same families?"

"I beg your pardon?"

Niémans pushed the papers nearer to him.

"The men and the women in these files got married. I suppose they belong to your famous university elite. They must be professors, researchers, intellectuals . . . Look at their names and tell me, one by one, if they also happen to be the parents and grand-parents of this new generation of supermen who win all the sports prizes."

Luyse grabbed his glasses and lowered his eyes.

"Um, yes, that is correct. I know most of these names."

"And you would agree that the children of these couples are extraordinarily gifted, both intellectually and physically?"

Despite himself, Luyse's tense face relaxed into a broad smile. A smarmy grin of satisfaction that Niémans would have liked to ram down his throat.

"Yes . . . yes, of course. This new generation is very brilliant. Believe me, these children are going to live up fully to their promise . . . And, as a matter of fact, we already had a few such fine specimens in the previous generation. For our university, such performances are particularly . . ."

Niémans suddenly realised that he did not so much distrust intellectuals as detest them. He hated them to his very marrow. He loathed their distant, pretentious ways, their ability to describe, to analyse and gauge reality, in whatever form it presented itself. These poor jerks lived as though they were attending some sort of show, and always left more or less disappointed, more or less blasé. And yet he recognised that what happened to them, unbeknown to themselves, was not something he would wish even on his worst enemy. Luyse went on:

"Yes, this new generation is going to strengthen our university's reputation and . . ."

Niémans interrupted. He put his files and registers back into the box, and then spat out:

"Then you should be over the moon. Because these people are going to make your university a household name."

The vice-chancellor looked at him quizzically. Niémans opened his mouth, but he suddenly froze. There was a look of terror on the vice-chancellor's face as he murmured:

"But what's wrong? You're . . . you're bleeding!"

Niémans looked down and saw a dark puddle gleaming on the surface of the desk. The fever that had been burning his skull was in fact the blood from the wound, which had reopened. He staggered, stared at his own face in the shiny, flat mirror and suddenly wondered if he was not looking at the reflection of the last murder in the series.

He did not have time to answer. One second later, he was kneeling unconscious on the floor, his face pressed against the desk, down in the sticky looking-glass of his own blood.

CHAPTER 56

Light. Humming. Warmth.

Pierre Niémans did not immediately realise where he was. Then he made out a paper hat. A white coat. Strip lights. The hospital. How long had he been there, unconscious? And why did his body feel so weak, as though his limbs, muscles and bones had been replaced by some liquid substance? He tried to speak, but the attempt died in his throat. His fatigue was pinning him down onto the rustling plastic cover of his bed.

"He's losing a lot of blood. We'll have to perform a temporal haemostasia."

A door opened. Wheels squeaked. White lights passed above his eyes. A blinding explosion. A burst of energy that dilated his pupils. Another voice resonated:

"Begin the transfusion."

The superintendent heard a clicking sound and felt something cold move across his body. He turned his head and saw some tubes connected to a fat suspended pouch, that seemed to be breathing, as it moved in and out, prompted by an automatic air-pressurised system.

Was he going to stay there, wandering through unconsciousness, in that antiseptic stench? Fade away in that light when he knew the motive of the murders? When he at last understood the secret that lay behind that series of slaughters? His face twisted up into a sardonic grin. Suddenly, a voice said:

"Inject the Diprivan."

Niémans grasped what was meant and sat up. He seized the doctor's wrist, which was already clutching an electronic lancet, and panted:

"I don't want an anesthetic!"

The doctor looked was taken aback.

"No anesthetic? But ... you've been cut almost in half, my friend. I'm going to have to stitch you back up."

Niémans found the strength to mumble:

"A local one ... Give me a local anesthetic ..."

The man sighed, shifted his chair back in a shriek of castors and said to the anaesthetist:

"All right. Then give him some Xylocaine. The maximum dose. A full two hundred milligrams."

Niémans relaxed. They moved him under the multi-faceted lamps. The nape of his neck was propped on a head-rest, so that his skull was raised as high as possible toward the light. They turned his face, and then his view became obstructed by a curtain of paper.

The superintendent closed his eyes. As the doctor and nurses started to busy themselves on his temple, his mind began to drift off. His heartbeat slowed, his head no longer tormented him. A delicious feeling seemed about to engulf him.

The secret . . . Caillois's secret . . . Sertys's secret. Even that was becoming vague, strange and distant . . . Fanny's face occupied his every thought . . . Her body that was so dark, muscular and curvaceous, as soft as volcanic rock that had been bronzed in a furnace, by the waters and the wind . . . Fanny . . . The visions filling his skull were like murmurs, the rustling of cloth, the whispering of elves.

"Stop!"

The order echoed across the operating theater. Everything came to a halt. A hand tore away the curtain and, in the wave of light, Niémans saw a devil with long locks, waving a tricolor police card under the noses of the astonished doctor and nurses.

Karim Abdouf.

Niémans glanced round to his right: the tubes were already gushing into his skin, into his veins. The elixir of life. The sap of arteries.

The doctor was brandishing his scissors.

"Hands off the superintendent," Karim panted.

The medic froze once again. Abdouf approached and examined Niémans's wound, now sewn up like an oven-ready roast. The doctor shrugged.

"I'm going to have to cut the thread."

Karim peered distrustfully around.

"How is he?"

"Solid. He's lost a lot of blood, but we've given him a hefty transfusion. We've stitched up his wound. The operation is not quite over yet and . . ."

"Have you given him any junk?"

"Any junk?"

"To knock him out."

"Just a local anesthetic and . . ."

"Get me some speed. Some stimulants. I need him back on his feet."

Karim's eyes were fixed on Niémans, but his words were meant for the doctor. He added:

"It's a matter of life and death."

The doctor stood up and searched through a chest of narrow drawers for a blister pack of tablets. Karim grinned fleetingly at Niémans.

"Here," said the doctor. "With this, he'll be up and about in half an hour's time, but . . ."

"Good. Now, move along."

The Arab yelled at the little group of white coats:

"Fuck off, the lot of you! I need to talk to the superintendent."

The doctor and nurses vanished.

Niémans felt the needles from the drip being pulled out of his arm and heard the paper sheeting being pulled away. Then Karim was handing him his blood-stained coat. In the other hand he was weighing the batch of little colored tablets.

"Your speed, superintendent." A grin. "Just for this special occasion."

But Niémans was in no laughing mood. He grabbed Karim's leather jacket and, his face ashen, murmured:

"Karim . . . I've . . . I've worked out the conspiracy."

"What conspiracy?"

"The conspiracy of Sertys, Caillois and Chernecé. The conspiracy of the blood-red rivers."

"WHAT?"

"They . . . they were swapping babies."

XII

CHAPTER 57

Eight o'clock in the morning. The landscape was black, shifting, unreal. The rain had started to pour down again, as though to give the mountain a final polish before daybreak. Translucent shafts broke through the shadows like funnels of glass.

Under the boughs of a huge conifer, Karim Abdouf and Pierre Niémans were standing face to face, one leaning on his Audi, the other against the tree. They were stock still, concentrated, as taut as wires. The Arab cop observed the superintendent, who was slowly recovering his strength, or rather his nerves, thanks to the effect of the amphetamine. He had just described the murderous attack of the Range Rover. But Abdouf was pressing him to tell the whole tale.

Through the din of the downpour, Pierre Niémans began:

"Yesterday evening, I went to the home for the blind."

"On the trail of Eric Joisneau. Yes, I know. And what did you find out?"

"The director, Champelaz, told me that he looked after children who had contracted hereditary diseases. And that they always came from the same families, those of the university elite. Champelaz explained the phenomenon this way: it's an academic community which, through its isolation, has worn thin its blood and become genetically poor. The children born today are destined to be extremely brilliant and highly cultivated, but physically weak and impoverished. From one generation to the next, the blood of the university has become corrupted."

"But what's that got to do with the case?"

"At first sight, nothing. Joisneau had paid a call over there to find out about eye problems, which might have some link with the mutilation of the bodies. But that wasn't the point. Not at all. Champelaz also told me that this inbred community had also been producing extremely vigorous offspring over the last twenty years or so. Intelligent kids, who were also capable of walking off with all the sports prizes. Now, this fact doesn't fit in at all with the rest of the scenario. How can the same community produce a line of runts and also a batch of absolute supermen? Champelaz had looked into the origins of these remarkable kids. He consulted their medical records at the maternity clinic. He examined their backgrounds in the hospital archives. He even had a look at the birth papers of their parents and grandparents in the hope of finding some indication, some genetic clue. But he found nothing. Absolutely nothing."

"And then?"

"Then, last summer, something strange happened. In July, a routine investigation in the hospital archives turned up some old papers, which had been forgotten in the basement of the old library. What were they? The birth papers of those very parents and grandparents of our supermen."

"Which means?"

"That there were two copies of these sheets. Or, to be more precise, that the records Champelaz had looked at in the official files were forgeries, and that the genuine papers were the ones that had just been discovered in some boxes belonging to the university's chief librarian: Etienne Caillois, Rémy's father."

"Shit."

"Quite. Logically speaking, Champelaz should then have compared the records he'd already examined with the ones that had just turned up. But he didn't. He didn't have time. Or couldn't be bothered. Or, more like, was scared. Of finding out the horrible truth about the Guernon community. So, I compared them."

"And what did you find?"

"That the official records had been forged. Etienne Caillois had imitated the handwriting and, each time, changed one detail in comparison with the originals."

"Which was?"

"Always the same one – the baby's weight at birth. So that the figure would match the data in the rest of the file, when the nurses weighed the baby again during the next few days."

"I don't get it."

Niémans leant forward. His voice was expressionless.

"Listen to me carefully, Karim. Etienne Caillois forged the first pages in the file to conceal something inexplicable: in these records, the weight of the baby was never the same the next day. The infants lost or gained several hundred grams in one night. I went to the maternity clinic and asked an obstetrician. He told me that such rapid changes are impossible. So, I took the only explanation left: it wasn't the weight which had changed in one night, but the baby. That was the terrible truth which old man Caillois had been trying to conceal. He, or more likely, old man Sertys, a night auxiliary at the Guernon University Hospital, swapped over babies in the delivery room."

"But . . . why?"

Niémans grinned horribly. The rain, blown in on the wind, was slapping at his face like a flail. His voice was wearing thin on the rock of his conviction.

"To regenerate a worn-out community, to pump new, vigorous, healthy blood into the intellectual community. Caillois's and Sertys's technique was simple: they replaced certain babies born to university families with children from the mountain stock, who'd been selected according to their parents' physical profile. In that way, strapping, powerful bodies suddenly became part of Guernon's academic circle. New blood percolated into the old in the only place where the inaccessible university elite crossed the path of humble farmers – the maternity clinic. A clinic which handled all of the children of the region and which made these exchanges possible. I then guessed that Caillois and Sertys shared a common

306

goal. Not only did they want to regenerate the professors' precious blood, they also wanted to engineer a breed of perfect beings. Supermen. People as beautiful as those in the photographs of the Berlin Olympics, which I'd noticed in Caillois's flat. And people as brilliant as Guernon's most distinguished academics. That's when I realised that those lunatics wanted to bring together the gray matter of Guernon and the bodily vigor of the outlying villages, to fuse together the academics' brain power and the natives' physical prowess. If I have understood correctly, they perfected their system to such an extent that they not only programed the births, but also the couples, by setting up marriages between selected youngsters."

Karim swallowed down these pieces of information one by one. He seemed to be silently, intently digesting them. Meanwhile, Niémans's feverish monologue went on:

"So how to make the right people meet? How to organise the marriages? I thought about the jobs Caillois and Sertys did, and the limited responsibilities they held. I was sure that it was precisely thanks to their obscure, humble positions that they had been able to carry out their scheme. You remember what was written in that exercise book? 'We are the masters, we are the slaves. We are everywhere, we are nowhere.' This seemed to imply that despite their lowly jobs, or rather because of them, they were able to control the destinies of the inhabitants of an entire region. They were lackeys, but they were also in charge. Sertys was a mere auxiliary nurse, but he changed the fates of the area's babies by swapping them over in their cots. As for the Caillois family, they set about organising the next part of the program – the arranged marriages. But how? How did they go about it? I then remembered Caillois's personal files in the library. We had checked which books had been consulted. We had also gone through the names of the kids who had read them. There was just one thing we hadn't looked at: where the readers sat, those little carrels where the students work. So I hurried back to the library and compared the lists of seating positions with the falsified birth papers. They went back over thirty, forty, even fifty years, but the whole thing matched, down to the last name. The kids who had been swapped over were always placed in the reading-room facing the same members of the opposite sex – who were offspring coming from the most brilliant families on the campus. I then did some checking at the registry office. Things didn't fit precisely, but most of those couples who had met in the library, through the glass panels of their carrels, had subsequently got married. Which means I was right. The 'masters' had first changed the kids' identities, then arranged who they would meet. They placed the swap-overs – mountain dwellers' children – in front of bright sparks who were the real offspring of the academic community. And so they gave birth to a superior cross-breed, bringing together the 'body' blood and the 'brain' blood. And it worked, Karim. Our university champions are none other than the children of those programed couples."

Abdouf remained silent. His thoughts were crystallising, as sharp and daggered as the needles from the larches as they mingled with the raindrops.

Niémans continued:

"I put the pieces together and, little by little, completed the jigsaw. I then realised that I was following the same path that the killer had taken, that the story about those old papers turning up in the library, which had been mentioned in the press, had tipped the murderer off. He must have compared the two sets of documents as well. I suppose he must already have had his doubts about the origins of Guernon's 'champions' and is almost certainly one of the champions himself. One of those lunatics' creatures. He then worked out how the conspiracy functioned. He followed Rémy Caillois, the son of the man who'd stolen the birth papers, and discovered his secret relationship with Sertys and Chernecé ... Who, I reckon, was only an extranumerary. A nutty doctor who had, while treating blind kids, stumbled on the truth and decided to join the genetic engineers rather than turn them in. So, our killer unearthed the three of them and went about wiping them out. He tortured the first victim, Rémy Caillois, in order to get the whole story.

He then simply mutilated and killed the other two."

Karim stiffened. His entire frame was trembling under his leather jacket.

"Just because they did a bit of baby swapping? And got couples together?"

"There's something you don't know. The villagers in the surrounding mountains suffer from an extremely high infant mortality rate. This fact is inexplicable, particularly as they are strong and healthy. But we can now guess the reason. Not only did the Sertys family swap babies over, but they also smothered the kids who were supposed to have been born to the villagers – but who were really the academics' runts. By depriving the mountain folk of their offspring, they were certain that they would try again and so provide even more fresh blood to be poured into the valley's academic families. They were fanatics, Karim. Madmen and murderers from father to son, ready to do anything in order to create their superior race."

Karim panted hoarsely:

"If these murders are revenge killings, why are the victims mutilated in such a precise way?"

"It's symbolic. The idea is to wipe out the victims' biological identities, to destroy the signs of their origin. Which also explains why the bodies were positioned in such a way that they were first discovered via their reflections, and not their actual forms. It was another means to dematerialise the victims, to disembody them. Caillois, Sertys and Chernecé robbed people of their identities. And they were made to pay in the same coin. As though it was an eye for an eye, a tooth for a tooth."

Abdouf got to his feet and went over to Niémans. The rain-laden wind beat against their ghostly faces. The condensation formed a pale mist around their heads, Niémans's bony crew cut, and Abdouf's long, soaking wet dreadlocks.

"You're one hell of a cop, Niémans."

"No, Karim, I'm not. Because even if I found out the killer's motive, I still don't know who it is."

The Arab sniffed icily.

"No, but I do."

"What?"

"It all fits together now. You remember my own investigation? Those demons who wanted to obliterate Judith's face because it was a piece of evidence, proof against them? Well, those demons were none other than the victims' fathers, Etienne Caillois and René Sertys, and I know why they had to wipe out Judith's face at any price. It was because that face was going to give the game away, to show up the nature of the blood-red rivers and this business of exchanging babies."

It was now Niémans's turn to be astonished.

"WHY?"

"Because Judith Hérault had a twin sister, who had been swapped over."

CHAPTER 58

The rain seemed to be abating at the approach of dawn as Karim began his explanations. He spoke in a serious, neutral tone of voice, his dreadlocks hanging down like an octopus's tentacles in the early light.

"You said that the conspirators picked out the babies that interested them according to their parents' profile. They were obviously looking for the strongest, most agile kids the slopes had to offer. They were after mountain creatures, snow leopards. And so they must have noticed Fabienne and Sylvain Hérault, a young couple living in Taverlay, in the heights of the Pelvoux, at an altitude of over five thousand four hundred feet. She was six feet tall, a giantess and splendid with it. A dedicated primary school teacher. A virtuoso pianist. Silent, graceful, vigorous and lyrical. Believe me, Fabienne was already a bit of a strange breed herself.

"As for her husband, Sylvain, I don't have so much info about him. He spent his life on the tops of the mountains, digging precious crystals out of the rocks. A real giant, too, who made no bones about clambering up the highest, most inaccessible peaks.

"And, superintendent, if our conspirators were going to steal one baby from the entire region, then it was obviously going to be this extraordinary couple's kid, whose genes contained the strange secrets of those lofty heights.

"I'm sure that, like true genetic vampires, they waited impatiently for a babe to come along. Then, on 22 May, 1972, the long-awaited night finally arrived. The Héraults turn up at Guernon University Hospital. That enormous, beautiful woman was on the point of giving birth. But after a pregnancy of only seven months. The child is going to be premature.

"Still, the midwives reckon that there won't be any insoluble problems.

"But, things don't go as planned. The child is in the wrong position. They call in an obstetrician. The machines start beeping like crazy. It's two in the morning on 23 May. And the medic and the midwife end up sorting the chaos out. Fabienne Hérault is not about to have one child, but two – a pair of homozygous twins, who are wrapped up together in her uterus like two halves of a walnut.

"They anaesthetise Fabienne. The doctor carries out a caesarean and manages to extricate the babies. Two tiny little girls, as identical as peas in a pod. They've got breathing problems. So they're urgently given to a nurse who takes them away to an incubator. Niémans, I can see in my mind's eye those latex-gloved hands that picked up those girls, just like I was there. Jesus. Those hands belonged to René Sertys, Philippe's father.

"He's totally out of his depth. His job was to make off with the Hérault couple's kid, but now there are two of them. What is he supposed to do next? As he washes those premature twins down, he breaks out into a sweat – they are two perfect miniature specimens, two masterpieces for Guernon's new blood bank. In the end, he puts them in an incubator and decides to swap just one of them over. Nobody's had a good look at their faces yet. In all that gory panic in the theater, nobody's noticed if they really are alike. So Sertys risks it. He plucks one of the twins out of the incubator and exchanges her with a little girl who's been born to one of the academic families, and who more or less resembles the Hérault kids — same size, same blood group, approximately the same weight.

"He now realises that he's got to pluck up his courage and kill the other baby. He's got no choice. He can't let a so-called twin survive, who has nothing at all in common with her sister. So he smothers her, then calls out in fake panic to the doctors and nurses. He plays his part excellently. The remorse ... My God, however did it happen? I just don't know ... I just don't know ... Neither the obstetrician nor the paediatricians have a clear opinion. It's another one of those sudden cot deaths that have been afflicting the mountain villagers for the last fifty-odd years. The hospital staff reconcile themselves to the fact that at least one of the girls has survived. Meanwhile, Sertys has a happy laugh to himself. The other Hérault is now part and parcel of the Guernon clan, via its adopted family.

"I worked all this out thanks to your discoveries, Niémans. Because the woman I spoke to earlier tonight, Fabienne Hérault, still knows nothing about this insane conspiracy. And on the night in question she saw nothing, and heard nothing. She was under the effects of the anesthetic.

"When she wakes up the next morning, she's told that she has given birth to twin girls, but only one of them has survived. Do we grieve for someone whose existence we hadn't even suspected? Fabienne accepts the news with resignation — but she and her husband feel totally confused. A week later, she's allowed to go home along with her little girl, who's now brimming with life.

"Somewhere inside that clinic, René Sertys watches the couple as they leave. In their arms, they are holding the double of a baby he's swapped over, but he knows that that wild couple live over thirty miles away and have no reason whatsoever to come back to Guernon. By letting that second child live, Sertys has taken a risk, but it's only a slight one. He supposes that the twin's face will never return to unmask the conspiracy.

"But he was wrong about that.

"Eight years later, Taverlay School, where Fabienne teaches, closes down. She is then transferred – the only coincidence in this entire business – to Guernon's prestigious Lamartine School, the place where the children of the university's lecturers go.

"So it is that Fabienne discovers something weird, incredible. In the CE2 class which Judith attends, there is another Judith. A little girl who's the carbon copy of her daughter. When she's recovered from the shock – the school photographer meanwhile has time to take a class photo, in which both of them can be seen – Fabienne thinks things out. And there's only one possible explanation. That identical child, that double, must be Judith's twin sister, who has in fact survived and was, for some strange reason, given to another family.

"Off she goes to the maternity clinic and explains what's on her mind. She's greeted with icy suspicion. But Fabienne is a hard woman and not one to let herself be easily intimidated. She insults the doctors, she calls them baby snatchers and says she'll be back. René Sertys presumably witnesses this scene and senses danger. But Fabienne is already long gone. She's decided to go and see the university family who are supposed to be the second twin's parents. Her usurpers. She cycles off with Judith toward the campus.

"Then, suddenly, terror strikes. As night begins to fall, a car tries to run them down. Fabienne and her daughter roll down into a ditch on the side of the rock face. Hidden in the ravine, with her child in her arms, she sees the killers. Two men, holding guns, leap out of their car. Horrified, Fabienne wonders what is going on. Why this sudden outbreak of violence?

"The murderers finally give up their search and leave, presumably under the impression that mother and daughter have fallen

313

to their deaths. That night, Fabienne goes and sees her husband, who still lodges in Taverlay during the week. She explains what has happened. She thinks they absolutely must tell the police. But Sylvain disagrees. He wants to get the bastards who tried to kill his wife and daughter himself.

"He takes a gun, gets on his bike and goes down into the valley, where he comes up against the killers much more quickly than he would have liked. They're still out on the prowl, spot him on the road and run him down. They drive over the body several times, then make their escape. Meanwhile, Fabienne has taken refuge in Taverlay church. She waits for Sylvain all night. The next morning, she learns that her husband has been killed by a hit-and-run driver. She immediately realises that her children have been victims of some sort of manipulation and that the men who eliminated her husband will also do away with her if she doesn't disappear at once.

"She and her daughter go into hiding.

"You know the rest. How the mother and daughter holed up in Sarzac, over one hundred and eighty miles away from Guernon. How they fled again when Etienne Caillois and René Sertys came looking for them. Fabienne's attempts to wipe out all trace of her child, convinced that she was the victim of a curse, then the car accident in which Judith finally died.

"Since that time, the mother has lived a life of prayer. Several possible explanations occurred to her. But her main hypothesis was that her second twin's adopted parents, a powerful and evil university family, had organised this whole plot in order to replace the daughter they had lost and that they were quite capable of murdering her and Judith so as to cover up their tracks. She never worked out the truth, the real reason for this exchange. Or the real reason why the two conspirators hunted her and her daughter down across the whole of France, for fear that she would reveal this terrifying scheme and that her child's face would be a vital piece of evidence.

"Our two investigations have now joined up like two rails

leading to death, Niémans. Your hypothesis corroborates mine. Yes, the killer looked through the stolen papers this summer. Yes, the killer followed Caillois, then Sertys, then Chernecé. Yes, the killer uncovered the plot and decided to exact a terrible revenge. And that killer is none other than Judith's twin sister.

"A homozygous twin who acted just as Judith would have done, because she now knows the truth about her origins. That's why she uses a piano wire, as a reminder of her real mother's virtuoso talents. That's why she killed her victims in the rocky heights, there where her own father used to dig out crystals. That's why her own fingerprints could have been mistaken for Judith's . . . We're looking for her blood sister, Niémans."

"Who is she?" Niémans exploded. "What new name was she given?"

"I don't know. Her mother refused to tell me. But I've got her face."

"Her face?"

"A photograph of Judith, aged eleven. And so, since they are completely identical, of the murderer. I reckon that with this picture we can . . ."

Niémans was trembling spasmodically.

"Show it to me. Quick!"

Karim produced the photo and handed it to him.

"She's our killer, superintendent. She's avenging her dead sister. She's avenging her murdered father. She's avenging those smothered babies, those cheated families, all those messed up generations for the last fifty-odd years . . . What's up, Niémans?"

The photo was twitching up and down in the superintendent's hands as he stared at it, his teeth clenched fit to shatter. Suddenly, Karim caught on and leant over toward him. He clutched his shoulder.

"Jesus Christ, you know her, don't you, superintendent?"

Niémans let the photo drop into the mud. He looked as though he was about to lose his wits completely. His broken voice croaked:

"Alive. We've got to capture her alive."

315

The two cops headed off through the rain. Gasping in shallow breaths, they did not exchange another word. They crossed several police road-blocks. The early dawn patrols glanced at them suspiciously. Neither of them suggested the idea of getting help. Niémans was off the case and Karim out of his patch. But still they both knew that this case was theirs, and nobody else's.

They reached the campus. They drove along its tarmac tracks, past its gleaming lawns, before parking and clambering up to the top floor of the main building. They strode on together down to the end of the corridor and, hidden either side of the frame, knocked on the door. No answer. They smashed open the lock and went inside.

Niémans brandished his Remington shotgun, loaded to the gills, which he had recovered from the police station. Karim was holding his Glock, pressed against his wrist by his torch. Two parallel beams of light and death.

Nobody.

They had just started a thorough search, when Niémans's pager bleeped. He was to call Marc Costes as soon as possible. He did so. His hands were still shaking and a terrible pain was gnawing at his innards. The young medic's voice was chirpy:

"Niémans? I'm with Barnes. Just to tell you that we've found Sophie Caillois."

"Alive?"

"Oh yes, very much alive. She was heading for Switzerland on the train."

"Has she said anything?"

"She says that she's the next victim. And that she knows who the killer is."

"Has she given you the name?"

"She'll only speak to you, superintendent."

"Keep her under close guard. Don't let anybody speak to her.

Don't let anybody go near her. I'll be there in an hour's time."

"In an hour? You're ... you're onto something?"

"Good-bye."

"Wait! Is Abdouf with you?"

Niémans chucked the cell phone to the young lieutenant and went back to his rapid explorations. Karim fixed his attention on the medic's voice:

"I've got the note of the piano wire for you," the pathologist said.

"B flat?"

"How did you guess?"

Karim hung up without answering. He looked at Niémans, who was staring at him from behind his rain-splattered spectacles.

"We're not going to find anything here," he exclaimed, striding toward the door. "Let's head for the gym. It's her hide-out."

The door of the gymnasium, an isolated building standing away from the campus, put up no resistance. The two men burst inside and spread out in a semi-circle. Karim was still holding his Glock just above the beam of his torch. As for Niémans, he had turned on the spot fixed on the top of his gun, following the line of the barrel.

Nobody.

They clambered over the floor mats, scrambled under the parallel bars and stared up into the darkness, where rings and knotted ropes hung down from the ceiling. Silence, as of the grave. The smell of cold sweat and ageing rubber. Shadows, patterned over with symmetric shapes, wooden forms and metal struts. Niémans stumbled into a trampoline. Karim immediately spun round. A moment's tension. A brief look. Both of them could sense the other's nerves giving off sparks like flints. Niémans whispered:

"It's here. I'm sure it's here."

Karim peered around again, then focused on the pipes of the central heating system. He walked alongside them, listening to the constant pumping of the boiler. He straddled a set of dumbbells and punch balls and managed to reach a grille of greasy metal bars, which was positioned plumb with the foam matting covering the walls. Without bothering about making a noise, he pulled away the grille and tore down the foam. This barrier concealed the doorway to the boiler room.

He fired one bullet into the notched opening of the lock. With an explosion of shards and metal splinters, the door blew off its hinges. He finished off the job by crushing the panel down with his heel.

Inside, everything was dark.

He stuck his head through, then immediately pulled it back. He was ghastly white. The two men dived in together.

A pungent stench gripped their nostrils.

Blood.

Blood on the walls, on the cast-iron pipes, on the rings of bronze lying on the floor. Blood on the ground, mopped up by handfuls of talcum powder, lying in stagnant, lumpy pools. Blood on the bulging sides of the boiler.

The two men had no desire to be sick, it was as if their minds were detached from their bodies, suspended in terrified astonishment. They went further inside, flashing their torches around them. Piano wires glistened, twisted about the piping. Jerry-cans of gasoline lay on the ground, corked with stoppers of blood-stained cloth. The bars of the dumb-bells were stuck with scraps of dry flesh and dark blood clots. Rusty carpet cutters had been abandoned in puddles of solidified gore.

As they ventured further and further inside, the wobbling beams from their torches showed up the panic that was gripping their limbs. Niémans spotted some colored objects on a bench. He knelt down. Iceboxes. He pulled one of them over to him and opened it. Without saying a word, he shone his spotlight into it for Karim's benefit.

Eyes.

Pale and bulbous, glittering with dewy brightness on a bed of ice.

Niémans was already opening another icebox. This one contained the blue forms of frozen hands. Their nails were darkened with blood, their wrists marked with incisions. The superintendent drew back. Karim took him by the shoulders and groaned.

They both now realised that they were no longer in a mere boiler room. They had entered inside the murderer's mind. Within her secret lair, where she had decided to slay the baby-killers.

Karim's voice rang out, piercingly:

"She's long gone. Nowhere near Guernon."

"No," Niémans replied, getting to his feet. "She wants Sophie Caillois. The last name on her list. They've just brought Sophie into the station. And I'm sure she'll find out – or knows already – and is going to go looking for her."

"With all those road-blocks? She won't be able to make a single move without being spotted and . . ."

Karim fell silent. The two men looked at each other, their faces lit up by the rising beams of their torches. With one voice, they murmured:

"The river."

The obvious place was on the edge of the campus. There, where Caillois's body had been discovered. There, where the current fell away into a small lake, before resuming its course once more toward the town.

The two policemen drove down to this limit, skidding over the grass slopes, taking the one that led down to the river bank. Suddenly, as Karim was braking alongside the stone parapet, in the light of their headlamps they saw a figure dressed in a black, glimmering oil-skin, and wearing a small rucksack. A face turned round and froze in the blinding beam of light. Karim recognised the helmet and the balaclava. The young woman was untying a long red inflatable dinghy, and pulling it toward her with the rope, as though mastering a frisky horse.

Niémans muttered:

"Don't shoot. And keep your distance. I'm arresting her on my own."

Before Karim had time to reply, the superintendent had leapt out of the car and dashed down the last few feet of the slope. The lieutenant brought the car to a standstill, turned off the engine and watched. In the ray of the headlights, he saw the superintendent running toward her and yelling:

"Fanny!"

The young woman was getting into the raft. Niémans grabbed her by the collar and yanked her back toward him. Karim sat there frozen, as though hypnotised by the strange ballet those two figures were performing. He saw them embrace – at least that was what it looked like. He saw the woman throw her head back, then bridle up in a savage movement. He saw Niémans stiffen, arch over, then draw his gun. Blood was spurting from his lips and Karim realised that she had just ripped his guts out with a stab from a carpet cutter. He heard the muffled sound of the shots, Niémans's MR73 finishing off its prey, while the two figures were still gripped together in a kiss of death.

"NO!"

Karim's scream died in his throat. Gun in hand, he ran toward the couple who were now swaying by the edge of the lake. He tried to shout again. He wanted to run faster, to run back through time. But he was too late to stop the inevitable. Pierre Niémans and the woman tumbled down with a ghastly splash.

When he reached the bank, it was only to see the two bodies being carried away by the gentle current toward the outlet. The interlocked corpses floated gracefully and sweetly on past the rocks before vanishing into the river which ran down to the town.

The young cop remained motionless, staring fixedly at the current, listening to the rushing of the foam, which murmured on behind the rocks beyond the edge of the lake. But then, suddenly, as though in a never-ending nightmare, he felt the blade of the carpet cutter dig into his throat, piercing his flesh.

A swift hand passed under his arm and made off with his Glock, which he had put back into his holster.

"Nice to see you again, Karim."

The voice was soft. As soft as a ring of pebbles placed on top of a tombstone. Slowly, Karim turned round. In the gloomy light, he immediately recognised that oval face, that dark complexion, those bright eyes, misted over with tears.

He knew that he was standing in front of Judith Hérault, the doppelganger of the woman Niémans had called "Fanny". The little girl he had been looking for for so long.

The little girl who had grown into a woman.

And who was very much alive.

CHAPTER 60

"There were two of us, Karim. There were always two of us."

It took the lieutenant a moment before he was able to pronounce a word. He finally murmured:

"Tell me, Judith. Tell me everything. If I have to die, I want to know the truth first."

Her hands clenched round the Glock, the young woman was still crying. She was wearing a black oil-skin, diver's leggings and a dark close-fitting fiber-glass helmet, which sat like a hand poised over her head of wild curly hair.

She suddenly started to speak:

"In Sarzac, when Maman realised that the demons were after us, she also worked out that we'd never be free of them . . . That the demons would always be on our trail, and that they'd end up killing me . . . And so she had a brilliant idea . . . She reckoned that the only place they'd never come looking for me would be in the shadow of my twin sister, Fanny Ferreira . . . In the very heart of her life . . . She reckoned that the two of us, my twin and me, should live one single life together, unbeknown to everyone else."

"And the other parents . . . Did they play along?"

Judith laughed fleetingly, between her sobs.

"No, you idiot . . . Fanny and I had got to know each other at Lamartine School . . . And we didn't want to be separated . . . So

321

my sister agreed to the idea at once ... That we'd both live one life as two people, in the greatest possible secrecy. But the first thing to do was to get rid of the killers, once and for all. We had to make them believe I was dead. Maman arranged the whole thing to make it look as though we were running away from Sarzac ... Whereas, in fact, she was leading them toward our trap – that car accident ..."

Karim had to admit that he, too, had fallen into the same trap fourteen years later. His opinion of himself as a brilliant cop suddenly collapsed. If he had been able to retrace Fabienne and Judith's trail in a few hours, then it was simply because he had been following the signposts which had been left. The same signs that had fooled old Caillois and Sertys in 1982.

As though reading his mind, Judith went on:

"Maman tricked the lot of you! She's never been a religious maniac ... She never believed in demons ... She never wanted to exorcise my face ... If she chose a nun to get the photos back, then it was to make the whole thing memorable, you see? She was pretending to wipe out our trail, while in fact she was digging out a deep open track so that the killers would follow us until the final scene ... That's also why she confided in Crozier, who's about as subtle as a bull in a china shop."

Once again, Karim ran through the various clues, each of the details which had allowed him to trace the two women. The doctor consumed by remorse, the bribed photographer, the drunken priest, the nun, the fire-eater, the old man on the autoroute ... All of them had been Fabienne Hérault's "signposts". The pointers which were to lead Caillois and Sertys to the faked accident. And which had, in a few hours, guided Karim to the autoroute service station and Judith's last moments.

Karim tried to disagree.

"Caillois and Sertys didn't follow your trail. No one mentioned them to me while I was looking for you."

"They were more subtle about it than you! But they certainly did follow us. We had a few dicey moments, believe me ...

Because, when we stage-managed the accident, Caillois and Sertys were onto us and about to kill us."

"But the accident ... How did you fake it?"

"It took Maman more than a month to prepare. Especially the way she smashed the car against the wall and got out unhurt."

"But ... what about the body? Who was it?"

Judith sniggered. Karim thought of the blood-stained iron bars, the gasoline cans, the pools of blood. He was now sure that Fanny had merely abetted her sister in her schemes of vengeance, and that the real torturer had been Judith. A mad woman. Fit for the sanitorium. And obviously it was she who had tried to kill Niémans on the bridge.

"Maman used to read all the local newspapers on the look-out for accidents and obituaries ... She went through the hospitals and cemeteries. What we needed was a body of about the same age and size as me. The week before the accident, she exhumed a child who'd been buried over a hundred miles away from where we lived. A little boy. Just perfect. Maman had already decided to declare me officially dead under the name 'Jude', as the final touch of her ruse. And, anyway, she was going to completely crush the body. The child would no longer be recognisable. Not even its sex."

She giggled strangely, choking on her tears, then went on:

"There's something you have to know, Karim ... From Friday to Sunday, we lived with that corpse in the house. A little boy who'd been killed in a motor-bike accident, and whose body was already in a terrible state. We kept it in a bathtub full of ice. Then we waited."

A question crossed Karim's mind:

"Did Crozier help you?"

"During the entire set-up. It was as if he was hypnotised by Maman's beauty. And he felt that this whole horrible business was only for our good. So we waited. For two days, in our little stone house. Maman kept on playing the piano. On and on she played ... That same Chopin sonata. As though she was trying to drown out that nightmare ... As for me, that rotting body in the bathtub started to drive me crazy. The contact lenses were hurting my eyes. The notes of the sonata hammered into my brain like nails. My mind shattered, Karim ... I was scared, so scared ..."

"What about your fingerprints? How come your fingerprints were on the autoroute records?"

Judith, her curls flashing, smiled through her tears.

"That was child's play. Crozier took my fingerprints on a fresh card and swapped it over with the one kept in the service station. Maman didn't want to leave anything to chance, just in case the demons came back to check that it was really me."

Karim clenched his fists. It really had been child's play. He reproached himself for not having thought of that.

Suddenly, an image flashed into his mind. That bandaged hand, holding his Glock in the rain.

"So, that night, it was you?"

"Yes, sphinx eyes," she laughed. "I'd come to sacrifice Sophie Caillois, that little whore, who was so in love with her husband that she never dared tell on Rémy and the rest ... I should have killed you ..." Tears spilled out from her eyelids. "If I had done, then Fanny would still be alive. But I couldn't ... I just couldn't."

Judith paused, her eyes blinking beneath her cyclist's helmet. Then she started speaking again in a rushed whisper:

"Immediately after the accident, I went to join Fanny in Guernon. She had asked her parents if she could live as a boarder on the top floor of Lamartine School ... We were only eleven, but we managed to live as one immediately ... I lived in the attic ... I was already an excellent climber ... I went down to see my sister over the joists and through the window ... A real little spider girl ... And nobody ever noticed me ...

"The years went by ... We took turns to be present in different situations, with the family, at school, with friends, with boys. We shared the same food, we swapped days. We lived exactly the same life, but one after the other. Fanny was the bright one, so she taught me everything about books, science and geology. And I taught her to climb mountains and navigate streams. The two of us made one incredible being ... A sort of two-headed dragon.

"Sometimes, Maman would come and see us in the mountains and bring us some provisions. She never spoke to us about our origins, or those two years spent in Sarzac. She thought that this ruse was the only way for us to be happy ... But I hadn't forgotten the past. I always carried with me a piano wire. And I continued to listen to the sonata in B flat. The sonata of the little corpse in the bathtub ... Sometimes I flew into terrible rages ... Just by gripping that piano wire, I cut deep weals into my fingers. Then everything came back to me. How frightened I had been in Sarzac, when pretending to be a little boy, those Sundays, near Sète, when I'd learnt to swallow fire, and that last evening, when I was waiting for Maman to leave with the little boy's body.

"Maman never agreed to tell me who the killers were, those bastards who'd pursued us and run over my father. I scared her, yes, I scared even her ... I think she realised that, sooner or later, I was going to kill those murderers ... My vengeance was awaiting a little spark ... All I now regret is that those birth papers came to light so late, after old Sertys and Caillois were already dead."

Judith stopped speaking and took a firmer hold of the gun. Karim remained silent; and his silence was an interrogation in itself. Suddenly, the young woman started to yell:

"What else do you expect me to tell you? That Caillois admitted the whole thing and begged for our forgiveness? That this crazy business had been going on for generations? That they were continuing to swap over babies? That they were planning to marry us off, Fanny and me, to one of those decadent university runts? We were their creation, Karim ..."

Judith leant forward.

"They were nuts ... Total madmen who thought they were working for the good of humanity by creating perfect genetic mixes ... Caillois reckoned he was God, with his people under him ... As for Sertys, he raised rats by the thousand in his warehouse ... The rats stood for the population of Guernon ...

Each of them was named after one of the families, doesn't that remind you of anything? Do you realise just how warped those bastards were? And Chernecé rounded off the picture . . . He said that the irises of the superior race shone in a particular way, and that he would be a real fly on the wall, at the threshold of the world, brandishing his eye-shaped torches in the face of humanity . . ."

Judith knelt down on one knee, the Glock still aimed at Karim, and lowered her voice:

"Fanny and I really put the shits up them, believe me . . . The first day, we started off by sacrificing young Caillois. And our vengeance had to be at the same level as their conspiracy . . . The biological mutilations were Fanny's idea . . . She reckoned that we had to annihilate them totally, just as they had destroyed the identities of the children of Guernon . . . She also said that we ought to smash their bodies into a set of different reflections, like the shards of a broken mirror . . . I was the one who thought of the locations: water, ice and glass. And I was the one who did the dirty work . . . Who made the first of the fuckers talk, with iron bars, fire and carpet cutters . . .

"Then we stuck his body up in the rock and went to smash up Sertys's warehouse . . . After that, we engraved a message into the librarian's wall . . . And signed it Judith, to scare the bastards really shitless, to show them that the ghost had risen from the grave . . . Fanny and I knew that the others in the plot would then rush back to Sarzac to check what they thought they had known since 1982 – that I was dead and buried in that lousy little tip . . . So we got there first and emptied my tomb . . . Then we filled it up with the rats' bones we'd found in the warehouse – Sertys used to label them, just like a real fucking nasty fetishist . . ."

Judith burst out laughing, then yelled once more:

"Just imagine their faces when they opened the coffin!" She then became serious again at once. "They just had to be taught a lesson, Karim . . . We just had to make them understand that the time for revenge had arrived . . . That they were going to die horribly ... That they were going to pay for the harm they'd done to our town, our family, us, the two little sisters, and to me, me, me..."

Her voice grew softer. The daylight was glinting like mother-of-pearl.

Karim murmured:

"And what now? What are you going to do?"

"Go back to Maman."

The cop pictured that huge woman, surrounded by her sheets and brightly colored rags. He thought of Crozier, the loner, who must have gone to join her later the previous night. The two of them would be locked up, sooner or later.

"I'm going to have to arrest you, Judith."

The young woman sniggered.

"Arrest me? But I'm the one who's holding the gun, little sphinx! One move, and I'll kill you."

Forcing himself to smile, Karim approached her.

"It's all over now, Judith. We're going to take care of you, we'll ..."

When she pressed the trigger, he had already drawn the Beretta he always carried strapped to his back, the Beretta which had allowed him to overcome the skinheads, his last card.

They fired their bullets and two gunshots rang out in the dawn. Karim was unscathed, but Judith fell back gracefully. As though borne away by the rhythm of a dance, she wobbled for a few seconds, her throat rapidly reddening with blood.

The young woman dropped the automatic, staggered slightly, then flopped down into the void. It seemed to Karim that a smile flickered across her face.

He suddenly screamed and leapt up over the rocks to look for Judith's body, the little girl whom he had loved – he knew that now – more than anything else in the world for the past twenty-four hours.

He spotted the bloody form as it floated off toward the river. He watched it draw away to rejoin the bodies of Fanny Ferreira and Pierre Niémans. In the distance, a brilliant dawn was rising, searing through the darkness of the mountains.

Karim took no notice.

He wondered how much sunlight would be needed to chase away the shadows that were folding around his heart.